agony angel

agony angel

So you think you've got problems...

Cesca Martin

Copyright © 2007 Cesca Martin

The moral right of the author has been asserted.

Apart from any fair dealing for the purposes of research or private study, or criticism or review, as permitted under the Copyright, Designs and Patents Act 1988, this publication may only be reproduced, stored or transmitted, in any form or by any means, with the prior permission in writing of the publishers, or in the case of reprographic reproduction in accordance with the terms of licences issued by the Copyright Licensing Agency. Enquiries concerning reproduction outside those terms should be sent to the publishers.

Matador
9 De Montfort Mews
Leicester LE1 7FW, UK
Tel: (+44) 116 255 9311 / 9312
Email: books@troubador.co.uk
Web: www.troubador.co.uk/matador

ISBN 978-1906221-102

All the characters in this book are fictitious, and any resemblance to actual persons, living or dead, is purely coincidental.

Typeset in 11pt Stempel Garamond by Troubador Publishing Ltd, Leicester, UK
Printed in the UK by The Cromwell Press Ltd, Trowbridge, Wilts, UK

Matador is an imprint of Troubador Publishing Ltd

Dear Angel,

I met this boy the other day and thought he was lush. I asked him out but he said no. I'm so depressed. My friend said he wasn't right for me. But how do I know when I find the right person?

Anon

There are some things in life I don't like: the word gusset, coach stations, memorabilia porcelain, little dogs dressed in tartan, people who paint themselves silver to pretend they're statues and flashbacks from May 14th 2001...
    That was a bad day. Just terrible.
    Now I haven't got the energy to go into all the details right now so I'll bypass the finer points and just give you the background so you're up to speed. Picture the scene: I am at a party with my best friend Suzie. Well, my best friend at the time, at university. (She's still a really close friend, but some of my other friends might be upset if I described her as my best friend now, as, well, you know what it's like). Anyway, the point is, I was on a night out with her and, at that time, she was my best friend. We are in a trendy bar in an IKEA sort of way – all tan leather sofas, big mirrors, pictures of blobs in colours like 'hemp' and 'cord'. We are drinking alcohol. We have dressed up for the occasion (smoky eyeliner, killer heels, wearing skirts that my mother would describe as 'little more than a belt'). We are both having a really good time. You get the gist. May 14th 2001. It had all started so promisingly.
    Suzie was spending the evening on a singular mission. She'd been trying to ensnare some poor student into her web (of love) for the past two months. I'd learnt a little from her about the man under scrutiny in that time. He was on her course, always sat in the back row at lectures, was tall with blonde hair and

wore a bottle green jumper which apparently 'really brings out his eyes'. Thus, he had been christened 'Gorgeous Green Jumper Boy'. To me this sounded dubious; students were scruffy enough but one jumper definitely hinted at a distinct lack of effort and questionable personal hygiene. To Suzie however he – and his jumper – stood for all that was fine and proper about her English lectures. He was the sole reason for her consistent attendance rates this year. Her parents would thank him on Graduation Day. It had been he that had dropped hopelessly unsubtle hints about the party we were now at and Suzie had responded by embarking on a high scale seduction programme, starting with a frantic early morning shopping trip to purchase just the right outfit for the occasion (the belt/skirt).

So far it hadn't been a particularly unusual evening. I'd been chatted up by a couple of men; one from the maybe-if-I-keep-drinking category and one in the no-way-never-not-even-if-all-other-men-are-wiped-out-by-a-freakish-natural-disaster category. The latter man has been talking at me for at least five minutes and is dressed in a leather jacket and a T shirt that says 'Don't Sweat It Baby'. This however was not the sole reason I rejected him on sight. I'm not that shallow. No, the main reason was his hair. He had a lot of hair; although that wasn't the reason I didn't like it (I am sometimes a fan of Big Hair see; David Hasselhoff, Simon le Bon and Mick Jagger in his earlier years). No, it wasn't the size of the hair that bothered me, it was the layout. He had managed to gel it – all of it – into a large sideways quiff. No wind, rain or other element had a hope of being able to move it. It was firmly stuck there, poking out to one side. And although it made for an impressive engineering feat it was not a nice hairstyle. So I was keen to see the back of him, not to check out the hair, but in the traditional meaning of this phrase ('to see the back of someone'). Sadly Gel Boy looked set to stay and started inundating me with his very best Saturday night chat. Topics ranged from the imaginative 'What music do you like?' to 'Do you come here often?' I had made the error of asking him what he did (zoology student) and before I knew it he had taken my continued silence as a green light and begun reciting his dissertation at me – something about the female ferret dying if she doesn't have sex in a year. It was all getting a little weird and slightly creepy so throughout his spiel I was desperately seeking out Suzie for a speedy exit.

Suzie however had chosen that moment to leave me snogging 'Gorgeous Green Jumper Boy', who had a moments before. (The belt/skirt never fails). I was momenta relieved for her, she had been after him for a long time, but th. soon passed as Gel Boy's sentences came wafting over me, 'You see they are seasonally polyoestrous and spontaneous ovulaters...'

I started to look around worriedly for someone else to get me out of this mess.

'...that can then cause bone marrow suppression and in certain ferrets this can lead to non-regenerative anaemia, and ultimately death.'

An attractive man with shoulder length hair and a suede jacket had just taken up a handy position leaning on a nearby pillar. I didn't hesitate,

'Andy,' I yelped at him.

He looked baffled. Gel Boy stopped mid-sentence.

'Andy,' I repeated, nodding at him encouragingly. He looked from me to Gel Boy to me. I gave him a please-go-along-with-me-look as Gel Boy darted his beady little eyes over at him. 'Andy' continued to look confused and then checked behind him for signs of any real Andy's, of which there were none.

'Andy, how are you?' I said my glare getting more insistent. Gel Boy, realising he was in no imminent danger, chose this moment to continue his ferret chat,

'So you see the female actually DIES if she doesn't mate,' he stressed a serious glint in his eye and then a lingering glance up and down my body. I shivered and realised I'd have to make a run for it.

Then a loud voice piped up, 'Oh my god is that you?' 'Andy' had cottoned on and was moving towards me. My shoulders sagged in relief.

He went on, 'I'm sorry I didn't recognise you with that.... that...,' he paused, starting to flail. I nodded at him, willing him to continue.

'That um.... Hair,' he said pointing at my head. Good work.

I smiled. 'Oh yes' I said patting my hair, 'It's a new look I decided to... to... tie it back,' I finished triumphantly.

...d staring at my hair, then 'Andy' and then me, ...rinkling with the effort to keep up. ...'Andy' went on moving in for a hug. ...look a little surprised as we embraced and he ...OK?'

...so much to tell you Andy,' I said gushing and patting him playfully on the chest. I turned to Gel Boy, 'I am so sorry but Andy and I go way back, do you mind?' And with that Gel Boy, realising defeat, turned and left.

'Thank you, thank you, thank you,' I said turning to him and grinning, 'I'm Angel,' I said, offering him a hand.

'I'm confused,' he replied, taking it.

I filled him in on the whole female ferret sex chat and when I was done, and he had closed his mouth, he started laughing. And when he stopped laughing he looked straight into my eyes. I felt a jolt. On closer inspection this man wasn't mildly attractive. God no, he wasn't attractive at all, he was absolutely, utterly, incredibly delicious.

'Can I buy you a drink,' he asked.

'Sorry,' I whispered.

'A drink, can I buy you one?'

'Oh yes, of course,' I said smiling.

We went to the bar and ordered two strange green cocktails and then we went to sit down on a tan sofa, underneath a picture of a blob. We chatted for a while, eagerly swapping stories and information about each other's lives. I felt so happy. And then suddenly, as I looked at him talking, it hit me. I had fallen in love. Love at first sight. He was the Man of My Dreams. I'd found him. He placed his hand on my arm and I looked up at him expectantly as he said, 'I've got to go to the toilet Angela, Angela, ANGELA... ANGELA, ANGELA.'

* * *

The tender voice of the man I loved morphed into a loud shouting directly in my ears. I tried to block out the screeching but it was useless. The voice was calling out my name determinedly and it wasn't the voice of Dream Man. Oh no, this voice was lodged in reality and I was brought back down to earth with a bang.

'Angela, ANGELA, ANGELA.'

'What, god, what,' I jabbered looking up to find an enraged woman staring back at me where Dream Man had been moments before. Oh god. The real world: in the present. My job. And Victoria my boss.

'Oh, I'm so sorry,' I flushed, 'I don't know where I was.' I said scrabbling around my desk for the pen I'd been chewing on. Well I did, I had been with my Dream Man, at a party, in heaven. But I didn't think mentioning it would help me right now. I sneaked a look through my lashes at Victoria's stony glare, and then shuffled my notes as if to prove I was back to work, focused and in control. She wasn't convinced.

'Look Angela you have got to get your page done. The subs need to work out the layout and they can't do that until you give them the text. We have got deadlines on this magazine, or has that word just passed you by?'

'No of course not, you are absolutely right, I'm so sorry.' My babbling continued as she remained motionless, 'There was a particularly interesting letter and it got me thinking about the poor girls' plight...' I began on a pitiful tale bound to evoke anyone's sympathy.

Not apparently Victoria's who interrupted the story before I'd even warmed up, 'I don't want to hear it Angela. Just finish the page and hand it in to the subs. Now.'

I rifled the papers around me with a stern expression muttering 'Of course, of course, so sorry,' in a repetitious pattern and then, when I realised I couldn't push bits of paper from one side of the table to another anymore, I coughed to signify it was time for her to stop glaring crossly at me. She sighed heavily and turned away. I smiled at her back weakly and watched her as she crossed the room to her desk a fairly safe distance away. I glanced over at Suzie for some friendly camaraderie but noticed her busily pressing various buttons on her telephone unable to register my grimace.

I would never have guessed one day, and one day had come surprisingly quickly, that we would be working in the same room once more. To be accurate we had never really worked in the same room together at university. We had gossiped, giggled, argued, eaten, partied and pretended to work in the same room but what I meant was I never thought we'd end up back in the same room together out in the real wide world. We had both started out in wholly different directions.

We'd both left university a year and a half ago with matching 2:1's, what any self-respecting student hopes to achieve after three years of eating pizza, drinking vodka and cramming exams. We'd immediately headed off to our illustrious capital; our heads full of childish dreams and hopes for the future. We had degrees for goodness sake. The world was our oyster, we were small fish in a big sea, big things come to those who wait etc etc. We knew it all. It had been a Dick Whittington style journey, to do as he had done and find our fortunes on the streets of London town. Instead of a talking cat named Puss I had taken two goldfish on the adventure who had miraculously survived their years of student living. Budweiser cans in the fish tank, that kind of thing. They certainly deserved a treat and I couldn't bring myself to get rid of them. This wasn't due to any particular attachment I had for them but an attempt to null the enormous guilt I still suffered due to a bizarre childhood habit of flushing all our family pets down the loo. Although I wasn't too concerned about the fish that might have swum to safety it was still a tragedy that Hazel the Hamster had gone the same way. Bless that rugged rodent, may he rest in peace. Anyway cats, Dick Whittington and, oh yes, our arrival in London town.

We had arrived in the capital buzzing with aspirations and fresh-faced enthusiasm. I was confidently seeking an agent, a life on the stage, a successful move into television, a film or two, a gorgeous flat, thousands of pounds, the cover of Vogue. The usual. I'd soon realised the endless search for an acting job wasn't quite as easy as I'd initially imagined. I'd gone from various castings, workshops, auditions and struggled as I found unpaid parts in London's fringe theatre. I had done a thousand part time jobs to pay the bills but had suffered from a massive crisis in confidence after yet another rejection. Slowly I had stopped applying for jobs and started complaining about my lack of regular income.

Meanwhile Suzie had sensibly accepted a work experience placement on a teenage magazine. She'd been offered a permanent position and two years later had been made Deputy Editor. Just like that. She'd been totally supportive of my bid for stardom; accompanying me to auditions, moaning with me about the various horrors of the Entertainment industry. And when times looked really tough and I was living on bread alone, she'd wangled me a job on the magazine. I'd never thought I'd ever use my Psychology degree for anything practical but it had come in surprisingly handy when applying for the post of Resident Agony Aunt. So now I worked in the office of 'Sweet SixTeen' writing problem pages for concerned thirteen year olds. I had temporarily shelved the acting ambitions for the need to make a bit of money. And although I didn't mind writing my column 'Ask Angel' I was often fantasising about an alternative existence as a glamorous actress.

At that moment Suzie looked up from her desk and noticed my forlorn expression. She winked at me and then carried on tapping away at the telephone. I nodded miserably back at her and tried to focus on the letter in front of me that had prompted my trip down memory lane. Ah yes, the all-important 'how do I find the right man?' question. Oh dear. Did this girl not realise from the various dating agencies, lonely hearts columns and escort services that every woman on this earth is asking the same thing? The search for the right man took a little bit of time. You had to put the effort in. And most women who had got to this conclusion had given up, hence the high sales in vibrators. Best not write that though. Still without mentioning sex toys to under-14's I placated her with a brief reply along the lines of 'How she would find the right man in time ya dee ya dar,' 'how she had to focus on other things in the meantime etc etc' and lastly 'how she might want to consider the fact that many women were now remaining single way into their thirties. In fact the largest social group in London were single people in their thirties, marriages were getting later, divorces were becoming more frequent, you will find yourself in excellent company...' I crossed the last bit out. Perhaps best not to depress her at too young an age. And anyway, maybe things would be different for her, maybe she would find Mr.Right. I had. I leaned back in my chair, sucking on my biro to show any observers I was deep in intellectual thought. I always went back to that night out with Suzie. That had been my one chance to be with The Man of My Dreams. Some might argue I didn't know him that well, that ordering two green drinks together is not a solid foundation to build the perfect partnership etc., but they were wrong. I knew he wouldn't have disappointed me. He had been my idea of the right man. In danger of floating back to his embrace I picked up the next letter purposefully and forced my concentration to focus on the scrawl.

Dear Angel,

I've been out with a gorgeous bloke twice and everything seemed perfect. But it was three days ago that I last saw him and although he promised he'd phone me, he hasn't. I've left four answer phone messages, but no joy. Should I leave it or try again?

Pippa, Cambridge, 17

I looked at the letter aghast, had this girl no shame? I started scribbling a reply offering her ingenious ways to distract her from humiliating herself further. Could she tape a note to the phone saying 'Do not call him'? Could she arrange a night out on the tiles with her friends? Could she throw herself into her schoolwork? Could she forget him until he rings? At the bottom of the letter I wrote in capitals, 'DO NOT UNDER ANY CIRCUMSTANCES BE TEMPTED TO PICK UP THE TELEPHONE AND DIAL HIS NUMBER.' She hadn't exactly been the coolest of customers up to now, but she could still make a last ditch effort to try. Familiar bells were ringing in my own ears as I wrote all this out. I shifted uncomfortably in my seat as my mind drifted from the reply, to the truth of the night I had met my Dream Man. I tried to suppress my train of thought but I suppose there are a few things I had omitted from my initial remembrance of May 14th 2001. I promise to now tell you the whole truth, and nothing but the truth, so help me god. It hadn't been a totally open and closed book. In fact I'd just left you after the opening chapter...

So back to me gazing into Dream Man's lovely eyes as he excused himself to go to the loo. I watched him manfully manoeuvre his way through the room and sighed as I fiddled with the straw of my drink. It had been such a lovely evening. We'd been chatting for a while and had discovered we had all kinds of things in common. For example he was heavily involved in the Jazz Society at the university and I had always fancied taking up the sax. He liked to visit the art museum in town and I lived only two minutes down the road from it! He was born in Nottingham and my granddad used to own a house there. It was spooky how well we meshed together. He was lovely, and witty and gorgeous. I sighed again for a bit of theatrical effect, and to show passers-by I was deeply immersed in my own little fluffy cloud world and not a sad loser with no mates. Everything was going to plan.

Cue Irish Guy who decided to step in at this point in the story, taking up the recently vacated spot to try his lucky Irish charms out on me. He settled himself in the chair and started speaking in a lilting Irish accent. I was still moonily gazing into the distance and gradually turned to take in the change of table companion. From what I could gather he was in the midst of an endearing speech along the lines of 'wasn't I pretty' and 'how nice I looked,' which I felt I couldn't really interrupt so waited for him to finish. I momentarily realised this little tête-à-tête might look a little dodgy to Dream Man, who had only been gone a matter of seconds, but he wouldn't be back for a while and the topic was to my liking. The main gist of it focused on the theme of me and how wonderful I was, and I could always spare someone a moment or two to chat about that. However time passed by gradually and I realised Irish Guy looked a tad too comfortable and any moment now Dream Man would be back to claim the chair, and my affections. So I jumped on the chance to be free of him by agreeing that he might buy wonderful little me a drink. As we walked towards the bar however I took a tactical fork to the left and watched as he blended into the gathering never to be seen again. Cunning. I straightened up. At that moment Dream Man came up behind me and steered me gently by my elbow towards the other side of the bar enquiring as to who the stranger was.

That's when I panicked.

'Oh er... oh um...' I rooted around for a gem of an excuse and voila, 'Oh he's my ex-boyfriend. You know what its like.' I chuckled with a look that said of course you know what its like. His blank face suggested he didn't seem to however, so I ploughed on, 'You know, you can never quite get rid of them. Always turn up at the wrong time,' I continued, carefully studying the cocktail menu as if it was some vital document I needed to learn by heart. 'But he's gone now, obviously got the hint,' I added staring directly up at him in a meaningful way. I saw Dream Man visibly relaxing and inwardly congratulated myself on such excellent handling of the situation, and after so many of the green cocktails too. Hurrah. I selected a drink and as Dream Man turned to order I checked over my shoulder briefly for any Irish folk nearby. I was distracted from my search fairly abruptly as Dream Man placed his hand in mine. I thought I might die right then and there. Not that that would have been the cool thing to do, and probably not the reaction he'd been going for. His manly hand claimed me. Yes, he wanted me. Me. Me. Me. It was all going so swimmingly. I felt his arm snake around my waist and I relaxed into it. Then suddenly another hand thrust a drink under my nose. I jerked a little. Three hands. My Dream Man had three hands. A freak. I knew there had to have been a catch. He'd been far too perfect. Oh god. I turned in horror to get a glimpse of this weird appendage and stopped short in my tracks to see Irish Guy grinning at me like a lunatic. It was his hand snaking around the small of my back. Ah.

What followed could have been described as a slightly awkward moment. It could also be described as an excruciatingly awful awkward moment, but I don't want to scare you. I turned to see Irish Guy, Irish Guy turned to stare at Dream Man and Dream Man turned to stare at me. Weirdly we were all still connected with hands and waists and drinks and arms. To any outsider the scenario could possibly have been described as a touch confusing.

Then before I could think up anything to say Dream Man had given him a withering look and stepped forward piping up, 'So you're the ex-boyfriend right?'

Irish Guy looked a little perplexed, not totally unsurprising seeing as we'd known each other for five whole minutes. Then there was another few seconds of horrible silence as Irish Guy looked questioningly at me. As did Dream Man. In fact they both stared at me, as if I had all the answers. Ridiculous. The tense silence was still there and I tried to explain everything coherently.

'Er...' I giggled a touch nervously, 'Well, er... no. Not exactly, actually um...' And I trailed off mumbling and glancing around the room for any kind of inspiration, or possible escape route. Suzie waved at me energetically from the dance floor, writhing around her catch. Not helpful. Before I could think of a better way to expertly blag myself out of the awkwardness Dream Man had rejected my hand and stalked off.

'Shit,' I muttered, and turned to take chase to explain to him that it had all been a big misunderstanding. But then there was Irish Guy still looking expectant and I realised I had better drink his drink and be done with him. So I knocked it back, wincing at the taste, and still trying to keep an eye on Dream Mans' route. However impeding my progress was Irish Guy who just wouldn't leave me alone. I took the first opportunity I could to try and make a run for it.

'I've just got to go to the loo, won't be long,' and legged it into the room dodging and ducking about until I reckoned my trail was truly hidden.

'Disaster, bloody, bloody disaster.' I stamped around a bit trying to catch the eye of Suzie who was now slow dancing with Gorgeous Green Jumper. I was simultaneously scanning the crowd for Dream Man and on Security Alert for any Irish people. During my somewhat frantic checks someone managed to slap me playfully on the bottom and I spun round, full of hope that the chauvinistic move might be Dream Man with a sign saying 'All is Forgiven' and a footnote that read, 'Be with Me Forever.' But it wasn't. It was Rick. With no sign. Darn. Rick was one of my best friends at university. He was very loud, very camp and not a man to run into in a crisis. For me this summed up how badly things were going. Even fate was against me. I didn't need Rick, I needed Rikki Lake. I needed to solve this dilemma. However beggars can't be choosers and seeing as Rick was the only advisory option, I had a go. I explained the whole nightmare scenario to him and he nodded and oohed when I got to the best bits. Trouble was he was less interested in helping me and more keen to discover just how dreamy Dream Man was. Then just as I was nearing the end of my anguished tale I spotted Irish Guy roving close by anxiously searching for me.

'Shit.' I muttered, and then hit upon a great idea, 'Rick. Quick. Kiss me.' And before he could argue I lunged at him pretending to give him the most passionate of all snogs. Long enough so that Irish Guy sees and short enough so Rick doesn't have heart failure. As I de-tangled myself I get shot a nasty look from Irish Guy, who thank god took the hint and departed forthwith. Giggling I wiped the lipstick from Rick's face.

'That got rid of him,' I said triumphantly. Then with horror I spot Dream Man out of the corner of my eye staring at me with a look of pure contempt on his face, 'Shit that's him, RICK' I nudged him, 'That's HIM.' But Rick was rubbing his neck in confusion.

'Er Angel,' he started, 'I don't know what to say. I don't. I mean. You know I'm gay right.' I stared at him disbelievingly, then kissed him quickly on the forehead and yelled, 'Of course gorgeous' over my shoulder leaving Rick to mull over the significance of the snog. I hadn't time to waste analysing my actions. That was for class. Spotting Dream Man making a hasty exit I gave chase. I saw him push his way through the revolving doors and tottered after him.

'Excuse me, schuse me,' I yelled, propping myself up on the way by any bodies in my path. I reached the revolving door in record time and pushed through it. The icy cold hardly hit me so consumed I was with my chasing game and, lets face it, more than a bit pissed. I saw him getting into a nearby taxi and rushed after him, my new heels fighting against the urge to start sprinting and tripping me up as best they could. Bloody things. At this point I was now yelling his name and such comments as 'you don't understand; he's gay' to make me seem less mad. He was quickening his pace and looking worriedly over his shoulder. He jumped into a vacant taxi and sped off. Left standing unsteadily in the middle of the road I slumped disappointed as I saw him disappear out of my life. Then my fighting instinct kicked in and I realized; I couldn't lose him. I was in love with him. He was right for me. With fresh determination I lurched into the pathway of another taxi which magically was empty and magically didn't run me down. I dived in on my mission.

'I want you to follow that taxi,' I gabbled confidently at the driver, 'Now,' I finished pointing in its direction like I was the main character in NYPD Blue and my next line was 'Step On It.'

The taxi driver, recognising a woman on a mission, and relishing the tense atmosphere got quite into his role. He raced after the other cab, flashing at it with his head lights on full beam and beeping his horn frantically. We gained a little ground but Dream Man's taxi picked up the pace and suddenly I felt like we were in a full blown car chase. I could almost hear the camp 80's beats as we sped down the road. Sadly the taxi man wasn't keen enough on his role as my gutsy partner in crime that he ignored traffic lights turning red and I screeched at him to keep going as the tyres ground to a halt. He also didn't take too kindly to me screaming at him, 'Move the fuck on, that's the love of my life,' at the top of my voice. We got to the part in the movie where the police woman is ejected from the taxi for abusive, aggressive behaviour. Oops. Miserably I see the fugitive as a small dot in the distance and realise the futility of further chasing. I pay my driver in a grump and step unsteadily out of the Bat Mobile.

I stood silently in a dark street feeling lost. If only I could have explained everything to him. If only I had been able to tell him about my epiphany (him being the man that should be with me forever). I looked around to get my bearings and realised I'd been dumped near my university building. And then a thought occurred to me. What a brilliant plan! Before I knew it I was tapping in the security code to the door for our computer room, conveniently open 24 hours a day for last minute essay writers and drunk girls on a mission. Throwing myself into a seat I switched on a computer, a groggy looking man clearly trying to get his essay finished in time for his deadline the next day looked up at me confusedly. I suppose I did seem a little over dressed, and over excited, for a late night internet session. I gave him a shrug of the shoulders and he went back to his work. Miraculously I managed to remember my password and soon I was roaming around the university website with one thought in my mind. I typed in 'Search' and then 'Philosophy' and then 'Undergraduates.' Hurrah, only 174 names popped up. One was the Man For Me. I didn't hesitate. I wrote a group email, forwarding it to every single Philosophy Undergraduate at the university. It read,

Dear Dream Man from Jennys partyt (?). I thjink I love you. Let me explain. You see he was gay and its not what it looks like you see no ecboyfirend just irish. Lets get tohether. I love. Uo[angela xxxcx

Send.

I bumped into him again weeks later. It wasn't good. In fact I've never seen a man so afraid. I guessed he was one of those people who thought cracking onto ex-boyfriends, snogging randoms, screaming at him down a road, chasing him in a cab, emailing him and all his fellow course mates in the dead of night, informing him I loved him, and all after a half hour introduction, not the best first impression. Bizarre. So I suppose that was the truth of the night I met Dream Man. It hadn't been a complete success.

And I was still searching for him. Well not specifically that Dream Man, as I had to face facts, he had probably taken out a restraining order against me, and undergone vital plastic surgery in an effort to stop me tracking him down. So it wasn't him specifically I was searching for, it was all that he represented. The whole package. Just perfection. I had had a glimpse of it that night. Could it really be that hard to find again? Because next time I was sure I'd know how to behave...

* * *

All these profound questions were interrupted by flecks of spit falling onto the page in front of me as a figure in a fit of coughing stood over my desk. I looked up to see a nasty nylon suit and shiny purple tie staring back at me. Groaning inwardly I plastered a sickly smile on my face and raised my gaze further.

'Hi Richard.' I said, not meaning it in the least. I didn't mean 'Hi' I meant 'what the hell do you want spluttering at me over my desk? Why, why do I need this today? What have I ever done to you?' But 'Hi' seemed easier somehow.

'Morning Angela,' he replied, his suit shimmering in the harsh overhead lighting every time he moved.

Richard was the Features Editor for the magazine and also, joy of joys, the magazine's Agony Uncle. He had a small column running down the side of my page where he answered problems for the teenage boys that wrote into the magazine. Personally the fact that he had a column on my page gave me the impression that I was more important than him. Sadly this didn't translate in his head. He thought this bought him the right to pester me daily on any topic in a smugly superior way. Tomayto, tomato.

'How's your column going?' I asked in a bored voice not

bothered if the column was finished, half-done, or naked running around the office.

He delivered the usual patronizing sneer, 'Oh God I finished it off on Monday. As you know I'm ridiculously busy editing with Features and haven't got time messing about with some stupid twelve years old's worries about his acne.' He smirked like he'd just cracked an enormously funny joke. I looked blankly back at him which irritatingly didn't seem to put him off continuing, 'Honestly they are such a bunch of sad losers. It's not difficult to think of replies. I just give them the usual 'you'll be fine, talk to your teacher' bollocks to them.'

'Well, well done you,' I said sarcastically.

He ploughed on oblivious to my tone, 'I heard you haven't finished your page yet though. Pushing it a bit fine aren't you?' he said awarding himself first prize in the pointing-out-the-painfully-obvious contest.

I gritted my teeth, 'Yes Richard. I deliberately push myself to the edge to test my creative abilities and nerves of steel. Satisfied?' I finished, a petulant pout playing on my lips.

Richard backed off my desk in an over the top panto gesture, placing his hand on his chest and trying to look affronted, 'Ooh bit touchy today aren't we. Is it somebody's time of the month?'

I looked at him incredulously. Un believable. Un-bloody-believable. I forced myself to stay calm and do as I always did, imagine him standing there naked, which always cheered me up. He was probably covered in boils. This man was a first class pratt and I had the misfortune to work with him.

Weirdly the rest of the office appeared to be completely unaware of his despicable nature and he might actually be described as 'popular.' Amongst the Features desk he was even promoted to the status of an attractive man. Debbie, with the bi-focal lenses, tried to hide her desire for him but any idiot could see she was head over heels. You would think that someone with such sharp eyesight would know better. She thought she hid it well but I'd noticed her breathing thicken every time Richard leaned over her to fiddle with her mouse. I was convinced he only applied for the job to up his chances of finding some poor soul to pose as a girlfriend. The office was made up almost entirely of women; the laws of probability were definitely on his side. Even though most of my colleagues proved to be way out of his league i.e. had a pulse, rumours abounded that he was now seeing the receptionist with the peroxide hair. Lucky girl. He was convinced she was seeing him for his dashing good looks, great sense of humour and sharp suits. I was convinced she was only seeing him to ensure she had enough to moan about to her friends on the phone all day. Debbie was convinced the rumours were totally untrue. Denial, poor thing.

Looking up I realised Richard was still talking to me. Suddenly my phone started ringing. I rolled my eyes and reached out for the receiver, 'Oh I'm terribly sorry,' I said waving him away mid-sentence, 'Do you mind.' A look of irritation crossed his face. Ha ha ha. He stalked off back to his desk and I raised the receiver to my ear not caring if the person on the end of the line was telemarketing or trying to sell me windows. I was free of him.

'Hello lovely,' giggled a voice down the line. I squeaked with delight. Victoria looked up sharply from the photocopier. I remembered to tone down the squeaking and try and sound business like and professional. I'd already been in trouble today.

'Mel, how are you? I thought you'd gone to Majorca with Peter?'

'We did,' sighed the voice on the end of the phone.

'So why are you back here? Don't say you got homesick.'

'Yeah that was it Angie. I got to Majorca, sat in the 30 degree heat and thought damn I wish I were back in England sitting in traffic, watching the rain and going to work.'

'Well, why are you back?' I asked again.

'Well the flight went well, we got on the plane, we landed and then we all watched Peter, pissed as a newt from all that in-flight booze, trip at the top of the aeroplane steps, bounce down the top three, land on the bottom three and break his leg on the ground.' She sighed theatrically and started to giggle, 'Honestly Angie I've never been so pissed off. He managed to land on some glass and I spent the first half of the week holding his hand in the hospital as the nurses tried to inject him in the arse and the second half sitting next to him by the poolside as he moaned he couldn't get his cast wet. It was too much so I booked us a flight back a week early. Honestly one day that man...' She trailed off and I was left to sympathise.

'Oh no, poor you Mel. So how's Peter now?'

'He hasn't told work he's back so he's lying on the sofa and I'm still playing Mother Teresa.'

'Well it can't be much fun for him,' I said.

'Rubbish, he's loving it. He's found a little hand bell from somewhere and keeps ringing it at me when he wants something.'

I grinned down the phone as she went on,

'And earlier he actually asked me to feed him grapes... and I did,' she groaned.

I giggled imagining Peter shamefully milking the situation for all its worth. Mel changed the subject to stop me chuckling at her plight.

'So what have you been doing all day? Answering all the troubles of the teens, eh?'

'Something like that,' I said.

'Look as I'm back early and have a vague suntan I was thinking I might want to branch out and go for some lunch. Can you be tempted?'

I sighed, 'I wish I could but I've got to finish my page for the magazine, the deadlines today. How about I call you over the weekend?'

'Alright don't work too hard.'

'Same to you,' I said hearing a bell ringing in the background.

'My master is calling for me' Mel's voice sighed. The bell became more persistent. 'I better go. Bye Angel.'

I put the phone down smiling. Poor Mel.

I pictured her rushing back to check on Peter and smiled. What's worse was in a few short hours her seven year old son Zac would be home from school to join the list of demands. I never knew how Mel managed to juggle her life I thought with a sigh. At 28 she was a few years older than me. She'd been doing her MA in Psychology when I'd met her at university. She'd been going out with Peter since she was eighteen, had had Zac when she was twenty and was then training to be a child psychologist. In between all this she'd found the time to practically pass my degree for me, breaking down complicated theories and making the most dull topics seem absolutely fascinating. Peter and her had stayed together, despite both their families' miserable predictions that they would never make it. They had only been going out eleven months when Mel had found out she was pregnant, but nearly eight years later and they all live in relative domestic bliss. Mel's mother has stopped forecasting imminent doom and now spends most of her free time planning a wedding that is always 'just around the corner.' Peter doesn't seem in any rush to propose. Mel's mother has nothing to worry about though. They might not be married but they are in the most stable relationship I've ever known. Including my parents. I was convinced they would stay together forever. Not that I had much reason to complain. I myself boasted the beginnings of a long term relationship. And, my mood lifting at the thought, I was meant to be seeing my boyfriend tonight.

The man in question weighs in at six foot two, around 170 pounds, sports clean, blonde hair and a respectable job as a trader for a big City firm. He's twenty-eight years of age and hails from the nice bit of Essex. Nicholas Sheldon-Wade, or just Nick. His credentials include four A levels (although one is General Studies), a degree from Durham University and an annual salary of over £50k. His interests include squash, going out, seeing me and Verdi.

I hadn't spoken to him for a little while actually. The poor lamb had been inundated with work. He'd mentioned something about an important account he was trying to close or trying to, well to be honest I might have slightly switched off to the finer details of the workload. Not that I didn't care. I had just let my mind slightly wander and before I'd known it he'd finished his sentence and my line was next. I think I'd said, 'hmm,' but very knowingly. He hadn't noticed my lapse in attention which assured me he still respected me as a mutual financial enthusiast. Which of course I was, or would be if I took more of an active interest in finance. To be truthful I shied away from the topic, normally due to the fact that personal finance had never been a priority and certainly never an interest with which I'd speak enthusiastically of. I'd usually pushed money issues to the back of my mind where they'd remained happily snuggled up with career issues, educational issues, political issues, that kind of thing. But back to the point. Busy. Nick. Poor him. I was suddenly gripped by an overwhelming urge to hear his voice and automatically reached out my hand for the receiver. But then I remembered I couldn't call him at work. Well to be truthful it wasn't that I was physically incapable of calling him at work so much as I wasn't allowed to phone him at work anymore. It had all been such a silly misunderstanding. I hadn't been thinking straight, I'd panicked. It was a one off. You see it dated back to a little episode in the first tentative week when we had been "seeing each other". I had thought it a fun game to call him at work as a surprise. I'd dialled his number enthusiastically, automatically assuming his dulcet tones would answer the call. So imagine my surprise on hearing a snappily efficient female voice on the other end pick up. I nervously asked to be put through to Nick and waited patiently to be transferred.

'And who shall I say is calling?' came the snappy efficient woman.

Caught off guard and realising from her unwelcome tone that obviously work calls weren't the done thing in The City I'd panicked and before I knew it blurted out, 'His wife.' Sure enough I was put straight through. An hour afterwards however I received a cold phone call from Nick who'd said he'd been fielding questions about his other half, who (by the way) he'd known nothing about, all morning. Thus work calls had become pretty much a no go area. I toyed with the idea of breaking this tradition but realised if the clock was correct I really didn't have long until my deadline. My page for the magazine was due in a few short hours. I went back to focusing on the letters in front of me.

Dear Angel,
I think I'm in love with my cousin...

Around lunch Suzie came by.

'So are you going out later? I thought I might call Rick and see if he's around. Fancy joining us for a drink or two?'

'Very possibly' I said, not looking up.

'Don't get stuck with that Nick or I'll never see you.'

'I won't.'

'Do you want...'

'Look Suzie I'm really busy,' I said pausing in my writing.

'Do you want some lunch?' she asked, choosing to ignore my slight.

'Can't. Haven't got time,' I said abruptly, back to scribbling.

'Victoria told me you're pushing it a bit fine,' she said.

I rolled my eyes at her, 'Don't lecture me Suzie.'

'I'm not going to lecture you don't worry, I just wondered if you wanted me to get you some lunch.'

'No honestly I'm fine. I'll grab something in a minute.'

'OK. See you later,' she said, in a voice that implied she was used to customary strops around deadlines. I looked up again to apologise but she had already gone.

I instantly regretted being so brusque as 1) Suzie was one of my best friends and didn't need me snapping at her and 2) I was actually very, very hungry. As soon as I could I rushed out to grab a quick sandwich and a coffee... and a Kit Kat and a Bounty if I'm being honest and detailing all food purchases, then raced back in to complete the 'Ask Angel' page. I smiled at Suzie on the way in to double-check I hadn't caused any permanent damage. She gave me a wave of assurance and I went back to being fervent. The day swept by and I tapped the last dot on my final reply with a satisfied sigh at 4.30pm. I checked it over for any overtly ridiculous spelling mistakes and double checked the phone numbers for the appropriate help lines. I had a good range of problems answered; the 'I'll never find a man' headed the page with 'my friend's anorexic' tick, the age-old 'Should I sleep With Him' tick, 'I'm depressed and alone' tick and 'My mum's leaving him' all present. It all seemed there.

I got up to deliver the pages to Victoria who would scan them and then hand them to the subs to type up and format, which was technological language for 'make look pretty.' Victoria's office was in the corner of the room. Although I could see she was not busy, and looking at me expectantly through the glass windows, I still knocked on the door. Feeling a mite silly when her efficient bark of 'yes' came immediately, I stepped inside.

Victoria's office instantly makes you feel uncomfortable. Everything within the office has a neat precision and place. Surfaces gleam. Ring-bind folders are stacked on the shelves in yearly order. Pictures are hung straight. Cacti stand poker straight in their pots. An air-purifier whirs in the background. The room shouts control and efficiency. I noticed her pencil sharpener was one of those electronic ones. Every pencil was hacked to a uniform length, drilled and sliced to look like all the others. I stared at the machine mesmerised, imagining her laughing evilly as she spliced each one shorter and shorter...

I dropped off the pages with a nervy smile and then tried to leave as quickly as possible with a 'have a good weekend' exit line all prepared.

'Angela,' she said.

'Hmm...' I said

'Thank you, but please try and make sure it's not such a rush next month.'

'Yes I'm so sorry I will.'

'OK then, have a good weekend,' she said, nicking my prepared line. Bitch.

Flummoxed I could only come up with a muffled 'Fanks yeah I will.'

As I left the office I deliberately ignored the nearby Features desk knowing instinctively that Richard would be looking at me with an 'oh-dear-just-finished' glint in his eye. Seconds later my head spun round unwillingly and sure enough Richard was staring at me with with an 'oh-dear-just-finished' glint. The world was as it should be. I raced to my desk, threw everything into my bag and headed for the door. I gave Suzie an 'I'll-call-you' mime on the way out of the office and then left the building to be hurried along the pavement to the tube station by the rest of central London.

* * *

Aaah. Rush hour by tube, the perfect way to end your working day. When I had first arrived in London I hadn't understood the urgency of my fellow tube riders. The Underground had seemed like such an amusing novelty, and I had skipped off to join the fun and "ride the tube". No one had warned me. The pace was unbelievable. Masses of bodies jostled and shunted through the ticket barriers, knocking aside fellow travellers with a quick flick of a handbag or a full body blow by a carrier bag.

I'd quickly learnt that it was the survival of the fittest in the land of the London Underground. You snooze, you lose. In my early tube riding days I had often waited politely for the people to get off at their stop before I made any effort to get on. But no longer. I'd learnt my lesson. How naïve I'd been. As I had been waiting patiently for the commuters to emerge, thousands of professional tube-takers had rushed past me, so that when I next looked up the seats were full; men, women, children were squashed up to the glass windows and I'd been left on the platform edge. 'Next train to Brixton, 12 minutes.' Dammit. After being patient three more times and watching three more trains leave with everyone aboard aside from me I'd cottoned on to the game. No more did I stand aside as people stepped off, no more did I wait for the doors to fully open, no more did I care if a little granny looked set to be trampled in the fray. That little granny knew tricks. Now I waited eagle-eyed for the overhead sign to announce '1 minute.' The next few seconds would be a nail biting wait, eyes shifting left and right to see the possible impediments to my route. Bodies coming at me from either side, people trying to overtake me by stealth, anyone with a large suitcase: that kind of thing. I eyed up a girl side stepping her way closer to the platform edge. I gave her 'a look' to show she hadn't got away with it. She froze mid-step. It was a cruel, heartless world out there on the platform. My heart beat faster; it was a matter of seconds now. I could see the trains' headlights in the tunnel. A hush descended. Formerly friendly, chatty people become a silent throng taking up their positions, like sprinters on the starting blocks. I stared stonily ahead without a word. The train doors opened and the race was on. People squeezed past in both directions, I moved forward blindly until I was standing bag crushed uncomfortably into my stomach, face staring directly at another commuter's armpit.

Success.

After exiting the tube the rain had begun to spit down and I vainly tried to protect my head from a soaking using my handbag that was little bigger than a matchstick box, and just as effective. I arrived in our street with my hair frizzing and my clothes taking on a soggy feel. We live in a second floor flat in an old Victorian House. Our street is deceptively plush looking. On the day of the viewing I had positively skipped along the tree lined road with relief, counting the house numbers down until I had looked up to review 48, Marmion Road. Not the prettiest on the block. The paint on the door was peeling off, and cracks in the brick work, that I had thought made it look 'ancient and mysterious,' to the building inspector had meant 'damp and barely habitable.' Still I had been blinded by a sunny day and a depressing three weeks of looking at characterless flats in yellow Lego land type complexes. The house wasn't yellow, the road was decent and we couldn't afford any better. I put the key in the house lock and half-heartedly sifted through the post on the side shelf. Most of the envelopes looked fairly ominous, brown with typed addresses and words like 'Confidential' stamped on them, so I left them to simmer a while longer. The hall walls were peeling a little where the damp was seeping in, and the carpet, a mustard-coloured throwback from the 70's, had fraying edges and faded flowers. Trudging up to our flat on the first floor I thought of the weekend stretching ahead, and a renewed vigour lifted me. Suddenly the carpet didn't seem so stagnant and the walls could peel off for all I cared. I opened the door and heard Ellie busily clattering around in the kitchen.

I've known Ellie for years. And not in a kind of 'oh yah I've known Ellie for yaaarrs,' I've really truly known her for years. We'd lived opposite each other in the suburbs of Guildford. We had gone to the same primary school. She'd known me in my 'I want to challenge Annika' phase. Together we'd perfected the Care Bears Stare (circa 1985). I'd beaten her at the egg and spoon race (Sports Day, 1987). She'd poured the cherryade into the kettle and I'd pressed the 'on' button. We'd both been grounded for ruining a perfectly serviceable carpet. We'd made a telephone using two plastic cups and a bit of string. When these failed to produce little more than a mysterious rustling we'd invested our pocket money in a couple of walkie talkies and spent the summer perfecting Morse code. We'd both made identical fashion faux paus's simultaneously believing slouch socks, polka dot leggings and glitzy ra ra skirts the way to go. We'd both got a perm, and admitted they didn't make us look anymore like Kylie. We'd weaved each other friendship bands with the promise that 'Here's your band, put it on. We'll be friends forever long.' We'd both cried when Daphne died in Neighbours. We had both thought the Rubix Cube a startlingly clever invention. We'd both given Barbie a bob and regretted it. We both rated 'Rainbow' as Quality Entertainment. We had both known that Captain Planet He's our Hero was 'gonna take pollution down to zero.' We had agreed the special effects in 'Back to the Future' would be the most advanced we'd ever know.

As time had gone by we'd remained close friends in our rebellious teenage years. We'd both snogged a guy (with tongues) at the school Christmas Party, 1992. We'd both got braces in Year 9. We'd both sent love letters to Mr Price who taught Art. We'd both put lemon juice, toothpaste and toilet bleach in our hair to streak it blonde. We'd both been lucky to retain a full head of locks. We'd both tried smoking together in the woods by our house. We'd done GCSE's together, A level revision. We'd dated brothers. We'd shared an 18th party. And though we'd got into separate universities, we'd both agreed to live together afterwards. So I've know Ellie for years. And she has known me. We'd lived in the flat for coming up to two years and Ellie had been unemployed for the last six weeks.

She'd been working as the receptionist for a large advertising firm. However after just over a year of loyal receptionist work they'd suddenly announced they were 'ringing in the changes,' 'down sizing,' 'moving in a different direction,' which translated into the common tongue as 'so you're fired.' She had always insisted the job was only temporary work whilst she looked around for what she really wanted to do. The only trouble was she didn't appear to have anymore of an idea a year on. She had tried a range of temporary work. The best being two weeks spent in a Knightsbridge boutique spritzing perfume on rich shoppers and the worst ranging from a mind numbing telesales job selling oven cleaner to bored housewives, stacking shelves of feed for a large pet shop and lastly waitressing in a dusty looking burger bar. The manager had been a skinny, spotty little figure of a man with nicotine stained hands and wandering eyes. She'd turned up looking neat with an enthusiastic smile stuck on her face and he had offered to give her the tour of the kitchen. After showing her how to use the deep fat fryer he ran through the process of making a burger. Having cooked the meat and toasted the bun he'd demonstrated how they placed the gherkin in the burger. Picking up two slices of gherkin he lay them next door to each other on the meat.

'You see Eleanor the gherkins do not sleep together,' he shook his head then laid one on top of the other and looked her in the eye meaningfully, 'They make love.' Ellie had run out of the trader's entrance after 1 hour and 47 minutes of employment.

'How was your day at work dear?' Ellie's voice floated along the corridor. Trundling into the kitchen I discovered her already covered in flour and attempting to make pancakes. I smiled at her dishevelled state,

'Ah the usual. Those poor teenagers desperate for help and advice from a wise and worldly woman of wisdom.'

'You mean your help and advice,' giggled Ellie looking at me with a raised eyebrow, 'I really worry for them, 'she said stirring the mixture in a bowl and doing a fairly good impression of a 50's house wife. 'Pancake?' she asked, holding out a plate on which lay a little stack of previous efforts.

'God Ellie we're never going to eat all of them.'

'I know,' she said, 'but I was bored and pancakes seemed like the answer.'

I relieved her of the plate and flung my bag onto the table, 'So are you going out tonight then?' I asked taking a first bite.

'I think I'm going to stay in,' she said pouring more batter into the frying pan. 'I went to the video store on the way home actually.'

'Ooh anything good out?' I said, all thoughts of a hectic social night out on the streets of London sinking fast into the background.

Ellie shifted a little, 'Hmm, not really. There was a lot of um... stuff we've seen. Are you not going out tonight then?' she enquired, her eyes darting from me to the table back to me nervously. I looked at her suspiciously.

'Ellie what have you hired out?'

Reaching into her bag on the table I saw her turn and a floury arm raced to stop me, 'Nooo, Angel. Ang. It's...' she trailed off as I opened the case.

'Ellie. It's Pocahontas II.' I stared at her in disbelief.

'Well,' she said defiantly, 'Well... I liked the first one and I wasn't in the mood for anything too deep.'

'There's no danger there then.' I giggled holding up the DVD with a scornful smile.

'Sure you don't want to join me?' she asked, whilst simultaneously covering a pancake with the remnants of a Nutella pot.

'Er, I think I might see what Nick's doing...' I said getting my mobile out of my bag and walking through to the living room '...Tempting though it is.' I flung myself down on the sofa and dialled his number. Even after six months of going out I still found this moment made me a little nervous. What if it was a bad time? What is he was busy? What if...

'Hello,' a voice cut through my insecurities.

'Hi Nick,' I said putting on my cool girlfriend voice. It was a cross between my polite work telephone manner and what I thought adult phone line people sounded like. A bit of hoarse sexiness to remind the man in my world I am the girl to be with.

'Who is this?' asked Nick, the voice obviously not ringing too many bells with him. I could hear the familiar background sounds of bar-after-work. The clutter of glasses and conversation meshing into a hubbub of noise I could never hope to penetrate.

'Angela,' I said, shifting out of sexy phone voice and into embarrassed he-didn't-guess-immediately-it-was-me voice.

'What sorry? Who?' he repeated.

'ANGELA,' I called a little louder down the phone.

'Right,' he said, still sounding uncertain and forcing me to repeat it once more and then finally spell it out.

'A-N-G-E-L-A.'

The phone call was starting to remind me of Christmas day calls to grand parents, who spent the first five minutes wondering who I was as I squawked at them down the line, and the rest of the call wondering who they were. But that is another story.

A breakthrough seemed to have occurred and recognition was granted, 'Oh Angel baby. How's it going?' A bellowing reply came down the phone.

I started to shout a little down the receiver, still trying to sound coy, sweet and attractive. It was quite a mission.

'Hi Nick. Just wanted to ring and check in with you.'

'What babe? I can't hear much. You want to do what with me?' A loud guffaw and I could hear Nick shouting to someone called Bobby/Nobby/Kobby, 'She wants to do something to me,' followed by an infantile 'Wooo.' I tried again.

'So where are you tonight? What are you up to?' I said, still screeching to be heard, all hopes of sounding laid back and breezy forgotten.

'Babe, I really can't hear you. I'm having a few drinks with the boys; I'll call you later if you like. We might go on to a club or something.'

'That would be COOL,' I shouted, feeling more than a little silly as Ellie popped her head round the door, 'I'll talk to you later then.'

'What Babe, what was that? You're going to climb me then? You're barking sweetheart.' More laughter.

'No,' I interrupted, 'No I'll TALK TO YOU LATER,' I said yelling down the phone.

'You do what you like darling.' The familiar guffaws accompanied this comment and I started to say goodbye.

'So I'll SPEAK...' I suddenly realised he'd gone. I held the receiver in my hand and blinked at it. Then I started as I noticed Ellie looking questioningly at me.

'So, is the lovely Nick taking you out?' she enquired.

I put the phone down and sunk into the sofa, 'Well he's a bit busy now but I'll probably see him later.'

'Hmm...' she said stiffly.

'What?'

'Let me guess. He's getting drunk with the boys?' she said rolling her eyes at me.

'Look Ellie he's had a stressful day at work and wants to unwind with his colleagues. That's fair enough. We don't know what it's like working in The City.' I said this in my most reverential voice. The City. It all seemed so grown up. Granted most of my preconceptions were based on watching Michael Douglas in 'Wall Street' during the late 80's. But I had to admit phrases like, 'Lunch, lunch is for wimps,' had stayed with me reminding me just how tough it all was. And my boyfriend worked there. Ellie handed me a pancake soaked in lemon and sugar.

I continued, 'Anyway he said he'd call later. So I might join them at a club or something.' I stuffed the pancake into my mouth. I hated excusing myself in front of Ellie; she had some crazy idea that Nick wasn't good enough for me. As if to prove this point she was looking at me in a way best described as 'with concern.'

'Stop staring at me weirdo and make me another pancake.' I pointed her to the kitchen; she dropped the quizzical gaze and went back to behaving like a domestic goddess.

I switched on the television and spent a few moments channel-hopping between various programmes. I was momentarily distracted by a news item on a woman from North Virginia who'd apparently just given birth to a frog but even the finer details around that story failed to keep me entertained for long. I remembered I'd promised to call Suzie and walking through to my room I waited for her to pick up.

'Hello Missie, are you out and about yet?' she asked as she answered.

'Hey, no I'm still at home but might be out later.'

'Excellent well Rick and I are in the Fleece and Firkin in South Ken and planning to stay here till closing.'

I could hear Rick bouncing around on his seat in the background. His entire demeanour resembled a Duracell bunny on speed. 'Come on Angel, come out and play...'

'Well... um...' I hesitated.

I could hear a groan from the other end, 'Let me guess. Nick?' she asked. I sat on my bed fiddling with my duvet.

'Well I'm waiting for a call from him and then I might join him at a club somewhere later, so I better just wait and see where he's going.'

'Fine, well we're here if you want to join.'

'OK... great. Well I'll probably see you soon, but if he's far away I might not make it in time so...'

'Alright, alright honestly Angel that's fine. I'll speak to you later.'

'OK, love to Rick,' I called.

On hanging up I heard a melancholy gay man saying, 'Is Angel pants not coming out to play?' and felt a pang of guilt.

'Angel, I've put the DVD on if you're interested,' Ellie called from the living room. I sighed and wrenched myself up off my bed to rummage through my chest of drawers. It took me under two minutes to dress in my finest around-the-flat attire, namely a pair of holey tracksuit bottoms and a nasty white T-shirt with the letters 'Purrfect' scrawled in pink across it. It had been a present from my little sister, which could obviously never be worn in public in the presence of actual living people. I wandered out of my room to the kitchen wondering if the Pot Noodles had finally run out. Ellie had settled herself down on the sofa expertly arranging various foodstuffs around her to ensure access to everything you could desire when camping out by the television. A bottle of wine was open, microwave popcorn stood steaming in a bowl and stray chocolate bars were scattered at every angle. The only thing missing was a man giving a foot massage. It was a tempting sight.

The action on the screen seemed standard Disney stuff. From the small bit I watched from the doorway of the kitchen I gathered it was winter in the New World as Pocahontas was sporting some pretty nice new snow boots for the sequel. The little racoon was involved in some kind of amusing snow ball fight with the pug faced dog and the kingfisher was buzzing around them both.

'I think Pocahontas looks fatter in this one,' Ellie said with some concern.

'Probably comfort eating coz she's single again.' I said stuffing a mouthful of Pot Noodle in my mouth and sinking on to a nearby chair.

'Maybe all the stress over whether she was going to get the sequel,' giggled Ellie handing me a newly opened bag of crisps.

We were introduced to the new love interest. He was a brunette with a pony tail and a cut glass English accent. He seemed arrogant and ignorant, never the best mixture.

'But better looking than the blonde in the first one,' I said pointing with my fork to the screen and sinking onto the arm of the sofa.

'I don't know,' said Ellie uncertainly, 'John Smith was a lot burlier, more manly. I liked his muscles.'

'I suppose this one is a bit weedy looking.'

'Too public school,' Ellie said shivering.

'What's wrong with that,' I said a little too defensively, 'Nick went to public school.'

Ellie mumbled something I couldn't catch. After another few minutes mulling over the action on the screen we both agreed that Pocahontas hadn't got the best taste in men, but also agreed she did pretty well for a girl stuck out in the middle of nowhere. My hand automatically reached for a stray Crunchie nearby and I settled snugly into the chair. The film was a sort of Crocodile Dundee-goes-to-New York type. Pocahontas packs herself off to London to sing a few songs and liven the place up a bit with her new boots and crazy loveable animal friends.

Hysterical. There was also a moral message flung in at the end but Ellie and I were too busy screeching 'SNOG, SNOG' in the closing scene to let it have much of an impact.

'Gah. I can't eat anymore. I can't drink anymore. I think I might live here for the next couple of days.' I said stretching my legs out and watching in amazement at the bump of my stomach. Not a pretty sight. 'I vow to never eat again.' I said doing my best to perfect a scout's honour.

'Do you want a hot chocolate,' Ellie asked getting up.

'Oooh yes.'

Ellie looked at me and laughed, 'What? It's a liquid,' I protested innocently. 'It's...' I was interrupted mid speech by a loud bang of the front door. Muffled footsteps could be heard on the floor below and then the downstairs flat door banged shut.

'Kevin's home,' I giggled nervously at Ellie. Kevin was the weirdo who lived downstairs. Kreepy Kevin as he'd been so imaginatively nicknamed by me. He was always dressed in the same checked faded yellow shirt and dark sludgy cords. He sported a large dark beard that Santa himself would have been proud of. Not that Kreepy Kevin was anything like Santa. Santa spent his days frolicking with Mrs Santa in Lapland, laughing and joking with his elfish community and looking after reindeer. Kevin was a man who lived alone, in a basement flat, rarely spoke to a soul and looked after a snake. He was like Santa for the devil child. In fact the snake discovery has been placed high up on my Bad Days Of This Year list, and Kevin and I have not spoken a syllable to each other since.

Six months ago our flat had been knee deep in dust and Ellie had borrowed a hoover off him for our first, and only, spring clean. I had been in charge of returning the machine. I had dragged it down the stairs, pipes and leads wrapping themselves round my legs as I shifted it, and rung his flat doorbell. Moments later Kevin had emerged with a bloody great reptile draped casually around his neck and I had scrambled backwards straight into a heap on top of hoover, pipes and leads, a scared squeaking noise escaping my lips and a cracking from the plastic vacuum cleaner somewhere beneath me. He looked at me slowly, stroking the snake. Behind him on the walls of his flat were framed snake skins glimmering in the semi darkness. I hadn't hesitated. I had raced back up the stairs as fast as I could, muttering about buying him a replacement hoover and not daring to look back. I had locked myself into the flat and waited by the door for Ellie to return home.

From then on in I had done my best to avoid him as much as possible. This wasn't too hard as he seemed to sleep through the day and only go out to engage in some kind of bizarre nocturnal activity in the cloak of darkness. I had no idea how he paid his rent. Probably drug dealing to his dirty tramp friends. No doubt they met in some seedy hole, or dark alley to conduct their business. Although admittedly he didn't appear to have an abundance of friends: even dirty tramp ones. I'd only ever seen one visitor to his flat; a surprisingly well dressed and attractive young woman. Social services perhaps.

Ellie interrupted my musing by handing me a mug of hot chocolate. We chatted a little bit. Ellie had spotted an attractive man buying a sandwich in the deli down the road and described him in minute detail. She also told me she'd bumped into an old school friend of ours who was in another play in the West End. I felt a bubble of envy and changed the subject quickly. Just as we were finally gearing ourselves up to go to bed we heard the downstairs flat door open again and the familiar muffled footsteps cross the hall, then the front door slammed shut. Silence.

'He's gone out again.'

'What the hell does he do walking around London at night?' I wondered out loud.

'Maybe he has a night job?' Ellie suggested. 'Or is a postman.'

'A postman?' I said sceptically.

'Well don't they get up early?' she protested.

'Early. Ellie it's...' I checked my watch '...It's half midnight. What does he do down there all day? With his snake.' I shivered.

'I'm going to bed,' Ellie laughed getting up from the debris. 'Sleep well,' she said walking through to her room.

'You too,' I replied, trying to shake off all thoughts of snakes and weirdoes before I gave myself bad dreams. 'See you in the morning.'

I crashed out on my bed quickly and as I was drifting off I realised Nick had never called.

* * *

I was woken the next morning with a call from Suzie. She'd gone on to a club with Rick, and as she so charmingly put it 'got lashed and got laid.' After a brief summary of events and a few groans and 'Oh my head's' she settled down to talk, 'So where did you end up last night then eh?'

I diverted her attention, 'So you saw Rick. How is he?' I asked quickly.

'Oh the usual – in love with some blonde guy. But apparently the blonde's already in a relationship, of three months, which Rick reckons is the straight equivalent of two years.'

'Really.'

'Sooo what did you do missus?' she asked, psyching herself up for a long, giggly hung over chat. 'You sound croaky...'

I sat up on my elbows and tucked the receiver under my ear.

'I stayed in.' I said, trying to sound proud.

'Oh,' Suzie said, clearly disappointed that I hadn't been raving around the streets of London.

'Sounds mental Angela, you mad cap party girl you, so anything exciting happen at all?' she asked.

'I watched Pocahontas II.'

'You watched what? Angela, I can't believe you write problem pages. I'll be over later,' she said aghast and then added, 'That is as long as you're not too busy watching the Muppets?' and hung up laughing.

Even on a Saturday after a big night out Suzie swept in looking immaculate. She was carrying the Times and the Telegraph under her arm and let me and Ellie rush around talking about nothing and making brunch whilst she criticised the actions of most of the world's leaders. Suzie could be very direct and slightly intimidating at times but she was loyal and amusing and a very good friend to me. I often thought how different she and Ellie were: Ellie with her bouncy homeliness seemed in total contrast to Suzie of the Pinstripe Suit, but seeing them cheerily greeting each other I wondered why I'd ever been concerned.

The weekend stretched ahead and we were all in a good mood cooking up bacon, sausages, eggs and sipping at tea. During the midst of this Rick flew in in a whirl of disorganisation, flinging a bag down on our sofa and flinging himself into a chair.

'We missed you last night. And I met someone,' he cooed moving straight into his favourite topic, his love life. 'He's so pretty,' he said sighing theatrically, 'a dancer with such a cute arse. Hi Ellie.'

'Hi,' Ellie replied instantly sitting down to hear more about the dancer.

'He is sweet, and funny and over 18. So it's legal,' he hoorayed, clapping his hands together enthusiastically.

'Sausage?' Suzie offered, thrusting the plate under his face.

'Suzie you're disgusting,' he said picking up a sausage delicately and nibbling at it.

'Ooh I forgot I'm not allowed to eat meat' he said stopping his chomping.

'There goes your social life,' smirked Suzie going back to reading the papers.

'Ha ha.'

'Why are you off meat?' asked Ellie trying to block out all the crudity.

'When have you ever been vegetarian,' I chorused in disbelief.

'Since now,' said Rick pompously, 'Some foods are not good for my digestive system. Some meat contains so much saturated fat and I'm concerned that it'll build up in my arteries...'

'Sounds painful,' giggled Suzie.

'Oh not this again,' I said cradling my head in my hands.

'Don't belittle my medical problems Angel,' said Rick haughtily.

'I'm not,' I said from my folded arms, 'I'm just blocking them out.'

Desperate to put off real life for another few years Rick had made the rash decision of signing up for five years of medicine at London's UCL. He was coming to the end of his second year and every week seemed to see him panicking over the latest new disease he'd learnt about.

'Honestly Angel, I've got a lot of the qualities of someone prone to blood clots and aneurysms. Fat can build up in my arteries and then one day it's boom, bang, over,' he described medically.

'What qualities have you got then?' I asked wearily reading the leaflet he'd just whipped out of his bag on 'Heart Attacks- Are you about to Have One?'

'A lot,' he said tapping the leaflet and then turning to Ellie, 'My have chest has been aching a little recently, sometimes it can be a really sharp pain...'

'Indigestion?' queried Suzie not looking up.

'And I sometimes feel shivery up my arm,' he went on, 'so I'm looking into family records, weak hearts can be hereditary you see, and I think my granddad might have died from a clot. It was that or the cancer that killed him, we're not absolutely sure...'

'Poor you,' said Ellie genuinely concerned.

I flicked idly through the information.

'I know it's terrible,' he nodded solemnly, 'but I'll get by. So Angel,' he said bouncing around to look at me, 'how is the lovely Nicholas? Still gorgeous?' He asked, obviously momentarily distracted from his symptoms.

Ellie got up and went through to the kitchen.

'He's fine. I was going to join him somewhere last night but he never called back.'

'So you didn't see him last night?' asked Rick confused.

'No I didn't meet him in the end.'

'She stayed in and watched Disney instead,' scoffed Suzie from her reading.

'What? Which one? Was it 'The Lion King'? Simba is so sexy,' Rick sighed.

Suzie looked up, 'You two really deserve each other.'

'I'm quite cross he didn't call actually,' I said venting a little frustration.

'Do you think its wrong to fancy a lion,' Rick mused.

'You should keep him in check Angel,' warned Suzie, 'Once he does this once he'll get worse and worse.'

'Once!' I laughed, 'He's done it more than once.'

'Apparently they based the face on Brad Pitt.'

'What?' we both looked at Rick.

'In the Lion King, apparently Simba's meant to be Brad Pitt,' he said quietly.

'We moved on from that conversation Rick. Come with us,' Suzie beckoned with her hands. 'Now we're discussing Nick and the fact that he didn't bother to call Angel last night and flaked out on their plans together.'

'Right. Got you,' said Rick clicking his fingers at her.

'So what do you think she should do,' Suzie asked.

'Well you shouldn't let him get away with it Angel,' said Rick firmly. 'You should call and give him what for.'

'Yes do Angel, call him. Call him now. He really can't get away with behaviour like that. It's a slippery slope,' she warned.

'Maybe you're right,' I said feeling a burst of confidence, 'I will call him.'

'And be cross,' said Suzie

'And indignant,' added Rick.

'Right.'

I pressed Nick on my mobile. He answered with a quick 'Hello.' I launched my attack.

'Nick,' I said in a chilling way. 'How have you been?'

Suzie and Rick both gave me an enthusiastic thumbs-up for my tone. Nick, clearly trying to ignore the fact that I seemed a little frosty, soldiered on.

'Angel babe, what a surprise. How you doing?' he asked.

I looked across at Suzie and Rick who were both intensely trying to listen in.

'Well I was a bit annoyed at not seeing you last night. You promised you'd call.'

Suzie was nodding at me and Rick was mouthing, 'Let him have it.'

'And you didn't.' I finished.

'Oh babe I'm sorry I went out with the boys after work and I don't remember much after eight o'clock. Hey I'll make it up to you.'

'Right,' I said not wanting to cave in quite so easily in front of my friends. 'Well... as long as it doesn't happen again,' I said warningly.

'Never babe, course not.'

'Good.' There was a brief pause before I continued, 'So am I seeing you tonight then?' I said confidently after such a brilliant performance of Angry Yet Forgiving Girlfriend.

'Er... babe can't tonight the football's on.'

'Right,' I said disgruntled. Suzie and Rick looked at me waiting to understand what was going on.

'Well I'm going out anyway,' I said breezily.

'Oh good. Alright Angel, babe, well I better go I'm...'

'How about tomorrow night?' I burst out quickly. 'We'll go

out, have a few drinks, some dinner.'

'Yeah probably. Speak then yeah, to arrange it.'

'OK. Well have a good night.'

'You too babe.'

I hung up smiling round at them both. 'Well...' I clapped my hands.

'You showed him,' said Suzie and then Rick and her snorted with laughter.

We stayed in most of the day eating, watching videos and lounging about. Rick was half-heartedly looking through some medical journals and being easily distracted. Ellie had gone off to spend the evening with her older sister who spent most of her life improving her already impressive home. As it was getting darker my stomach rumbled.

'Let's go out for dinner,' I said brightly.

'OK,' agreed Suzie.

'OK but its not going to be a big night, I've got revision I have to do,' moaned Rick, 'On circumcision and infections of the genitalia.'

'Thanks Rick.'

'What?'

'I was eating,' said Suzie coldly indicating her half-eaten sausage.

It turned into a brilliant night, sipping away at wine, eating steak and swapping stories. I gazed around at my two friends in a pleasantly fuzzy daze. Then when we'd all had enough to drink and Rick had started describing more of his diseases in greater depth we agreed to go our separate ways. I jumped into a taxi and sat back in the leather feeling slightly queasy. Just as I had closed my eyes I was rudely jolted awake to be told we'd reached my street.

I tumbled out of the taxi and searched around for the relevant change in my bag. Realising I didn't have any relevant change, indeed any change, in my bag I tumbled right back into the taxi and informed the un-amused taxi man to take me on a cash point search. Half an hour later he was speeding off into the night and I was clawing my way up the steps outside our house. I was pretty pissed I realised, stumbling on the steps. Glaring bleary-eyed at the keyhole I poked cluelessly at the lock when suddenly the door swung open and I plummeted unsteadily through the doorway and landed in the hall. I briefly considered passing out there but the bristles of the door mat were digging into my cheeks and my eyeball was inches from a mammoth sized shoe. I covered my head quickly with my hands as the giant scuffed shoe next to me moved. Cowering in a ball waiting to be stepped on I realised the shoe had moved away from me. I splayed my hands across my face and peered through my fingers nervously. I focused on a pair of corduroy legs and a large dirty mac the type favoured by tramps, train spotters and perverts. It was Kreepy Kevin, staring down at me.

'Oopschy,' I laughed nervously, slowly manoeuvring myself upright and grabbing the wall for support.

Kreepy Kevin still seemed to be eyeing me dangerously as I backed along the corridor away from him to the stairs. Like a dangerous animal at the zoo I remained eye contact as best I could, which was difficult as my eyes were fighting the urge to blur into a haze. Never show fear, never show fear. They can smell fear. I felt around for the bottom of the stairs with my foot and then turned and clambered quickly to the first floor using both my arms and legs like a drunk baboon. I didn't dare look back, or slow up, in case he suddenly decided to take chase. Whipping out my key and finding the lock successfully I raced in to our flat and breathlessly slumped against the door listening out for any noises outside. Was he still lurking in the darkness? It was all quiet. Then downstairs the front door slammed shut. He was gone.

I passed out on my bed fully clothed, waking only when the rising sun threatened to boil me in my bedclothes. My mouth was dry and my lips still had a faint tinge of red wine. A plume of stale smoke seemed to hang round my bed in a fog. I groaned as the phone rang. I knew instinctively it would be for me. Only one person would call before eleven o'clock on a Sunday morning. My mother.

'Angel' Ellie called in a slightly resentful voice, 'It's your mum.'

I wrapped myself up in my duvet and moved through to the sitting room.

'Morning Mum,' I said stifling a yawn.

'You sound a little croaky darling. I hope you're not coming down with something.'

'No I'm fine I've just woken up.'

'Just woken up on a lovely day like this.'

'Yes mother. I know. It's a crime.'

'Honestly you're just like your sister, lying about all day and...' I cut off the lecture with a swift explanation.

'I went out last night mum, so what did you call to say. Anything serious?'

'Well I didn't call you about the weather,' she bristled realising her rant had been shortened somewhat. 'I called to ask whether you'd remembered.'

My head was chugging slowly into first gear and then froze.

What had I remembered? I began to rack my brains as her voice continued to rattle on at an alarming pace in the distance. Was it her birthday? Possibly. I didn't think it was a wedding anniversary as we'd only just celebrated one of them recently. Maybe it was my birthday I thought hopefully, no, I knew that was wishful thinking; my birthday was months off. Still I could hear the distant squawking of my mother slow down a notch and realised I was going to have to go for something. So I plumped for a birthday.

"Yes of course I remembered, Happy... birthday..." I ended uncertainly.

"Birthday? What are you talking about darling, it's not my birthday and it's not your father's. Are you getting confused darling? Oh of course, are you talking about Elsie's birthday dear? You know Elsie, lives at number 95, gorgeous rhododendron bushes. Anyway she's going to be ninety next week. Can you imagine? Ninety. Her daughter's organising a little party for it and pretty much the whole village are invited, are you coming down for it dear, how sweet of...'

I hadn't a clue who Elsie was, or what my mother was on about. I started to regret ever picking up the receiver. This was far too much of an ambitious activity for a Sunday morning. Fortunately Dad came on the line as a blessed relief from all the birthday chat.

'Hello love, good of you to welcome us home.' And then I remembered. They had been away on holiday, Mauritius, or the Maldives, well somewhere exotic beginning with 'M' anyway. And I was meant to have recorded University Challenge in their absence.

'So did you remember? It was the semi-finals you know' continued my mother.

'Oh university challenge. Oh our, our television's broken,' I said uncertainly.

'Broken.' My mother sounded suspicious.

'Yes the aerial um... the aerial has gone.'

'Gone. What do you mean gone?'

'It's gone... off,' I said without confidence.

'I knew you wouldn't remember. I said to your father you wouldn't remember.'

'It doesn't matter Barbara, I'm sure she tried.'

'Sorry Mum,' I said feeling instantly guilty. I hadn't tried anything.

'...So I asked Marjorie Allen next door to do it as a back up because I knew you wouldn't remember. And I said that to Marjorie too.'

'Oh,' I said slightly riled that my mother had that little faith in me.

'So there's no problem love,' said my Dad trying to make me feel a little better.

'That's not the point Michael. I knew she wouldn't remember. I told you. Didn't I tell you?'

'Yes you told me.'

'Well at least you've got it,' I chipped in, desperate to steer the conversation away from my failings as a daughter, 'So how was your holiday?'

'... It was obvious the Oxford college were going to win it anyway. That is a real university,' said my mother, 'None of this business of polytechnics trying to pretend they are real universities. In our day it was Oxford, Cambridge, or nothing.'

'Holiday was lovely thanks Angel,' said my dad on the other line. 'Beaches, sun, sea. Excellent food.'

'Hold on Angela I'm just putting the kettle on.' Mum disappeared from one of the lines.

'So was everything alright? How did Mum get on?' I asked.

'Yes she was fine. There were a couple of moments.' He paused, 'Well she was a bit afraid of the water, you know of shark attacks and the such. Watched Jaws too often if you ask me."

'Oh well did that stop her swimming?' I asked, secretly sympathising with her.

'Well I was chatting to another chap staying at the hotel who told your mother she was more likely to be hit on the head by a coconut than eaten by a shark.'

'Oh good did that help?' I said. My father sighed.

'Not really she just spent the rest of the holiday walking around the paths of the resort shielding her head in an attempt to avoid her likely demise by a stray coconut.' We both started giggling at which point my mother's voice suddenly cut through the laughter, as she piped up on the other line.

'1 in 200 apparently,' she said haughtily.

'What?' I stopped mid-giggle.

She went on indignantly, '1 in 200 are the odds that you could be hit by a coconut and, as I've explained to your father, they're very heavy. It was just lucky that neither of us were hurt.'

'Oh honestly Barbara we've been over this...'

'So were there any sharks there?' I asked.

'Yes darling, I read a bit about it in the travel guide. Reef sharks mainly but you never know...'

'They're not man-eating though are they...' chipped in my dad.

'Well I still wouldn't want to be swimming around there with them, honestly it's...'

'Absolutely, right, well, welcome home,' I said trying to escape the inevitable argument about sharks and coconuts.

'But you don't necessarily read about all the attacks do you?'

'I'm glad you had a good time, best go now.' I went on helplessly. I didn't think it had sunk in.

'Reef sharks are harmless. You're more likely to be killed by an angry crab...'

'OK. Well speak soon. I'm off,' I repeated.

They snapped to attention.

'Right Angel we'll see you soon I hope and lots of love from us' said my dad.

'Bye Dad, and Bye Mum. Welcome home,' I said in my best flight attendant voice.

I went to replace the receiver. It was at this point my mother suddenly remembered to tell me all sorts of pointless little facts I never needed to know so that saying goodbye took at least twenty minutes. How she managed to retain such useless information was beyond me, I could only guess she stored it all specifically to bring out when I wanted to put the phone down. Somewhere amongst the chatter about a leaking roof and the fruit cake at Alice's Garden Party I agreed to come home next weekend.

As I replaced the receiver I was reminded of a vague hang over I was having. I moved through to the kitchen for a pint glass of water and smiled as I imagined my parents on holiday. My mother had always been slightly hectic to say the least but she behaved like a true Brit Abroad when let loose on holiday. With the dictionary of the native language tucked under one arm she would often resort to yelling things slowly in English rather than attempt a translation, in the hope that if the sounds were slowed down they would be easier to understand. Most of the people she was shouting at were so used to English tourists that they could understand every word. Of course when it came to haggling over the price, or complaining to the hotel they suddenly became experts at feigning ignorance, much to the exasperation of my mother who would then start on an elaborate mime. My father pottered along after her picking up rare shells, little pieces of local information and the bills.

My Dad was a calm man who spent most of his time nodding along to my mother's various rants about technology/my sister/petrol prices/the council. Little riled him. In fact his only pet peeve was the neighbours' cat who had recently made it its mission to foul Dad's precious lawn as often as possible. This had led to an uncharacteristic outpouring of feeling on the matter over the phone to me the week before. Otherwise, as I said, he was a tame individual. I was soon distracted from thoughts of my family by my mobile phone flashing its envelope at me.

'Cum round 7 & bring food. Nick.' Short and sweet. He had a very dry wit.

I spent much of the rest of the day beautifying myself in preparation for the night. The usual shower, shave, tweeze, wash, exfoliate, varnish, was extended to include a face mask, aromatherapy bubble bath, bikini wax and fake tan. Five hours later I was packing a little bag and yelling a quick good bye to Ellie as I set off for his flat in Maida Vale. I was reading horoscopes on the journey there and was encouraged to see that it was a good week romantically for the Piscean. Apparently Sagittarians like Nick were going to need to focus in the workplace as things were looking worryingly bleak. Which was bad because he might be fired and good because he would have more time to spend with me.

I gazed up at the imposing house with its smart black iron balconies, white columns at the entrance, crisp clean brickwork and views over North London. I buzzed his flat tentatively, butterflies flapping around a little in their best effort to distract me. His confident drawl crackled over the intercom.

'Hello,' he enquired. In a slight fit of nervous excitement I put on a bad cockney accent and piped up, 'Pizza delivery for Mr Nicholas Sheldon-Wade.' The intercom was silent and I bit my lip wondering whether that had been a bad move.

'What?' came the abrupt reply, 'I haven't ordered anything.'

'Er no, it's just Angel,' I said in a small voice, the pizza gag apparently lost on my boyfriend. Another slight pause as this piece of news was digested and then voila, 'Oh hey, alright babe, come up,' and he pushed the buzzer for entrance to the house.

I got up to find the door left on the latch. Slightly disappointed that he hadn't greeted me lovingly at the threshold I scolded myself for being so childish and bustled through the doorway with assorted bags, coats and paraphernalia.

I found Nick sprawled on the sofa. It was a large black leather sofa that took up most of the front room. It faced a wide screen television that cost about as much as the flat Ellie and I lived in. Underneath was the all essential item, the X Box, which depressingly I noted was switched on, possibly suggesting I was in for a bit of a wait before Nick could function as a walking, talking member of the human race. I would be expected to endure at least an hour of shouting, squirming, swearing and annoyance unless it was 'accidentally' switched to off. Mission Number One.

'Hello,' I said in a sing songy cheery voice, as if I were in the midst of auditioning for a part in a musical. It always took me a while to wind down at Nick's house. Everything about the flat appeared to have the sole purpose of intimidating me. The modern swirls of art work on the white expanse of wall, the aluminium artefacts placed about the room like part of a spiked obstacle course. The folders of important documents. But in the midst of all this was Nicholas, my Nick. I practically launched myself on the sofa to be beside him.

'Hey gorgeous,' he said seeming to move in for a cuddle. I relaxed into the sofa waiting for his arms around me, but he'd been reaching for the remote. I flicked open one eye open and leant over to kiss him.

'Could you grab me the paper?' He asked forcing my kiss to brush roughly against his cheek.

'Sure,' I said.

'Thanks babe. Oh, it's in the kitchen.' He added nonchalantly.

'Right,' I got up off the sofa and walked through to the kitchen, a room straight out of the centrefold of the IKEA catalogue. Lots of silver items that gleamed from lack of use and the cleaner Betsie's weekly visit.

I spotted the paper, or rather I saw the Daily Sport, which was I assume what he meant by paper. I wasn't totally convinced he'd get many powerful political messages from that. Although Polly from Lancashire was doing a grand job of showing off her concern for fading patriotism dressed in a fine pair of union jack pants and nothing else.

'Here you go,' I said handing it to him and settling myself once more by his side.

'Angel,' he said in his favourite little-boy-lost voice (he knew it was a winner with me) 'I'm hungry. Did you...'

He trailed off looking at me expectantly, like a child on Christmas morning who knew presents were a sure-fire thing.

'Ah Nicholas. Tonight we shall be having a dinner of Sainsbury's finest. Unless you want to go out?' I added, wondering if he had booked a quiet dinner for two on the sly as a surprise. It appeared he hadn't.

'I don't want to go anywhere darling.' I inwardly glowed with the suggestion that he wanted to spend the evening alone, with me. His voice continued in the midst of my day-dreaming, 'I had plans but was so knackered, thought I'd just have a boring night in.' Choosing to not sound too affronted that I was presumably the star attraction at the glamorous sounding Boring Night In I curled up to him and asked after his week. After a couple of minutes of economic chat my eyelids were drooping from the need to keep up. I was relieved from duties as an economic sound board by a blessed phone ringing back in reality. Nick stopped mid-sentence, or what I thought was mid-sentence, and I was jolted upright as Nick reached to grab the phone from the mess of a coffee table. He answered the call with a roar of recognition.

'Nobby mate how goes it?' The reply was sufficient enough to prompt Nick into some heavy chuckling and a few accompanying snorts.

'That good eh mate, so what are you up to tonight?' Another bout of chuckling and a couple of 'yeah' 'yeah's' were thrown in.

'No mate. I was going to hit 171 with Barney and a few others but I've got the missus round to make me some food.'

I bristled slightly but Nick looked up at me, winked and squeezed my thigh playfully. He was only joking of course, I could be so sensitive. I snuggled back down on to his shoulder.

'No, no mate. She doesn't feel up to it.' I could hear a babbling from the other end and then Nick laughing and saying, 'Yeah, women eh.'

After a few more minutes of boy chat I thought I might as well make a little food to pass the time and I heaved myself out of the sofa to start unpacking the bags in the kitchen. I opened the fridge to be faced with a familiar sight. Can of lager, can of lager, pack of sausage, can of lager, half a pizza, can of lager, unidentifiable dairy item, can of lager. I laughed at the state of it all. This man.

The kitchen was never quite an area I excelled in. I was a member of the 'if you can't microwave it what is the point of it?' category. Recently however I'd tried to take a keener interest. The way to a man's heart and all that. But cordon bleu I was not. Anyway I'd boiled the odd egg and heated up the odd baked bean can. I was still young. I read the back of the packet of pasta carefully. Boil for six minutes seemed simple enough, but I had always had an incredible knack for burning things. Bacon, toast, waffles, soup, you name it I've probably destroyed it. As the kettle boiled I leaned back against the counter and flicked through Heat magazine to pass the time. They were showing pictures from the Oscars and I stared enviously at the actor's and actresses grinning assuredly from the red carpet, clutching their golden statues and wearing Gucci.

Nick called out from the living room, 'Angel as you're up will you get me some crisps – so go on mate did he take her home?'

'Nick, we're just about to eat dinner. Can you wait five minutes?' I hollered back.

'He did – No it's a starter babe. I'm so hungry. Please darling – and twice bloody hell.' I sighed and shook my head in a 'oh pesky kids' kind of way.

'Fine,' I muttered putting down Heat to rummage in the cupboard. I took them through to Nick still deep into the catch up with Nobby.

He raised a hand and waved, 'No Angel darling – yeah go on mate,' he handed me back the packet, 'salt and vinegar babe – so she went back with him,' he carried on. I dutifully replaced the packet with the correct flavour. Nick was engrossed in the conversation. I went back to the kitchen to check on the pasta, which was happily bubbling away. After a few moments of herb wizardry and cheese grating I had finished. I drizzled a bit of melted butter over both plates and stood back to admire my work. Cheese and asparagus stuffed pasta with mange tout and baby sweetcorn. Lovely.

Carried through the pasta and heard Nick finally signing off on the phone. Just in time. I ran through to grab the pepper and a couple of candles I thought I'd light. I emerged back into the living room carrying the lit candles triumphantly...

'Absolutely... Alright... I love you too...'

I paused, frozen on the spot, the candles wobbling uncertainly in my grip. A thousand pounds said that wasn't Nobby on the end of the phone. Nobby was a 6ft 3 inch public school boy rugger bugger, no doubt with built in homophobic tendencies. Who was Nick talking to so lovingly? He hadn't said those words to me yet. He'd said 'Angel I love puddings,' 'Angel I love your breasts,' 'Angel I love Chelsea...' but never 'Angel I love you' full stop, end sentence. But wait... Nick looked up at me, did he seem guilty? Not in the least the bastard, he remained completely unflustered. I on the other hand was going a nasty shade of pink, what should I do? Throw boiling candle wax at him and storm out? Start sobbing in the middle of the living room? Call out repeatedly, 'You bastard, you nasty bloody bastard'? Wait for an explanation?

'Alright, alright,' he continued, 'Tell Dad it's on the 16th. Fine I'll tell him, alright. Gotta go mum.' Wait for an explanation. The correct answer. Win fifty pounds. My whole body relaxed, and I saved the candles from a messy demise.

'Alright, bye mum.'

I made some space on the coffee table; it would have been way too ambitious to suggest a move into the kitchen, and twisted the pepper over the plates.

'So how's your mum?' I asked innocently. I had never met the woman but was keen to be updated as to her well being at regular intervals. Know thy enemy routine.

'She's fine,' Nick answered getting up from his home in the sofa and coming over to the table. 'I'll just get some wine,' he said going back through to the kitchen.

Poor Nick, probably trying to forget all about her. I wouldn't make it worse by enquiring further. From what I had gathered from past conversations Nick had had a fairly traumatic childhood. He had been brutally flung into a prep school at the tender age of eight. His parents had divorced when he was only twelve and he had lived out his teenage years between feuds and upsets. They had had to sell their eight bedroomed detached home in leafy Suffolk and Nick's first speed boat had been auctioned off. Things proceeded to get worse when his dad cut off one of his two allowances and his mother remarried an Australian called Paul. They had replaced love with money and often spent Christmases away skiing in separate parts of the globe. It sounded horrendously bleak. Nick seemed to survive though, brave little soldier. I watched him with a concerned eye as he poured the wine and tucked into his food.

'Angel what's that?' he asked poking at a piece of stray asparagus and lifting me out of my reverie.

'Asparagus,' I said.

He looked at me dumbly.

'A kind of vegetable,' I went on, realising immediately this wasn't selling it to him.

'I know what an asparagus is Angel. The point is why are we eating it? Do I look like a beardy weardy veggie?'

'No,' I giggled imagining the sight of Nick in his pin stripe engaging in a bit of tree hugging round Hyde Park.

He pushed the rest of the pasta to the side of his plate, 'I might order a pizza. This can't fill me up.'

I swallowed my mouthful slowly. Oh damn.

'Well there's always pudding,' I said hopefully, quickly piling our plates up and taking them through to the kitchen. 'I got Vienetta.'

'Excellent. You're such an Angel.' Gah. If I had a penny for every time I'd heard that line I'd be... well at least £1.64 in profit. I carried out the Vienetta and watched in amazement as over the next few minutes Nick wolfed down half the slice. Poor baby he was obviously so hungry. I'd remember next time to buy some steak or other manlier dish.

I left him to finish off the ice cream and started wiping away any signs that I'd cooked in the kitchen. Marble surfaces were scrubbed and pans were dried and hung back up to sparkle. I could hear Nick switching on the television and took him through a Stella before he would need to get up. Finally when I thought the kitchen looked tidy enough to be seen by the cleaner I went back through to the living room and cuddled up next to Nick.

'Oh Angel you didn't need to do the washing up,' he said stroking my hair distractedly.

'That's OK.'

I stayed curled up in silence for a few minutes. Content. Nick appeared fairly engrossed in the programme, some kind of opera from the sounds of things. I listened hazily to the dashing tenor churning out the standard pained love solo and watched a large fat woman sing right back. Poor bugger. After a few more minutes like this I began to feel incredibly restless. I realised it was still only about seven o'clock and the evening sky peeking through the gap in the curtain looked inviting. 'Nick,' I looked up at him, 'Do you want to do something? Let's go somewhere. We can't stay locked up here all day.'

'Why not?' Nick muttered from his frozen stance on the sofa.

'We just can't,' I said suddenly bouncing up in an overly enthusiastic school girl way, 'It's a really nice evening. Let's go for a walk at least. Get some fresh air.'

I could see my ideas were falling on deaf ears. Nick didn't appear to have taken his eye off the fat woman's heaving bosom.

'Nick,' I said. 'Nick,' I repeated, this time nudging him on the shoulder to ensure he couldn't pretend I was a nasty figment of his imagination. 'Pleasssseeee,' I pleaded in what I hoped was a cute, endearing way.

'Oh Angel. I've got a long day tomorrow and...'

'And so have I.' I interrupted firmly.

He snorted at my remark and muttered something incomprehensible. 'Yes darling, but...' Realising he might not win this one, he changed tack. 'But darling. We never see enough of each other and I invited you over here to spend a bit of one-on-one time together.' He pulled me down on to his lap, 'You see sweetheart, what's the good of running across London together when everything we need is right here.' I looked around sceptically at the sofa, lightly sprinkled in the remnants of salt and vinegar crisps, Nick resplendent in tracksuit bottoms and a can of Stella by his side. However before this image had digested he made his point by kissing me firmly on the mouth. I responded in kind and soon we were writhing about remembering why we were so good together. We didn't even need to leave his living room. Twenty or so sweaty minutes later I was adjusting my bra and he was back to watching the fat lady singing.

It was a slightly awkward situation getting ready for bed around a boyfriend. In the early clothes-thrown-everywhere phase we had cut through the embarrassment with ill-disguised lust. Now it was me skirting around him with a little bag of toiletries, 'oh do you mind if I use the bathroom,' 'can I borrow some toothpaste,' 'is this my towel...'; that kind of thing. I had always wanted to be one of those girls who whispered seductively in the ear of the boyfriend the promise to go and 'slip into something more comfortable' emerging moments later in a cloud of perfume and red satin. But I wasn't one of those girls so I tucked up next to Nick in a simple cotton vest top and low slung pyjama bottoms. I lay in bed dozing in and out, Nick idly stroking my arm as he read some sheet for work. It all seemed so adult. Frightening. As Nick was occupied I focused on some of my best day dreams to pass the time. Nick and me splashing in a turquoise sea, Nick feeding me marshmallows by a crackling fire, Nick and me meeting George Clooney. Nick and George duelling for my love, in breeches. Sigh. Nick was still busily studying the sheet of figures and I let my mind wander over the last seven months. The dates we'd been on, the sex we'd had, the first night we met. I loved that story. The Night We'd Met by Angela Lawson. There had been nothing very adult about that. I smiled at the memory.

It had been seven months ago, on a blustery night in November. Suzie and I had been invited to a house warming party in Kensington hosted by one of our richer friends from university who had borrowed a bit off daddy to buy a little apartment of her own. That's independence for you. The theme had been 'schooldays' and so, with hair in pigtails and pleated tartan mini skirts, we'd set off into the night. After stopping briefly to purchase a bottle of wine we'd approached the flat with some trepidation. The usual sounds of house-party-in-full-swing (heavy beats, yelling, laughing, vomiting etc) seemed lacking in the air around 56b Clarence Mews. Still not dwelling too much on it; perhaps the walls were very thick? perhaps the flat was towards the back of the house? perhaps they were all in the garden...? we traipsed in.

A quick scan could conclude that normal house party elements were absent from the event. No mass of heaving bodies, no passed out rugby boy in a corner, no jiggling to bad music and no cans of lager scattering the floor. Odd. Instead we discovered one or two nervous looking individuals sitting on a smart new sofa carefully avoiding eye contact and sipping frantically at their plastic cups of punch. After a few brisk minutes of doing the same Suzie had deduced this party was not going anywhere and announced we suddenly needed to be somewhere.

'Don't you remember Ang?'

I had played along with lots of 'Oh of course er... Cynthia's meeting us for a drink... yes, er... Cynthia goes way back... so I suppose... we must dash terribly sorry... GREAT party by the way... byeee' and escaped into the night swigging at our wine and high fiving our lucky escape. And we didn't high five a lot; they were reserved for special occasions only. We wandered the streets a little wondering where we should end up when our minds were made up for us. Up ahead in the street a group of men, many in smart looking suits and ties, were making their way into a bar on the other side of the road.

'Bingo,' I pointed.

'Good plan,' added Suzie linking arms with me, 'Let's go.'

Adjusting our ties and straightening our shirts we approached the bar the group of men had disappeared into. Inside was a throbbing mass of Friday night revellers and through the crowds we could just make out the disappearing train of our boys. We followed as best we could. Cute school girls no longer we used our elbows to jab any obstacles/people out of our path and finally arrived at the stairs where the men had walked moments before. As we went to follow suit our biggest obstacle yet intervened.

'Excuse me ladies it's a private party tonight I'm afraid. Stag do.' We looked up at the bouncer who had spoken both simultaneously assessing whether we could take him out. We couldn't. Suddenly our pursuit seemed to stumble and flail.

'Oh yes, yes we know. We are... we are...' Suzie was struggling now for time. I stepped forward quick as a flash.

'We're the strippers.' I finished the sentence for her, and tried to divert attention away from Suzie's look of shocked horror, 'Yes, yes. And we're late I'm afraid. So if you could just let us up there,' I said indicating the room above. 'We'll get on with our job.'

'Of, of course, sorry girls. Should have known from the outfits.'

'Thank you' I said pushing past confidently and looking back at Suzie, 'Come on Sandra we're late.' A bewildered Sandra followed me up. Reaching the top we were giggling with relief.

'Christ Angie now I know why you are going to be such a great actress.'

'Desperate times,' I said shrugging my shoulders and smiling.

We pushed open the door and were hit by the whiff of Lynx and the pumping music and lights. A guy sidled uncertainly up to us, a glass of beer in his hand.

'SCHOOL GIRLS' he yelled, 'THERE ARE SCHOOL GIRLS IN THE HOUSE,' and promptly passed out beside us. Suzie gingerly stepped over him and made her way determinedly towards the bar. As I was following a hand reached out and turned me round.

'Alright there. I'm Mike, best man, and who might you be?' he asked.

'Oh er... we are the strippers,' I said trying to sound convincing.

Mike looked momentarily confused, 'I didn't know I ordered any.'

'Oh yes we got a call from the er... agency and they said get down here for eleven.'

'Wicked', he said turning around to holler at the room of heaving men, 'Boys the strippers are here.' Those in hearing distance raised a cheer and I scarpered before Mike could turn back around to question me further or ask me for a sneak preview.

I made it the bar and immediately located Suzie which wasn't at all hard as, although she wasn't the only one in a skirt, she was certainly the only one who looked good in a skirt. After a few minutes we were surrounded by men vying to buy us drinks. Men with balloons up their tops and lipstick smeared over their faces, some with plastic devil horns perched on their heads, some holding large inflatable penises, most with beer dribbling down them. The odd few still looking fairly respectable in shirts, ties loosened at their necks, were too busy playing catch up to get close to offering us a beverage. Fairly typical I mused.

'One drink and then we better leg it or they'll want us to start taking clothes off,' I whispered at Suzie as she accepted another free shot off the bar man. She downed it in one.

'Absolutely Angie. Absolutely.' A shot was thrust into my hand and as I knocked it back I realised we might be in a spot of trouble.

'Hey I'm Nick. And I think you must be the girl of my dreams.'

I turned round about to roll my eyes at a Nick that would use that chat up line and then jolted upright. Hello Mister.

A tall, well built, man in a suit was standing on the spot where the corny line had been delivered.

He laughed immediately, 'What? I had to get your attention somehow.'

'Does that line ever work?' I said doubtingly.

'To be truthful it hasn't enjoyed a 100% success rate but it does better than, is your father a thief?'

'What?' I said looking bemused 'Is my father a thief.'

He leaned in, 'Well someone stole the stars and put them in your eyes.'

I groaned.

'You see!' he said triumphantly, 'What's your name?'

'Angela, or Angie, or Ang or Angel,' depending who you are.

'Angel,' he repeated, 'Can I buy you a drink?'

He had light blonde hair, cut short, suntanned skin and a straight Greek nose. His eyes were startlingly blue and direct. He wouldn't have looked out of place in a 1930's Nazi propaganda poster. He exuded confidence. I didn't normally go for such Arian male stereotypes but I reckoned I could definitely make an exception for him. He turned around to order from the barman and I admired his shoulders, muscular and athletic looking. I hurriedly looked away as he turned back to hand me my drink.

'So you sexy schoolgirl have you got your parents permission to be out this late?' he asked with a gleam in his eye.

'Absolutely not,' I said looking affronted, 'I clambered out of my bedroom window using pillow cases tied together. Us school girls, you see, are very resourceful.'

'I'm sure you are, and when can we expect to see what's underneath those neat little uniforms,' he said traipsing a straw along my neckline. I looked at him challengingly.

'I'm afraid only very good boys ever get to see what I hide under here... I didn't get my prefect's badge for nothing you know.'

He laughed and returned my confident gaze. The electricity crackled between us. Sadly at that moment Mike, best man, chose to stumble between us. Clasping my shoulders he yelled loudly to the room, 'Alright lads, the strippers are going to do their thing.'

Suzie was looking sheepish beside him. Her tie was askew, her eyes slightly glazed and she'd already stained the front of her shirt with drink. She didn't look completely with it.

'We're just going to get our music,' I said and grabbing Suzie's arm pushed her unsteadily to the DJ's box.

'Shit,' I said giggling 'What the hell are we going to do now?' Neither of us could speak properly through our giggles but we whispered to the DJ and got out two stools ready for our act. The boys had formed a semi circle around us and we waited for the music to begin. The first chords of 'You Can Leave Your

Hat On' started up and we tried to look as sexy and appealing as we could as we moved past each other, swinging our arms, to the beats. Taking off our ties one by one and unbuttoning the tops of our shirts we waited for the chorus to start up and side stepped slowly towards the door undoing the remaining buttons. The boys, expecting us any minute to return and take off the shirts entirely were momentarily confused as the seconds ticked by. At this point we were racing down the stairs faster than two greyhounds round a track, frantically doing up buttons. We pushed and prodded our way back through the crowd. I looked round just as we flung ourselves through the doors of the bar to spot a confused Nick staring around the room. Suddenly his eyes lighted on me and I hurriedly rushed through the door. Suzie was up ahead in the street clutching her sides, tears in her eyes, as she laughed and laughed. I was breathless with all the running. It was more exercise than I'd done so far that year.

'That... was...' I puffed stopping briefly to wipe my eyes. 'Hysterical.'

Clinging to each other and wiping the tears out of our eyes we started moving away.

'ANGEL.' Came a shout.

'Wha...' I said looking around. Nick was standing in the doorway of the bar.

'Who's he?' giggled Suzie.

'Angel,' he called, jogging up to me with his gorgeous lean body. I realised immediately there was no point making a run for it. He could outstrip us (excuse the pun) within seconds.

'So you naughty schoolgirl, not really a stripper are you?'

'Not exactly no,' I said laughing.

Suzie spotted the rest of the boys emerging now from the doors of the bar, 'Quick Angie, let's go,' she said tugging my sleeve.

'Oh god,' I said looking over to see Mike and the others making a wobbly beeline for us.

'If they catch you they'll make you dance,' Nick said grinning.

'Here quickly what's your number?' he asked whipping out a sleek little mobile from an inside pocket.

'Um...' Suzie had started to veer down the street again holding up her hand for a nearby taxi, 'It's 07867 243...'

'Angie get in,' screeched Suzie flinging open the cab door. Mike and co had picked up their pace,
'67...' I said in the direction of Suzie. Mike and co began jogging.
'ANGIE.. NOW,' she squealed.
I jumped in the back of the taxi, '8.' I finished.
'I'll call you,' he yelled as we screeched off.
Looking out of the back of a taxi I could see Nick standing watching it leave, the assortment of weirdly dressed boys finally catching up with him. I turned to Suzie with a grin plastered over my face, 'I think I'm in love,' and then we both collapsed into the leather seats and started cackling once more.

* * *

Monday morning. The Bangles wrote a song about it, its existence is legend. Monday morning. What is good about it? Mine was spent in an uncomfortably frantic rush running around the room picking up clothes and searching for edible food. Nick had already showered and left at dawn. Only noisy birds and city traders were up at that hour. I looked around for a note on the pillow but it must have fallen off in the confusion of waking up.

Faces on the underground escalator did little to convince me that any soul was merry on a Monday morning. Blank looks stared past adverts promising cheap flights, car hire and a tan like the girl in the photo. My eyes swept across them listlessly lighting only on the smiles of numerous musical theatre stars, all happily singing their heart out in the West End. I looked at these pictures longingly. I missed acting. It had been so long since I'd last auditioned for anything. I felt a pang as I remembered all the high hopes I'd had, the roles I'd had at school and university, the endless singing lessons, the praise from examiners, teachers, and parents. All that had given me a firm belief that I would find success on the stage, I would make it in the acting world. Pah what did they all know? I'd spent months roaming London sending out head shots, begging for auditions, with no success. The agent who I'd signed with so enthusiastically had lost interest in me after a couple of months and I became another CV in a mounting pile. I knew my work as an agony aunt had been a temporary fix. I knew I had to juggle both, but life in London had suddenly got busy. I had a job, friends, a boyfriend. I had bills to pay, reality to consider. A small voice inside me scoffed at these thoughts and I diverted my attention to the car adverts. Less likely to prompt a life crisis at 8.30 on a Monday morning.

I walked out of the underground and turned right. The building I worked in was a looming, character less grey concrete block with dirty windows and graffiti sprayed outside, but on the plus side was a mere stone's throw from the tube station. I pushed through the heavy glass doors of the building, gave a half hearted smile at the porter, who in turn did little to acknowledge me, and then crossed the floor to the lift. Various people were waiting at the lift doors, some rummaging in hand bags and others already on mobile phones sounding important. Standing in the drab steel elevator we stared wearily ahead as the doors opened on each level and various people left and arrived. The atmosphere had a glum early Monday morning feel to it and there was absolute silence. Finally we reached the fourth floor and I moved to the front to get out. As the lift doors opened my black and white world was suddenly promoted to Technicolor. Like when Dorothy arrives in Oz. Characters popped off the page, rooms seemed cartoon like in their appearance and everything had a sparkly, youthful feel to it.

The reception desk was large and oval and draped in fairy lights. It twinkled at me on arrival. A bright blue neon sign across the desk was emblazoned with the word 'Sweet SixTeen.' The trendy looking computers, all see through backs and light blue plastics, completed the upbeat youthful effect. To the right of the desk was a waiting area, complete with bright cushy sofas and littered with glossy magazines. In the middle of both were the double doors to the office beyond. I nodded to the receptionist, who was already absent-mindedly flicking through a magazine and looking well at home, as I walked past.

It was a large open plan office. A path of clear carpet ran down the right side of the room. All the front covers from previous editions had been framed and placed in rows along this wall so that the faces of various teenage models grinned toothpaste smiles back at you. Under these photocopiers, faxes and computers endlessly came to life, spewing out page after page. The room was abuzz with movement and business. I made my way towards the back of the room. We sat in blocks, or 'teams,' as Victoria always described. Features, sub editing, Health, Lifestyle My 'team' was situated at the end of the room. The smallest team ever. A two man team. I sat opposite one half of Fashion.

I reached my desk and dumped my bag, immediately about-turning for the little kitchen and the first of a compulsory injection of caffeine. I suppose kitchen seemed a little over-enthusiastic a description. If any of my friends were the proud owner of a kitchen like this I'd persuade them to immediately sell up and move out. The room was home to brown flaking walls covered in notices, a pile of empty cardboard boxes and a counter smeared with remnants of crumbs and unidentifiable jams. A single fridge and a kettle were the only hints that something culinary could happen in here. This morning a miniature pocket-version of a girl, wrapped in a hooded jumper, hunched up waiting for the kettle to boil was the only added addition to the decor. The girl turned her head a little and stared at me vaguely through bloodshot eyes.

'Hectic weekend,' I commented.

Obviously moving her head had proved quite an extraordinary feat and she had dropped her gaze once more to let out a slight grunt of assent and continue to watch the steam rise.

Tally sat opposite me as one half of 'Fashion.' She was usually the friendlier half, having been known to lend me clothes from the magazine's wardrobe at a moments notice. The magazines were lent things for modelling shoots and as long as things weren't lost or destroyed you could borrow them without much fuss. Tally herself never looked in need of anything new. She was the type of girl who made her own clothes, always looking ridiculously trendy in things that would make normal people just look silly. Note today's outfit: Purple leggings, a puffy skirt, some kind of netting under it, a well fitted green coat with patch work flowers and long blonde hair on the way to becoming dreadlocks. She was a girl who would fit in in Camden town.

I joined her watch and we waited in silence for the familiar bubbling and click of the kettle to announce 'off.' After pouring a cup of coffee she added a little cold water and then gulped it down.

'Thass a bi' better,' she said wiping her mouth with the back of her hand. Obviously shocked by her ability to form half a sentence she quickly poured herself another cup of coffee and turned to me sipping at it slowly. I had made the mistake of opening the fridge in a feeble search for a carton of milk and was now considering gagging from the smell. Instead I poured a coffee and joined Tally to stand sipping, sighing and smiling every now and again. This calm little interlude was abruptly shattered by the arrival of Claudia, Beauty, carrying a nasty leopard skin hand bag in one hand and a plastic carrier bag in the other.

Claudia did not carry off clothes well. She was a brash, opinionated woman who your mother would describe as 'tarty.' She was also an anally retentive bitch. So not the best person to bump into first thing on a Monday morning. She slammed down her carrier bag, removed a carton of Soya milk and one of those weird little vitamin yoghurts, and then turned to root around in the fridge.

'Honestly who the hell looks after this place? It's absolutely disgusting,' she said recoiling from the smell.

Tally and I looked at her, looked at each other, rolled our eyes and went back to sipping in silence. The fact that neither of her listeners were able (Tally) or wanted (me) to contribute to her rant did nothing to slow it down. She went on, oblivious to the fact.

'Well there's nothing edible in there,' she said banging the fridge door shut, 'I'm glad I brought in my own foodstuffs. I only ever drink fat free Soya milk anyway so there's no real harm.' She reached over and grabbed the kettle sloshing water into a mug and popping a green tea bag in that turned the water a kind of unpleasant vegetably colour. 'The way they let this kitchen go really makes me cross, it doesn't take too long to get someone in to give it a bit of a scrub once a week but, oh no, they just let it...'

'Do you want some bread?' I asked thrusting the loaf towards her in the hope of ending this monologue.

'God no,' she cried, clearly offended, 'I don't eat wheat. And I avoid red meat, dairy, and of course alcohol,' she finished looking in Tally's direction critically.

'Right,' I said, wondering quite what was left to consume

once you'd deleted them off the menu.

She peered intrusively into my mug and then looked at me with a shocked expression. 'Black coffee,' she stated.

'Yes,' I said, 'Very good.'

She glared at me.

'There's no need to be sarcastic Angela. Don't you know coffee ages you? It is a drug Angel. It is a known fact that it has links with raised blood pressure, heartburn, headaches, insomnia, dehydration, infertility, digestive ulcers and not forgetting the fact that...'

During this lecture Suzie rushed in, flung down a bursting carrier bag and before even a 'Morning' had passed anyone's lips had scuttled back out to the office. 'Back in a minute, I bought doughnuts,' she called over her shoulder.

I dived on the carrier bag with relish.

'I wouldn't,' Claudia said through pursed lips, 'Think of the calories.'

I lifted a doughnut out of its box.

'There's probably around 400 in that alone. I feel faint,' she said dramatically.

'Here,' she was rummaging in the leopard-skin bag, 'Read this, I always carry it around with me.' She whipped out a little pocket book from the bag like a magician conjuring a rabbit.

'Here,' she said waving it in front of me desperately, 'Please borrow it.'

I took it out of her flailing hands and read the title. The ominous sounding, 'Calorie and Fat Gram Guide.'

'It's like a bible,' she said reverentially.

The Calories and Fat Gram Guide was a frightening read. Numbers, food names, everything was written out in tiny, specific detail. Fortunately I had no frame of reference. I read with fascination that bacon, back, fried contained 460 calories and 40 grams of fat. Bacon, middle, fried was a slightly more substantial 470 calories and 42 grams. But what was middle/back? Does every bit of fried back bacon contain 470 calories? Would you be eating 920 calories if you had two pieces? And was 42 grams a lot of fat? Do you even need fat grams? Would you pass out if you bypassed them completely? The name was definitely off-putting. No girl I knew would want to fill herself up on fat grams. They didn't exactly imply they came from a healthy food group. But then butter beans sounded wrong and by all accounts were actually nutritious and good for you. A complicated read. It appeared counting calories could form an A level in itself. I handed the book back to Claudia.

'No that's fine,' she said with what I was certain might have been a sneaky glimpse at my midriff, 'you borrow it.'

'But won't you need it?'

Claudia gave me a knowing smile, 'Of course not.' She plucked my piece of toast out of my hand, 'White medium slice bread 80 calories, and 0.5 grams of fat,' she sniffed at it, 'Flora Light, 357 calories and 38 grams of fat per 100g. Raspberry Jam, 47 calories per 100g.'

'Oh,' I said. We were all looking at her in absolute disbelief.

'Apple,' I said.

'68 calories.'

'Weetabix,' I continued.

'476 per 100g.'

'Custard cream,' whispered Tally.

'78.'

We both fell into a respectful silence. Claudia sighed.

'Right, must get on. See you two later,' she said whisking out of the kitchen.

I continued to peruse the little book of figures. There was a section on biscuits. I scrolled down to T but they had left off Trackers. My favourite biscuit. I concluded they must just be very, very good for me. I'm possibly losing weight just by chewing on them.

'Right,' I said throwing the paper cup in the bin and moving to the door. 'Hope you feel better later,' I said looking back at Tally.

'Hmm,' she mumbled working her way back down to monosyllables after the morning's onslaught.

Dear Angel,

My friends keep calling me 'Fatty McFatison' as a joke coz I'm Scottish and large. My mum says it's just big bones. I don't want to be overweight but then I don't want to watch what I eat all the time. What can I do?

Cheryl, Glasgow

Poor old Cheryl. I knew what she meant about watching what you eat. I'd always half-heartedly aspired to be a girl that watches what she eats. And I do watch. I watch closely as I cut the chocolate cake slice off, I watch it as it is placed on the fork, I watch it as I manoeuvre it to my mouth. I like my food. I always hoped I might develop a bout of anorexia at some point but no such luck. I blame my stable upbringing and solid family background. Up until the age of 19 I had boasted a slim physique, not having to care what I ate, when I ate or how much I ate. But as I moved into my twenties I noticed a distinct swelling around most of my body parts. The trouble was looking good was always such a massive effort. I didn't know how people found the time. Surely you would have to give up full time work to stand a hope of joining the parade of women with smooth legs, straight hair and varnished nails. I also didn't see myself as someone who could carry off the impeccably polished look. I worked hard at perfecting the sexy mustered 'what, this old thing' look.

Hi Angel,
Both my best mates have boyfriends and whenever I ask anyone out they say no. I'm so depressed because I'm over weight.
Lauren, 13

Dear Lauren,
Might I suggest you invest in the Calorie and Fat Gram Guide? This ingenious little book will tell you exactly what you are putting into your body. Do some exercise, cut down on snack food and drink lots of water. Good Luck Lauren.
Angel

Today was going to be a fairly relaxing return to my usual work. I'd finished the page for the magazine on Friday so now I was focusing on answering all the letters we were sent last month. Everyone who wrote to the magazine got a reply; just not all of them were published. This job was entirely less stressful than ensuring the magazine page was completed and readable. I felt more at liberty to be myself in the home replies and often they just wanted a bit of friendly reassurance and to know someone had listened.

Dear Angel,
I had sex with my boyfriend and now I think I might be pregnant. I don't know what to do and don't tell me to tell my mum coz she'll go mad. Help.
Debbie, Portsmouth

Oh dear! Twelve years old and pregnant. Now don't worry Debbie, there's no need to panic.... Christ I can't believe this child. Twelve years old! When I was twelve years old my biggest fear was whether slouch socks were still in. What should I write? I turned around to the fat guy giving out the sandwiches in the office, 'Nigel.' He looked up from his sea of cellophaned snacks and gave me a nervy smile,

'Nigel, if you were a twelve year old girl and you were pregnant, what would you do?'

He looked at me uncertainly, cocked his head to one side, as if that might help his thought process, and repeated slowly, 'If I were a twelve year old girl?'

He paused again. 'Er...' he blustered, 'Well...'

By now Fashion and Beauty were both surreptitiously hovering over their work and craning their ears anticipating his reply.

'Er... I would probably... Er...'

'Oh come on Nigel, what do you reckon? Tell your teacher? Kill yourself? Go windsurfing? What. Help me pleaseeee,' I pleaded. He was turning a deep shade of pink now; I could see the fear rising in his eyes. Tally had nearly fallen off her chair giggling.

My phone started ringing. Nigel's entire body relaxed and he slumped over the sandwiches delivered from my inquisition. I picked up the receiver.

'This isn't over Nigel,' I said, smiling at Tally.

'Hello.'

'She'll know the answer Michael it's silly to try and call again they're obviously not goin...'

'Hello,' I repeated cutting through the monologue on the other end.

'...to do anything about it. Right, Angela it's your mother.'

Surprise.

'Hello mother. Problems?' I queried, wondering exactly

when I had handed my parents my work number and whether I had really thought it through.

'Angela, what type of computer do you have at work?'

'It's a DELL Mum, why?'

'Because I'm ringing round everyone we know to make sure they haven't got one of these new fangled see-through ones. We should never have bought the thing.'

'Right. Well mine's a DELL and it's been fine so far so...' My quick exit was denied.

'... Ours has gone at home and I have spent all morning ringing their services department. Or should I say trying to ring their services department – all I'm getting is little robots telling me different numbers to press.'

'Oh dear,' I said holding the phone a little way away from my ear and clicking on my email icon.

'... I'm still hoping on hope that maybe, just maybe, someone might actually pick the phone up to talk to me. Just now they told me their website address so I can get help on that. As if anyone with a broken computer can get onto their website. At the moment all I'm getting is a plain blue screen. It was the reason I dialled the ruddy number in the first place.'

'Can Dad help at all; you see I'm at work and...'

'Your father is no help, he keeps telling me to call in a professional. They cost sixty pounds to call out, at least. He doesn't care; he's gone out to the garden now. Keeps muttering to himself about that cat from next door. Honestly it's all that man ever talks about...'

I didn't dare point out this was due to the fact that my mother was usually on full rant about the rest of the globe's issues. This was a time to placate her.

'Well Mum look, maybe Dad's right. Maybe you need a professional. It could be a virus,' I suggested, playing on one of her worst fears.

'A virus,' she paused. She hadn't thought of that. 'Alice's husband got sent a virus and he lost all his files... everything,' she told me in hushed tones.

'Well Mum it could be something like that I'm afraid,' I went on, 'They're very common. I suppose the only way you'll be able to know is by getting someone to fix it for you. It could be serious,' I ended dramatically.

There was another long pause on the end of the phone. Computer viruses were a force to be reckoned with. My mother felt out of her depth.

'Maybe it wouldn't hurt to get it looked at,' she capitulated.

'Hmm...' I muttered, not wanting to say anything more in case it distracted her.

'Yes I think it's best. Well thank you Angela.'

'That's OK Mum; I hope it gets sorted out.'

'So do I,' she said solemnly.

'Bye then.'

I popped the phone down relieved to have thought of such a prompt solution. I went back to the pregnant girl's letter and tried not to sound too disapproving or too shocked by her age. I then replied to a letter about depression and a letter about being afraid of the dark. Was 'buy a night light' not taking it seriously enough?

The day dragged by lightened briefly by the decision to 'Go Large' in MacDonald's at lunch time. The Calorie and Fat Gram Guide simply reminding me of the food I was really craving. Back in the office, and after another few replies, I was getting distracted. In the midst of giving out some advice about dealing with bullies I found myself gazing off into space. Tally was fixing the hem on a skirt for a future photo shoot. She looked up, noted my bored expression and asked,

'If you could choose would you have snake skin as skin or spaghetti as hair?'

This was not unusual. It was a game that had kept us entertained on many a rainy day and I looked at her with relief for the distraction. Two choices and you absolutely have to choose one.

I mulled the choices over, 'Spaghetti as hair' I concluded.

Tally wrinkled her nose.

'How about you?'

'Probably the same and I'd just go for regular hair cuts.'

'Hmm.'

She went back to sewing and I went back to gazing.

I looked back at her moments later,

'If you had to choose would you have the bark of a dog on every other word or a forked tongue?'

She was pondering this when my phone rang.

A No Caller ID came up on my phone. A stalker. Brr... I answered with a cautious, 'Yes.'

'Hello is that Angela Lawson.'

'Yes.'

'Hello my name's Sam I'm calling from BOS Productions; you sent your CV in to us a few months ago now. We're holding auditions next month for our new theatre season and we'd like to invite you in to see us.'

'Oh,' I mouthed, not quite believing what I was hearing.

Tally had poked her tongue out at me and was pointing to it. I gave her a quick thumbs up to show her I'd noticed and tried to focus on what he was saying.

'I know it's a little way off but are you available on the 20th?' he asked.

My mind raced. Why was he ringing now? I haven't sent anything out in months. I haven't even thought about acting. Well, I hadn't done any acting in ages. I missed it I thought with a pang. But I was working full time now and I had a busy life. And I'd only go and be rejected again. I couldn't do it, I was constantly being told no, always second place, always the wrong hair colour, the wrong height, too English looking, not English looking enough, too loud, too quiet, too... I realised he was waiting for a reply.

'Oh um... no, I'm probably working.'

'Is there any chance you can get out of work?'

'No... no probably not,' I said.

'How about the 21st? Any better for you? That's a Thursday.'

'No... I can't.'

'That's a shame. I very much liked your CV. Are you working on anything particular at the moment? TV, theatre, film?'

I realised with dread he had assumed I was still acting. Feeling ridiculously like a failure I muttered a curt, 'No.'

It would be good to start trying again though I thought with a panic. Why had I just said no? Maybe he would like me, and I had had roles in the past. A couple of years ago I was always appearing in various fringe productions and we'd often had great reviews. Why had I suddenly given up on it all?

'Well if you do find yourself available, feel free to give me a call. We'd love to see you.'

'Thanks, thank you. I will,' I said hurriedly hanging up on him. I sat idly doodling for a while, my mind a little blank. Then I miserably pushed the phone call to the back of my mind. I had other things going on now.

'Would you have boils all over your face or a third arm?' asked Tally not noticing my dismal expression.

* * *

A lot of Ellie's temporary jobs involved evening work. This left her free in the day to look for a suitable career. She spent a lot of time on the computer. She spent much of it playing Solitaire. The arrangement also meant she had unwittingly become a firm follower of most day time soaps. Except Hollyoaks which cast an unreasonably high proportion of attractive women for a British soap and was therefore to be boycotted. What she hadn't realised was I had worked all this out.

Her guise for these useless day-time activities was ingenious – she would sit on the sofa, lap top perched precariously on her knees five minutes before I was due home and pretend to be working on her CV. Of course I'd dutifully swallowed this for a while, but when you're spending three weeks and three days honing a Curriculum Vitae you might dare to expect a little more than 300 words. She didn't insult me however by beginning a new lie. Or she simply couldn't be bothered. So we went through the routine like any well-established evening ritual.

'Hey Ellie.'

(Ellie looks up from frenzied typing with studious expression on face)

'Oh hey Angel. I didn't hear you come in...'

(Ellie resumes frenzied typing waiting for me to ask...)

'How's the CV going?'

(Ellie rolls eyes and rubs the back of her neck)

'Oh... OK I'm having a little trouble with Hobbies and Interests.'

I pause here. This was the test. The test of Good Friend or Bad Friend. Would I be tempted to tell her to cite Day Time Television and Computer Games with Toby our goldfish as her reference? Or would I sweetly navigate around the potential minefield? I followed the latter to the ticket. I achieved top marks in the test. I was a good friend.

'Why not write something a bit random to show you've got 'personality'' I emphasised the last word in a cheesy voice and then continued, 'How about synchronised swimming suggesting you are both nimble, lithe and work well with others. No one would ever make that up...'

'Hmm...' Ellie murmured distractedly, her eyes flicking back to the action on the television. I looked up from my musing over an assortment of weird hobbies; fire eating (indicating a daring edge, ready to tackle a challenge), train spotting (suggesting the ability to sit for long hours waiting for fuck all to happen but seeming fairly upbeat about the whole thing- important in most temping work), bear baiting (indicating the ability to hold your own against threatening challengers) taxidermist (suggesting...) but Ellie didn't appear totally focused on the topic. I glanced at the box. Ah. Neighbours. How stupid of me. I wouldn't get any sense out of her for another twenty minutes. So I moved away into my room, leaving Ellie transfixed to the screen, all thoughts of a career suspended until tomorrow.

I checked the answering machine, 'you have no new messages.' I checked the pad by the answering machine where we write messages, blank. I check behind the table just in case a message about a message has fluttered off and become lost, there is nothing. I come to the conclusion that Boys are Mean. What's silly about it is that we know this and yet it still bothers us when they are mean. They also know we know this so you'd think they'd stop being mean, but that's a perfect world. Nick said he'd call. He said we'd do something this week. But he hasn't called. And fine it's only Monday night, fine. But it still bothers me. We are surely past the dreaded 'I'll-leave-it-three-days-before-I-reply' stage. I've heard him fart, I've seen him do a number two (I know I sound six years old) I've smelt his sweat, I've felt him come. Not to be crude about it, he does nice things too, but my point is I know him well now. We shouldn't be playing games. Not that I'm overly worried. It would just be nice to hear from him. Ring me, ring me, ring me dammit.

Ellie immediately picks up on these negative vibes. It's

intuitive. OK fine, I had to throw about five saucepans around the kitchen and stomp child like to the bathroom but then she said, 'Angie, is everything ok?' Such a good friend. Of course I tried to put on a brave face, I did the small half smile, the little shrug of the shoulders and the slow sigh of, 'Yeah... (long exhale, sad eyes) I'm fine.'

'Are you sure?' she asked, sensing incredibly that maybe I was just being strong. It's lucky she knows me so well, I fling myself down on the sofa and yell, 'He hasn't called, he said he'd call, he hasn't waaaahh.' I plunge my head onto a nearby cushion and stay there waiting for her sympathy. Disappointingly she remains silent long after I'd finished my tirade. She then strokes my hair. I wait for the accompanying soothing words. She continues to stroke.

'Er Ellie, what are you doing?' Silence.

'Well to be honest I think you should play it cool. Leave him alone for a bit.' Hmm... This hadn't been part of my plan. I was planning on calling him up, begging him to get over now and pay me some attention.

'I know you don't want to hear it Ang but he can take you for granted.' La la la la la la la not listening. La la la la.

'You've got to make him realise he misses you,' she continued. Would she ever stop? Who does she think she is: Oprah? 'Make him do some of the running. Then you'll know how much you mean to him.' Hmmph.

I know all this is really quite logical sound advice. This doesn't stop me from floundering on and asking, 'But what if I don't mean much,' in a small voice.

'Then,' she sighed, 'he's not worth it Angel.'

I digest this piece of news. Then I reject this piece of news. It seems a little extreme; we are talking about a very busy man here. And a very attractive, amusing man. He has a lot of pulls on his time. A party here, a function there, work to do, people to impress. It was a heady world. It wasn't surprising he often forgot to remember little me. So it was my job to remind him. And anyway it was only Monday night.

After half a pizza and some curling lettuce with mayonnaise I thought I'd call Suzie. She was constantly flitting from one man to the next; she'd know what to do about a missing boyfriend. After the initial, 'Angie it's been one day. He's a man, what were you expecting' she began to realise I was more concerned by the pattern emerging.

'He often waits for me to call. He never stays here. Sometimes he doesn't return my call for days. He...' Realising I was bordering on neurotic I left it at that, finishing with the latest theory, 'So Ellie reckons I should start to play it cool,' I said laughing heartily to show that I was pretty cool already. 'Reckons I should let him come to me.'

Silence from the end of the phone. This was getting awfully familiar.

'Well she's probably right Ange.' Oh. 'There's always that stuff in self help books. Men are like elastic bands; let them go into their caves. Bla bla bla...'

'What?' I asked confused as to what I was supposed to be letting him do in a cave with a bunch of elastic. 'Why would that help?'

'Well you know. If you leave a man alone a bit, let him pull on the elastic band as it were, he'll come springing back to you.' I had little idea which books she had been reading but it sounded suspiciously like self help for those involved in arts and crafts.

'And what's the bit about the cave?' I said, willing it to be more logical than the pinging plastic.

'That's where they think,' she said almost triumphantly. 'They go and think and then come back to you all loving because they've thought it through.'

'Righttttt,' I said not entirely convinced that she hadn't been reading the book upside down.

'You are like a radiator' she said warming to her topic, 'You exude warmth and energy. He needs to see that.'

Excellent, OK, well thanks for all that.

'Do you see what I mean Angie?'

No, I think you sound mental.

'Yes, he needs to see... my warmth?'

'Exactly!' She sounded like she'd just solved the issue of world famine. This gave her an added spurt of confidence to continue coining out advice.

'Nick needs reminding that you have a life too. Next time he calls be busy.'

'But why? I'm not busy.'

'I know but you have to make him think you are. That you

could be somewhere else. With cooler people. At a party.'

'Ooh a party where?' I said getting excited by her plans.

'Well there's not actually a party,' she said.

'Oh, oh right, of course not,' I continued. Damn no party; that had sounded fun.

'But he needs to think there is, so you are unavailable, unobtainable and therefore a better catch because of it. Angel didn't you cover this in psychology? It's basic stuff.'

'Really,' I said wondering why the hell I'd wasted three years of my degree focusing on reviewing the memory process and seeing how visual information is perceived. This information was far more practical.

Within seconds of saying good bye to Suzie the phone had trilled again. NICK it said. HA! I scooped up the phone. ALLELUIA! Playing it cool worked! Oh. I didn't have my contacts in. RICK it said.

'Angel pants. I've just spoken to Suzie. She's totally right.' He carried on before I had time to get cross at the speed my news travels. 'Play the ice maiden darling, every one knows that the ice maiden is a winner. Totally ignore him. Nick who. It will make you gloriously inaccessible and...'

I cut him off petulantly, 'I don't want to be inaccessible.'

'Of course not darling, but he'll love you more for it,' said Rick slowing down his speech a little so that it had a better chance of sinking in.

'What if he just doesn't call... ever'? I said dramatically, not really believing this could happen.

'Well you're right darling he might not.' HUH?!

'But then you'll know he's not Mr Dreamy won't you, and darling don't worry there's plenty more ass out there?'

Sensing the silence from my end Rick managed to change the subject and spent the next five minutes convincing me that he was coming down with a rare disease in the intestine. Before he went to take his temperature he reverted back, 'Promise me Angel pants, ice maiden. Who are you darling? Say it out loud.'

'Er...'

'Come on darling, who are you?' He said sounding a good bit like an American in an AA meeting.

'I'm an ice maiden.' I muttered, sounding more than a mite silly.

'Louder,' he teased.

'Fuck off,' and giggling I replaced the receiver. Rick was shouting, 'Perfect darling, just like that.'

Exhausted from the onslaught I went and made a hot chocolate with extra Baileys. They were both right. It couldn't do much harm to leave it for a bit, make him make a bit of the effort. I joined Ellie in the living room. Playing it cool, the new plan. To confirm this course of action I made Ellie watch Thelma and Louise. They were playing it cool. Oooh Brad Pitt's fit. Not that I was bothered. Men no longer affected me. I was an ice maiden.

'Angie are you muttering into your mug?' said Ellie looking over at me.

Realising I might be saying my new mantra out loud I went crimson, 'No, I was just... wondering whether... we had any ice... in the flat.'

Before Ellie could probe further, and after Thelma and Louise had driven to their deaths, my mobile was flashing 'HOME.' I watched the car go over the canyon and gulped. The ultimate way to play it cool and achieve absolute Ice Maiden status. Unobtainable was now their middle name. I pressed 'Yes,'

My mother was already in the midst of a babble. Something about the downstairs loo and toilet duck. Nice.

'Hi Mum,' I interjected, trying to divert her off the subject of bathroom freshness.

'Hello Angela darling. Just wondering if you were coming home at all this weekend. Edward's still home and we haven't seen you in a while. If the train fare's a problem I'll get your father to pay, I can't believe how the prices have just gone up and up. Only six months ago it was a pound sixty cheaper...'

'Mum, mum.' She paused to inhale air, I took the opportunity to step in, 'I think I'm going to stay in London this weekend but maybe next...'

'It's that boyfriend of yours isn't it? Nick. Are you busy doing something nice with him?'

'Er... no not exactly I just have a lot to do at the moment. Actually I'm playing it a bit cool with Nick at the moment, getting him to make some effort you know.' I immediately shut up, had I just outlined the Ice Maiden Plan to my mother? Doof.

'Oh good idea darling. Let him stew.' Which I think actually meant she was agreeing with me and not telling me to make him some kind of a casserole dish.

'Your father was always pestering me after I'd left him a little while. Men are so stupid darling, that's what we all have to remember.'

'Right. Absolutely.'

'Well good luck and let us know when you are coming home. I've got to clean the bathroom now. You know your ruddy sister only went and...'

I let her carry on a few minutes with the latest in a long line of little sister related rants. She was playing the bane of my mother's life particularly successfully. Apparently when my parents had been away she'd gone out, got drunk and passed out on her bed. Her best friend, assuming she was choking on her own vomit by now, had got the police to smash their way in to check on her.

'...So we spent a hundred pounds on a new window. Honestly that girl. Anyway darling I better go, can't chat all night. Your father sends his love.'

'Love to him too, Bye mum.'

Ellie looked over at me curiously, 'Go on, what's your sister done now,' she asked. I repeated last week's saga for her.

'Oh, God, brilliant,' she said shaking with giggles.

All the phone calls had made the evening fly by and I was soon woozily wishing Ellie a good night. Getting ready for bed that evening I counted the hours. Ooh – I'd been playing it cool for a good three hours and twenty minutes. Fairly impressive stuff. Just see how they come running. Suddenly my mobile phone started rattling out its jaunty tune for the fourth time that evening. My stomach lurched as I crossed the room to dive on it. But no, another false alarm. 'MEL.' My phone line was starting to resemble a BT call centre. I hadn't realised I had this many friends. I answered it before it hit the chorus. It was Mel wanting a moan before bedtime. Seems Zachary had been painting the house red, literally, using a Crayola Crayon.

'He's going through a really naughty phase and today he pointed at Peter's mum and said, 'Granny why have your legs got all those blue lines, can you not wash them off?'

'Oops,' I said giggling and secretly congratulating myself on avoiding having children thus far.

'The trouble is I can't tell him off. I've sent him to the naughty corner so often he might as well camp there.'

'Make Peter do it.'

'He's not here and he's been so busy at the moment catching up from the holiday we hardly see each other. We haven't been out in ages.' This rung a familiar bell. I was back on safer ground. Seven year old boys were not an area of expertise but The Disappearing Man was tonight's central topic.

'I know he has to work,' she continued, 'But it still gets boring.'

'My advice to you is to play it cool Mel.'

'What?' came the dubious reply.

'Well make him miss you. Let him come to you. Be cool.' I said educating her in the new ethos.

'Angela I've had this man's child, I gave up the right of cool seven years ago pushing something the size of a watermelon out of my vagina in front of his very eyes.' Hmm... coarse but fair. I did wonder whether that experience in itself was to blame for current events but sensibly chose not to throw that idea out in the arena.

'I live in his house, I mother his child, I wore a breast pump around him. Cool is simply not an option,' she went on patronizingly.

Hmmm... fine.

'No,' she carried on, 'I'll just make us some time. Make him a meal or something.'

I accepted defeat.

'Oh, OK that sounds like a nice idea. Anyway you too are great together. Everyone knows that. He's probably just as frustrated being so busy with work as you are.'

'You're right Angel. God I'm being silly. Look I'll call you in the next couple of days to make a lunch plan.'

'Brilliant.'

'Sleep tight.'

'Night.'

I put down the phone feeling a warm glow. I knew it would be fine. They had been together so long and Peter absolutely worshipped her.

The warm fuzzy glow threatened to weaken my resolve. Do not call him. I rushed through to the kitchen and ate a Tracker to distract myself. It didn't do the trick so I popped in some Pringles. Better. I shouted goodnight through to Ellie. As I brushed my teeth I reckoned I've done a pretty good job of it. Four hours and thirty six minutes without texting him. To celebrate I type in the message I would have sent. 'Really want to see you soon. Call me. Sleep tight. Love Angel xxx'

But I don't send it. See how cool I am.

I wait ten minutes. Then I send it.

Doh!

* * *

A minor slip up to the plan, and I don't tell anyone. To make up for it I spend the rest of the week not ringing Nick. Which turns out to be far more exhausting than just simply calling him. I think of ringing him, I scroll down to his name on my phone, my finger hovers dangerously, and then I sigh, go for a run, eat cake and sleep. Mostly in that order, ok fine, I made the running bit up. I think of ringing him, I imagine him answering, I hear his voice which varies between comments such as 'Angel I've missed you' through to 'Angel I want you/need you/can't live a day without you.' In all our conversations he is lovely, flirty, cheeky and... unreal. The only shortcoming I might add. I think of ringing him and then get cross when everyone else rings me, usually to tell me not to ring him.

Work is a fairly good way to eat up the vast amounts of time in between stressing about calling/not calling Nick. It provides a distraction. I'm deep in the midst of dozens of home replies and dolling out some good sound advice to the teens of today.

Dear Angel,
My fiancé has to work late a lot. We often argue about it. I don't want to keep fighting but how can I get him to see that although I think his job's important I miss him and wish he'd spend more time with me?
Clare, 18, Wrington

Dear Clare,
Oh dear! Up until now you have played into your boyfriend's hands slightly. By agreeing to marry him you are

immediately shouting, 'I really like you, I depend on you, I need you.' You've lost the upper hand. Relationships are games that we need to win. Although your boyfriend says he is 'working late' he is also sending a subliminal message to you which says 'I am better than you, I own you.' Perhaps on these late nights you should go out with your girlfriends, don't answer the phone, keep him waiting- retain the air of mystery. Otherwise he'll be walking you down the aisle and then walking all over you,
   Good Luck!
   Angel

I stopped the letter to check my mobile. No sodding messages. Sighing I picked up the next letter on the pile. It seemed to be of a similar theme. I set to work.

   *Annie, Men need to be taught that we are capable of getting on with our lives without spending every minute of the day obsessing over them and...*it is so unfair that I am always wondering if he'll call... *you need to make sure he realises that...* none of my other friends do this so why am I being a ridiculous... *you are not always 'just there' as his play thing, you are a...* loser about it all. He's just busy; I need to get over it and... *warm, loving individual with your own needs...* concentrate on other things... *and if he doesn't start to respect that you should seriously consider where your relationship is headed.* Why doesn't he ever ring, just to say hello, just to check if I'm having a nice... concentrate on other things Angel. Concentrate.

   Berating myself I looked down at the next envelope. I instantly recognized the familiar scrawl. Mary, 47, Hull. She was the only over 18 to write to me. Her niece had left the magazine lying around after a visit and she'd found my page and decided to send a letter. She'd first written nearly a year ago and after an indignant reply from me she had kept up a fairly regular run of correspondence. Most of her predicaments usually involved her evil husband Bernard, his bitch of an ex-wife, and a steady stream of mistresses. In one recent episode the latest bit on the side had turned up berating Bernard for taking Mary to a cheese and wine do at 'their friend's house.' I'd seen her through this trauma and through the humiliation of Bernard ending her membership with Weight Watchers after four sessions (and when she'd lost 4lbs) so she would be home to cook for him. He put her down, he flaunted his other women around and he made her feel fat, ugly and dull. Every now and again there'd be silence from her and we'd assume she was coping, but then the letters would start up again. She sometimes wrote a quick note to tell me that things were getting a little better. The length of this letter suggested it wasn't going well now.

I raced over to Suzie's desk to show her the latest.

'She's written again' I said with a flourish, 'It seems Bernard has run back to that girlfriend of his again.'

'The one he met on the internet?' said Suzie looking up from her work.

'No the one from Tesco's. Patisserie Section apparently.'

'I knew he would, I bloody knew it. Her last letter was way too upbeat, poor Mary. God he's such a bastard.'

'We're all doomed. DOOMED,' I spat as I read out the latest instalment in my hands.

I gasped, 'She says here that she returned home to find him sleeping with her in their bed. And the woman was wearing her dressing gown.'

'Oh Christ that is wrong,' said Suzie appalled.

'Right something has got to be done,' I said drawing myself up straight. Poor Mary. It just didn't deserve to happen to her. Was it always going to be this struggle to keep down a man? Mary seems to be a loving wife, always cooking, ironing, washing and tending to the cheating snake. How did this happen to her? I spent much of the rest of the day drawing up an in-depth action plan for her. Her self-esteem would be desperately low and I was racking my brains to think of things she could do to make herself feel better. Spa treatments, lunch with the girls, long walks, a personal trainer, a break away, a return to work...

In the midst of writing out my Action Plan for Mary my mobile phone flashed. The little text message envelope appeared on the screen and I clicked OK.

'Dinner tomorrow night. I'll pick you up at 7pm. Nick.'

I hugged my phone to my chest; thank goodness. I wasn't going to end up like Mary quite yet. Nick wasn't absolutely cuddly with his messages but he didn't need to be. Dinner. With him. Hooray. He had got in touch. He'd thought of me. He wants me. He loves me. Well, I corrected myself... soon he will love me.... Ha, ha, ha, ha!

* * *

Thursday dawned bright and sunny. With thoughts of the evening's dinner still putting a little spring in my step I strolled care free down the office corridor. Getting to my desk I found a pile of letters with a single post it note from Agony Uncle Richard (I'm-a-waste-of-space-Winters) instructing me to 'Reply Immediately.' Searched on the note for a please, a thank you, a you-are-so-lovely-Angela and was shocked to the core to discover there was none. I craned my neck round the desk to sneer at him but realised the effort was useless as he had his back to me. He was jabbing at his keyboard surrounded by his Features groupies no doubt all furiously researching their latest shocking tale to make the most grabby headline. My Father Tried To Eat Me, Shoes: How to Wear Them etc, etc. They all gave such a great impression of being so busy, well I was busy too so I picked up the bundle and pushed my way over to Richard (I'm-a-frustrated-individual-Winters) desk. I stood tapping my foot at their table waiting for one of the gang to inform me when I may begin talking to their demi-god Richard. No one looked up from the tapping and I began to slightly lose my nerve, but then, huzzah and bingo, the man himself raised his gaze.

'Angela, what a pleasure. And what can we do for you?' At this all the groupies looked up, keen to watch him in action. I assumed he had only deigned to talk to me to humiliate me in front of the adoring clique.

I started protesting, 'Richard I've just found all these letters on my desk. I can't answer all of them I haven't got time. I've got to research my column and do all my home replies.'

'Look Angela, I spoke to Victoria and she agrees I haven't got time to waste replying to these kids all week when I should be working on important feature articles for the magazine.'

'But I...'

'You do all your home replies and it won't take you long to knock off mine will it. It's bad enough I have to waste time writing the 'Dear Richard' agony column let alone waste more time writing to them all in their homes.'

'But I...'

'Look Angela,' the groupies were in raptures, 'It's not my problem anymore, you scuttle off and complain about it to Victoria. She'll tell you just what she told me.'

'Well you be assured that I will be speaking to Victoria on this matter,' I said waving the letters around.

'I will be assured,' he said looking solemnly at me. I think he was taking the piss. I got back to my desk silently fuming, which was difficult to do as I was really very, very angry. I pulled out my chair and threw myself down fairly petulantly. That was more like it. Stupid, nasty, mean little man.

I remembered the initial pleasure I had upon hearing my agony aunt would indeed have her own perfect partner. What every agony aunt needs, an agony uncle. I'd been so excited about meeting my fellow problem page-writer. Agony Uncle Richard appeared to be quite attractive if his passport photo above his column was anything to go by. He had stubbly good looks and a twinkle in his eye. Yes, I imagined we'd get on well together. Not that I had intended to jeopardize my newly acquired professional role by lusting after my co-worker, but I assumed a little friendly flirtation would only be expected. It would have been rude not to. We were going to be partners in crime, side-by-side into the fray, ordering Indian takeaways when working late together, going for long lunches to giggle about the more ridiculous letters under the guise of going on some kind of agony solving course. That kind of thing.

I had it all sussed and ensured I dressed appropriately for our first meeting. I had to look cool, confident, and, as a given, gorgeous. In my favourite black A line skirt and knee boots I was feeling confident. He needed to meet me, feel comforted by my equal good looks (he wouldn't want some sad fatso following him around the office 24/7) and develop a brutally intense crush on me. He would obviously be forced to suppress his feelings so that only I would be aware of his wanton desire. I would look at him fleetingly every now and again so he'd hope upon hope that one day I'd cave in and abandon my professionalism to be with him forever. All the sexual tension would build and build; he'd ask for my advice on the trickier letters, search out my womanly opinion, listen carefully to my replies watching me closely, he'd want to stay late and.... Oh I was off. In fact I was just rushing through the various exciting scenarios involving myself, Richard, a large tub of Haagen Daaz and the office photocopier when a horrible streak of dirty blonde man shoved past me through the revolving door. I'd met him then.

A cheap nylon suit, slightly shining, and something even Jonathan Ross might turn his nose up at, was the first thing to hit me. The dirty blonde hair desperately spiked up with glossy gel in an attempt to distract from the fact that the owner was sporting the finest in receding hairlines, was the second. Passport photos should be banned. In fact I was considering asking him whether he had asked his flatmate/older brother/father/ granddad to pose for it as the reality was so far removed. He was around 5ft 7' and sometimes wore cowboy boots in an attempt to gain an extra inch or two. Worst of all however was his decision to sculpt the stubble of facial hair into a tuft of spiked beard protruding from his chin. To my horror I soon discovered he dyed this a different colour each month. I supposed it was a sort of amusing take on Billy Connolly's disastrous experiment with the pink beard, only worryingly Richard wasn't joking.

I balked at the number of replies I needed to do. There must be some mistake. He must be wrong. I knocked tentatively on the door of Victoria's office. Within five minutes I was stomping back to my desk, only making a detour to moan in Suzie's ear about all the injustices in the world. Predictably within minutes he was standing by my desk. I pretended to be deeply involved in reading a letter in front of me. I was staring at it so hard any passer by would think I was suffering from terrible dyslexia. I didn't look up. This didn't stop him talking to me.

'And what did Victoria say?' he said. I looked up at him with a murderous face. As if he couldn't guess.

'See I told you,' he said, obviously relishing his new role as Hardened Task Master.

'Fine Richard, I'll do them.'

'Oh come on Angel there aren't that many,' he smirked popping a fresh pile of letters addressed to him on my desk.

I gaped at him. He was just calmly doubling my workload. Not only was I going to have to write the home replies for my own page, I was going to have to write his too.

'Well see you later then,' he said, unable to stop himself from a smug smile as he left.

I glowered at his departing back.

'OK then. Bye Dick,' I muttered under my breath. He spun round and gave me a glare as I neatly placed a wide-eyed look of surprise on my face, 'What?' I asked in innocent protest, 'Is there something wrong?' Childish I know but he reduced me to infantile tactics.

I grumpily picked up the first few letters and scanned down the typical worries of thirteen year old boys, and then one of them caught my eye. A few moments later I had started to scribble furiously and soon a satisfied smile crept across my face and I sat back to admire my handiwork. Perfect. I re-read it for any grammatical errors and my own satisfaction.

Dear Richard
I was in the boys' showers the other day when my mates made fun of me...

Dear Daniel,
Don't worry I often get letters from boys worried about the same thing. It is a lot more common to worry about this than you think. Many boys do not develop at the same rate, and this often means some do not develop as soon as they like. I myself have a surprisingly small penis for a man of 29. So don't worry Daniel you are not alone.
Richard

Still giggling I picked up another, within seconds I was signing off with a flourish.

Hi Richard,
I've got a big problem. I recently kissed a girl but I didn't know what to do with my tongue. She put hers in, and then took it out when I didn't. Do you do it one after the other or at the same time? Help!

This is a common worry among teenagers. I myself have had a massive difficulty trying to improve my technique over the years because I have no one to practise on! The one girl I kissed got cross by my 'washing machine' method which is when you move your tongue round in an energetic circle. I thought it was working wonders. So sorry mate, just try your best, I'm no help to you at all.

Richard

The day's work was completed fairly promptly. There'd been hardly any need for research as most were written entirely inspired by petty revenge and an intense dislike of Richard (I'm-a-loser-Winters). I smiled generously at him as I sent them down to be posted. He did a double-take. My good mood remained even when I discovered there was a tube strike and I had to take about five buses going via Birmingham to get home.

An hour later, hot Ribena in hand, I went to collapse on the sofa next to Ellie. As I had just eased myself into place and rested my head back an announcement on the news infiltrated my consciousness. I darted to an upright sitting position.

'Shit Ellie what night is it?'

'What are you talking about Ang?'

'Night, what time, evening,' I stuttered as I raised myself off the sofa faster than a speeding light. 'Night, I mean, what day is it?' I didn't give her time to reply, 'Shit its Thursday it's actually Thursday.'

'Is that a problem?' Ellie enquired with a confused look. She popped another load of Pringles into her mouth and added, 'Great television, they're doing a Midsomer Murder special.'

I shot her a scathing look, 'Bloody Nick is going to be here any minute. We're meant to be going out to dinner. How the hell did I forget?' I said rushing around the room as if doing a circuit of our lounge was going to help the matter.

'Bloody hell Angie, sit down. You're making me feel panicky.' She said curled up on our sofa, a mug of steaming tea in her hands and a rug draped over her legs. She couldn't have looked less panicked if she tried. Cool as a bloody cucumber in fact. She clearly did not get the seriousness of the situation. I spelt it out for her.

'Ellie,' I began in a dangerously tight voice, 'The man I'm in love with,' at this she rolled her eyes in a not-so-subtle-way, I chose to ignore it. Too little time for a full-blown fight about it.

'The man I'm in love with,' I repeated, 'Is about to arrive any minute now and take me out for an expensive dinner. Do you see what I'm wearing? Not exactly bloody evening wear is it?' She looked at my Snoopy Pyjama top and grey tracksuit bottoms with a critical eye. By this point I'd taken up the rushing around again, and legged it through to my bedroom with Ellie yelling, 'Unless he likes the just-got-out-of-bed look' unhelpfully at my departing back.

Moments later I was crossing her path with a pile of plastic bottles in my arms in the direction of our bathroom. Only the essentials obviously. I went back to get the second pile.

I stared at myself in the mirror. My hair was scraped back into a messy pony tail, my eyeliner was smudged and my foundation was barely still apparent. I set about my transformation as quickly as I could. Foundation, smoky eyes and pale pink lips. Time for clothes. With few minutes to decide what to wear I relied on an old favourite, throwing on my black halter neck top and green knee length skirt. I found my black heels nestled underneath my bed and popped them on, hooking in some gold earrings to complete the look. As I scooped up a bracelet I heard the flat buzzer go.

I heard Ellie letting him in to the flat. A muffled, 'Hello' and a muffled reply of 'oh it's you. Hi' and then silence. I looked at my reflection for any last minute changes.

'Angie Nick's here,' came the announcement. My stomach flipped over.

'Just coming,' I yelled, bronzing my cheeks within an inch of their lives in nervous excitement.

'Angel,' Nick called, 'The taxi is waiting.' I knew this last comment hinted that I was suddenly meant to have miraculously finished my preening and emerge calmly in a pouf of perfumed air to announce in a tinkly voice, 'darling sooo good to see you' before lightly brushing two kisses in the air around his cheeks. Instead I flew into a general panic, flapping around the bedroom flinging various items in my bag and yelling, 'Two seconds, I'm just finishing my nails.' As I said the words I realised I sounded a good bit like a character out of Brookside and any minute would be leaving the flat kissing my three illegitimate children goodbye.

I scurried out of my bedroom blowing on my left hand, which was painted a beautiful shade of red, and hiding my right hand, which was bare as a baby's bottom. Nick was perched on the arm of our decrepit sofa fidgeting, checking his watch and clearly resenting the fact that my nails were costing him valuable time and money. He was so attractive brooding on our flea-ridden furniture I mouthed thank you to my god at my good fortune in nabbing such a creature. The moment he saw me he sprung up, pecked me on the cheek and flung a coat around my shoulders. Ellie's coat, but the fact that he'd picked it out so meticulously stopped me protesting. He obviously thought I suited it. Bless him. It was only during my coat pondering that I realised he had legged it down the stairs to the waiting taxi and I almost pulled a muscle jumping two steps by two after him.

'Bye Ellie,' I screeched, plummeting to the landing floor and only narrowly missing spraining an ankle in the effort to keep up. I got into the taxi as the meter clicked to 80p, Nick raised one eyebrow at me and I sunk low in the back seat to feel guilty for the rest of the journey. After a few good minutes of solid remorse I tried to buck myself up by discreetly attempting to finish the right hand of nails, but I hadn't counted on quite so many speed bumps down Melville Road. I looked down to quickly inspect my handiwork and realised with horror that the skin of my right hand was now streaked in scarlet red as if I'd been butchered in the back of the cab by a psychopath. The taxi braked just before I could try and fix the damage. I plunged the hand into Ellie's coat and hoped Nick wouldn't notice anything was amiss.

Nick hopped out on to a small cobbled side street in quite a trendy part of town where a crowd were smoking and laughing and chatting outside an entrance. I went to leave the cab after him but the driver was gesticulating with his hands and repeating, 'Monee, monee' at me. With one foot on the street outside I twisted back.

'Oh of course, so sorry,' I said craning my neck around for Nick who had disappeared into the throng outside.

'Monee, monee, monee.'

I reached into my bag and pulled out my wallet whilst simultaneously scanning the crowd for the return of Nick with a pile of cash.

'Monee, monee.'

'Yes I know, hold on,' I said rummaging for cash. I handed

him a twenty pound note abstractedly. Where had he gone?

'No change, no change.'

I turned back to the driver, 'Hmm?'

'No change, no change,' he said waving the twenty pound around.

'Right,' I said looking frantically in my bag again. I checked for Nick. I'd lost him now. Which bar had he gone to? Was that him?

'No change, no changeee.'

'I know,' I screeched groping fruitlessly for change that didn't exist.

'Oh fine, fine, just keep it,' I said clambering out and slamming the door. Straightening my skirt I looked around the hubbub outside for a tall, devastatingly attractive man. No where to be seen. I got out my phone to call him, then right on cue he appeared at my side looking a little put out.

'Angel where did you get to?' Nick asked obviously ignoring the fact that he had disappeared into a crowd of revellers the moment the taxi had drawn up. Not waiting for a reply and distracted by the gang of suits he called, 'Well are you ready to go in?' over his shoulder. Not wanting to argue about it I nodded and traipsed after him, 'Absolutely, so sorry,' I muttered.

He put a hand on the small of my back, 'That's ok sweetheart, oh hold on, just going to say hi to Fizzy.' And then I was whisked into the crowd.

It took us about forty-five minutes to reach our table. Nick knew practically every other diner within a fifty metre radius. We stopped for air-kissing and chats with many be-suited men and their suspiciously blonde and young 'wives.' To be truthful Nick did most of the air-kissing and chats while I stood tucked behind him nodding at his braying companions in an earnest way and laughing politely whenever they made a joke (usually relating to accountants or the stock market. How many accountants does it take to change a light bulb, that kind of thing. Terribly amusing). Poor Nick was obviously so eager to get us quickly to our table to be alone, for the start of our romantic dinner together, that he tried to save time by not involving himself in lengthy introductions. In fact he didn't introduce me to one of the braying companions. He did manage to find an extra ten minutes or so to shake his head and discuss knowledgeably the falling something-something shares and the rise in whatsit-whatsit's prices but I could see he was trying to escape all the talking shop as soon as he could. I often forgot that his job was highly stressful and important. He never found it funny to joke about his clients or his day at work. I had discovered that early on. The City was not a laughing matter.

We finally sat down at our table and got comfortable. Nick shifted his seat slightly to be 'out of the way of the draft' just in front of a mirror behind me. We spent a few tense minutes trying to catch the eye of a waiter. Every time I tried to start some light chatter Nick would crane his neck round to continue the hunt, which would silence my efforts. Finally a waitress casually sauntered over, seemingly completely unaware of our desperate search. I idly wondered if the dress code for waitresses included her bare minimum approach to dressing. Her skirt, if indeed it existed at all, was a simple strip of black underneath a white shirt that acted as shirt and mini dress in one. Ingenious. I self-consciously slipped my skirt up a notch, and then realised the futility of the action as my legs were safely hidden under the table. Damn them. A fleeting temptation to whip them out and display them right across the starter and soup course gripped me as Nick's eyes kept wandering during our order, but I restrained myself and placed a fixed toothpaste smile on my face during the whole ordeal. I was going for 'yes I'm cool with this' but the smile, possibly a little psychotic I realised when Nick turned and flinched a little, obviously wasn't doing the best to convey my laid back non-threatened image. She barely bothered to look in my direction but drawled the days specials so quietly to Nick that I was forced to crane my neck and lean across the table to hear. Not totally effective as all I ever picked up was 'salmon, herb, asparagus' intermittently, so anything special from the kitchen was going to have to pass me by. Nick was nodding animatedly at her as she read from the list, no doubt to ensure she didn't spit in our soup (such a clever guy) and she melted in his presence. When she started laughing at a comment he'd made (something funny about the prawn vol-au-vents apparently) I realised they'd formed some sort of intimate members only club, and I didn't know the secret handshake. Nick ordered for both of us, salmon en croute with dill sauce. I wasn't a fan of fish in general but kept quiet. He did know the restaurant better and the days specials had just been whispered in his ear. It must be delicious.

When the waitress had exited, with one final giggle and wiggle at Nick, we sat looking at each other, as two relatively new young lovers should. I realised we'd been going out for over seven months now (seven months and four days to be truthful to you) but actually we didn't get to spend that much quality time together. I valued nights like this. But seven months was a long time. I looked over at him and considered blurting that out, but managed to restrain myself just in time. Be cool I breathed. Be cool. He was wearing a crisp pale blue shirt and a steely grey jacket that gave him an air of class and sophistication. His hair was newly cut and he had an emerging line of stubble on his chin. I thanked my lucky stars again for the presence of this dashing hunk of a man. All mine. A lovely, straightforward, upright, individual. He was fiddling nervously with the napkin in his lap, which was so endearing. His face was screwed up in concentration, as he clearly tried to muster up the courage to begin our evenings chatter. Few often got to see how nervous he could be and I settled back in my chair and gazed at him.

He looked up abruptly, sensing my melting eyes on him, 'Christ Angela, why are you staring at me, it's off-putting. I'm trying to text Chris,'

'Oh,' I flushed caught off the hop and suddenly realising the nervous fiddling was in fact tapping on a mobile, 'Oh... so... Chris from... the office,' I said weakly.

Nick didn't bother to look up, 'Yeah, he's recording the game.'

'Ah,' I nodded. Past experience told me I should not ask what game this was. Replies to questions such as these usually involved a loud snort and a patronizing 'Jesus-you-don't-know-what-it-is' roll of the eyes. I waited patiently for him to finish by pretending to develop an urge to study the room with a sudden intense interest in architecture. Marble columns by reception, hmm, very interesting. A sign for the Toilets written in an italic scroll, very nice. A mahogany bar with red velvet covered bar stools, fascinating. Finally he finished and I looked back at him with a startled try at 'Oh you're still here, silly me I was too engrossed by the decor.' Cool you see. That's me. Nick placed his mobile to the left of his fork on the table, no doubt just to make sure anyone urgent could contact us in an emergency, and looked at me. I sighed inwardly and waited eagerly for him to speak and then when time had ticked by a little over the comfortable silence barrier I piped up, 'How was work.' Darn. Dazzling Question Number One I thought. However seeing his face light up like I'd just asked him what he got from Santa made me realise I couldn't have made a better enquiry.

'Yah it was OK. Hectic obviously, but fine. We didn't lose too much, the Telecoms were down and everyone's a bit worried about that. But I knew they'd come down once the American stock market looked set to fall. I said that to Clive and by lunchtime I was proved right. And I knew A.G and P.H.Y.P were never going to merge. Stupid buggers putting all their...' And he was off. I watched his fervent expression and admired the way his face became increasingly animated with every word. He looked to be getting a little more excited as the seconds went by. He kept repeating something about playing footsie with me, but all the economic jargon had slightly knocked my concentration. Dutifully I reached my leg out underneath the table and stroked his ankle as he spoke. He slowed down a touch, it was obviously working as a minor distraction, and I placed my chin in my hand on the table and looked at him seductively though strands of hair. His speech slowed down further, and suddenly it stopped. I was left smiling coyly at him, my foot now running up and down his calf. I was glad he was so keen to be affectionate. He was so naughty.

'Angela, are you even listening – what are you doing?'

I looked at him slyly through lowered eyelashes, 'I'm doing just what you asked,' I purred in a husky sort of a voice. Very sex kitten. I was hot. Nick however was still looking at me strangely, as if the husky tones had not sent him off into an orbit of pleasure. Odd.

'What do you mean what I asked?'

Slightly distracted my foot was now just rubbing one particular spot on his leg as he went on, 'I was just talking about the terrible decline in my client's shares and you are rubbing your foot up and down my leg.' Ah. This wasn't quite the reaction I'd been going for. My foot had stopped its wiggling now and rested itself until it had the green light to go.

'But you wanted to play footsie,' I giggled and then tried the sultry look once more. Anything to defrost the icy glare he was sporting at that moment.

'Footsie, Angela. Footsie?' He said aghast.

'Er yes,' I replied, my confidence faltering a little now, and my foot ready to move away from his side of the table.

'I think you'll find,' he began in a tone best utilised when teaching five year olds, 'I was talking about the FTSE, the Financial Times Share Estimate, and not asking you to participate in a childish game of...'

Beep. Beep.

Suddenly the phone was beeping and he dived on it. 'YES, YES, YES,' he said punching the air. My foot was flung aside in the madness.

'Good news,' I enquired politely but Nick was involved in another run of frenzied texting. To improve my mood the waitress in the mini dress chose that moment to reappear with the salmon. Of which fortunately there appeared to be one ounce. Minimalist obviously being the general rule around here.

'So they did it,' she said laughingly at Nick and dumping my plate down unceremoniously before me, 'I watched extra time in the kitchen. It was a great goal. Brilliant.'

Nick grinned at her, 'See you doubting Thomas, what did I say, I knew they'd come through.' Oh god, it was that members only club again and this time they had passwords.

'Hmm,' I said chipping in, 'Great... er...' they were both staring at me now, 'Great... restaurant. Love the... décor.' I said with a flourish of my fork. They looked at me then they looked straight back at each other.

'So how did it go in?' Nick asked her enthusiastically.

'Graves crossed the ball. I thought the cross looked off but Hobbs made such a great header.' I assumed they were still talking about sport, but I couldn't be certain. After another bout of hearty giggling and sporty chat she finally decided to make her exit.

'Better get on; I have got other customers you know.'

Nick nodded at her back.

'Nice girl,' he said as she crossed the room.

'Hmm... I said not trusting myself to speak. Because if I did it would be along the lines of 'cow, cow, cow, cow, cow, bitch, cow' and that wasn't mature or clever. She was not good to have around on a date. In fact on my list of Things You Want On A Date 'Pretty waitress' is a fairly low priority.

After all the excitement, and the waitress and the game Nick had fortunately forgotten he had been in the midst of lecturing me about, 'You see Angela, the FTSE is...' Oh god no. I tried hard to look interested.

'It's extremely vital to know what is happening in...' As he spoke I realised I was left with few options before me. It was either option a) gouge my own brain out with the remaining silverware or option b) knock back the House White. I decided on the latter and after a while everything became more amusing. I was not a dingus. And footsie's were vital to the stock exchanging. The F stood for Fuck what did the F stand for again. Wasn't Fuck I knew that. Oh bugger! Two identical, and equally attractive Nick's, were leaning across the table at me. Oop, now there appeared to be three. He was right, finance was important. Realising he might have to distract me from refilling my glass a further time, and guessing that my interest in London's stock market was ebbing in the face of this liquid opposition, he turned the attention on me, and enquired after my day.

In my highly alert state I noted that the three Nick's were looking right at me and I opened my mouth to gobble an ungracious 'What?' at them, but then I heard the question. Light travels faster than sound you see. How. Was. My. Day. Gottit. I started gabbling, 'Well I got another letter from Mary, you know the lady from Hull whose husband keeps messing her about saying he'll leave her unless she loses weight, and she...' I noticed him snorting a little into his glass '...and she reckons he'll go back to his mistress again if she stops going to her weekly sessions at Weight Watchers but he is refusing to pay for them and...'

All the Nick's were laughing now; I bristled with sensitivity, 'That was just what it was like.'

'I don't doubt it Angel. Those people, Christ, how tragic. Tell the fatty to lose some weight.' he guffawed. 'Poor bastard lumbered with a big moaning wife and having to live in Hull. Can't be hard to sort out though?'

'What do you mean by that?'

'I mean, my darling, that your job is not exactly high brow is it.' Press pause and rewind. He called me darling. Nick Sheldon-

Wade called me darling in a public area. In daylight. Relatively sober. I am Nick's darling in a relatively sober daylight world open to the public. I went back to thinking about Nick before I could confuse myself further about who was sober or darling or living in daylight. I just knew for sure that he had said 'darling' to me. I was his darling, his sweetheart, his dearest, his beloved. I was pretty bloody chuffed about it too. This was significant. This hinted at long term surely? Hurrah! I also recalled he had slagged off my job, but right now I was still on the darling high so I let it slide.

The evening swam by. From what I remember I reckoned I was on pre-tt-y good form. I had needed to keep up the entertainment as at one point during the main course Nick had nodded at so many people over my shoulder I started to worry that he was developing a weird nervous tic.

A trolley piled high with sumptuous looking puddings was wheeled past us as we finished the salmon and I looked longingly after it. Desserts were a massive weakness of mine. Cooking I wasn't a fan of but when it came to baking a good cake I was your girl. I didn't know you had to remove that string on the chicken but I did know how to whisk egg whites into a light and fluffy syllabub. If it contained cream and a few pounds of sugar I paid attention. The waitress ambled over to speak in tongues with Nick. After a few minutes she looked up at us both.

'So would you like any coffee or desserts?' I opened my mouth to speak but was too slow.

'No we're fine, just the bill please.'

I closed my mouth again. Oh.

'Alright babe,' he said smiling at me over the table.

'Hmm... fine,' I said, 'It's been really lovely and so nice to see you and the restaurant is...'

'So a few mates are going to go on to a club or something. Do you want to come?' he said, signing the check with a flourish and getting up from his chair. I nearly pulled off the tablecloth in my haste to get up. Then I felt dizzy.

'Oh. Well, I don't know Nick I've got to get into work and it's already late. Can't we just go home?' I said with what I hoped was a sexy little smile.

'Oh babe, I feel pretty pumped up you know. Need to work off some energy. Do you mind if I go?' My sexy smile slumped.

I didn't want to act the possessive girlfriend, but then I couldn't face a night of cocaine, drum and bass and small talk with Nobby, Lobby and Wobby.

'Sure, OK. Of course you can go.'

'Alright babe, well, I'll call you a cab,' he said indicating to the porter to order me a cab. 'I'll call you tomorrow,' he said kissing me briefly on the lips.

'Right... have a good night then,' I pushed open the heavy glass door numbly and stepped out into the night alone. I could hear Nick chatting to the waitress. He called her darling. I got in a taxi and went home.

* * *

Why had I got in a taxi and gone home? Why, why, why? He probably took the waitress home. I would have taken the waitress home I was so pissed. Damn, damn, darn and damn.

'Morning dearest,' came a call from the kitchen. 'How was the night out with Mr. Thoughtful?'

'Not right now Ellie OK,' I called gripping my head as if it would fall into pieces if I didn't. Which it probably would.

Must get out of bed and dress in clothes. Must get grip. Must. I looked down to see I was in fact wearing clothes, last night's clothes to be precise. For a fleeting moment considered just leaving them on but then my mothers face set in a stern grimace entered the fog of my mind and I got up to change like a good clean middle class girl. I had to stop going out on week nights. Not good.

'Gah,' I said as I entered the kitchen. This translated as Tea. Must Drink It. And Ellie, fluent in this type of language, had already popped up and put the kettle on. I sat at one end of the table nursing a glass of water and rubbing my temples as if that might magically make my hangover disappear.

'So, where did you go? Did you have a good night? Has Nick already left for work?' Ellie's questions were fired at me like bullets from a machine gun. It was too early for this kind of an attack.

'No he went on to some club I think. I was pretty pissed. I came home.'

The machine fire rattled on, 'Oh so you didn't go with him.

But doesn't he have work today? Was it a nice night though?'

'I'm late Ellie; I'll talk to you later alright,' I said scuffing the chair on the floor as I left.

I could still hear the machine fire as I was leaving the flat, 'Well I'll see you later. We'll catch up then. Have a good day.'

I didn't have the energy to pipe up more than a whispered 'hmm.'

My head was pounding slightly as I hurried along to the tube. There was no point making a massive dash for it as unless I was suddenly able to scale buildings I was definitely going to be late. Better to be a little bit later and much less sweaty. I blocked out the journey and managed to make it into the office without really concentrating on anything bigger than right foot goes there, place left foot a little bit ahead of that, right foot again. As ever the reception was its usual assault on the senses but I hurried past, head down until I was safely in the kitchen.

After downing a pint of water and a black coffee I felt a little bit more able to deal with the day ahead. As I sat down at my desk I remembered pieces of the conversation at dinner the night before. Today was the day when I proved Nick wrong. My job was... my phone was ringing. I answered.

'Angel,' Mel chimed.

'Mel,' I said in exactly the same voice as a mortally wounded soldier has as he lies dying.

'Morning,' she sounded like an overly enthusiastic children's TV presenter.

'Oh morning, yeah,' I said not quite matching her on enthusiasm.

'You sound chirpy.'

'Sorry I went out last night,' I said hoping she wouldn't ask me to embellish further. It seemed like a fair explanation in itself. She rattled on oblivious, 'I just called for a quick... oh it's obviously not the time, why don't I call back later.'

'No, no, it is' I said weakly.

'Look why don't I pop over for lunch and we'll chat then,' she said, 'Gives you a couple of hours to feel more human. Meet you at that café round the corner from you at one, Ricardo's, OK?'

'That would be good,' I whispered.

'Sorry Angel I didn't catch that, OK. One cough for 'yes,' two for 'no'.'

I started giggling in spite of myself.

'I'll see you then. One o'clock. Lovely.'

'Can't wait,' she said back on the kids presenters couch, 'Byeee.'

The morning moved by in a nauseous drag. I could barely be bothered to continue with Richard's letters and gave most of them fairly short shrift. I felt a little better leaving work and walking in the breeze to lunch. I arrived at Ricardo's early to see Mel sitting fiddling nervously with her napkin, a glass of wine half empty next to her. Had anything happened? I suddenly thought back to our earlier conversation on the phone. Had she seemed upset? It was all a bit fuzzy but I was fairly sure I would have noticed if she'd been in a state. I walked straight over to her, 'Mel are you alright?' I asked, seeing her starting to shred the napkin in her hands.

'Angel,' she said getting up and enfolding me in a massive hug, 'It's so good to see you.'

I was even more worried now, 'Mel are...'

'Would you like a drink madam,' asked the waiter interrupting.

I looked up, 'Oh um... yes... a latte please. Semi-skimmed milk. Thanks.'

'Could you also bring her a glass for the wine,' Mel indicated the bottle.

'No Mel I couldn't,' I said balking at the sight of alcohol so soon.

'You have to Angel, you'll want to toast me,' she said her face suddenly breaking into a massive grin.

Moments later I was staring at her mouth agape.

'Can you believe it Angel?' she said still tearing at the napkin in an excited way.

'Really?' I said staring at her, 'But when, how, who... tell me everything,' I said in a rush, all tiredness forgotten.

'He proposed last night.'

'How?' I said instantly.

Mel laughed, 'It was sweet really. He had put the ring on a plate and called me in with his little hand bell and was there on bended knee when I arrived.'

'And then...?' I said.

'And then I said yes immediately,' she finished, her eyes

twinkling with happiness, 'We stayed up all night planning the wedding. I kept checking that he was sure but he seemed as excited as me.'

'Of course he is.'

'Can you believe it?' she rushed on, 'It's going to be in September. We know it's soon but it seemed silly to rush it. My mother's so happy we're not living in sin anymore she practically had a coronary when I broke the news.'

'Wow,' I said, really meaning it, 'That is brilliant Mel.'

'I bought these just now,' she said producing bridal magazines from her bag with a flourish. 'I can't wait, there's so much to do and Zac is going to look so cute in something like this,' she said pausing to tap the model page boy on page 5 in 'Bridal You'. 'It's not going to be huge, just our close friends at the wedding and then a reception afterwards,' she gushed on.

We looked through the magazines for ages, pointing at the loveliest dresses, some with huge trains, sequinned bodices, puffy skirts. It was enough to turn any girl on to the idea of matrimony. She wanted a handful of close friends, her parents, Peter's parents and of course Zac at the actual ceremony. Her sister was the Maid of Honour and fortunately had the responsibility of organising the finer details. When we'd exhausted the catalogues and finished our omelettes we sat in a relative calm. Mel, aware that we'd been moonily discussing her future for the majority of lunch, turned to me.

'And how about you? Is everything going well at work? How's Nick? How about the acting? Have you got any shows coming up or anything we can see?'

I laughed at her eagerness to be a good friend, 'No, no acting right now and work at the magazine is ok. Nick's great, it's going well.'

'Good, I can't believe I still haven't met him.'

'I saw him last night actually,' I said coyly, realising her elation was contagious. 'He is lovely,' I sighed.

'Your ears are burning Angie. Someone's talking about you,' she said waving at my ears with her fork. I blushed, thinking immediately that Nick was probably having a similar conversation with one of his friends.

'So go on,' Mel prompted, 'What did you do?'

Angel: We went out for such a lovely dinner.
Nick: Went out for a meal with the missus yeah.
Angel: He looked gorgeous and we had so much to catch up on.
Nick: I couldn't believe how good it was.
Angel: He really is a sweet guy and so nice to everyone we met.
Nick: It was awesome. Such a surprise.
Angel: I can't believe I'm still seeing him.
Nick: I just didn't think it would be possible.
Angel: To get on that well with someone, it's so rare.
Nick: But it was incredible, seriously special.
Angel: Just thinking about him gives me goose bumps. He's absolutely brilliant.
Nick: From a corner in the 92nd minute. Who would have thought? Fuck it was brilliant.

'I'm so glad you've met someone decent Angel, your last boyfriends' have been an interesting bunch,' she cackled.

'Hey,' I said smiling.

'Do you remember that guy you were dating in your third year of university,' she said trying to jog my memory. 'Black hair, square glasses, you thought he looked like a tortured artist.'

'Oh god,' I groaned burying my head in my hands.

'He invited you round to watch a video, you assumed it would be a drama, a romantic comedy something like that...'

'And instead he sat me down in front of a black and white film about a man who experiments on brains in sinks,' I finished the story for her shivering, 'It was gruesome. I thought he was going to suggest we swapped vials of our blood or something...'

Mel laughed.

'Honestly Mel I can safely say Nick is nothing like that. He is lovely.'

'Well we'll have to meet him sometime,' she said already firmly set in the third party.

'Actually I'm planning on having a dinner party next week,' I said out loud realising that I hadn't planned anything of the sort but would now have to start.

'Oooh that sounds lovely.'

'How about Saturday night. I'll have to check with Nick of course.'

'Of course,' she said in true couple's mode.

'But he should be free. We can celebrate your engagement properly.'

'Brilliant. Well I'll arrange a baby sitter, but that would be great.'

We hugged good bye and Mel practically skipped off to the tube station. I smiled as I watched her go. I was so glad that Peter had popped the question. It was absolutely right. Mel and Peter had always had a successful relationship, despite their families' initial concerns. She was suited to him. They complimented each other. She was laid-back and he was always bouncing around in an enthusiastic way. They both seemed to have a healthy regard for fun with a capital F, holding dinner parties at their flat, taking Zac to the zoo, the park, kite flying that kind of thing. They were a good team. Even when she moaned about him I could tell she wasn't really annoyed. He was thoughtful and good to her and she deserved him.

That was their secret – compatibility. I thought back to the night before. Had I really tried to connect with Nick? Had I really taken an interest in his work? I needed to be a little bit more suitable for Nick I realised. He was suave, sophisticated, he understood wine lists and wore designer suits. He worked hard and played hard and took life seriously. I was more on the hippy side of things, slightly disorganised and hectic. If I wanted to keep my man happy I had to become a little more like his cup of tea. It was clear that I had to behave a more like the girls I'd seen in the places Nick and I went to. The girls in suits, who oozed confidence and ambition. The girls who made £50 k plus a year, and were called 'women,' even though they were still under the age of twenty-six.

With all this in mind I was inspired to spend the weekend in a very life style improving way. Rick popped over to offer encouragement and gifts. He produced the ingenious 'Hollyoaks Dance Workout' video from his rucksack and insisted that we begin with that. As we soon discovered it was neither a dance nor a workout. It was three fit girls bouncing around in disco lights. Still it was strenuous enough for me. The last time I moved this many muscles the Berlin wall was being pulled down. In the midst of some lunges Rick announced that he was concerned he was damaging his bones and stopped. I continued to jog on.

'I'm just a bit worried Angel,' he said chomping on a Kit Kat, 'I don't want to overdo it.'

I had moved on to squats and was breathing steadily; I could do little more than look at him witheringly.

'I'm sure I haven't had enough protein in my diet and my bones might definitely be weaker than most. You can develop osteoporosis later in life if you are not having enough calcium,' he went on.

'Or scurvy,' I said laughing.

'Scurvy,' he repeated, instantly sounding fretful, 'Do you think that would be possible?'

'No Rick,' I gasped, 'Scurvy is something sailors got in the Middle Ages.'

'I don't know Angel. I was reading this medical journal the other day and one woman's condition was so bad her legs were completely bent inwards.'

'Isn't that rickets?' I asked confused.

'No scurvy. Oh,' he paused looking increasingly nervous, 'I'm not sure. Oh god is rickets more common?' he fretted.

'Either way you won't have either of them Rick. You're diet is fine, you are fine,' I repeated.

'I'm just erring on the side of caution Angel,' he said solemnly popping another Smartie in his mouth as I soldiered on sweating.

With Rick gone and Ellie out I got ready for bed early with a green tea. Sitting up on my pillows I drew up a little weekly schedule. Work, gym, Work, run, Work, gym... It seemed depressingly sparse, but I was determined to stick to it. Then I snuggled down to sleep feeling relatively satisfied that I was making a transformation into a new Angela, a better Angela.

What seemed like a couple of hours later I got up bleary-eyed and managed to move into some vaguely sporty clothes for my first ever early morning jog. And on a Sunday too. Beneath the feeling that I still hadn't had enough sleep and shouldn't really be wearing my old school tennis skirt for such strenuous exercise I was also a little chuffed that I was still being so motivated. Downing a glass of orange juice and chomping on some cereal I got up to go. I emerged into the cool morning air. The sky was a cloudless light blue and birds were chirruping happily as if they had been up enjoying dawn for hours. I began to feel a little more alive and dutifully began doing some stretches by our front door. Turning my head to stretch my neck I noticed a figure moving steadily up the street in the early morning light. His steps were slow and slightly uncertain. He was wrapped up in a dark winter coat and clutching something in one hand. I squinted to get a better look; he must be a tramp I reckoned. As he neared our house, horror upon horror, he stopped. Then he turned towards me. What was in his hand? I suddenly panicked, maybe it was a knife? Great I was going to be stabbed to death dressed in a tennis skirt. I looked quickly round for a nearby weapon. A bin lid seemed my best bet. A possible shield I reckoned. Now my attacker was moving up the steps towards me. Well I am definitely going to die. I could see his face now, hold on, it was familiar...

It was none other than Kreepy Kevin. He looked a mess. And more of a mess than usual. His eyes were swollen and red. He looked glazed, staring off into space. I thought he would look up and scowl at me but he didn't even acknowledge me, just walked straight past me up the steps and let himself in. I looked at the object in his hand. He was holding a few dead plants tightly in his grip. He looked like he'd been up all night. Where had he been? What had he been doing?

I shivered.

Only when I heard the door of his flat shut could I finish my stretches. I set off pounding the curiosity out of me as I jogged along the streets.

Arriving home an hour later (yes, an hour later) and after a shower and a bowl of Special K (yes, Special K) I headed to Victoria. Now I know I've mentioned this already but I have to stress it again. I do not like coach stations. I dislike text message language (how r u, Im gr8 :), c u 2morow) but I really hate coach stations. Probably more than anything else in the world, although people who pretend they're statues are pushing a very close second. I hate the stations but I need to get the coach home to Guildford. It's a bind.

I'm now sitting quietly on cold steel, surrounded by activity and the lingering smell of hot dog onions meets sick meets smoke. Pigeons are feeding on the filth around me. Every now and again one swoops down in an attempt to dive bomb me, just for kicks. I can hear a general hubbub of noise but today, and today is not unusual in any way, I am sat next to a man who smells, a woman who can't STOP coughing and two seats down from me a man yelling, 'Are you looking at me?' to himself. As he rocks. Nearby a man in a neon yellow works jacket is pointing and shouting at three people who don't even speak the language, let alone are able to decipher 'WHATDOYOUMEANYOUHAVEN'TGOTATICKET,' because I barely can. Another guy further along is bleeping his mobile and simultaneously increasing the volume on his ipod. Next to him a woman is rustling her brown paper bag and dropping sausage roll pastry EVERYWHERE. And finally opposite her a mother keeps yelling 'Charlene It's SHAN'T not shall not,' (which it isn't, Charlene is absolutely correct). I'm not going to point this out however. Just like I'm not going to tell the woman who is coughing up phlegm to a) stop and b) desist from feeding the fucking pigeons. Who continue to feed on the filth. This is all happening within fifteen fect of me. They are SO CLOSE. And SO LOUD. I'm going mad, I'm losing it – I feel like standing up, throwing my bag to the floor and yelling 'SHUT UP, JUST SHUT THE FUCK UP, SHUT UP, SHUT UP, SHUT UP.' Instead I sit and let my blood boil. I grit my teeth. I wait for the hands to slowly tick to eleven am, I wait for the man in his little blue jacket to tell me I can get on the coach and I try very hard to block out all the noise. So I bloody hate coach stations, but trains are just so damned expensive.

Fortunately I have a whole hour to calm down before I am whisked home to face another mad house. Mine. When I arrive there my mother informs me that my sister has just left. With her new nose ring, which will not be coming back to the house, thus prompting my sister to tell her that neither is she. Dad has pointed out that my sister has not taken a bag, and though she is not a total stickler of fashion she would never leave home without her Led Zeppelin T shirt. Because I haven't been home in a while my mother, pleased with the novelty, doesn't take too long in calming down. Dad has been handing out Earl Grey like it's a medicine and now we're all sat round the table focusing on other things.

'How's Nick?' My mother asked almost immediately.
'He's fine,' I answered.
My mother nodded, clearly hoping for a little more.

'We went out for dinner the other night,' I mentioned.

'That's nice,' she said encouragingly.

'Hmm.'

'What did you have?' she asked. This was a particular habit of my mother's. Wherever I'd been, she wanted to know in detail what I had consumed there.

'Er fish.'

'You don't like fish,' said my mother wrinkling her nose in confusion.

'Well it was salmon,' I explained, as if that made a difference. It seemed to, she had moved on.

'So when is he coming to stay? We want to meet him,' she smiled.

'There's no rush Barbara, when Angel's ready,' chipped in my Dad looking up from the crossword.

'Oh soon I'm sure,' I assured them, 'he's just very busy at the moment. You know, the City.'

My parents had both seen the film 'Wall Street' too and nodded in respect.

'And what about the acting darling? Are you still doing anything to get work? What's your agent up to?' fired my mother.

'Nothing,' I muttered.

'Oh dear,' said my mother pursing her lips together.

'She's very busy at the moment Barbara with this magazine job,' said Dad.

'Yes Michael I know, but she's very good,' said my mother, turning to discuss me as if I wasn't there.

'I know, but it's up to her isn't it,' said my Dad nodding his head in my direction.

'Shouldn't you be trying to get some evening work perhaps in a show?' she suggested turning back to me.

'I know, I know. I need to send off some CV's, but it's been so busy at work and I'm really getting into my job,' I lied, thinking back to the phone call from BOS Productions. Why hadn't I called him back? I should go to the audition on the 21st. They'd liked my CV for goodness sake.

'So you're going to stay on the magazine. Give up on the acting?' asked my mother.

'No I'm not giving up on it, I just, I'm not doing anything

right now,' I explained.

'Well Alice from down the road, her niece is trying to be an actress and she says it's awfully difficult, but I'm sure you are a lot better. She butchered that Lady Macbeth speech.'

'Wasn't that in junior school?' I frowned.

'But you can tell,' my mother said knowledgeably, 'And ever since we watched you perform Shepherd Girl Two at school we knew you were good. Very realistic with the sheep. You must keep trying.'

'Don't pester her Barbara she's got a lot on her plate,' my dad said.

'I'm not pestering her, you're just a very good actress Angela, everyone says so.' By everyone she meant Uncle David, Auntie Jane and cousin Lizzie with the wonky eye.

'You are good Angel,' said my dad. A rare compliment. Had he guessed my confidence had plummeted to rock bottom? Did he mean it? 'You were excellent in that play we saw last summer and the reviewer was extremely complimentary,' he went on, bringing in a professional to back up his statement.

I changed the subject quickly, 'So what's Ed up to?' I enquired. Ed was my little brother who was barely around and when he was you'd barely notice.

'Oh I am worried about him,' gushed my mother, 'Hardly speaks. I'm worried what he's thinking about all the time,' she fretted.

'He's at his friend's for the weekend,' answered my dad.

'Well I hope he talks to them, I can't get more than a few grunts out of him,' said my mother.

'Boy's just shy,' piped up my Dad, 'no wonder with all these women around,' he smiled at me.

'Nonsense,' snorted my mother.

My dad and I exchanged a smile.

Fortunately she was interrupted from further analysing by a buzzing from the timer and rushed off to remove a large joint of beef from the oven. She managed to produce a spectacular roast lunch; Yorkshire puddings, peas, carrots, parsnips, roast potatoes, all the trimmings. We sat in a satisfied quiet digesting the meal and half heartedly helping Dad tackle the crossword. When we'd finally given up on seven across it was getting late and I had a quiet walk with my dad around the village. The peaceful chat was only blighted by a long speech about the neighbours' cat who could be seen slinking through a fence ahead of us. Apparently it was persisting in fouling on the lawn, even after dad had been round to complain about its lack of toilet training.

'Knows things that cat does,' he grunted at the end of his lecture.

I kept silent and walked on as he simmered down once more.

We returned to the house in time to hear mum chiming, 'You'll be doing no such thing madam,' down the phone and then replacing the receiver.

'That was your sister,' she explained. On hearing she was due to return home in an hour, 'for her things' I decided to head back to London before it all kicked off once more. Dad decided this was an excellent plan and instantly offered to drop me at the coach station.

It had been an exhausting day playing the dutiful daughter but I was glad to have spent some time at home. There was still no word from Nick, but I'd show him. The weekend had been a warm up to my metamorphosis. Tomorrow was the official start of the new improved, low fat me. I collapsed into bed and shut my eyes thinking about the changes I'd make. I needed to take my life more seriously. I needed to dress better, read intellectual literature, understand Nick's job, become a fascinating factual machine, enthral people with witty stories peppered with long words and complicated metaphors. I needed to work on my career, take my job more seriously, gain respect from people in the work place. I imagined everyone's admiring glances as I became Angel, Agony Aunt Extraordinaire. I pictured Richard and Claudia kneeling before me chanting 'Angel is our god' 'Angel is amazing' and then realised I'd fallen into dreams.

* * *

I'd set the alarm for 6.30am and almost propelled myself out of bed on the first buzz it made. I'd never prepared for a day at work on this scale. It was extraordinary. I flung the curtains open in a fit of new me energy and then turned to my wardrobe. I needed to dress properly for the day. I decided to opt for something a little edgy. Something that shouted, 'I am sharp dammit.' I rifled through the hangers realising I might be forced to settle for something that had been ironed in the last couple of years. I didn't see this as a set back though, a reason to give up, oh no. New me embraced the challenge. No clothes, pah, we'll see about that. I'll find the correct outfit. And what's more when I've found it, I'll put it on, go out, and buy an iron in it. That is how new I am. I knew somewhere in the mess nestled a little pinstripe number I'd purchased in my 'I'm moving to the big smoke' shop. I'd assumed that those there city folk were all going to be clad in the same uniform attire, and I must fit in. Ah! Got it. I pulled out the skirt and jacket combo and selected a shirt to go with it. I dispensed with my usual contact lenses and popped a pair of tortoise shell square rimmed glasses on the end of my nose. I scraped my hair back into a very neat ponytail and spritzed it with hairspray for that sleek hair-advert look. Very secretarial I thought as I looked into the mirror in my most chilling way. But something was missing...

I felt around in the back of my cupboard for an ancient black briefcase, which had been purchased in the same spree as the pinstripe. Slightly dusty but it still sprung open. I upended the contents of my trusty Louis Vuitton hand bag (fake) and transferred most of the debris. House keys, sweet wrappers, glasses case, mobile, all nestled into the base of the briefcase. The various compartments stared at me longingly and I popped a pen in one of the more pen shaped looking ones and stood back to admire the effect. The sad little pile of items didn't shout 'Organisation is my middle name' so I removed a few of the scraps of paper and ancient shop receipts and popped a calculator on the top. For effect. Then I set about placing my belongings into neat groups, which I imagined was the done thing with these working girl types.

'Ugh. What's all the noiseeee?' wailed a voice from the corridor and my door was pushed open. Ellie stood in a T shirt rubbing her eyes with her fists and yawning, 'Why the noise, why the noiseee...' Mid-sentence her eyes widened as she took in the array of clutter, the briefcase, the suit...

'What are you doing Angie, and why the hell are you dressed like Lois Lane?' she giggled obviously taking in my newly sleek look, the skirt, shirt and glasses combo. 'Are you making some kind of fashion statement? Are you auditioning for a part in a play? If you... ooh I like that,' she said scooping a top out of the nearest mound of clothes and holding it up to herself. 'So Lois why the change?' she said peering at herself in the mirror.

'I just felt like being a bit more formal for work,' I shrugged, wondering if wearing a tie was going too far.

'Snazzy briefcase,' Ellie giggled.

I proudly showed off my morning's work, 'I've got my letters in this section, unanswered in here, and answered in this bit. Then there's stationery, nibbles, medical, cosmetic, essentials and lastly miscellaneous.' I pointed to the last with a flourish.

'Er... very organised,' Ellie said as I nodded sharply and snapped it shut, mixing up the combination on the lock with the palm of my hand.

'Well best get on,' I said straightening my skirt and smoothing my hair in the mirror.

'Right.'

I stalked out to the kitchen. Instinct drew me to the bumper size carton of 'Coca Pops' but today was a new day, I was 'turning over a new leaf,' 'putting my best foot forward' and that. I fumbled in the dismally sad little fruit bowl and unearthed an apple that didn't look totally unappealing. Ellie was now gaping at me from the doorway obviously unwilling to step into the kitchen in case she caught something in the air around me. Not enjoying the attention much I half heartedly munched on the apple and headed for the door. Ellie pressed herself up against the wall as I headed out.

'Bye Ellie. Have a good, constructive day,' I yelled.

'Er... I will,' came the uncertain reply behind me.

I banged the door shut and trotted down the stairs. A pile of mail swarmed over the doormat and I sifted through it. Most of it was large A4 official envelopes for Kevin. Obviously not being much of an early riser due to his weird late night outings I put them in a neat pile on his doormat. Brownie point number one: Being a good neighbour, check. I looked around at the street and allowed myself to be momentarily impressed with my efficiency. It was at this point of the day I was usually dashing from one corner of my room to the next swearing and stubbing toes in a frantic rush to find clean pants. I started a brisk walk in the direction of the tube, my heels click clacking in a satisfying rhythm down the street. I made my way into the tube and paid for my Travel card.

On the way to the ticket barrier I caught the eye of the newspaper man standing behind his counter. He smiled at me and I walked over with purpose. I scanned the rows of papers. Daily Telegraph, The Guardian, The Times, The Mirror... I looked up. Newsagents mans eyes were expectant. I scanned the rows again, The Daily Mail, Daily Express, Financial Times. What should I be reading? Hmm... that looks interesting. I reached out a hand and then snatched it back. Did this magazine represent the old me? What would the new me be reading? Something to improve her life prospects perhaps? Something to organise her finances? Something to inspire home improvements? Whatever it was, I realised with a sinking heart; it wasn't Heat magazine. I frantically looked around for other newspaper reading commuters. They were few and far between. There was a small child with single mother. Single mother: No paper – No time to read it poor thing. Small child: No paper – No literacy ability. Old frail lady: No paper. Plastic bag full of cans though – No sanity perhaps?

Then I hit upon a man nearby with a folded (I craned my neck sideways) Daily (I tipped a little more) has an 'I' in it and what looks like an R, two R's. Daily Mirror, I finished looking, my neck now at an uncomfortable angle. At the back of my mind somewhere I remembered Nick's snort of derision about 'tabloid Mirror readers.' Something about being left wing. But was that bad? To my right a woman in an inoffensive navy trouser suit was also asking for the Mirror. She didn't seem like the extremist sort. But you could never be sure. The newsagent man had now dropped his gaze and was half heartedly rearranging the chewing gum into uniform rows. As I looked up he glanced at me again and smiled encouragingly. I opened my mouth and shut it. His smile faltered, he looked disappointed. I went back to scanning and he went back to sorting out rogue packets of chewing gum. I wasn't ready for this; I wished I hadn't walked over to the stand at all. But his friendly smile had beguiled me and now I had to buy something. What did it matter, most looked like they were saying the same things anyway. News was news after all. Who would care? Who would notice? It was too early to deal with this kind of pressure. I looked up.

'I'll have...' my voice faltered, 'I'll have... some chewing gum please.'

Arriving in Oxford Street Tube my feet were already starting to ache from the power heels. I itched to get to my desk and sit down as the lift slowly chugged past floor after floor. Finally the familiar ping announced its arrival on the fourth and I pushed my way through the doors. I emerged into the neon world otherwise known as the reception area of 'Sweet SixTeen.' Richard's not-so-secret girlfriend was already whining into her telephone in her distinctly nasal voice. Something about the Portuguese and bad sea food from the snippet I got. I hurried through the push doors before she could finish her call and whine to me in the flesh.

As Resident Agony Aunt I found that, like doctors, people told me things. Things I often didn't need to know. And often things I didn't want to know. They unburden themselves, letting me listen to the clutter of their existence. I didn't dare tell them that I felt totally and utterly under qualified to deal with the disasters that passed as their lives so I often smiled encouragingly and 'oohed' at the important sounding bits.

As I made my way past the smiling pictures of Leonardo de Caprio, Jude Law and Johnny Depp I noticed a few admiring glances in my direction. I slowed my pace a little. I thought I saw Clive with the big hair (Features) doing a double take. Oh, he was just heading to the photocopier. That's OK though Ian (IT Support) definitely just looked over my way. New respect. I could sense it in the air. They were sitting up and taking notice. This must be what they call 'Girl Power.' I obviously exuded it.

I settled myself at my desk and rather like at the start of an A level exam looked up at the clock just as the hand clicked on to eight thirty. Paper was arranged neatly before me and I went to click open the briefcase for the first letter. Before I had snapped it open however Suzie came over in her coat looking curious.

'Angel what are you doing here so early? Has something happened?' she asked, her eyes full of concern.

'Absolutely not,' I said brusquely shifting the briefcase towards me.

'Oh well that's good...' she said as I finally turned my attention to her.

'Am I not allowed to be punctual for work anymore' I asked innocently.

'Oh no absolutely, it's great. You've changed your hair style, it's very nice, and glasses Angel...'

'Well,' I leant back in my chair and sucked on a pen which I thought made me look pre-tt-y darn industrious, 'I had a back log of letters to work though (back log- good word) and thought er...' I fumbled around for the appropriate phase, 'best do today what you sometimes put off to tomorrow...' I filtered off sensing the phrase hadn't gone quite as well as it might.

'Well good for you,' she said laughing, 'I'll see you later, have a good day.' I watched her go and then reached out to open the briefcase.

Shit! What was the combination?

I started randomly typing in four digit codes. None of them appeared to be the magic numbers. I resorted to brute force. But after a few minutes jiggling it around and trying to force it with my feet, nails, hands, teeth I had to give up. I'd deal with it later. The minutes were ticking by and I had work to do. It might not have been the best start to the day but I wasn't deterred that easily. Oh no. I plucked a letter from my in tray and picked up an abandoned biro.

Dear Angel,
I'm so depressed and don't tell me to talk to my teachers as they think I am thick and that is why my school work is going so badly. But it's actually because I can't stop thinking about this boy at school. He is the only person who seems to notice me and I think it's just pity but I hope its not. Should I tell him? I think about him all the time.
Carly, Bristol

Dear Carly,
We have better things to focus on in life than mere emotional worries. Why don't you try and spend your time learning a new skill, focusing on other aspects in your life. It is a shame to wile away the time by day-dreaming about boys who may, or may

not, like you. Focus on your studies and become the kind of girl no one will ever pity.

Angel

I could hear my mobile faintly ringing in the briefcase. Some people were glancing around for the cause of the noise. I looked as mildly irritated as they did. Honestly, tsk, some people are so thoughtless. I realised it might have been Nick ringing me and I allowed myself a moment to mull that over and then shook myself. I must work hard, be impressive, start to behave like the woman he would want. I sucked on the end of the biro thinking how best to end the letter. This girl seemed like a pretty useless time waster. I wanted grittier, more hard hitting problems. Something that would be worthy of an Eastenders sub plot. This girl should just get a grip and... I suddenly noticed a bitter sensation in my mouth. This wasn't metaphorical, I quickly realised the biro was leaking into my mouth. I whipped out the pen before I gulped down anymore ink and placed a hand over my mouth to hide the rivets of pen dribble escaping. I needed to make my way to the bathroom and assess the damage. I got up from my desk surreptitiously, pretending to be lightly coughing. I could see the little lady sign on the door, I had so nearly made it there when, disaster, I was accosted on the right by Richard I'm-here-to-make-your-life-hell Winters. I clamped my mouth shut and prayed none of the blue had spread to my lips.

'Well good morning Headmistress,' he chuckled his eyes working slowly up my body and making every piece of flesh crawl in disgust. Unable to retort with a sharp put-down, in fact any kind of a noise, I could only glare at him in what I hoped was a withering way. I sped up my pace. Richard however was enjoying the sport of Angel Baiting and jogged along beside me.

'So why the change? Trying to get a bit of class? Aiming for a promotion? Going to a fancy dress party?' My eyes flickered dangerously and I half mumbled, half breathed insults through pursed lips. I'd nearly made it to the loo door.

'Why no speakeee Head Mistress? You need to punish me. I've been a bad boy and need a good caning...'

It was too much. I burst into a loud sarcastic laugh, spitting blue saliva as I yelled, 'You wish. I think you'll find I have better taste than...'

Just at that moment Victoria appeared from around the corner, 'Good morning Richard.'

I paused, mouth agape, in the midst of my rant.

'Angela I...' She trailed off mid sentence as she took in the scene, 'Angela, what is wrong with your mouth?'

'I, I, well...' As I shuffled and well-you-see'd for a few more seconds Richard cocked his head to one side enquiringly.

'It was my pen,' I said admitting defeat and holding up the offending biro, Exhibit One.

'Well get cleared up. Honestly,' she said, clearly exasperated by the scene. Richard rolled his eyes with her. I skulked off to clean myself up in the bathroom. Richard smirked and slunk away to his desk to swivel and be smug in his chair.

I wanted a swivelly chair to look smug in I thought as I furiously swilled my mouth clear of blue. After a few days at 'Sweet SixTeen' I'd realised that there was some kind of warped hierarchy going on with the seating arrangements and what you sat on was a direct representation of your place in the pecking order. It was clear that the more important you were the more swivelly your chair was. Mine, needless to say, was a plastic moulded black chair. It did not swivel. Richard as Head of Features and Agony Uncle sat on a plush, cushy, swivelly one, brand new. It was rumoured the Editor's chair could do three and a half rotations at a push. That was power. I assumed Fat Nigel had a beanbag with a hole in off eBay. I spat out the water. After the new me really kicked in I would be swivelling away in no time.

It was exhausting being efficient I thought as I signed off another letter. This feeling was not a usual feeling I had. My hand was slightly aching, my eyes were feeling strained and I had the start of a headache. This was labouring. This is the kind of feeling Bill Gates, Richard Branson and that women who set up that dot com thing must have. The kind of people who get up at dawn to go to the gym before work and eat wholemeal bread and energy drinks. Or to call them by another name: Freaks. Although I couldn't deny my Day As A Keen Bean Eager Beaver was giving me a little glow of satisfaction. I was like City Girl, wrestling with deadlines, playing with the big wigs, living on the edge, working gruelling hours, right through lunch hour. A lunch break. Pah. Lunch breaks are just ill-disguised excuses to slack off.

'Slackers,' I muttered under my breath as a mass exodus passed my desk. Lunch breaks, who needs them? I asked my computer screen. Lunch breaks are, lunch breaks are... I looked longingly around the office, my stomach rumbled in delight. No, I couldn't. I mustn't cave in. Temptation. Bad. Lunches, temptation bad, bad, bad. Lunch breaks were for old me, new me was more efficient. Focus on the letter, focus on the letter and don't think of hmm... lunch. My stomach rumbled again. 'Come on Lady,' it seemed to be saying, 'Get some din dins in me' (my stomach apparently being the stomach of a five year old child). Think he might have been concerned about the lack of action all day, by now he normally had his work cut out. A biscuit here, a cup of tea there, half a snickers, a custard cream, a nibble of Twix, a few crisps – he was obviously missing the work out. What harm could a little lunch do? I rummaged in the kitchen's pathetic excuse for a fridge and unearthed a pot of coleslaw. Grabbing a plastic spoon and a plastic cup of squash I went back to my desk. I ate the coleslaw, drunk my squash and got lots done too!

Victoria came over to me at the end of the day and when I glanced up and noticed her there I automatically flinched. What had I done now?

'Angela,' she began ominously.

'Yes... anything wrong?' I asked nervously, surreptitiously wiping a bit of coleslaw off my desk at the same time.

'I wanted to congratulate you on your work ethic today. I've noticed you've been working particularly hard and I want you to know that it has been noted. You've taken on a lot of extra responsibility taking on Richard's' workload too. And we are very grateful.'

'Oh. Well thank you,' I said not quite believing the praise.

'Well have a good evening, I'll see you tomorrow,' she turned to go, 'Oh and Angela...' I looked up. Worried again.

'Nice suit.'

I blushed; I was taking another step towards that swivelled chair.

Straight after work I headed to the gym. I had to blow a layer of dust off my gym card as I produced it from the back my wallet. I was almost expecting to be re inducted I'd been away so long, but the receptionist handed me a towel and waved me through. I walked past the little crèche and the window out on to the indoor pool. An aqua class appeared to be going on in the shallow end. An instructor was dancing around by the edge of the pool and a lot of eighty year olds were waving their arms in the water copying her moves. I thought most were probably trying to signal their imminent heart attack but she appeared oblivious and kept them bopping away in the shallows as Girls Aloud screeched out at them. It seemed a pretty terrible way to go.

After changing and stashing my bag in a locker I hit the gym with a determined air. A bit of cycling and sit ups were first on my list. After ten minutes on the running machine I was beginning to feel like giving up for the night but then I noticed a little crowd forming outside Studio 1. Feeling my self motivation draining away I walked over curiously to discover which class they were waiting for. 'Body Combat' announced the timetable. Suddenly the doors opened and a group of ladies stepped out carrying gym bags, water bottles and some strange speckled blocks of foam. I looked at them curiously, what had been going on in there? What cult was this? Had little time to ponder this as I was herded in with the rest of the queue by an overly enthusiastic girl in a red vest top and combat trousers. Worryingly I noted she had a prominent pot belly and a couple of frighteningly muscular shoulders à la Gladiators. Was instantly concerned that by following her moves I would become like her.

'OK everybody find a space,' she said into her mouthpiece.

The instruction was followed and soon we were warming up with some jogging on the spot. The class sounded vibrant and youthful. Something Lara Croft would turn up to, if she felt so inclined. A place where people in shiny tight fitting cycling shorts clearly felt at home. I looked around me warily noting the figures of the lesson-takers. Although most were clad in unnecessarily tiny athletic gear no one appeared to be size 20 plus so I figured the class must be doing something right. Half an hour later I was doing jump kicks, upper cuts, scrunches, round house, jabs, hooks, punches and all the other moves you've seen on Sega Mega Drive games. The hard core atmosphere was only dampened when the pot belly girl tried to get us all to start shouting 'Hey' every time we punched the air. Most could only struggle out a weak yelp. I made a noise somewhere between a whispered 'Ha' and what I think a dying shrew might sound like.

I didn't get home until 9.30pm and by then I was ravenous so rushed into the kitchen to pop some pasta on.

'Did Nick call the land line?' I asked Ellie from the kitchen, 'I haven't been able to check my mobile.'

'No, no one called. Oh actually your mum did. She said how do you work the bread oven you gave them for Christmas but she called back and said don't worry she'd worked it out after all.'

'Oh,' I said disappointed, 'Nick said he'd call over the weekend and I still haven't heard from him.'

'He probably doesn't know your mobile's not working. Why don't you ring him on his?' said Ellie not looking up.

'I have,' I muttered.

She was standing in the doorway of the kitchen.

'How many times?' she asked, sensing I sounded a little shifty.

'Oh... A couple,' I admitted.

'A couple meaning...'

'Two.'

She looked at me.

'Fine three.'

'I don't know why you bother.' She sighed sitting at our kitchen table nursing a wine glass.

'I have to. He's very busy,' I argued.

'So are you. Why should you do all the running,' she asked.

'Look Ellie you don't know him like I do. He tells me a lot of things and I can understand, because of the problems in his past...'

'Problems,' Ellie interjected with a snort, 'What problems Angel? That man has had everything delivered to him on a silver platter. Not to mention you constantly serving yourself up as dessert. Honestly that...'

I stopped her in her tracks, 'Look Ellie, we don't know what its like to come from a broken home.'

Ellie sneered. 'A broken home? Oh poor little Nick. Was he t...t... taken into care, did his foster parents b...b... beat him?' She stuttered over her words like an extra in 'Oliver' and then started laughing.

'It's not funny Ellie. His parents divorced when he was twelve. That's a very impressionable age. The poor mite wouldn't have known what was going on and it's affected his relationships as an adult. He's had trouble committing because he sees how hard it was for his parents.'

'Unlikely. It's just because it doesn't get any better than this. He can go to work, go out, never call, stride in whenever, cast you off and you are always there being understanding. Ang, she said more gently, he's taking advantage of you.'

'Look Ellie I read Psychology, and it's all over the letters I get. Some people have real difficulty in expressing their emotions. We are one of the lucky ones Ellie. Nick didn't have the same chance...'

She groaned, 'Angela you've gone mad. That man can do nothing wrong. He's not good enough for you. You scurry after him like an eager puppy. You have to play it cool, you watch yourself. You don't dare voice an opinion... look at you in that suit. It's about him, its not who you really are.'

'We have to make some compromises,' I said tugging at the briefcase.

'And what compromises has he made for you Angel.'

I was silent for a little bit.

'I'm going to get changed,' I said moving into my room. I fiddled with my CD player and lay down on my bed letting Robbie Williams make me feel a little better. A few minutes later there was a timid knock and a piece of white tissue on the end of a straw was pushed under the door as a surrender flag. Ellie stepped into the room uncertainly and held out a steaming mug of hot chocolate in apology.

'I'm sorry Angie,'

I looked at her and smiled weakly, 'That's OK...'

'I just don't know why you let him treat you like that...' she said handing me the mug.

'Ellie don't start. I know...'

'OK, OK,' she interrupted her hands raised in surrender, 'I just think you are lovely and he should show you a bit more respect. Just don't let him make you miserable, alright.'

'I won't.'

'Good. Your pasta's ready,' she said.

Ellie had been single for more than three years. She didn't know. She'd never met anyone really special. She'd never really been in love. She didn't understand. He could be lovely. In the first few months he had rung all the time, he had checked on my day, he had invited me over for dinners. He had been attentive. It was just recently he had become slightly distracted by work. Well, more distracted by work and other engagements. Yes he could be lovely. And I didn't want to be alone.

* * *

The next day I woke, a little groggier but still determined to make a go of the new efficient me. I was working away by nine and trying to ignore the constant ache of my thighs. I thought back to what Nick had said about the letters not being high brow. I'd show him. I knew they were already educational – do this, don't do that, but perhaps this practical everyday advice could be worded better. The letters could become a form of literature. I just needed to slightly tweak the vocabulary and my page would read like a Bronte novel. If indeed the Bronte sisters ever did concern themselves with drug problems, sexuality quandaries and snogging technique.

Dear Angel,
At the moment life is good as I am popular at school and quite pretty and have a boyfriend, but I'm worried about choosing my GCSE's. I know I am fairly academic but I don't want to make the wrong decisions. How will I know what to do?
Louisa, London, 14

Dear Louisa,
Is it not 'Proverbs Chapter 25: Verse 16' that says,
'Hast thou found honey? Eat so much as is sufficient for thee, lest should be filled therewith, and vomit It.'
I think you'll agree the statement still holds relevance for today. Your problem can be solved applying this wisdom. Do not fill yourself up with 'honey,' or you shall regret it. Take heed of this lesson and good luck in your future endeavours.
Angel

Slightly obscure perhaps but Nick wouldn't be able to tell me I wasn't high brow now. Look at the vocabulary. Would my meaning be clear? Did I understand my meaning? Ah well, I shrugged, she was the academic, she could work it out. I popped that one to the side. I was on a roll now.

Dear Angel,
My sister is a year older than me and always makes me look stupid when her friends are round. Then when we are alone she tries to be nice to me. I now don't trust her and we don't talk much anymore. How can I make her see it hurts me?
Kate, 15, Poole

I racked my brains for an answer, and then, delving into past memories I thought back to the play I had done last summer. A bit of Shakespeare, that's what was needed. I scanned the internet for a copy of the script and began to write.

Dearest Kate,
It was in the Midsummer Nights Dream that Shakespeare talks of a 'wall.' Although it was manifest as a physical object in this play, it can clearly be seen to become relevant in an emotional sense. We all put up 'walls' in our everyday lives Kelly. You need to get past the wall, see through it. Just like the Mechanics managed to do in... (I scrolled down to the relevant page) *...Act V Scene I. Thanks for reading.*
Angel

To Angel,
My boyfriend is lovely. He tells me the whole time how much he loves me. The trouble is (and don't tell me to talk to her because I have and she won't admit it anyway and my mum says just drop it) I think my sister really likes him. They are always laughing together and I came home from school and he was showing her his art. I don't know what to do.
Felicity, 14, Bournemouth

Dear Felicity,
Was it not, if I am not mistaken, a chapter in Proverbs (Chapter 26 Verse 25) that told us, 'When he speaketh fair, believe him not: for there are seven abominations in his heart.' This is a warning for us all. Tread carefully around this man, he might shower you with compliments but is his heart true? As for your sibling this is an absolutely disastrous plight! I hope...

No that won't do. I highlighted hope on the computer and clicked Thesaurus. Hope = expect, trust, anticipate, wish, look forward to. None sounded particularly high brow so I plumped for the word with the most letters. Anticipate.

I anticipate... doesn't that mean something different to hope? *I anticipate that you will be able to locate a resolution to your disquiet by and by...*
Angel

After an hour and more than 30 searches of the thesaurus, an Internet Bible and a couple more online Shakespeare plays I had finished. I popped the replies in their envelopes and went to make a much needed coffee. High brow I now was. Intellectual and well reasoned – that was me. I'd never worked so hard. I returned to the office after lunch feeling drained of energy. I resorted to my old style to finish off the pile of letters in front of me. Being intellectual was extremely time consuming. Fortunately after reading the next letter I realised I was back on more certain ground. I'd answer this and then make my way home.

Dear Angel,
I'm 14 and my boyfriend and I have been going out for three weeks. I love him loads but I'm worried when I don't see him that I think about him all the time. It's affecting my school work as I miss him so much. What shall I do?
Vicky

I know exactly what you mean Vicky. I often curl up on my bed and fall into a day dream about my man. He's called Nick and he's a trader in the City! We've been seeing each other for eight months and I am really starting to think it could be long term. He hasn't said anything of course but sometimes when he looks at me I just know, you know. He is good-looking and confident and everything I could want in a man really (It's no wonder I day dream about him all the time!)
Sometimes I worry that he isn't thinking about me as much as I'd like, but then it isn't a perfect world is it? And men are useless at expressing their emotions so maybe he's thinking about me but not sure how to say it. My flat mate thinks that he's being a b*****d but I think he's probably just not the expressive sort. I'm sure he is often wondering how I am and thinking about the

last time we saw each other. I think my flat mate's probably a bit jealous coz she's been single for nearly three years. That's probably it.

I'm sure your boyfriend thinks about you too so don't panic, Angel

I regretted mentioning anything to Ellie. I had been trudging wearily up the stairs to the flat after the exhausting day of thesaurus searches and research. Before I had even turned the key in the lock, the door had swung open and she had loomed large, hands on hips, prepared for battle.

'So did he call today?' she demanded.

I straightened up, mind racing for a cunning excuse.

'Look Ellie,' I flustered, 'I've, he's, well, I've just got back from work and it's been a really long day and...'

She interjected, 'So he didn't. There's a surprise.'

'Ellie, that's not fair it's just well, look I'm tired and...' as I spoke I spotted an opening to her left and without warning lunged at it in an attempt to get pass her door inquisition. It failed and my knee was now half crushed between her leg and the door frame. I tried to look laid back about this, as if it had been part of my plan.

'I told you Ange, I knew he wouldn't, he's so bloody arrogant. How many days has it been now? Six, seven, ten? Hmm, how many?'

I felt more than a mite silly standing at my own door arguing with a 5ft 4" bouncer in blonde pigtails, complete with cartoon comedy sized slippers.

'Look Ellie, give me a break, he's obviously been really busy with work and...' My protest was silenced by the pitiful look on her face.

'Work?'

'Yes Ellie, work, where I've just been, a busy place with computers, windows, pens and telephones. A place I go every day and...'

'I'm not saying you don't know what work is Angel, but Mr. Thoughtful doesn't appear to have a diligent bone in his pathetic little body.'

I raised my voice a little at this, 'That is not fair Ellie; Nick does not have a pathetic little body. It's a lovely body...'

'Oh god Ange I don't care, I'm not discussing Nick's glorious physique I'm discussing his inability to function as a decent member of the human race. He can't treat you like this just because he's going off for long boozy lunches in the City.' Her voice softened slightly as she added, 'You are worth more than that.'

'He's just busy. He works hard...'

'Yes but he doesn't work hard at being with you does he? He just flies in and out of your life at his own convenience. Never assuming for a minute that you might, god forbid, have other plans.'

There was a noise below us and we both turned to see Kevin standing in the stairwell looking up at us both. There was a brief pause as I nodded and Ellie smiled at him nervously. He moved back into his flat. Somebody pressed 'Resume' and we carried on where we'd left off.

'OK just promise me you'll make him make a bit more of an effort,' she said.

'He does make effort,' I argued.

She looked at me in an irritating way.

'Fine,' I said, 'I'll talk to him. Now let me in.'

She moved to one side, satisfied that her work here was done.

I knew Ellie was wrong. It hadn't been that long since I'd last heard from him. And we had a laid back relationship. Sometimes I'd wait a few minutes before I returned a call. Once I left it a good half hour. He was just a busy person, and that was good, I didn't want to be with some one who sat around all day doing nothing. I liked the fact he was motivated to go out and hang around at London's finest bars and clubs. He was just young and full of life. And so was I. I wasn't exactly waiting for his call every minute of every day. I only thought about it a bit because I liked him so much, not that I was actually bothered. I mean, as I've mentioned, we are in a laid back relationship. It's fine. Absolutely fine.

* * *

I walked into the office the next morning still pondering all this. Maybe it would be nice for him to just text occasionally saying how he is and when we were next going to see each other.

It would be nice to feel that he was thinking about me, even when he was being busy. But then I couldn't ask for the perfect man, there were so many good qualities he had that I had to forgive him for one bad thing. I had to be thankful that he was an upright, employable, good looking, articulate go-getter. It could be a lot worse. He could be an unemployable, ugly no hoper. And he wasn't. The usual morning hubbub of office noise managed to permeate these thoughts. People were already tapping away at computers, talking on their phones and I was relieved by the distraction. I popped my bag down on my desk and went off to make toast and drink tea.

On the way to the kitchen I over heard Katherine (Features) talking to Louise (Fashion) about a nasty thing she'd read in the paper. As I walked past hearing the hushed tones, the sympathetic sighs, and the 'oh how terrible' comments I realised I was being a bit melodramatic about everything. Terrible things were happening to people all over the world and all I can obsess about is my boyfriend.

The June issue of 'Sweet SixTeen' was open on the kitchen counter. As I waited for the kettle to boil I scanned the page. The article centred on one man's escape from a guerrilla gang in Thailand. Apparently Paul and his girlfriend Janine had been back-packing around the country when they'd been held up by four gunmen. They'd taken Paul away and threatened to kill him. He'd managed to escape and now they were both safely back at home. Janine was quoted as saying, 'Being away from him made me realise how much I loved him...' They were planning to marry the following year. I stared at the photo of the smiling couple. They looked extremely in love. I sat back at my desk thinking about the article and trying not to burn my tongue on my tea. It did seem strange that Nick hadn't called. I sighed. Maybe Ellie was right, maybe he did just take advantage of me. I picked up the first letter of the day and read it through.

Dear Angel,
My ex boyfriend keeps calling me telling me he loves me. It's becoming really annoying as my new boyfriend thinks I still love him but I don't. I can't stop him ringing though even though I've told him I don't love him anymore. My mate said I could ask the police to put him on a restraining order or something where he is

forced not to ring. I don't want to ring the police but how can I make him stop calling?
   Sally, Wokingham

How ironic.
   I started scribbling a half hearted reply along the lines of 'oh no poor you having men calling you the whole time' without sounding too unbelievably envious. A stalker: I wish. My phone was so quiet I thought it was on permanent silent mode. I signed off the letter. Why couldn't Nick be a little more considerate I raged. But then the article in the magazine, the hushed tones in the office... I jolted upright, what if something had really happened to him? What if they had been speaking about a disaster he'd been involved in? That thought had never crossed my mind. I'd assumed he just hadn't rung, but what if...
   I mentally scrolled back the time. I knew he'd been away to play rugby in Nottingham that weekend and I knew I hadn't heard anything from him since. A slight panic gripped me. Maybe he wasn't able to call me. Maybe he'd had an accident, been knocked out unconscious. He might have been concussed, not remembered who he was, or where he was. He could now be stuck in some nasty hospital in the Midlands, bedridden, and wishing he could remember my name and my telephone number so that I could take him home. Or he could have had one of those freak heart murmurs you're always reading about where the player just drops dead. Or maybe he'd been shot or mugged (everyone knows that Nottingham is the new gangland). So many new, more frightening scenarios flooded my mind. No, this was ridiculous. He is just busy. But I found my finger clicking on the Internet Explorer Icon. Best to have a little check, just to be on the safe side. I flicked to the BBC website for any telling head lines, 'Man in 20's in fatal accident,' that kind of thing. 'Man leaves nothing but note for lover,' 'Man's dying words, 'Tell Angel I love her'.' Nothing. Well not nothing, apparently a brother and sister in Germany are having an affair and it's sparked a huge debate about German incest laws. But that wasn't relevant right now. Anyway Nick might have been in yesterday's news. I went on a search for Debbie with the bi-focal lenses. I didn't want to stereotype but she looked like the kind of girl that read the papers.

'So anything horrible happening in the world?' I said as a hearty, if not slightly warped, opener. Debbie looked at me startled, which wasn't totally surprising as I'd rarely said more words to her than 'Hi' at any one time, and now here I was demanding a brief synopsis of the week's current affairs.

'I'm sorry?' She looked confused as she inched the bridge of her glasses up her nose a fraction and peered through them.

'Any big events in the news, around the Nottingham area perhaps, any serious muggings or events...'

'Sorry?' She repeated, the glasses already slipping back to place.

'In the news, is there anything significant in the news?' I asked in a tone that implied surely-you-understand-that.

'Significant,' she repeated, 'Er... well there's been a terrible flood in Turkey,' she said looking up hopefully, keen to please.

'Oh dear. No, no I mean any kind of local events?' I went on sweeping the flood story away in a millisecond.

'Er... a woman was attacked in a park in Turnham Green...'

'That's sad but no, not quite what I was looking for,' I said getting more impatient. Debbie looked distraught, she realised she was getting the wrong news items; she started reeling off facts like a newsreader on Fast Forward. House prices going up in the West, a coach accident in Switzerland, unrest in the Middle East, the assassination of some obscure member of a council in a country I couldn't pronounce. All the while I was shaking my head. As her pace increased I realised I better be a little bit more specific. This girl was like a google search engine flinging up obscure web link after obscure web link. None of them correct.

'No.' I said finally, 'Anything concerning a man called Nicholas Sheldon-Wade. Anything about him at all?' I asked.

'No um... I haven't seen anything about him.'

'Oh,' I said disappointed, and then of course quickly relieved, he was alright after all.

I went back to my desk trying to concentrate on the letters in front of me. I sent him another text message, and got nothing back. I doodled, I scribbled, I fidgeted, I flicked unseeing through the pile of teenage angst.

Dear Angel,
My boyfriend has just confided in me that he has been

attacked by a group of lads who go to our school. He started crying when he told me. I don't know what to do. I think they did more than just hit him you know, but he won't tell me. He's become very quiet and.......

Agggghhhhhh.

'Sorry, Hi, me again,' I said waving at Debbie like a long lost friend. We'd never bonded this much in all the months I'd worked there. Debbie herself looked like a bunny caught in headlights.

'There's nothing about him. I checked, really, nothing,' she stammered.

'Yes I know but well, have you got any of the papers?' I asked.

'Oh yes I'm sure I could... hold on,' she said scampering about collecting bits of newspaper from her desk. 'Here you go,' she said handing me a bundle of papers at lightning speed. I went back to my desk. Honestly that girl needed to chill out.

I started scanning the pages for any obvious stories Debbie could have missed. Anything with a particularly small print the lenses might not have coped with. There was no joy, so I flicked quickly to the back to check on the Births Deaths and Marriages section. Sheldon-Wade didn't appear to be there. I closed it with a sigh. This is ridiculous but then I wouldn't be able to live myself if I just stood by and did nothing. London was a frightening place. Any number of disasters could have occurred. Only yesterday I heard about a man who had been attacked outside a petrol station for a chocolate donut! It was a crazy, unstable world out there and I'm sure I'd read that white, male men were actually the most frequent targets for London crime. Maybe something had happened to him; maybe he'd been mugged or beaten up, or fallen down or knocked down or run over or...

In a fit of nerves I dialled his work number. It rung a few times and I waited, heart racing, to hear his secretary come on the line. She'd be the one to break the sad... sad news that...

'Hello,' came Nick's distinctive drawl.

'Oh,' I said completely startled.

'Hello, who is this?' asked Nick. It took me a few seconds to register what he'd said.

'It's me. Angel. And it's you, you're alive,' I said, instantly covering my hand over my mouth in horror. What was I saying?

'Yes Angel I know that.'

There was a pause.

What was I doing?

'Angel did you ring just to tell me that, because I'm very busy and I know I'm alive so if that's all...'

I was too embarrassed even to try a nervous giggle.

'Oh yes of course I knew that, it was just my little joke Nick, I hadn't heard from you and...' and STOP TALKING ANGEL STOP, SSSH, HANG UP, LEAVE, GO NOW. 'And um...'

'Yes,' he said as I filtered off into silence.

He hadn't called, I'd been texting him, I'd worried about him.

'Look I've been really busy this end, babe. Hey, why don't you come to Bar Nectar tonight?'

My mind briefly flickered back to Ellie and last night's conversation, 'Nick how do you know I'm free tonight?' I asked sheepishly.

'What do you mean babe, I have got a lot to get on with this end.'

'Oh nothing, nothing. It doesn't matter. I'll see you tonight,' I babbled in instant agreement.

'Right I'll put you on the guest list, see you later then.'

'Alright but it can't be a late one. I've got work tomorrow and...' As I rattled on I realised he'd gone. I finished my sentence anyway just in case anyone was listening in, so with a fake 'Alright Nick, have a good day,' and an 'I miss you too,' tacked on for good measure I replaced the receiver. He was fine, and I was seeing him tonight. Then I realised what I'd done, groaned and put my head in my hands.

After the small you're-not-dead faux pas I realised I had a bit of work to do to regain some Cool Points with Nick. I needed to work on being trendier, more aloof, and more desirable. I needed to show Nick that other men wanted me. I needed to salvage a bit of control. I didn't have time to think it through properly but I knew tonight required a definite Plan Of Action.

I picked up the next letter. It was date marked four days ago and I opened it hurriedly. Mary, 47, Hull writing about her cheating husband Bernard who was sleeping with the bakery woman. I briefly hoped this was a letter to inform me everything was OK but instantly realised from the slightly blotched and messy scrawl it had been written in an emotional rush. What had happened now?

Dear Angel,
Thank you so much for your letter. I tried a few of the things you suggested. I went to the spa with a girlfriend and I went shopping and brought a top which was nice. But I don't feel better. I think he's still with her. I haven't said anything to him yet. I can't. Particularly not after what I did the other day. I made a right fool of myself. I just wanted to catch a glimpse of her. I wanted to maybe say something to her, tell her that I knew about her and it wasn't on, going off with someone else's husband. So I went to Tesco's to see if I could spot her and when she turned around to serve me in the Patisserie section I totally bottled. I couldn't do it. So I jumped behind the pyramid of baked beans and hid. I couldn't go through with it. And she could see me standing there with my basket, because people kept taking the cans away. And she thought I was some local patient from the hospital (we have a mental health care place around the corner from us) and I'm sure she would have called security if I hadn't stopped watching her and left. And even though she was wearing one of them hats with the netting I could see she was Bernard's type. He always has liked blondes. Angel I don't know what to do. I feel useless. And she seemed a really confident type. How can I compete?

Poor Mary. I tried to write something encouraging back, but the situation did seem beyond hopeless. I imagined her crouching by the cans and cringed. How could we all stoop so low? When you're desperate all reason seems to fly out of the window. I felt sorry for her. I also felt like I couldn't become like that. My are-you-dead phone call was close enough. I really had to get a grip on myself or I'd turn into a Mary. Tonight was the night I would prove I could behave myself. I walked back to the flat that night planning what to wear and what to do to gain back some ground.

I could hear voices inside as I walked wearily up the steps to our house. Putting the key in the house lock I pushed the door and stepped inside. Instantly the voices stopped and I looked up to see Kevin standing outside his flat with a girl in a smart grey jacket. She was the woman we had seen visit him before. They looked an unlikely pair. She was smartly dressed, neat hair, polished nails. He was... Kevin. They were both looking at me as if frozen in speech. The girls' mouth still formed an 'O.' There was a tense silence and I could see her fidgeting nervously. Kevin didn't look up. I gave both of them an embarrassed nod as I scuttled past them up the stairs to our flat. As I neared our flat door I heard both of them muttering to each other in low voices.

Who was she? His hand had been on the door frame, as if blocking her entrance to the flat. Why hadn't he invited her in? Were they not friends? Why did they seem so familiar? What had they been arguing about?

The moment I was inside I didn't think much more about it. I wanted to wake myself up and get going for the night ahead. Concerns about Kreepy Kevin were low priority now. Ellie was busily chatting on her mobile for most of the evening so I was left to focus solely on pampering and preening myself for the night ahead.

I went in to say good night to her before I left, nervous as to her reaction after the last couple of night's lectures.

Ellie looked up at me, 'Angie you look stunning,' she said, immediately melting away any remnants of frostiness. She grinned at me, 'Go and make that boy toe the line. Hotton cotton to it skip, aye aye, port to starboard.'

'Alright, alright I get the message Ellie. I promise I will talk to him. No more soldier sailor talk.'

'Aye aye, cap'n,' she said saluting me with her hand. I looked at her pityingly. She bent her head down, 'Maybe one day I'll find someone,' and then lay back down on the sofa.

I laughed 'Bye Ellie.'

I got the tube into Leicester Square and called Nick's mobile. No answer. He must already be there. I set off in one direction and asked a few people for the location of the illustrious club. Their faces were blank as I rattled away in my native tongue. None of them appeared to speak English. I was starting to worry a little now. Where was it? Was it one of those underground places you heard of, where you needed to be sent the message in advance? Or was that just for raves? I was running late now. I approached the most English looking person I could, no obvious headdresses or wicker shoes and a distinctly suspicious look in the eyes. As if I was about to steal his chips. Excellent. Got him. With no pretence at looking anything other than smug he pointed across the street to a large neon sign that, of course, announced 'Bar Nectar' in bold fluorescent letters. Blushing I thanked him and then darted into the traffic to create some distance between us.

Neatening my hair I strolled up to the outside to join a small queue forming. The door staff were checking their lists and intermittently nodding and undoing the sacred rail that separates plebeians from the mighty clientele of their exclusive establishment. I could see two guys up ahead looking a little nervous, signalling to the list, to the doors, and then, from what it looked like, to God above. I watched, cruelly fascinated as the signalling got increasingly frantic. But with a single shake of the head, and a threatening step forward, the bouncer dispatched them both back onto the streets. Their names clearly hadn't made the grade. I unbuttoned my coat a little and pushed my breasts together. It seemed obvious but an admiring glance from one of the door staff assured me this was the best course of action. Wild gesticulating to Lord Jesus was now way down the list. I got to the front of the queue and looked as pouty and adorable as I could.

'Hi it's Angel, Angel Lawson, I'm a guest of Nick Sheldon-Wade.'

'Alright love we've got an Angel,' said the door staff who'd admired the breasts. I giggled a little and said thank you in my most coy voice. In one swift moment I'd undone most of the good work of the Sisterhood in the 60's. This was freedom. I scuttled in before they could change their minds.

Depositing my coat with the bored looking beauty behind the desk I headed towards the mill of people perched by the bar. One of the first people I noticed was Nobby. Unmistakable as he towered over everyone else in the bar by a foot or so, width and height. Nick must be close by. They went everywhere together. I, on the other hand, was never going to be one of Nobby's bosom buddies. On our first meeting he'd asked me if I dyed my hair. I told him I did and his follow up question had been the much under rated, 'What colour's your growler then?' I was left speechless. Nick assures me he's hysterically funny and girls 'just don't get him.' I assure Nick that girls do get him; they are just too polite to pretend otherwise.

'Hey,' I said, pausing as I tried to bring myself to say 'Hey Nobby.' I just couldn't.

There was no spark of recognition in his dull eyes.

'It's Angel,' I went on. No sign of life. Clearly hit once too often on the head by a rugby ball.

'Angel. Nick's bird,' I persisted cringing.

'Oh Nick's bird. Gotcha,' he said clicking his fingers at me in a way that suggested his next word might be Ciao.

'Well hi,' I said keeping it simple for him.

'So Angel, can I buy you a drink?'

I smiled, taken aback, 'Oh that would be lovel...'

'MATE,' he yelled making me jump in fright. Before I knew it he had lumbered off to embrace MATE who he'd spotted over my shoulder and I was left at the bar alone. I ordered a Double Vodka and Coke and downed it in one. Then I ordered a second one and turned to look for Nick.

An hour and a half later I was sitting perched on the corner of a large curved sofa spending most of my time getting up so that people could get out. Nick was in the middle looking hugely at home. Every now and again he caught my eye and nodded at me. Soon he would come over and sit with me. It was clear he was a bit stuck for time. One girl to his left appeared to be dominating his attention which seemed so unfair. It was clear he would much rather have been chatting to the man on his right who looked so interesting in his square framed glasses. The girl was actually behaving extremely rudely forcing Nick to turn his back on this man and lean in closely to her to try and catch her obviously insipid voice. Every now and again I glimpsed him throw back his head in laughter, no doubt to keep up the pretence that he could hear her at all, or to give her a bit of a confidence boost. He was such a warm-hearted guy.

I suddenly realised, on return from yet another loo visit to pass the time that I would have to strike up a conversation with someone, as it seemed to be clear that the very rude girl would not give up boring my poor boyfriend for the next few minutes. I turned to the guy sitting next to me staring into his pint and attempted a bit of small talk.

'So do you, um... are you a member of this bar.'

'What do you reckon sweetheart?' he slurred 'Of course I'm a bloody member, anyone who is anyone is a member.'

'Of course,' I continued with a tinkly laugh shaking my head, as if I was fully aware of this fact and anyone who wasn't was well... just plain stupid.

'But what I meant was...' He looked up from staring at his pint, possibly for the first time in over half an hour, and I suddenly realised I might have to complete the sentence I'd started, 'Well you know, what other kinds of bars are you a member of?' Looking appalled at the fact that he had bothered to raise his head for such a dull question he returned to viewing the bottom of his glass.

I sat there for a few moments longer, examining my nails thoroughly incase anyone wondered why I really hadn't got time to talk. When this got tired I started smiling at various people sitting around the semi circle in an attempt to start up a lively debate. Most just ignored me and one girl looked startled as I smiled at her in a sociable sort of way. Obviously friendly chit chat with strangers wasn't the done thing in Bar Nectar. The girl raised her eyebrow, turned to her friend sitting next to her and mentioned something about some lesbian who was around. I couldn't hear the detail, but for some reason the friend was looking right back at me smirking. I went back to examining my nails as if one was about to fall right off.

The Plan Of Action wasn't going totally smoothly. Nick was still looking fairly fascinated by the dull yet quite attractive evil girl and I was fast beginning to feel lost and a little lonely. Suddenly a glass came crashing down on the table next to me. Orange liquid swilled over the sides spattering on my skirt, and a pinstripe suit slumped onto a stool next door to me. The suit swayed precariously on the stool then turned to face me, taking a couple of seconds too long to focus on my face.

'This ish my seat where I left it.'

'Um... yes. Well hello,' I said in my over-nervous-small-talk voice usually reserved for kindly uncles and mad people.

'You're gooorgeous, haven't seen you here before. I'm Tom,' he held out his hand then slipped and used it to prop himself up on the table.

'I'm Angela,' I said trying to pretend I hadn't noticed the hand shake debacle. I knew this was my chance. I glanced at Nick and then back to Tom. He was dressed in a zipped up tracksuit top and khakis. If his eyes didn't look so glazed and his hair didn't look so wild he could have auditioned for a Gap advert. He would do.

'What did you say your name was? Angelico?' he slurred, not quite able to focus on my face, although managing to ogle my boobs quite successfully.

'Um... Angela,' I said realising for the seventh time that evening my glass was empty again.

'Would you like a drink Tom?' I asked looking over at Nick who didn't appear to be standing up to challenge Tom to duel for my affections.

'Alright Anika but I'm buying,' he said producing an embarrassing number of notes from a pocket with a flourish.

'Angela...' I corrected.

'Erica, I know, you said,' he said patting my bottom as I left for the bar.

I returned moments later with the drinks. Tom hadn't appeared to move an inch from the time I'd left him. I sat back down.

'So Anoushka, what do you do?' he asked, sniffing a little.

'Well I work for a magazine for now, but I'm trying to get into acting,' I tacked on, instantly realising this just made me sound like another desperate twenty-something wannabee. And right now it wasn't even true. How hard had I been trying? Not very. I had lost confidence. I had flaked out... I of course didn't need to tell him this. Tom slurped at his beer.

'Interested in acting are you? I work in PR, give me a call and I can set you up with the right people. It's just a matter of image. You know Kate...' he said.

'Angela,' I said patting him on the arm like a small child.

'No, you know Kate.'

'Kate?' I queried.

'Moss,' he finished.

'Oh right, of course Kate,' I said trying to keep up.

'Well she was a total nobody before she met me and then whoosh she went to straight to the top didn't she? Spoke to her last week actually and she said 'Tom. Thank you. You've helped me so much.'

'But I thought she was discovered by some modelling scout in an airport years ago?' I said a little confused.

He looked at me as if I was mental, 'And who do you think tipped him off? Christ I'm so used to hearing it. Like when I was out with Chris M and he was like...'

'M...? Moyles?' I ventured.

'No. Martin,' he said rolling his eyes.

'Oh right of course,' I said feeling uber geeky and still not totally sure who he meant.

'And he was like Tom, mate, Coldplay were nothing before you. And they say its coz they write good music. Bollocks,' he said shaking his head and laughing. He suddenly looked up at me, 'It's image.'

'Right,' I said.

'So babe just get in touch whenever and we'll sort you out.'

'Oh OK, well thanks, I will.'

After a few more drinks Tom started turning into a surprisingly amusing guy. I was fairly sure we were enjoying some scintillating conversation. We were such fascinating people. I was in quite the party mood. My high spirits were only interrupted by occasional glimpses over at Nick who was still settled next to the evil, dull but quite attractive girl. But then I headed to the bar and the world became a sunnier place.

At some point Tom was offering me some coke to help me keep up the pace. I'd never seen myself as a particularly druggy individual before. Far too middle-class. I still thought that skunk was a type of furry little animal. The pictures from soaps and budget British films hadn't exactly made the drug taking scene look glamorous. I re-played images of dirty girls, syringes stuck in their arms, and pale skinny men with shaved heads and bruised limbs 'shooting up' together in a dirty toilet. They were the kind of people that existed in fiction and nothing more. You read about them and every now and again you'd hear stories. Of course stories would be told; everyone had a story, a friend of a friend's cousin's mother. I knew of these stories. I'd watched the films with the pumping soundtracks. I'd heard and I'd watched knowing that these people would never really exist in my reality. In my cosy world of lattes and cappuccino's with people who call the settee the sofa and the lounge the living room. I simply wasn't hard core enough. In this setting however, surrounded by beautiful people wearing designer clothes and sipping Cosmopolitan cocktails, it didn't seem quite so sordid. Tom assured me the buzz was incredible. I turned around to see if it was time I muscled in with my boyfriend but no, he was still occupied. His head was now bent over her chest. He was looking at some kind of mole in between her cleavage. Benign I hoped. I held out my hand to Tom, my new best friend and recently appointed drug dealer.

I pushed my way over to the ladies loo clutching the foreign packet in my hand. I locked myself into a cubicle and tapped out the powder uncertainly. Getting out my credit card I divided it up into two lines, just like the movies. The disapproving faces of my mother, father and, bizarrely, Mother Teresa flitted across my consciousness. The catchphrase 'Kids: say No to Drugs' was being played on a loop as the background sound track. Then I pulled myself together, I needed to grow up. This was what all of London were doing. Crazy London, the real London, clubbing London. I snorted it up.

I splashed my face with water and stared back at my reflection, almost half expecting to look a thousand times cooler in an instant. I had surely become a girl who could repeat every line in an Eminem rap? Apparently not. My reflection confirmed I had become a girl with a wet face. Nothing more. I reapplied some eyeliner and headed back out to the bar.

I could see Nick still engrossed and was gripped by the urge to throw the wench off that sofa and drag him off to be with me, me, me. I'd sobered up fairly quickly (drenching yourself in tap water usually does the trick) and I was alert and ready to take Plan of Action up a gear. I scanned the room for Tom. He was soon by my side, sniffing a little, but ready to play his part in my Plan, albeit in ignorance. I yanked him on to the dance floor. It might have been memories of childhood dance lessons and routines to the Macarena or it might have been the cocaine kicking in. Either way moments later I realized I was one of the best dancers in Soho. I spent the rest of the night snaking around various people on the dance floor. Lucky things. Soon Nick was on the dance floor, no doubt tempted by my moves and obvious beauty. I wrapped myself around him and whispered in his ear. We looked so good together writhing about to the beats. I was feeling beautiful. The eyes of Bar Nectar were on me, me, me. I got drink after drink and danced and drank and partied and laughed and drank and danced. This was my life. I was accepted. These people were loving me and I was loving them. Must remember to become a member of these Members Only Bars.

The time swept by and by two in the morning I was outside the club, mystified to see I'd managed to sweat through my top without even noticing. My dancing exertions seemed like distant memories and I was suddenly over-whelmingly tired. And drunk. And shiny.

'I'm off home babe,' said Nick about to walk off.

I suddenly felt like a small child lost in a theme park. I panicked. Nick was going home, without me?

'Oh I'll come with you,' I said leaping forward and clinging to his arm, half for affection and half for support.

'Oh alright, if you like...'

'Shall we get a taxi?' I said dragging him off the pavement as I hailed a cab. I wasn't letting him go this time. 'Come on Nicholas,' I said pouting a little and stroking his arm. 'Maida Vale, please.'

We were safe in the cab. I sat back; head spinning, overwhelmed with relief. I was taking him home. How silly of me, we were always going to be going home together. I had just been paranoid.

I closed my eyes for a couple of seconds and listened to the sounds of late night London and Nick's voice filtering through the haze. He was talking about someone called Georgia and I was waiting for him to mention Tom. He had obviously seen his clearly flirtatious behaviour and I knew it wouldn't take long for him to ask me about it. Now he was babbling about some Greek Islands and I waited patiently for his story to end.

'So that was a good night,' I said, aware that I might be slurring a little.

'Yeah it was alright, thank god for Georgia or I would have had a shitty one...'

I gushed on, refusing to be interrupted, 'I had such a lovely evening chatting to Thomas, such a funny guy.' I paused and looked up to register the reaction.

Nick looked at me. 'Thomas, who?'

It was working; I could sense the jealousy.

'Oh just some guy I met,' I said breezily, 'Really amusing. Works in PR,' I dropped in.

Nick looked perplexed for a couple of moments longer, clearly battling with his inner emotions, attempting to keep down the envy and appear unbothered. The Plan of Action was about to celebrate its first victory.

'Oh god Tom, oh yeah I noticed he talking to you. Georgia and I were just waiting for him to fall off his fucking stool. So out of it. Such a wanker.'

My eager enthusiasm immediately deflated, my shoulders hunched. I closed my eyes and sat back as he went on gushing about Georgia and some yacht.

* * *

I groggily opened an eye five minutes later and moved one arm in a sweepy movement to ascertain Location Of Boy Friend. Arm reported back Sightings: Nil. I opened the whole eye. No Boy Friend. A question flickered across my consciousness; why were we lying down? I didn't remember lying down. And another one followed; why were we lying on a bed? I didn't remember lying on a bed. I remember we were sitting in a taxi, but I was definitely horizontal now, and not in a taxi. On a bed. Lying. Not sitting. But still definitely confused. How odd. From vague objects I could take in through the one eye I recognized Nick's bedroom. We must have just got back. He'll be in the bathroom. I shut both eyes again to block out the start of blood throbbing through head. Five minutes later I opened the eye again. No sight nor sound. Through the mists of objects I could make out some blurred letters, no, numbers. 8. 4. 7. I closed my eye again not wanting to overstrain the poor thing. 8. 4. 7. I sat up; way too quickly it transpired, as I grabbed my head in an effort to stop the room spinning. It didn't. My stomach lurched and I looked over. 8. 4. 8. These figures danced before me. 8, 4, 8. Actually 8:48. 8:48. It was 8:48. Fuck, oh, no, bugger, bugger. It really was absolutely truly 8:48. I had somehow lost a night. A night of precious, precious sleep. How, how had that happened? I had work in twelve minutes and I was lying, no sitting, on a bed far, far away.

I realised with a slow dread that I'd read about stories like these. People wake up unable to account for time, sometimes losing hours of their lives. Aliens take their bodies, experiment on them with silver instruments and return them back. They don't remember it but time has passed and it is the only clue to the hideous things they've just undergone. I felt sickened. Not particularly from the story but sickened in general. I'd felt pretty sick before the whole alien/silver instrument experiments thought. Although it hadn't helped make me feel any less queasy. God knows what those bastards did to me.

8:52. Agh. Agh. Why did it keep doing that? Damn time for moving on at 60 seconds to the minute. I had work in 8 minutes. I made a brief calculation in my head. I had work in 8 minutes + I was in a bed on the other side of London town + I was not superwoman = This is bad. Bleurgh. I celebrated this result, and the arrival of 8:54, by throwing up in the bathroom.

Sitting back on the bed I considered my options.

Option One: Call in sick to work.
Positive points: Get to not to go to work.
Negative points: Victoria would know and hunt me down with sniffer dogs. I was not exactly in her Little Golden Book of People I Love To Work With Right Now. In fact I had a sneaky suspicion I was headlining the book of People I Must Fire ASAP.

Option Two: Snuggle back down calling for medical assistance and possible pizza delivery, I added as an after thought.
Positive Points: People will bring me food and paracetamol and I will learn to feel alive once more.
Negative Points: The world will go on turning and Victoria will hunt me down with sniffer dogs.

Option Three: Get up and go to work.
Positive points:
Negative Points: Will have to get up and go to work.

I manoeuvred my body up and made my way slowly to the bathroom. Pulling on the light switch I was suddenly swamped in brightness. Blinking I groped for the sink. The face staring back was unrecognizable as last night's Femme Fatale. The smoky, kitten eyes were now panda patches of mascara – lashes clogged together and bloodshot whites peeking through. I half-heartedly wiped underneath them and splashed my face with water. Preening finished, today's approach to make up being the much underrated Bare Minimum Look. I stumbled back through to Nick's bedroom and realized my wardrobe choices were limited. Five minutes later I had managed to concoct an ingenious little outfit using Nick's bottle blue jumper and my short black skirt and knee boots of the night before. My hair, smelling of eau d'stale smoke, was hastily tied back into a ponytail. I was dressed. The only shortcoming of my chosen outfit was its ability to keep me warm. This is normally a vitally important function for jumpers but as I stepped onto the street outside, and into the blazing sunshine, I realised it wouldn't come in handy today. The trouble was I was wearing my backless glittering number from the night before underneath, so unless I could persuade the office it was National Fancy Dress Day I was doomed to sweat profusely in bottle blue.

I somehow managed to get into work and scuttle unseen to my desk. Convinced that I was moving around in a fog of smoke and alcohol fumes I kept a relatively safe distance away from, well, everyone. I had a lot of time to dredge up the events of the night before. I still had no idea as to how I had ended up at Nick's flat without remembering. I had a sneaking suspicion I had behaved badly. I'd taken some cocaine, I remembered that. And I'd drunk half their supply of vodka. And I'd spent the evening with that horrendous guy Tom. I groaned as I thought back. Had I even spoken to Nick all night? Had I flung myself around the dance floor quite as energetically as I recalled? Had I really begged the DJ to play Hanson's 'Hmm Bop' as a favour? I despaired of myself. I think I had some kind of obsessive compulsive disorder to humiliate myself publicly. Maybe I was sick? I clearly did not have an iota of self control. Why couldn't I have just gone out, behaved sensibly, put the sophisticated Plan of Action to work, chitted, chatted and charmed the table, floated seamlessly from conversation to conversation and overheard people whispering to each other 'That's Angel, she's Nick's girlfriend. Isn't she gorgeous.'

Why couldn't I be that girl? Just for one night? Hair smooth, make up un-smudged, clothes un-ruffled. A tinkly laugh, a delicate smile, an appreciative nod, a demure little walk...

I had to get a grip. Did I want to lose him? He was all I had at the moment. I needed to make more of an effort. He needed to be impressed by me. Not carting me home to throw up in his Maida Vale palace.

Dear Angel,
I love my boyfriend but he doesn't love me. He talks to my friends but not me. I just wish he would talk to me and I am getting bored as he never is around me. We have been going out for 8 months and the first few months were great but then it went hay wire. He doesn't hug me or anything and the last day of school he said he did not want to for a photo. Help!
Felicity, 14, Glos

Dear Felicity,
On reading your letter it occurred to me that you might not be making as much effort as you could. You say that your boyfriend talks to your friends and not to you. Are you trying to talk to him? Instead of getting bored when he's not there invest some time in learning about activities that interest him. Then when he talks to you he'll be interested by what you have to say. Support him in all he does. If he is a keen train spotter learn about engine size. Is he a car enthusiast? Learn about the intricate workings of the catalytic converter, the importance of having SatNav... Or is he a keen bird watcher? Ponder the wonders of the cry of the Green Woodpecker, see the Brown Owl's ruffled underbelly...
Maybe making a bit more of an effort will spark his interest in you once more and you'll recapture the magic of the first few months...

The abrupt ring of my phone interrupted my scribbling. Without thinking I picked up the receiver.

'ANGIEEEE,' came a wailing in my ear. I instantly regretted picking up my phone. Why couldn't I screen my calls? How had this squealing creature got my work number? I must have given it to her sometime. On a previous black day.

It was Imogen, an actress I knew from university. She launched into the main reason for her call.

'I really wanted to ring and tell you to turn on your TV on

Thursday. My show is finally being aired. 8pm. Prime time. I'm so excited.'

'Oh,' I said weakly, 'that is brilliant. How exciting,' I said trying to sound it. She was always quite sweet, a bit over enthusiastic and air kissey, but nice enough.

'How about you Angel? How's it going? I've really been off the grape vine what with doing that national tour. Have you managed to get anything good? Adverts? TV? I thought last time I saw you you were about to start some show at The White Bear...'

My heart sank further as I listened to her animated chat continue. All her successes were listed effortlessly and her enthusiasm threw me into a decline. It was obvious I was never going to get anywhere. I hadn't been to any castings, I hadn't called my agent. I hadn't rung back that guy at BOS Productions about that audition. I had lost it. What had happened to my initial excitement and confident assertions that I would keep trying whatever happened? What happened to believing that I was a good actress? I clearly hadn't been a good actress. I had obviously been terrible. Only ever cast in fringe shows and some short films, and fine I had made a few people laugh, but what did they know? I had never really achieved a glittering credit, or had a top agent scooting me round to the best casting directors. I was obviously destined to never make it. I was useless as an actress and had to move on and get over it.

'...You were great at university Angel. Oh and you know Ollie's been picked up by the BBC. They absolutely love him and are talking about flying him out to Prague for some period drama. Sounds amazing. Honestly it's all been such a whirlwind hasn't it? I can't believe we left university two years ago...' She rattled on oblivious to my lengthening silences.

Suzie had wandered over to my desk and was now waiting patiently for me to finish. Imo had interrupted her monologue to ask what I had been up to. I summed it all up succinctly.

'Well I've got a lovely boyfriend and I'm having a really good time at the magazine,' I said trying to sound as equally pleased with myself as she was.

'Oh but that's brilliant. I bet he's gorgeous. Well look we must meet soon and...'

Suzie picked up the letter I'd been writing with idle interest. My eyes darted up nervously. Imo was still blathering in my ear about a reunion. I suddenly didn't want Suzie to read that letter. Imo paused to catch her breath and I quickly jumped in before she could start up again.

'I've got to go Imo but I'll give you a call about that drink and that's great about your show, well done,' I said trying to get rid of her before Suzie started looking disapproving. Too late.

I noticed Suzie's face changing as she scanned my reply.

'Bye Imo, yes, Thursday night 8pm right. OK. Alright, yes, see you soon. Bye.'

'You can't send this,' said Suzie the moment I had replaced the receiver.

I looked guilty.

'You weren't going to send this were you?'

'No,' I lied swirling my foot around on the floor.

'Angel you wouldn't,' she gaped at me. Suddenly I was not her best friend. I was a naughty Year Nine and teacher was telling me off. I thought about distracting her by spontaneous crying but knew instinctively she was sharper than that.

'Angel what are you thinking? You can't write this. The poor girl just wants a bit of sensible advice...'

'I know I'm having an off day that's all,' I thought, surreptitiously pushing other letters out of view.

'You can't say THAT,' she yelped reading the letter feverishly.

Tally looked up from her desk opposite and gave me a quizzical smile.

'I wasn't going to send it,' I said sounding flustered.

'Oh my god,' Suzie muttered eyes darting across the page 'Catalytic converter...'

'I obviously got distracted,' I said pulling out a fresh piece of paper to prove I had learnt my lesson. I started writing a new reply.

'Look I'm starting again,' I said when she hadn't noticed. Tally started giggling quietly at her desk.

'Honestly Suzie you can stop reading it, I have been a bit preoccupied today that's all.'

She put the letter gingerly down on my desk. 'I see.'

I looked at her nervously; my pen still hovered over the paper.

'Right, well I'll see you later Angel,' she said looking worriedly at me.

'See you,' I said as cheerfully as I could.

As she turned around I grimaced at Tally.

'Right... lets read it then,' said Tally holding out her hand.

I felt momentarily guilty imagining the previous week's letters winging their way across the country. It wouldn't really matter though; it wasn't like they were relying solely on my advice. Most had friends, parents, teachers, they could turn to. They'd work it out.

Anyway I just don't care enough about their problems. I have my own problems. Most of their problems are so easy to solve. Obvious solutions. I mean how much heart ache can a fourteen year old really feel? Could a twelve year old really be that depressed? What ever happened to your youth being the happiest time of your life? They all seemed so down about it. I'd give anything to trade places for a day or two. They should try and sort out the mess I've made. Why they are asking me to help is also beyond me. Do they honestly think because I look like an adult I suddenly have all the answers? I know nothing. I am a state. I go out mid week, get drunk, get high and behave like an idiot. I'm a useless horrible person. I can't act, I can't write letters, I can't do anything. I can't even do this job right. And Suzie thinks so too. Everyone probably does.

I was sunk in a black hole of doom. Maybe I was experiencing a come down after my cocktail of drink, drugs and fast living. I had been behaving like quite the girl around town. And mid week too. Nick was all I had at the moment to keep me sane. He kept me happy. He was something I could focus on. Yet last night hadn't gone well. I was losing him to women with pearl necklaces and yachts in the Med. I re-read the letter in front of me and realised I needed to take my own advice. I had to become the woman Nick really wanted. It wasn't just about wearing pin stripe and learning to read the FT. I couldn't just dress up and hope to pass as her. I needed to really start to think like her. It was just like an acting job. I had to become the character. I vowed to go out and buy 'War and Peace' in my lunch hour. This weekend I would prove just how organised and industrious I could be. The dinner party I had planned would be my Trafalgar and I would conquer it. Yes, conquer it I shall. Because if I couldn't keep hold of my boyfriend I couldn't do anything right.

Dear Felicity,
You need to prove to him how much you love him. Cook for him to really show him you care...

* * *

The day of the Dinner Party dawned. I felt a little better after eleven hours sleep. Yesterday had definitely been a lapse in my general positivity. I felt a lot better with the weekend ahead and plans to be executed. Trouble was I'd had a list of Things to Do and was now 2 hours behind. The list, being a list written by me, wasn't exactly extensive. It included:

Shop
Make house look pretty
Cook
Make me look pretty

I knew I was already cutting it fine. I flung on some tracksuit bottoms and a T shirt and tied my hair back in a quick bun. I definitely felt ready to face the day. There was no feeling of imminent doom, no crisis in confidence, no black hole of despair. In fact I didn't appear to be suffering at all today. My outlook could be described as sunshiny with a light breeze. Things weren't the utter disaster I sometimes made out. In my quieter, saner moments I realised it wasn't all going too badly. I lived in London, in a flat, with a friend. I had a job, a few more friends and I had a man. Although life wasn't quite the rosy fairytale I'd been promised, it wasn't all doom and gloom. I could definitely do worse.

My boyfriend doesn't take heroine or steal cars. My flat mate isn't a cat-loving fifty year old called Maureen, my job is not cleaning loos at the local petrol station, my friends aren't a complete bunch of losers, in fact one or two are relatively well-to-do! With all these blessings in mind I headed off to the supermarket.

I pushed the trolley past other Saturday shoppers scooping up various ingredients when I saw them. It wasn't as easy as I thought. I was boggled by the choices of meats on display. Would it matter if the mince was organic and finely ground? Or would extra lean be better? How many would 300g feed? And at £2.99 a tub are olives absolutely necessary to the success of a lasagne?

I'd taken the recipe book and my mobile phone with me. When I wasn't reading from the book I was dialling my mother at home.

'So I can use chopped tomatoes? Right... Oh what kind of cheese is best for the sauce?'

'Plain cheddar will be fine darling... I'm glad you rung, your brother just called to tell us he needs to tell us something and you know he never rings...'

'Do I just throw it all together?'

'...I'm worried about him...'

'So the tomato sauce can be Dolmio? And are onions good to add in?'

'Yes fine darling. You just chop them thinly and pop them in. Oh, and drizzle a little butter over the mange tout. You need milk for the cheese sauce too... And your sister's only managed to have her tongue pierced. She can't eat, she can't talk. She keeps telling me to thalk to her. As if I know what that means. She can hardly say her s's and the swelling was meant to have died down after a couple of days. Her hand's still black from the dye you know. Yes, she managed to dye her hand. That girl...'

'Mum... MUM do I make that skimmed or semi skimmed?'

'Semi darling, and your father doesn't know what to do about these telephone masts. They're planning to get one put near the school. Can you imagine? Pauline and Malcolm live right next door. As if they want a ruddy great mast...'

'What so I buy the lasagne slices and then layer them across the mince sauce. And I'm making a pavlova for pudding, so I need cream for it.'

'Yes, yes darling. Although try reduced fat as no one ever knows the difference... and they've written to the council too. Honestly your father is not happy about it all and I've said if you are going to insist on....'

'OK Mum well you've been such a help. I really have to go now. OK love you too... Yup. OK. Fine. Tell him good luck from me. OK... will do. Fine. Right... OK. Bye.'

Three and a half hours later I was back in the kitchen, panicking at the array of items I'd purchased. What did they all do again? I cunningly managed to persuade Ellie to help oversee the operation. She was Head of Cooking The Mince and I was allotted Vegetable Duty. I informed her it was a necessary part of the process of flat mate bonding. We set to work playing Norah Jones in the background in a desperate attempt to exude some calming vibes.

The relative peace came to an abrupt halt with the arrival of Rick who decided to tell us both he was definitely developing a bad case of haemorrhoids, and then tried to show us his symptoms. Almost enough to put Ellie off stirring the mince. We'd managed to persuade him to stop worrying about his imminent demise and get dressed for the night. He was now happily grooming himself in my room listening to Will Young whilst he got dressed. The whole scenario seemed so gay I hadn't even bothered to make any sarcastic remarks.

A couple of hours later I was dressed and made-up. I'd straightened my hair and popped some dark grey evening eye make-up on ala James Bond Girl. As I finished curling my eyelashes the buzzer rang.

I opened the door with a grin on my face and, as it was later pointed out to me, flour on my nose.

'Mel, Peter, congratulations,' I said as they bustled in to the flat.

Mel thrust two bottles of wine in my hand.

'Angie this is so nice of you,' she said, 'And you look great.'

'Thanks.'

'So... er... what have you cooked up?' Mel said looking, if I'm not being totally paranoid, a little on the nervous side. I suppose I wasn't best known for my culinary talents.

I looked at her solemnly, 'Starter is Plain Salted Crisps and peanuts. Dry Roasted naturally.'

'Right...'

'Followed by toasted cheese sandwiches and jelly to finish.'

Mel's face looked momentarily speechless as Peter stepped forward laughing.

'Good to see you Angie. You never mentioned you were a cordon bleu cook. Sounds delicious.'

'Bitch,' said Mel hitting me playfully with her handbag, 'You had me worried.'

'Where is the trust?' I said hitting her back.

Half an hour later I surveyed the room with a small smile. Peter was being manly opening wine bottles and trying to talk about wine vintages with Rick who was too busy staring at his forearms to do little more than nod. Suzie had arrived and was deep in discussion with her date Chris someone (advertising) but more importantly I reckoned, as I saw him brush her leg (attractive). Mel and Ellie were discussing wedding dresses and flower arrangements. Everything looked like it was going to go well. The food was bubbling away, people appeared to be happy. Nothing had been spilt over any carpets and my mother's wine glasses were all still intact. Only one person was missing.

I went to check on the food. The door to the kitchen was open and I could hear them all chattering away. If only Nick would get here we could eat. He must have been held up.

'So when are we meeting this Nicholas character?' called Mel from the living room.

'Oh he'll be along any minute,' I said stirring frantically at the mince and reaching for my mobile. His answer phone. Again. He obviously hadn't got his phone on him. I really hate people that are permanently attached to their mobiles as if it's some essential life support. It would be nice for him to switch his on occasionally though.

'Hi Nick, it's Angel. Just checking you're on your way over. I've made dinner. See you soon then. OK.' I finished, impressed that I still sound breezy and laidback and then ruining this by tacking on the end, 'Can't wait to see you. I'm laid back though, so come whenever, well not whenever because (nervous laugh here) everyone else is here and the food will burn but... well see you. Right. Bye.'

I turned to see Rick gaping at me.

'Tell me that was just a rehearsal and not the real thing.'

I looked at him worriedly, 'Do you think I sounded tense?' I asked, back to stirring in an over zealous way.

'Er... no, chilled and laid-back darling. So... you never told me you were such a good cook...'

After laying the table, lighting more candles, making half-hearted small talk with Chris and checking the clock for the hundredth time I realised he wasn't coming. The hand ticked to 9.30pm and I knew I couldn't feed them salted crisps anymore.

'Well I suppose we better eat,' I said brightly.

Mel sneaked me a look of concern, 'Angel it's fine. We can wait.'

'No honestly let's eat, if he...'

Rick jumped up clapping his hands before I could finish, 'Thank god darling I'm starving.' He wrapped me in a hug and pecked me on the cheek, 'So where do you want me to sit? Ah here,' he said pulling out a chair next to Peter. 'Lovely,' he said settling himself down before I could provide him with an answer. Everyone else took their places. Ellie discreetly removed one of the table settings and came into the kitchen.

'He's just being thoughtless,' she said as she noticed me gloomily spooning out helpings of food.

'I know,' I said giving her a half-smile, 'He might have forgotten, or been tied up with work or...' I trailed off.

'Let's just have a good night without him,' she said putting her arm around me and squeezing me in a maternal kind of way.

'You're right.'

'Don't think about him, alright?' she said carrying through the dish of vegetables.

'I won't,' I said smiling at her weakly.

The meal was a pretty good success from what I could tell. There had been no need to call a take away and everyone seemed to be getting on. I'd been chatting a bit more to Mel about the wedding. They were just finalizing the plans for the reception and they'd booked a little church in Knightsbridge. They were picking hymns and some processional music that Mel's cousin was going to play on a harp.

'Angel I wanted to ask you something,' she said looking at Peter and turning to me, 'Would you do one of the readings at the wedding?'

I was overwhelmed and broke out into a surprised smile.

'I'd love to,' I said giving her a hug. 'Of course. Thank you.'

I felt genuinely moved to have been asked.

'Thanks Angel,' said Peter raising his glass to me.

I blushed. It was lovely of them to want me to read. I was already nervous about the prospect. I hardly heard what Peter was now saying to me.

'Oh yes and Angel a friend of mine saw you in a show a year or so ago in the White Bear and was wondering if you are still acting. He's just set up his own agency and they're seeing some new people.'

'That's great Angel,' said Ellie looking up pleased.

'I'll give you his number,' Peter said smiling at me. The familiar fear rose up briefly. I started procrastinating. How lovely. Isn't that nice. Would anyone like anymore? How could I tell him that I had lost any talent I had? Fortunately the need to put raspberries on the pudding distracted him from pursuing it further. But maybe I should take the number and give him a call. What harm could it do?

Half way through the pudding the buzzer to the flat shrilled and my stomach flipped. Finally!

I pressed on the buzzer to let him in. Immediately I heard muffled voices and clanking in the background.

'ANGEL, ANGEL, NOBBY,' came a slurred yelling. I didn't think much of it.

Another voice was hollering in the background and the voice repeated itself, 'ANGELLLL.'

'It's open,' I said pressing the buzzer again.

I could hear the hollering voice breaking into some kind of a chant and wondered if it was my Nick or in fact some mental Jehovah's Witness on a house call.

'Angel it's Nick. Let me in NOBBY.'

My brow creased. That wasn't quite the endearment I'd wanted.

The chanting stopped and I heard another voice interrupt, 'It's me Angel too... ANGEL.'

I instantly recognized the distinctive cut glass accent, Nobby was obviously with him. They sounded pissed. It should be fine though, I needed a gate crasher to ensure the party could be deemed an absolute success. However after a few more failed attempts to let themselves in; with me yelling 'Just push the door' over the intercom I realized there might be a problem. Everyone in the living room had settled into a post-pudding-pre-coffee lull, and were happily eavesdropping throughout the entire saga.

Any peace was absolutely shattered by the arrival of Nick and Nobby, clearly fresh from some private party in a pub. Nobby was swaying precariously around the living room and Nick was lurching towards me, an open bottle of wine in his hand.

'We bring you gifts Angel,' he said planting the bottle in my hand and surveying the room through squinted eyes.

'Ellie,' he cried lighting on a familiar face. He pulled up a chair next door to her and sat down with a sigh. 'Angel will you be an Angel and pour me some wine,' he said. I blushed and poured him a glass, knowing that everyone around was watching us like some scene in a soap opera.

'So where have you boys been,' I said, trying to sound jovial, as I turned to Nobby.

'They won,' came the muttered reply from his large frame which was now passed out on our sofa. 'They won.' His eyes fluttered and then closed. I lunged for the beer can in his hand, but too late, its remnants were flowing freely over our carpet.

'I'll get a cloth,' said Ellie getting up and going into the kitchen.

'Angie I think we'll go,' said Suzie sidling up to me as I was propping up Nobby's head on a cushion.

'Oh but it's still early,' I said, keen for my first dinner party to be a roaring triumph and keener for Nick to see just how popular I was.

'I know but Chris wants to go and see a friend DJing at Blue Bar and he said he can get me in for free and...' she leaned in so Chris was oblivious, 'he's delicious and I want to take him home. Please let me go.' She finished looking at me with saucer eyes.

'Fine,' I smiled.

'Thanks gorgeous,' she hugged me, 'And thank you for everything, it was delicious.' She looked back at Nobby whose head was lolling again, 'Good luck.'

Chris made a brief and formal thank you in my direction and then I watched Suzie drag him off into the night. I doubted they'd ever get to see his friend spinning the decks. The others still seemed to be happily chatting and I went to help Ellie clean up the mess.

I walked in to the kitchen to find Ellie and Nick wrapped around each other. Ellie was squashed up against the kitchen counter, her hands on my boyfriend's chest, and they both turned to see me walk in. The image didn't immediately digest and for a moment I look like a cartoon character when he realises he's suspended in thin air and is about to plummet to his cartoon death. Baffled. There was a silence as I tried to take in what I was seeing. Ellie was flushed in the cheeks. She'd whipped her hands away from his chest as I'd walked in. Nick had turned slowly as I came in. His hair was slightly ruffled, as if... I didn't want to think about it. He looked at me levelly. I found my voice.

'What the fuck is going on?'

'Why don't you ask your boyfriend?' said Ellie glaring at Nick and then at me. I flinch.

'Nick?' I looked at him.

'Oh I have to tell her do I?' he said turning to her.

'Well you're the arsehole with the wandering hands so, yes, you better tell her,' said Ellie.

Nick started laughing and I looked from him, to her and back again. 'Oh it's me with the wandering hands now. I see,' he said in a sarcastic tone.

'What's that meant to mean,' she spat.

'You know precisely what,' he said looking at her knowingly. It was apparently just me still in the dark.

'Angel, I think your friend has a little crush,' he laughed looking at Ellie patronizingly.

'What?' She burst out. 'As if I would ever touch you.' She turned to me, 'Angie he's lying. I was doing some washing up and he came in and lunged at me.'

'Bollocks,' scoffed Nick. 'That's bollocks. But you tell her what you want,' he said looking coolly confident leaning back on the counter.

'It's true Angie.'

I looked at them both. Nick was shaking his head slowly at her in disbelief and Ellie was a ball of emotion. Guilt? Embarrassment? I didn't know what to do. I couldn't think.

Rick walked in, looked around at us all and then ran away. I carried on staring at them.

'For fuck sake,' screeched Ellie, 'He's a wanker Angel. A total letching wanker.'

At this Nick turned to her, 'Just because I turned you down.'

'Nick what happened?'

'Angel, sweetheart, I...'

'Don't butter her up with...'

'Shut up Ellie,' I turned back to Nick, 'Nick what happened.'

'I came to get a glass and she tried to kiss me.'

'That's rubbish,' said Ellie.

'Maybe you should tell your flat mate what you said to me?' he said quietly.

Ellie looked at him, 'What?'

'You heard... What did you say to me when Angel was through there?' He pointed to the living room.

'Oh what did I say,' she said putting her hands on her hips.

'You told me you were so glad I'd come tonight, that you'd been wondering where I'd been...' He smirked at her.

'I meant for Angie. Angie I was glad he'd come for you,' she pleaded looking more flustered.

'Look why would I kiss you when my girlfriend was right next door?' asked Nick looking genuinely confused.

'Why would he Ellie?' I said looking at her beseechingly. Nick in turn was looking suitably indignant.

'Because he's a creep that's why? You're deranged if you can't see that Angel. He's a scumbag.'

'Don't call him that.'

'Yeah don't call me that.'

'Shut up Nick.'

'OK Precious.'

'But he is Angie. He's an arrogant letch and you're wrapped around his little finger.'

'That's not true.'

'Fine, you're right. I threw myself at Nick. I'm the bad guy. Christ this is pointless.' And with that she picked up her keys, stalked through the living room and slammed the flat door behind her.

The whole flat was silent. I entered the living room to see everyone either looking shiftily at their plate (Mel), gaping at the door (Peter) passed out on the sofa (Nobby) or looking curiously over-excited at me (Rick). Nick appeared in the doorway behind me. I looked mutinous. The silence continued for a few more seconds and then just as if a Director had yelled 'Action' they all jumped into simultaneous movement.

'Er, I'll go and see what that was about...' said Rick scooting off his chair.

'I'll get the car,' said Peter rushing out after him.

'Well it's late and we better be... the baby sitter will want to...' Mel started pointing and making frantic 'call-me' actions.

Within ten seconds the flat was empty of guests (Nobby was still passed out, oblivious, but he hadn't technically been invited anyway). I looked at my boyfriend, gazing around the room. He looked up and tried to give me a winning smile, as if the last ten minutes hadn't just happened. When I gave him an accusatory glance his shoulders slumped.

'What actually happened Nick?' I asked looking at him suspiciously. I didn't know what to think.

'I told you she kissed me.'

'What she just threw herself at you?' I said sceptically.

'Basically,' he said shrugging his shoulders.

I carried on glowering at him, determined to know the truth.

'Well not immediately. But I went into the kitchen and she started talking to me, telling me she'd always liked me and that I wasn't right for you. Then she just launched herself on me and started kissing me.'

'She says that you kissed her.'

'Well she would wouldn't she? But why would I kiss her when I'm with you?' He softened.

I was tired, 'Nick why don't you go? I'll call you in the morning.'

'No babe I'll stay with you. You're upset,' he said coming over.

'I just don't know what to think,' I said hopelessly.

'Poor baby,' he said drawing me to him. I leant against his chest feeling drained of energy. I didn't know what to think. I kept returning to the image of them together in the kitchen. She had looked pretty guilty. And Nick wouldn't just go round kissing other girls in my flat, I was here, he could kiss me. It must have been Ellie. I closed my eyes as he stroked my hair. I didn't want to think about it anymore.

'I wouldn't do that,' he said quietly.

And as he held me tight I believed him. It didn't make me feel any better though.

* * *

I didn't stay in the flat over the weekend. Nick and I spent a cosy Sunday in his flat, watching videos all day curled up on his sofa underneath a duvet. He made me a fry up for breakfast and was behaving impeccably. Finally we seemed back to behaving like we had in the first couple of months. It felt comfortable and as I stretched and nuzzled against him like a cat I blocked out all the unpleasantness of the party. I got back to the flat late on Sunday night and heard Ellie's door shut just before I'd arrived. I'd briefly lingered outside it and then moved into my bedroom. I didn't have the energy to start a row now. It had been such a lovely day and I could confront Ellie in the morning.

Of course it was raining the next morning. A gloomy Monday made worse by steady persistent drops of rain. The big drenching kind as well. The sky was grey and overcast and the streets were filled with running women with tiny umbrellas, men with tiny newspapers and granny's with tiny little rain hats done up in a bow under the chin. I arrived at the office feeling soggy.

Dear Angel,
My best friend is more interested in my sister than me. She's always talking to her, even when I'm not there and she meets her everyday. She doesn't care if I come out anymore. What should I do?
Lydia, 13, Newbury

Hmm... I confidently started to write.

Dear Lydia,
Best friends can often let us down. I myself have been unlucky enough to know girls in the past who have seemed like loyal, trustworthy people and turned out to be back-stabbing liars. It is hard to work out why friends can often hurt you so badly. It sounds like you are the victim here, and hopefully your friend will see that she's hurting you and stop. Try and find out from her why she is doing this. If this doesn't help and her behaviour doesn't change, dump her. You can get a new friend easily.
Angel

I felt a tinge of sadness as I signed off the letter. I couldn't believe Ellie and I were fighting like this. We didn't fight. We had the odd argument but nothing that can be defined as more than 'a tiff.' I couldn't believe we were fighting in the real live dictionary use of the word meaning 'To fight; to contend or struggle in war, battle, single combat etc'. I couldn't believe it. But I also couldn't believe Ellie would snog my boyfriend, a man she knows I am totally hung up on. Just because she is single and has been for months doesn't give her the right to sweep in and steal my man. She was obviously trying to hide the fact she fancied him underneath an ill-disguised contempt for him. It should have been so clear to me. Ellie had never disliked my boyfriends with quite the same passion. She was always rolling her eyes about him, urging me to ignore him, telling me to leave him alone, let him come to me etc. I thought of every time she'd been rude about him, telling me he wasn't worth it. No doubt she was biding her time, waiting patiently for me to mess it up, waiting for him to realise that I wasn't the girl for him, waiting so we'd break up and she could get her nasty little mitts on him. The tinge of sadness had quickly evaporated and I was left with raw anger again.

What would I do now? I couldn't live with Ellie after all this. I'd have to leave the flat. Where would I go? Could I move in with Nick I wondered? He had a big place; I'd be no trouble, cook his meals and keep the place tidy. Ellie would cry a lot, beg me to stay, tell me it was all a big mistake. But how could I go on living there and seeing Nick knowing that every time I spoke about him, saw him, she was there, in the background, loving him from afar and trying desperately to hide it? It would be too awkward. It wouldn't work.

And if Nick wouldn't let me move in with him I'd move to someone else's place. Set up with a newer best friend. Take the Guess Who board; take the Disney videos and the life size cut out of Johnny Depp. Actually I wouldn't do that; I'd make Ellie move out. She is the boyfriend snogger after all. By all rights she should be the one to leave and set up somewhere else. Alone. In a one bedroom flat. With dank walls. In a basement with little daylight and a weird smell. With no nice flatmate to drink hot chocolate with and talk about Eastenders to.

'You all right Angel?' said Tally sitting across from me noticing my dismal expression.

'What? Oh yes, I'm fine. Just work you know,' I said tutting and shaking myself, 'A sad letter you know,' I said as some kind of explanation.

'Oh right, why what happened?' she asked the picture of concern.

'Oh um... this girl... has... a problem with her... nose,' I finished.

'Sounds terrible,' said Tally going back to her work.

I couldn't talk to Tally about it all. I actually felt a little embarrassed. It all sounded so sordid, best friend and boyfriend triangles. I really needed someone who knew everyone involved, someone who had known me for ages, a real friend. I really needed Suzie. I looked over at her desk and then remembered with a sinking heart that she was out of the office. She was at some bonding management meeting brushing up on her management skills. Damn. She would usually work it all out for me. She'd at least get cross on my behalf. She would give me a consoling lecture about how Ellie had been a bad friend and she, Suzie, would never have behaved like that with one of my boyfriends.

But then a small bit of me doubted. Doubted Ellie could do something like that. This was a girl who had organised a surprise birthday for me, arranged a day at a spa when I got my first acting part, sympathised with me after every audition, exam failure, boyfriend trouble...

She was my best friend. She loved me. But then why would Nick say it? Why would he make it up? It didn't seem like there was any other explanation. And he was my boyfriend; I couldn't just ignore that fact.

I knew I would have to confront her. The very idea scared me. I was not a confrontational person. I remembered those girls in the park when I was younger. You know the ones. The girls who get cross with you because you're standing at the swings funny or looking at them in a weird way. 'What's your problem' they'd spit, waiting for a full level fight to break out so they could get involved and kick some middle-class butt. But I always scuttled off muttering, 'Nothing, I'm not looking at anything.' Hard core I was not. For this reason I spent a lot of time breathing levelly on the tube home. I thought about strong women, tough women with balls of steel like Germaine Greer, Clare Short and Lara Croft. The tube journey was all part of my mental preparation for the night ahead. Unless Ellie isn't at home and then all the psyching up will have been one long waste. I'll be forced to watch action movies to retain the pumping adrenalin until she's back.

I put the key in the lock and waited for Ellie to greet me in an emotional way, insisting it was all a horrible error and she's sorry. No running steps in the corridor, no door flinging open to welcome me, no frantic apologies as I put my bag down. She must be out, crying somewhere about being such a terrible friend. I briefly feel a pang that she's hurting and I can't help. But she isn't crying anywhere at all; she's sitting on the sofa. She's looking frosty and I look at her surprised. She is not winning me round with this approach.

'So did you speak to him,' she asks in the voice that accompanies the frosty look.

I don't expect this. A challenge, from a girl that has been trying to seduce my boyfriend. No tears, no desperate 'I'm sorry's,' no bumper size carton of Roses chocolates, nothing to suggest that she is in anyway gearing up for a massive apology. I didn't expect it. I feel cheated. Which is about the right emotion seeing as I have been, not just of the chocolates, but of my best friend. Cheated of a real explanation and apology for her behaviour on Saturday night.

'Ellie, he says he didn't do anything,' I argued.

She stared at me, forcing me to soldier on.

'He was as confused as I am.'

'He JUMPED ON ME Angel,' she shouted.

'He said you jumped on him,' I said in a quieter voice.

'And you believe him,' she said looking mutinous.

'Yes. I think I do,' I said looking back at her.

'I thought you might say that. Anyway I'm going out. I don't have anything to say to you.'

'Oh Ellie don't go. Please let's talk about this...'

'I have nothing to say. I would never do that and if you can't see that I don't know you at all.'

'But why would he, Ellie I, he wouldn't lie, is there another...' I was flustered.

'He IS lying Angel.'

I looked at her trying to work it all out.

'I don't even like him Angel.'

Her voice was measured and cold. I'd never heard her like this.

'What am I meant to do Ellie? Accuse him of lying?' I said.

'That would work,' she said and stalked out, slamming the front door.

Sniffling I call Nick. No answer, his phone's off. I was suddenly overwhelmingly tired. I felt miserable and alone. I curled up and watched a video without taking it in. It felt creepier being in the flat alone. I could hear noises from Kevin's flat downstairs. He was moving around preparing for his nightly trip out no doubt. Or dancing with his snake. Suddenly all the strange rattling noises, muffled cries and general madness didn't seem funny or anything to laugh about. It seemed frightening. I tensed as I heard him pacing for what seemed the millionth time that night. I'd never noticed so much movement before. I felt vulnerable without Ellie to tell me I was being silly. Or to get scared with me. In my room I turned on some music and lay in bed mulling everything over until I must have fallen into a restless sleep. I dreamed of drowning in a sea of blood. I reckoned that wasn't a good thing.

* * *

I woke to the song 'Aint no sunshine when she's gone,' which seemed suitably ironic. I'd hardly been in work for half an hour when Suzie could be seen stalking over to my desk. Before she was within a couple of metres of my desk she had started on me.

'I spoke to Ellie last night. She called me to check if you were OK.'

'Oh right.'

'Then she told me what happened,' she went on.

'I see,' I said levelly.

'Are you mad Angel? Of course Ellie didn't do anything with Nick.'

Tally, desperately trying to focus on sewing a button, almost jabbed herself in the finger with the needle she was concentrating so hard.

'She's distraught,' Suzie said, not mincing her words.

'Well I know. But after what she did it's only right that she's upset,' I muttered sullenly.

'Angel she wouldn't have done anything' she said scornfully.

I started to protest, 'But Nick told me she came on to him.'

Tally was now scanning some invisible document on her computer to block us both out.

'Well he's obviously lying.'

'You weren't there Suzie.'

'I didn't need to be there. There is no way Ellie would do that and you know that.'

I shrugged.

'Don't you?' she repeated looking at me.

I looked at her, 'But Nick said that she was all over him.'

'Of course he said that. He was cornered. Anyway he was so rude turning up late, he was drunk, and he hasn't been treating you well at all recently.'

'I know but he seemed so genuine,' I said, willing her to understand.

'He isn't trustworthy,' she said matter-of-factly.

'All men are snakes,' Tally chipped in, all pretence at not listening to us forgotten.

'Exactly,' said Suzie spinning around, glad for the back up.

'Fine I'll talk to him,' I said sulkily.

'Good, because Angel Ellie would never do anything like that. She's far too nice.'

'I know,' I said in a small voice.

I started psyching up the courage to call Nick. I suppose the little bit of me had known all along that Ellie had been telling the truth. I had just hoped otherwise. I sighed, realising I had to grudgingly admit that my boyfriend could in fact be a lying, cheating no good... the phone shrilled. It was Mel.

'How did it go the other night?' she asked in a small voice, trying hard not to sound too curious. 'I thought I'd give you a bit of space to sort it out. So has it all been um... sorted?' She asked hopefully.

'Not really.'

'Oh.'

'Ellie and I haven't spoken which hasn't been great and everyone has been lecturing me already, saying Ellie would never do that.'

'Suzie?' Mel guessed.

'Yes,' I giggled a bit.

'Well I hate to say it...' said Mel.

'Go on,' I sighed.

'But I think she's right. Ellie just wouldn't do that.'

'I know. I do know, I just...' I vented a bit of frustration, 'It's just so unfair.'

'I know it's shit. He is a shit,' stressed Mel.

'Anyway look I better go Mel. And I've got to do some work,' I said looking at the pile of letters left unread in front of me.

'Oh Angel before you go will you do me a favour?'

'Sure what is it?' I asked.

'Could you come and help me with Zac's party on Sunday? Peter's worried he won't be able to control them all.'

I was too distracted by my plight to make up an excuse, 'Yes sure. Fine. Give me a call later this week to remind me.'

'Thanks Angel and good luck with Nick. Hope it all works out.'

I hung up on her sighing. And what had I signed up for? A seven year olds birthday party. Sounded wild. Still Mel needed the support. I would cross that bridge when I came to it. My phone went off again. Rick was on the end of the line.

'I know what you're going to say,' I yelped, having heard enough for one morning.

'Oh Angel pants, Angel pants. What a dilemma.'

'I know,' I said miserably, glad that Rick was being so sympathetic.

'Ellie is so lovely,' he cooed, 'But then Nick is so gorgeous.' He paused, clearly torn in his loyalties for a moment. 'What are you going to do?'

'I'm going to confront him I suppose,' I said sounding more confident than I felt.

'Oh he's so pretty it's such a shame,' sighed Rick.

'It's not over Rick,' I said defensively.

'Oh I know but well... if he kissed her don't stick around for him to walk all over you.'

'I won't,' I sighed, 'It could have been a misunderstanding you know or... or... Well Ellie might have kissed him,' I said sounding desperate.

'You know Ellie would never do that,' Rick repeated.

'I know, I know I know I know, I know...'

And suddenly I really did know. I didn't want to know. Yes I was happy Ellie wouldn't have to move out and we'd still be friends but no I wasn't happy that Nick had lied to me. Why had he lied to me?

'Why did you lie to me,' I said the moment he picked up the receiver.

'What who's... ah, Angel,' the voice said, 'Hello darling. Didn't we discuss the fact that you weren't to call me at work?'

'Yes we did discuss the fact Nicholas (Nicholas? – he must be in trouble) but I want to know why you told me my best friend lunged at you when she did nothing of the sort.'

A pause.

I wavered; waiting for his explanation of why he did it. Why he had felt the need to behave like that? To lie? Maybe our relationship had all got too much for him? Maybe he needed to hurt others to ease his own hurt from childhood? Maybe he had wanted me to be jealous? Maybe he had been so drunk he didn't have any control over any of his bodily parts?

I was ready to hear it. I'd feel a little pain and then we could make up and move on. He could apologise, I could ooh and aah for a bit and then he could woo me once more and our relationship would survive its greatest test so far. We could work through this. It wasn't like anyone had done anything much.

Nick was still pausing.

'She kissed me Angel,' came the pitiful reply.

'Bollocks,' I scoffed, 'You were drunk and you tried to kiss her. What I want to know is why?'

He exhaled loudly down the phone. 'Why not?'

'I'm sorry,' I said momentarily confused.

'I said,' came a sneer, 'Why not?'

'What's that meant to mean?'

'So I was drunk and I made a mistake. I'm not perfect.'

'I know but I've just spent the weekend ignoring my best friend and...'

'Well it's not my bloody fault you're so over-emotional. It was one kiss for Christ's sake.'

'Yes but...'

'Deal with it,' and he hung up.

I sat staring at the receiver in my hand. A little voice within me told me that hadn't gone quite to plan. I lowered the receiver and stared at the phone for a few more seconds, not quite believing that brief phone call was it. His whole explanation. All I was going to get. I'd been hoping for some easily explained misunderstanding. He'd been reaching for a spoon, he'd tripped, he'd found himself wrapped around Ellie. She'd got the wrong idea and assumed the worst. I'd burst in on the scene before it could be explained. Silly him and silly us for falling out over it. We might even have laughed and japed about it in the future. That kind of thing.

I hadn't expected that.

* * *

I could see Victoria walking over to my desk and I tried to look more alert. She seemed to be looking at me. Maybe she had heard I had been a bit upset and wanted to offer me a shoulder to cry on, a place I could go for comfort and... Then I caught sight of her expression... Oh no, could my day get any worse...

'Angela I'd like to see you a minute please,' she said coming over to my desk. Her tone didn't imply she wanted to offer me a pay rise or a company car. My stomach plummeted. I felt like I was at school being summoned to the Headmistresses Office. It seems my day could get worse. I sneaked in feeling fairly nervous. Why was I here?

'Well Angela I'm sure you know why you're here,' she said staring at me as she sat down behind her desk.

Had she over heard? Did she know all about Ellie and Nick and...

'These came to my attention,' she said waving at some pieces of paper in front of her. I craned my neck to see what they were.

'Did you find it funny?' She asked, clearly bewildered.

'Funny?' I repeated, extremely confused now. 'Sorry I don't understand.'

'Shall I read one to you?' she asked coldly. Then I caught sight of what she was holding. It was a letter, in my handwriting. Ah...

I started to feel a little clammy.

'Let's see,' she said putting on a pair of glasses and reading, 'This girl wrote *'Dear Angel, I think my boyfriend is in love with his ex. He has a photo of her in his locker and talks about her all the time. I don't think he finds me as pretty or fun but I love him. What shall I do?"*

She looked up at me and I squirmed a little more.

'This is what you wrote in reply. *'Dearest Charlotte, It is potentially probable that your youthful gentleman harbours feelings for his previous beau. But I am unquestionably persuaded that the avenue to pursue is to converse in a discussion of your beliefs in the company of him. Solicit him to be honest, truthful, sincere, candid and frank and I'm convinced she will be converted into a phenomenon of yesteryear.*

Yours sincerely Angel'.'

Victoria looked up from her reading.

I shifted uncomfortably. This was clearly the pile of letters from the thesaurus batch. Victoria was obviously not a fan of my newly improved intellectual style.

'Why the five words meaning honest?' Victoria asked peering at me over the sheet of paper.

'Well I thought him being truthful was important so I highlighted it.'

She looked at me disdainfully, 'Highlighted it by using five different words that all mean the same thing Angela. Do you really think that was completely necessary?'

'Um... well... I thought perhaps...' I was floundering. She was waiting for my explanation. Maybe she would believe me if I actually spoke like the letters. That I was that intellectual naturally. I rooted around for some complicated vocabulary to convince her.

'Well you see I often peruse through the correspondence and er... realise that,' I was started to lightly perspire now, I hated being put on the spot like this... 'Realise that those who digest the... um... information regarding their personal development frequently discover the...'

'Yes Angela.'

'I just thought I should make it a little more of an interesting read. Thought- provoking. Our readers aren't stupid you know.'

'Yes thank you for informing me of that,' she said coldly.

'I just thought, well, the magazine's not exactly high brow is it?' I muttered mirroring the criticisms levelled at me by Nick.

'No Angela it's not high brow. It's not meant to be high brow. It's inclusive. The language we use is important. We are not writing for the readers of The Guardian. Our readers are teenagers and we need to use language they understand.'

I began to feel a little silly.

'You can't send any of these,' she said sighing, 'Honestly Angela I thought your work ethic this last week has been excellent. But then I read this and just think what a waste of time and effort...'

'I'm sorry,' I said interrupting her, 'I don't know what came over me. I wanted to try and make my letters a little more exciting.'

'Angel your letters are fine. Please go back to writing them in language we all understand.'

'I will. Absolutely. I really am sorry,' I said reaching out for the letters on her desk. 'I'll re write them.'

'Do,' she said and then gave me a little smile, 'Honestly Angel.'

I skulked back to my desk, relieved that she had seen the funny side.

Re-writing the letters took me the rest of the day and I managed to carefully avoid any conversation with people around me. I still couldn't believe that Nick had been so cold. The phone call had been so final. Was it really all over? Before I started fretting I forced my eyes back to the page in front of me. I had been lucky that Victoria had been so decent about the letters. She could have been much more severe. I couldn't even understand some of them. I definitely needed to abandon attempts to be an intellectual. I replaced them with simpler versions and shorter words. I left on the dot of five, escaping the office and Suzie's eyes before I would have to go into my day.

Ellie was already ensconced on the sofa when I wearily pushed the door open an hour later. She looked up, instantly on edge.

'So you got what you wanted,' I said.

'I'm sorry,' she said frowning at me.

I gave up trying to be spiteful. I was tired.

'Look Ellie I'm really sorry. I know he was lying. We broke up.'

'Oh.'

There was a bit of a silence.

'He was a git,' she said helpfully.

'I know.'

Then she came over and hugged me.

'I'm really sorry Angel.'

I sniffed a bit. Pitifully. 'I'm sorry for not believing you. I just didn't want to think he would do that and I...'

'I know, I know,' she soothed rubbing me on the back.

'No Ellie I really am sorry. I feel awful.'

'It's fine. Honestly. Come on I'll get some wine from the fridge,' she said plonking me on the sofa. 'We'll just stay in and watch a DVD.'

I nodded and sat back listening to her cluttering around in the kitchen.

I was relieved she had been so sweet to me about the last few days. She really was such a good friend. I felt tearful as I realised what a bitch I'd been. How could I ever have thought she would do that to me?

She handed me a glass and settled down in front of the television. We half heartedly watched a bit of the news and some show full of celebrities showing off their pets. It was good being back in the flat with no tension. I relaxed into the sofa and stared blankly at the screen.

After a while she had to ask.

'So what did he actually say when you called?'

I explained. When she heard about the phone call her mouth was raging in indignation. 'What! He just gave you no explanation, no reason at all.'

'None,' I said.

'What gave you no reason at all?'

I shook my head.

'None. Absolutely none,' she repeated clearly at a loss.

'God, what a bastard. Honestly Angel you can do so much better.'

'Alright Ellie,' I said giggling weakly, 'I'm not quite ready to start looking for a replacement.'

We sat sipping in silence.

'That's horrendous,' she fumed.

'Hmm...'

'God he's worse than I originally thought,' she said furiously.

'Hmm...'

'He's a pig.'

'Hmm...'

'No, that's too mean to pigs. He's a cockroach. A stinky, hard shelled, filthy cockroach.'

'Right,' I muttered.

'A cockroach,' she repeated nodding her head.

* * *

Hi agony aunt/uncle,
I am a male age 22 and never had sex in my life. Now I am getting married. My problem is that I have a small and bent penis. Will it be a problem in intercourse, plz explain clearly.
Patrizio, 22, Stafford

Dear Patrizio,
I'm sure it will be fine. If you are marrying her, she will be pleased. A lot of men shy from commitment, and though their genitalia is in working order, their capacity to love is not. I cannot see why your new wife will mind too much, at least you are there for her.
Angel

The week dragged by in a fit of nervous tension, constantly hoping that every phone call and every text message might be from Nick. Then hoping that every phone call and text message was not from my father. To compound my great mood Dad had chosen this moment to ring up and rant regularly about the neighbour's cat. I had to endure daily reports about the animal's activities and its deliberately malicious lavatorial habits.

At work my mind was constantly flitting from the letters. My new found industriousness was waning. I couldn't be bothered with all the teenage angst when my own life was falling apart. I put the small but bent penis reply to one side and stared at the next letter for a little. It was from a girl worried about her boyfriend. I rushed off a slightly half hearted reply, trying not to sound too bitter. At least Kimberley, 14, from Bolton had a man that loved her. And fine so it sounded like he was cheating on her with her mate from the orchestra but it wasn't over like it was for me. He hadn't told her it was done, finished, ended. He'd just wanted to carry on being with her, albeit with the flutist too.

With a little start I thought back to the memory of Nick and Ellie in the kitchen. What if there had been other Ellie's? Maybe Nick is seeing someone from an orchestra. Maybe he's happy right now and not worrying about me or feeling queasy at the memory. He'd dumped me; it was so unfair. He'd had longer to adjust to the idea, or maybe he'd just never cared. I steered away from further analysis. It was like a permanent repeat of Trisha in my head, the same episode over and over.

Apparently I wasn't allowed to mope about it too long. Ellie was on damage control. She had taken on the role Guardian of the Phone with relish. She'd taken to moving my mobile phone around the flat so that I had to keep ringing myself on the landline to find it. Any minute she'd start checking my text messages like some jealous lover. Although she really didn't need to. Any text message from Nick would be instantly reported in full, complete with a half an hour conversation wondering what the text meant; does he miss me? does he want me back? is it a subliminal message to get me to reach out and forgive him? should I reply? Etc, etc. I never got the chance to obsess though. He never texted. I was however texted by everyone else in my phone book, although they were mainly texting me to not text him and that made most messages a little frustrating.

'ICE QUEEN DARLING ICE QUEEN love Rick'
'I'll know if you have so you better not text him, Ellie'
'Don't bloody touch that phone to contact that snivelling little jumped up loser, Suzie'
'Hope you're ok; call me if you want to chat. Mel'
'I've made a casserole for this weekend if you want to come home, mum'

After days of absolute stubborn refusal to pick up a phone I started to weaken. I thought my silence would be enough to prompt Nick into action but my phone remained silent. And I'd checked with my phone operator and it was working. So that wasn't it. I checked with the network too, just in case, but apparently there were no unusual glitches in the system. So I came to the conclusion that he hadn't dialled my number. Then I wondered if he was waiting for me to call, but then I remembered the whole point of why I wasn't calling (because he is an adulterer and an Evil Man) and didn't give in. But my resolve was definitely weakening. I could feel my grip on reality slipping a bit when Heart FM played Bryan Adams. And then the moment came. I knew it would. One day.

It was a Thursday night. I felt lonely. There was no one in the flat. I was drinking Kahlua, (and only half-heartedly adding milk) straight out of the bottle. I'd just watched a countdown of 'TV's Most Romantic Moments,' so I really shouldn't be blamed. It just happened. My finger slipped m'lord. I sent a text message.

For a second I thought it might not have sent. This was the second in between me sending it and the delivery report saying it had sent. I'd rung the phone operator back to see if there was anything they could do to stop it being read the other end. Apparently they get this a lot. They said they couldn't help. They were "sorry", as if that were going to ease my state of mind. I polished off the rest of the Kahlua.

Then I wandered the flat.

I made myself a toasted cheese sandwich. I unravelled a thread in the curtains. I threw paper at the bin in the corner. I wrung my hands. I sighed. I drunk a bit more. I then reckoned work would be the best solution to my misery and looked around unsteadily for something to write with. Pen in hand and the back of a cereal box handy I started scribbling some replies.

'Dear Laura
I think its very sad that you are thinking you're fat but don't care what they all say your school I think you are lovely and I would want to be your friend as you are so nice and it doesn't matter if you are a bit pudgy or not.'

'Dear Paul it is a shame that you have a long nose but my mate who used to like the rolling stones had one too and he was fine and works in America now. So you'll be too I think.'

'Dear Angel, I am really embarrassed. My right boob is bigger than my left boob. I don't know what to do. Don't tell me to see my doctor. Cerys, 15.'

I re-read it. Then I re-read it. The pen I'd been writing with clattered to the floor as my hands flew to my top. I pottered unsteadily through to the bathroom clutching my chest. I stood in front of the mirror, looked all around me and tentatively lifted up my top. Note: buy underwear. Stared at boobs for about six minutes and by end was totally convinced that left breast was larger than right one, in unnatural and freaky way. Definitely. Oh god. How had I never noticed this before? It was there, the evidence right in front of me. I leant my face against the mirror in despair. Why was everything going so wrong? Clearly I was doomed to roam this earth with an unnaturally sized left breast. And Nick hadn't texted back so I was just some sad lopsided big left breasted loser who would never have a boyfriend and would have to join up with people on singles holidays and learn to play solitaire with marbles. I staggered back through to the living room feeling sickened and collapsed on my bed. Before passing out I called Rick. We arranged to meet the next day for an emergency coffee shop summit. I asked him to ring in the morning and remind me we'd spoken and then I don't remember the rest.

* * *

Rick did call to remind me and I managed to heave my Kahlua-filled carcass to the coffee shop just in time. Incredibly the urgent nature of my call had prompted us both to be on time. I saw him hurrying down the street with a suitably concerned look on his face. Or it might have been his urgent need to pee. Which he then told me about in minute detail.

'Is it normal Angel to have pea green urine? That doesn't seem right does it?'

I quickly reminded him I was not part of his medical fraternity and would he please stop talking to me about his faeces. Especially as I was feeling so delicate.

When I said this he looked at my reddened eyes, sighed and folded me in a massive bear hug. I quite clearly had Tragic Case written across my forehead. I wriggled out of his embrace and settled back down into my chair. I'd reserved us a table for two near the back and had already ordered a blueberry muffin to pass the time.

'Darling, can I get you a coffee?' he asked at the counter, giving eyes at the Coffee Machine Man who I'd hardly even registered. I say hardly because I was heartbroken, not blind. Even in my Emergency State the man was still a fox, and those kinds of looks can't go unnoticed. I still had a pulse.

'I'm fine,' I said nibbling sadly at my muffin. True friend Rick didn't linger or try to engage Coffee Machine Man in talk, he'd realised from my demeanour that now was not the time to hit on men. Now was the time to help me.

'So,' he said flinging his bag under the table and shifting his chair closer to the table for a more in-yer-face interrogation style chat. 'What's happened?' he asked. Suddenly everything seemed such an effort to muster up. My mind was fogged with thoughts and the face of Nick Sheldon-Wade. I smiled weakly and tried to change the subject.

'Oh not much. How are you?' I asked, adding a high pitched 'Hmm...' to lighten the effect. Rick just stared at me as if I was mad.

'Sweetheart who the fuck cares how I am, now spill the dirt. What's happened? Has that gorgeous Nicholas been a shit again?'

I cringed as he said his name so flippantly, 'No, no. Well we haven't spoken all week and... well... I didn't know what to do and so I...'

'Yessss,' he said ripping the Demerara packet with his teeth.

'I... I missed him so I thought it might be alright to get in touch and so I... I should have called him but I didn't have the guts, well, some things are better on paper you know and well, I thought I'd...'

'Yessss,' he said stirring the sugar in slowly.

'I texted him,' I ended finally, 'And I have a boob that is bigger than the other boob so now he'll never want me.'

'What? You texted him.'

'AND I have one huge boob and one little one,' I repeated.

'Don't be silly darling you have gorgeous boobs. If I was straight I would stare at them all the time. And that's not the point anyway what did the text say?'

'Nothing.'

'Angel, show it to me.'

'No I can't, anyway it doesn't matter I'm a one boobed freak. No one will want me. If you had one short arm and one long arm wouldn't you want it fixed?'

'What... just show me the text.'

'I'm a freak,' I repeated.

'Show me the text.'

'No.'

'Angel, show me it.'

'I don't want to. And one boob is huge and the right one is little. I'm never going to live it down. I'm considering surgery.'

'I don't want to hear it Angel, give me the phone.'

'No.'

'Well show me your breasts instead then,' he said sitting back.

'No.'

'Well then... phone,' he said reaching out.

'Oh fine,' I said huffily. I handed it to him and sat in a sulk.

I could see his face twitching as he scrolled down. I waited expectantly for the verdict, and panicked a little as the silence continued. He looked up at me and then reached out for my hand to stroke it.

'Aggh, that bad,' I said and banged my head down on the table. Then the tears came. Excellent, that would make me seem much less tragic.

After a few seconds of patting my head uselessly Rick swung to attention. 'OK. So courses of action,' he announced, mulling it over a bit. 'You must stop calling and texting him,' he said firmly.

'But I...'

'Ba ba ba,' he said hushing me, 'It's for your own good. No more communication from now on. Nothing in Morse code, no telegrams, love letters, things in Braille... nothing.'

'I get the picture,' I grumbled.

'And no pictures,' he added, concerned I had found the loophole.

I looked at him scathingly.

'Now next thing, you must not mull it all over, you have to get a grip. It's OK you crying in front of me in a coffee shop but other people won't be up for it.'

'Thanks,' I said feeling even more stupid.

'Stop wondering what he's up to and get a life of your own.'

'Yes sir.'

'Stop drinking by your self as that only ends in tears.'

'I never, well I usually never...'

'And you were drinking with who exactly last night?'

'Ellie was there.'

He looked at me disbelievingly.

'Fine, Ellie was there for a little while but... oh carry on.'

'You could write down all the things you want to do to him,' he said.

I looked up startled.

'NOT in a sexual disgusting way you filthy madam, surely

you feel like cutting his balls off by now?'

'I don't,' I said miserably.

'Well that will come, for now start to feel a bit of rage. You deserved to be treated with respect and he should be sorry.'

'He should be,' I repeated.

'And most importantly go out, look devastatingly gorgeous and bag yourself a new man.'

'I don't want a new man.'

'Yes you do Angel. Then you can flaunt him under the nose of the nasty Nicholas who'll be so overcome with jealous he'll either kill himself or beg you to come back...' he finished triumphantly.

I had to admit that this was a better reason than most for shopping around for a new boyfriend. But I was still not persuaded.

'I can't go out,' I said instantly feeling exhausted by the very idea.

'Yes you can, you have to have some fun Angel.'

'But I...'

'I don't want to hear it,' he said silencing me in what must have been his most masterful tone 'So first step,' he continued looking appraisingly at me in my sad little state. 'Look gorgeous.' The mascara in rivers down my face was certainly not helping my image as a sex kitten but after wiping them on the muffin napkin I was ready to hear about suitable outfits and hair styles. Rick went into some detail and after a few more minutes I'd started to think going out might just be the best solution. Like the old days, dancing into the early hours, knocking back cocktails and dressing up glitzy. We arranged to meet the next night and Rick promised he'd organize some others to join us. A small glimmer of excitement pricked through the Clouds Of Doom and I returned to the office feeling marginally better.

Dear Angel,
I broke up with my boyfriend a week ago and really miss him. I'm crying the whole time and my mates said he misses me too, what should I do?
Lucy, Bournemouth

Lucy I'm so glad you wrote to me. Do not worry. You are

feeling lonely but that will pass over time. You've got to remember that you're young and single. The world is your oyster. Move on! Don't spend your time moping around after some boy, get out there and have some fun. Hold your head high and other boys will come running. Good luck.

As I signed off I prayed I was right.

* * *

Saturday arrived in a burst of sunshine and weather reports announcing a mini heat wave. I instantly decided to celebrate the novelty of the glorious, sunshiny English weather with a day of sunbathing. Reclining deckchair under the one arm and Cosmopolitan under the other I headed straight for our little communal garden. No one from the flat above was down there and Ellie was visiting her sick Aunt. A figure was moving in the downstairs flat and I squinted my eyes against the sun. I thought I could make out a face in the small window, but it had shrunk back into the shadows before I'd had time to focus. Kreepy Kevin no doubt. He'd hung some wind chimes in one of the windows which gave out an ominous sort of low haunting sound every time the breeze blew. Typical. Today however was too nice a day to worry about him and his Kreepy ways so I went back to arranging various items around me in a summery way.

Sunglasses yes, pint glass of Pimms yes, sunhat yes, sun cream factor 15 yes. I settled down supping at the Pimms and idly flicking through the fashion pages of Cosmopolitan. It was bliss. In fact the only glitch in the day was the realization that most of my wardrobe appeared to have suddenly become unfashionable and now if I didn't have anything with tassels on I might as well be dead. Then spirits lifted when I remembered fashion moves in cycles so surely did not have too long a wait till I am cool again. Hooray.

Magazines abandoned I was enjoying draping myself on the reclining deckchair to sun my back. It was definitely getting warmer. I fell into a lovely daydream about sandy beaches, fresh water lagoons and a gorgeous boyfriend who looked just like George Clooney. Then he turned into Nick and my eyes jolted open. I picked up another magazine and started reading furiously. I was quickly distracted as the article was all about a woman who'd just had her stomach stapled by a surgeon who wasn't a surgeon, but was apparently a 'cowboy,' which hadn't made for the best results and now she was infected and was considering suing and... I'd forgotten all about my thoughts. The article had included photos. I lay back and relaxed once more now trying to block out thoughts of Nick, and fat women with infected, red bits.

I decided to try and develop an all over tan. The sun was getting hot on my back and I'd just read that strap marks were 'Out' (along with wedge heels and the colour green). Reached behind me to unclip my bra but, as I reached, weight unbalanced and chair decided to slowly tip backwards. I ended up horizontal, grass up my nose, legs waving in the air and neck set at a crazy angle with bra dangling half off. Realised Kreepy Kevin might possibly have witnessed the entire display, so couldn't just get up casually. Instead I pretended it was just what I had planned to do so, with neck still a little squiffy, rolled on to my side pretending to want to sleep. Cunning. Was careful not to flash breast-bigger-than-the-other-breast, which would lead to terrible unleashing of secret, so clutched top to me in weird pretending-to-be-asleep position. Soon got really uncomfortable though, and couldn't reach Pimms, so decided to exit in one swift movement so as not to expose myself to anymore unwanted attention. I ran, blushing, up to the flat leaving my belongings scattered around the garden. I vowed to return, at nightfall, to clear up the strewn mess.

Still determined that today would be a positive day I set about improving my life through the art of Feng Shui. Tally had given me the article on it, which was going in next month's issue of the magazine. I scouted for it in my bag. Steps needed to be taken to improve my general karma, and my room was a mess and needed a good clean. Either way it couldn't hurt to get some extra help from the cosmos. Looking around my room, crumpled article in my hand, I realised with slow horror it was no wonder everything in my life was going down the pan. Straight lines, dark colours, furniture facing in entirely the wrong direction – I had a lot of work to do. The first things to go were the arty long, dry twigs in a vase by the window. The spiky edges on each branch were apparently to be blamed for my terrible financial situation. They were probably costing me hundreds of pounds a year just sitting there and I was shocked to realise their fiscal power. I rammed them, and their spiky edges, into a black bin liner, never to cost me sterling again. Other sharp items were immediately removed (nail scissors were locked away, tweezers were put in my make up bag) just in case they embodied similar damaging power.

My goldfish were about the only positive in the whole room. I double checked they were still alive. The article informed me that living things encouraged a good flow of positive energy and, though the tank was a little grimy, I could still just about make out that they were half heartedly swimming about. I felt relieved. I reckoned dead goldfish would be a Feng Shui no-no. Then I turned my attention to the bed. Was concerned that the burgundy throw draped over it was causing it to be a 'stressful area' so folded it up and popped it in my wardrobe to be on the safe side. Dark colours were out and pale colours were in. As were round mirrors, pot plants and clocks. None of which I had. I unearthed an old watch, still ticking if you shook it, and placed it on my chest of drawers. Then I rearranged the furniture a little to look like the room in the photo. My bed was moved around to the east to improve my wisdom. I popped a couple of books on my bedside table to stress this fact even more. I was just dragging my rug around to a new spot when my mobile rang.

Sneezing from the dust I picked it up. It was my mother no doubt ringing for a weekend catch up. I answered.

'Mum.'

'How are you?' she asked, her weekend catch up question number one.

I was too exhausted to go into precise detail, so plumped for an 'I'm fine,' reply.

'What are you up to this weekend?' was her second question on the catch up.

'I'm Feng Shuiing my room,' I announced.

Silence from my mother who was obviously not a follower of the trend.

'And I'm going to go out tonight with some friends,' I added helpfully.

'What a lovely idea, after all that working. You need to let your hair down. Going anywhere nice?' she asked pleased to be on a topic she understood.

'No idea. Somewhere central I think,' I said lightly dusting nearby surfaces with a dirty rag.

'Well be careful Angel. I do worry about you being in London you know, all those muggers and criminals,' she said dramatically.

'I'll be fine Mum.'

'And who are you going out dancing with?' she asked.

'Rick.'

'Nick?'

'No,' I said hastily; keen to not go into recent events with my mother quite yet, 'Rick.'

'Have we met him?'

'No. I've told you about him though...You know I went to uni with him, blonde, camp, loud, slightly irritating,' I described.

'Is that your homosexual friend?'

'Yes mother.'

'Oh he sounds like a nice boy' said mum, keen to display just how hip and politically correct she was, 'And is Nick joining you there?'

'Hmm...' I muttered indistinctly. I took a tactical divert, 'So any news from home?'

'No. Nothing much around here. Well your sister has managed to hurt her back. She fell down some pot hole in a car park. Probably drunk,' she added, 'and Ed's on the seconds for cricket.'

'And how's Dad?' I asked.

'He's fine, well, he's still on about the cat next door. He nearly smashed the conservatory window today banging on it to scare it off...'

'Oh dear,' I muttered rooting around under my bed for a missing shoe, 'He told me it's been playing up.'

'He needs to calm down or he'll have a heart attack,' my mother warned, 'Doug from down the road had a heart attack at 63. So young. Lost all movement in his left side. Well I best get on,' my mother chirruped.

Poor Doug. I hadn't had time to register her exit and was left holding the phone in my hand and my yellow rag in the other. I finished up the clean, had a bath and prepared to get ready for a night out.

* * *

Yes I loved being single. I remembered now. I was singing along, screeching out the chorus to some Christina Aguilera and dancing around my new look bedroom in my underwear. A glass of wine sloshed in my hand and Rick was on the phone telling me to hurry up. I remembered the fun I used to have. Tonight I was going out with some of my best friends. We were going to go to bars, clubs; we were going to be spontaneous. OK fine we were going to be quite spontaneous but I knew we were heading to Roxie's around 10.30pm because it's really hard to get in there any time after that. Nights like these are what it's all about. We will meet people, chat in a sophisticated wine bar way about our jobs, our trendy social lives, whilst supping at Margarita cocktails and bopping to R and B. The single way of life, I love it.

I remembered to go and collect my things from the garden and went down to scoop them up before I left for the night. Someone had already placed them in a little pile, magazines tidily stacked and the rest in a neat little bundle. It must have been Kevin, no one else was in the house this weekend. I wonder what he'd been doing with my things. I imagined him rifling through my possessions on some dark purpose. I double-checked that everything was there. One of the free sachets of perfumes in Cosmopolitan had gone missing. He had obviously taken it for himself or was putting it on the snake. Eugh. I couldn't let the thought fester however as the taxi beeped at me from the street and I was off to be single and carefree.

Five hours later I am sitting on a bench outside 'Club Fiesta' gabbling words of Turkish to the doner kebab van man opposite whilst dribbling cheese down my chin. I've sunk to a new low. Rick is wrapped around a blonde with a tight t-shirt and spiky gelled hair. I've remembered, single is not fun. I hate being single. A taxi honks as it passes. Pigeons are feasting on the crumbs around my feet. How did I get here? I consider getting up from the bench. Rick is now snogging the blonde man.

Single at the end of a Saturday night. This is not what it's all about. The energetic singing is over and my outfit, that looked so good five hours ago, is looking tired and crinkly and stained. I suddenly remembered past nights like these. The night when my strap broke, the night in 'Vibes' getting hit on by lesbians, the night I fell pissed down some stairs. I got up and wobbled uncertainly over to the man in the van.

I looked at him blearily, 'Kofte Kebab.'

I hear Rick and the blonde giggling about something, 'Large please.'

I hand over my last fiver.

Muttering good bye to Rick I walk home. Kebab in hand and head trailing. Then it started lightly raining. Mini heatwave my arse.

I miss Nick. More to the point I miss being tucked up in bed with Nick, having sex with Nick and not bothering to have to go out to search for another Nick (not that I necessarily want a man called Nick, that would make the search a whole lot harder, but someone like Nick only not quite like Nick who dumped me and is a bastard, would do.) Then I'd be happy and not walking home with a handful of meat and some shrivelled salad items to pass out alone in old make up and three inch heels.

It was in this state of mind that I woke up, head pounding, mouth dry. I must win him back. I didn't want to be without him. Nothing else was going well at the moment with the acting, or the magazine job, and having a boyfriend had been something fun, something good. For the most part. Anyway I had proved I was useless at being single, I hadn't got the energy for it. I hadn't got the energy for much this morning. And worse it was Sunday morning and I was expected to be at Mel's for Zac's birthday party. Not good. The very idea of a room made up of thirty seven year olds and one clown filled me with dread. What had I been thinking signing up to that one? I couldn't face it. I was definitely too depressed. I reached out for my mobile but as if Mel and I were suddenly psychically one it started to ring and, sure enough, Mystic Mel was on the end of the line.

'You are not going to call me later and cancel Angel,' she said in an unusually authoritative tone.

'Er...'

'You are not,' she repeated. 'Right, I have to go I haven't got time to talk. It will be good for you to be there, take your mind off things...' she went on, 'So I'll see you in a couple of hours. Byeeee.'

So I was going then.

Three hours, a shower, five glasses of water, two

paracetamol and a mug of coffee later I set off for the party. I'd forgotten to get Zac anything so I stopped at the newsagents and purchased five tubes of Smarties on the way.

I rung the doorbell and was quickly bustled into the house by Peter, 'Hi Ang...'

The moment he opened his mouth he was instantly sprung on by a crowd of seven year olds who proceeded to attach themselves to every limb. I could hear his muffled yelling of, 'She's in the kitchen,' before he was overcome by the ambush. I gingerly stepped around the mayhem and went to find Mel and some refuge.

'Angel you made it,' she said as I pushed my way into the kitchen. She was surrounded by cakes and sweets and chocolates. It was like a diabetic's wet dream. She reached over and gave me a quick hug, 'How have you been?' she asked.

I tried to sound suitably buoyant for her and gave a hearty, 'Very well thank you.'

Mel looked at me with searing precision, 'You just need to take your mind off things,' she said confidently.

I was immediately put on spooning chocolate mousse duty. I had to dollop portions of the mousse into little plastic bowls with Mickey Mouse printed on the side. Mickey seemed happy. Big smile, a kick in his step, a twinkle in his eye. I wondered whether I'd ever be happy, like Mickey, again. Or was it the kind of happiness only mice can find? I wish I were a mouse. Is that enough mousse?

'Angel are you sure you're ok with that?' Mel asked from somewhere distant.

'I'm fine,' I said in a voice that instantly made me sound far from it.

'Angel?' she repeated slowly.

'I'm fine; really,' I said trying to perk up by thinking of Mickey, that jaunty little guy.

'Maybe spooning mousse is giving you too much time to dwell,' she said thoughtfully.

'Nick did love puddings,' I said nodding, voice instantly threatening to crack.

'Right,' she said wiping her hands on her apron, 'You go and help Peter watch the kids and I'll carry on in here alright.'

'OK,' I said dragging myself off to the living room.

Suddenly realised as the screaming got louder I might have led myself into a raw deal. I pushed open the door to find children dangling from chairs, balloons stuck on the ceiling, one boy licking a photo frame and one girl almost completely hidden under a sea of wrapping paper. Peter was busily showing five boys how to blow raspberries with their hands.

We managed to introduce some kind of order to the group by being assertive, in control and up for some bribery. Soon children were in a circle, music was playing, parcels were being passed and the more aggressive kids were clinging on longest waiting for the music to stop. Of course Peter and I were in charge of seeing that the aggressive children didn't open any parcels and the quieter ones all came out bewildered winners. With lots of shouts of 'no looking, no looking,' we paused the music so that everybody had a go. None of the children, aggressive or otherwise, thought to ever question the process. The magic of youth, so trusting. After a run of Grandmother's Footsteps, Musical Statues and Musical Chairs we were on to singing. We'd covered such classics as 'The Wheels on the Bus' and the ever popular; 'Heads, Shoulders, Knees and Toes' and I was beginning to feel a bit tired from all the exertion. It was when a 'Nick' won Musical Bumps that I spiralled into a bit of a decline. Mel spotted something was amiss.

'Get in here,' she said closing the kitchen door behind us.

'Sit,' she said pointing to a chair. I sat down without questioning her. Her tone was not one to reckon with.

'Are you OK?' she asked looking at me.

'I'm fine... honestly I'm...'

She cut me off abruptly, 'Angel I have never seen anyone look that depressed when singing "If you're happy and you know it clap your hands". You are miserable.'

I didn't have the strength to argue with her. It was a fairly obvious conclusion. She wasn't exactly Miss Marple material yet.

'Angel what's up? You're not normally like this over men, what's so special about this one?'

'Nothing. I'm being stupid. I'm sorry,' I said, feeling guilty for being such bad company.

'No really, what is it. Tell me Angel.'

'Well it's just, well, I really liked him and I thought he liked me but...' she looked at me sympathetically as I soldiered on, 'He just... he just doesn't want me,' I said helplessly.

'I suppose it's always harder when you know you like them more than they like you,' she mused.

I looked at her aghast.

'He didn't really make a massive effort did he?' she said probingly.

'I suppose not,' I admitted grudgingly, 'But he was busy with work,' I protested.

'Yes but they find the time if they want to don't they,' she continued in an irritatingly gentle voice, reaching to offer me a Fun Size Snickers.

'I just really liked him,' I wailed, 'and I miss him. A lot.'

'I know, and you've never had this before Angel. Men have always followed you around, so it's hard when you meet someone who doesn't make as much effort as you.'

'I suppose so,' I shrugged opening the Snickers.

'Believe me,' she said warming to her topic, 'I've got ugly friends who are like this all the time. They always fall hard and the bloke is just un-bothered. They are constantly heart broken and...'

I looked at her as she filtered off.

'Are you saying I'm ugly?'

'Oh shit of course not but what I mean is... you've never had this before but others have.'

'What ugly people have.'

'Well er... not always ugly people.'

'You said they were ugly. Do you think I'm ugly? Oh my god I'm ugly. Is that why Nick dumped me?'

'Of course not. Don't be ridiculous Angel, you're stunning. Anyway he didn't dump you he's just an arsehole.'

'He isn't.'

'Angel.'

'Fine he is, but I still miss him.'

'Fair enough. You're allowed to.'

'Mummmmeeeeee,' came a wail from the living room, 'Julie's got my Lego in her ear.'

'Coming,' she hollered back and then turned to me, 'Just don't mope for long, he's not worth it.'

'I won't,' I said giving her a weak smile.

Mel sighed and went back through to extract the Lego and ensure no one needed hospital attention.

I felt guilty for lumbering her with my problems. I didn't want to be this boringly unhappy. I thought about what she'd said. Nick had bothered me. It was true. I had to admit that past boyfriends had been controllable; I'd always known that they had liked me. But Nick had liked me, I thought fiercely. I know he had. When we first met he couldn't get enough of me. He'd thought I was living the high life, an actress schmoozing amongst celebrities and casting directors. Inviting people round for canapés and cocktails. Dressing up and hitting the tiles. His naughty little school girl. He'd called me every day, invited me out to every night and bought me presents. He'd liked me. I just didn't know when that had ended. Or why.

I could hear Mel next door grappling with control and tried not to sink further into my thoughts. I would help her out. I would be Super Friend, entertaining small children and keeping the peace. Within five minutes I found myself orchestrating a game of Sleeping Lions with the entire room of seven year olds. Mel was back to baking five hundred cookies, Peter was rescuing balloons and all of us were waiting expectantly for Cosmo the Clown, who was apparently stuck on the A303 in traffic.

After my stint as Grand Games Master we were all on a break for tea munching on chocolate crispies, sausage rolls, ham sandwiches and strawberry jelly. There was relative calm as they chomped on their E numbers and played with the new presents. I looked around the room pensively. Girls and boys were all playing together. Two girls and a boy were busily racing sausage rolls across the carpet and two others were popping bubble wrap pieces together. There was no sign of sexual politics. No sign that anything was unusual about this set up. Zac was sitting next to a girl called Charlotte and showing her his new red electronically controlled car. And it wasn't in a 'Hey, Char, see this car – it is an extension of my penis' way because he doesn't know he has one. Well not a working one. Well... you get the picture. He wasn't playing mind games with her. Charlotte wasn't sitting there going, 'Why is he showing me his car? Does showing me his car suggest that Zac likes me... like that?' No, she was just looking at the car. They were friends. I sighed. It had been so much simpler then.

I thought back to the time when men hadn't bothered me at all. When my stomach didn't plummet to a new low when their name was mentioned. When boys and men were brothers and fathers. When the telephone never rang for me; and that wasn't a problem. When my parents went out more frequently than me and that wasn't a big deal. Those days. I'd been oblivious to the grown up being that was Man. I knew nothing about him. I mean Barbie's Ken had been all smooth upfront. He'd been a eunuch for crying out loud – what was I supposed to know? Through school men hadn't bothered me. I'd played sports, did well in English classes, performed in the school plays, sung in the choir. I didn't fret about looking good. I hadn't concerned myself with Valentines Day or the boys in Form 5. I had just pottered about, perfectly content, collecting the Sylvanian Family and going to ballet.

Why couldn't I go back to Those Days? I could reverse the clock. Sign up to numerous extra-curricular activities. Become one of those women who had hobbies. I imagined myself now joining Salsa clubs, watercolour classes and poetry circles instead of worrying about my love life. I could probably become editor of the magazine in a year with the energy and time I'd save. I'd be able to get into work at dawn, leave at ten. I'd help the environment, recycle more often, give clothes away, enjoy emotional freedom and the occasional gin and tonic of an evening. I'd be one of those women who write to magazines advising other woman to put baking soda and lemon on it to remove the stain. I'd make people hand painted candlesticks for their birthdays and would laminate recipes to give to my friends. I smiled at Zac and Charlotte. I would be just like them. I would go back to having innocent, good old-fashioned fun. As I was smiling inanely at my perfect world Charlotte went to take control of the red vehicle and Zac pushed her down. She started crying. I sighed. Maybe nothing changes. It appears all men are mean from such an early age. I got up to separate them before any bloodshed could occur.

'That was bad Zac,' I said doing my best naughty-boy voice. I don't think it worked. Zac just called me a Fudge Head and went on his way. I checked on Charlotte who, despite wearing a salmon pink dress, seemed a sturdy girl and was soon wiggling out of my grasp to play with loo roll with the other children. Small pleasures I suppose.

Mel was right I didn't get like this over men. Maybe it was

because it had all ended so suddenly? Maybe I just needed closure? I realised I had to talk to him about it. He'd been so abrupt with me on the phone. I needed to know definitely that he did not want to be with me. Maybe it had just been a fight and he was waiting for me to initiate contact? Either way I didn't care. I couldn't keep moping around like I was. So first thing on Monday morning I called him, and we arranged to meet after work on Tuesday and I didn't tell anyone about it, knowing instinctively they might not see it as progress. But I hugged it close to myself all morning. And on top of the shame was a stronger, more positive feeling. It was Hope.

* * *

I had been carefully avoiding talking about Nick to both Ellie, because she hated him, and Suzie, because she would just tell me to get a grip. Suzie's heart was made of strong stuff; mine was a little more prone to breakages. So when she marched me off for lunch with her I immediately felt emotionally exhausted by the prospect.

'Angel,' she said peering at me over a Big Mac, 'How have you been?'

'I'm fine thanks,' I said looking down at my fries in front of me.

'Hey I have actually been worried about you, you know,' she said reaching across the table to pat my hand. Her sympathetic voice immediately melted me. I look up at her in what I know is a hopelessly pitiful way. I can't help it. Lately my expressions range from abused puppy in dogs home to injured puppy on roadside. I'm a walking personification of the word Melancholy. Which of course Mel finds really funny. Prompting jokes like, 'Now we're both Mel' to try and push me over the edge into suicide.

I tried to make a bit more of an effort or otherwise I knew I'd cry. And that didn't seem appropriate in a bustling McDonalds on Oxford Street. I tried a bit of distracting small talk.

'So what happened with Chris?' I asked her.

'Who?'

'Chris... advertising... fit... the one from the dinner party.' These were all the facts I could muster.

'Oh yeah' she mused, 'No,' she concluded. 'He was sweet, but a bit dull. I'm better off being single. And to be honest with you Angel I think it's actually a good thing that you're not with Nick anymore. You can do a lot better.'

'Hmmm maybe,' I muttered, wondering if I should tell her about the meeting I'd arranged for tomorrow.

'He really didn't seem to be that thoughtful. I think you're definitely better off without him...' she went on.

I better own up.

'...I mean to turn up half the way through that dinner hammered, not even apologise when you'd made all that effort and then try and pull Ellie.' I cringed from the comment, missing my opportunity to confess.

'It was just low of him and you need to be with someone better than that.'

She continued to spell out the many reasons why I was far better off without him until I could take it no more.

'I called him actually.'

She stopped mid-spiel.

'When?'

'This morning. I told him I wanted to meet up after work this week.'

'But isn't it over between you two?' she asked.

'Well sort of,' I admitted, 'but it was all so sudden I wanted to talk to him about it all.'

'So, what did he say?' she asked.

'Well I can't remember exactly what he said.'

'Well give me the gist.'

'Well I said, Hey Nick how have you been and he said Fine and I said I miss you and he said Angela I'm quite busy this end and I said Can we meet up some time and he said How about after work and I said when and he said Tuesday and I said Where and he said the bar round the corner from work and I said, the one on the corner of Temple Street and he said No Angela that's the Burger King and I said I know that I'm not stupid and he said I know and then he sort of sighed through his nostrils like this (I exhaled) and I said OK I'll see you there at six and he said Fine.'

'But you can't remember exactly.'

I blushed, 'I didn't... well anyway that's tomorrow, so what do you think I should do?'

'What do you mean do? Why are you going anyway?' she said looking at me.

'What do you mean why.'

'What's the point?' she shrugged.

'The point,' I repeated, clearly not on the same page.

'Yes Angel. Why are you seeing him?' she spelt out.

'I have to win him back,' I announced confidently.

'Why?' she said.

'What do you mean why?' I said, back to parroting her lines back to her, 'I think there's a chance we can salvage our relationship.'

'Your relationship,' she said sceptically, taking up the parroting for me. 'Angel he ended it with you and you were only together for six months.'

'Eight,' I corrected.

'Ooh,' she said with, if I'm not mistaken, just a hint of sarcasm.

'And you can get to know some one really well in that time,' I added.

'Yes but it's not exactly till death us do part stuff is it, you weren't about to marry the guy.'

I paused, 'I might've,' I said.

Suzie looked at me with as much disdain as she could muster, 'Angel you're twenty-six and you were seeing him for eight months, you weren't about to marry him.'

'Not immediately,' I agreed, 'But later perhaps.'

'Christ I would have married Chris 'later perhaps'.'

'Suze you went out with Chris for two dates, if that...' I argued.

'Ahhh, but later perhaps,' she sighed.

'It's not the same Suzie.'

'Fine. So you miss him. That's fair enough, of course you miss him. Everyone hates the end of a relationship,' she said matter-of-factly, 'But it wasn't a long term thing and he cheated on you Angel.'

'No he tried to cheat on me, that's not the same thing.'

'Fine he tried to, but tried with your best friend Angel, and god knows who else.'

'What have you heard,' I said looking up. 'What other woman were there?'

'I haven't heard anything I'm just saying that maybe Ellie wasn't the first.'

I sunk into my chair. 'We don't know that,' I argued, 'He might be feeling really guilty about the whole thing and want to explain'

'But Angel he hasn't called you to meet and explain has he, you called him.'

'Look I miss him Suzie what am I meant to do?'

'I know, and it's not fair, but you've got to leave it Angel he's not worth it.'

'I don't want to be single again?' I moaned, 'I've been there I've done that. It's not for me.'

'You're just mulling over the worst, think of the good things,' she said looking at me encouragingly.

'What good things?'

'The fact that you're free to focus on your career.'

I scoffed at this.

Suzie changed tack, 'You can sleep on both sides of the bed, you can eat when, where and what you like, you can go out whenever you like... those kind of things. And anyway there are other men out there you know, just waiting to screw us over.'

'Good to know,' I said glumly, 'Anyway I don't want anyone else,' I went on stubbornly.

'What! Ever? Don't be so dramatic.'

'No not ever, ever, but not for a while.'

'The best thing to do is to get back on the horse and ride it,' she said without a hint of irony.

'I did. I climbed back on the horse. I went out on Friday with Rick. It was rubbish. I hate being single,' I said stubbornly.

'Going clubbing with Rick is not the best way to embrace the single way. Did he take you to Vibes? Did he make you dance to the Macarena? Did he get off with someone and then let you walk home alone...?'

I sat in a stroppy silence as she ticked these points off on her hand. I hated that about Suzie. In her books she is always right, and what made it worse is the fact that she is actually always right. Hmmph.

'...Did he get the DJ to do a shout out for a new boyfriend for you?'

'None of this is the point.' I said ending her righteous spiel. 'I miss Nick.'

'Fine,' she said, 'See him, but you don't need to be with him, or anyone else for that matter. Don't let him walk all over you again.'

'I won't Suzie, I just want to see him and hear what he has to say.'

'OK, OK. All I'm saying is be careful. We better get back to the office,' she said looking at her watch.

* * *

I had one of those afternoons at work you dread. Lots of paperwork, lots of people to call, lots of people coming over to annoy you. By the time I got home that evening I was ready to collapse on the nearest squishy item to hand. Ellie had been in all day and was currently doing some vague dusting with a spray can and a mouldy looking yellow cloth. I'd nodded to her as I passed hoping she wouldn't try and make me join her.

After a little while I heard her holler, 'Angel come in here.'

I was in the midst of curling my hair. I sighed and put down the tongs. 'Coming.'

I imagined now I would be forced into a bandana and given an identical mouldy yellow cloth. However when I walked into the sitting room Ellie was on her hands and knees on the carpet, cloth forgotten and ear to the floor.

'What are you doing?' I asked standing over her.

'Ssh,' she hissed, 'Listen.' With her ear still on the floor she swivelled her eyes up to fix on me. 'Can you hear?'

I didn't need to put my ear to the floor to realise she was talking about the downstairs flat. Even from my standing position I could distinctly hear raised voices emanating from below.

'They're yelling,' I said stating the obvious.

Although we often heard movement, the weird wind chimes, rattling and water pipes, we had never heard yelling from downstairs. In fact I don't think we'd ever heard talking from downstairs. Ellie was squinting with the effort of listening in.

'I think it's a she and she said something about him being selfish,' she whispered, 'Or something about shell fish, I'm not absolutely sure.'

I strained to hear distinct speech but could just make out muffled yelling. Ellie was moving around the room now listening out for a clearer patch of carpet.

'Ellie do you think you should be...'

'Ssh.'

I shut up but, unable to make out any specific words, I got pretty bored pretty quickly. I walked through to the kitchen and picked up a glass. Seconds later I was crouching by Ellie's side.

'OK what have we got,' I said listening in. Ellie smiled at me.

'She's angry at him for something. I bet it's that blonde woman you saw the other day. Wonder whether they are going out?' she mused.

'Maybe I...'

'Ssh...' she interrupted me, 'Did you hear that?'

'What?' I asked, amused that Ellie had turned into such a nosey neighbour.

'He's yelling back. He's telling her to leave it alone.'

There was more shouting now, both had raised their voices. As I listened in I started to make out some words.

Half way through one bit I got confused, 'What did he say? He billed her?' I said wrinkling my nose.

'No.'

Ellie looked a little shaken. She had sat up. Her face was pale.

'He said he killed her.'

We both jumped as a door banged shut. I stared at Ellie.

That night I really missed Nick. It would have been good to have him by my side convincing me that I was being a crazy and over emotional female. Ellie and I had tried to convince each other we had simply misheard or misunderstood the conversation but we were still on edge all night. The flat downstairs had gone completely silent and we flinched any time the water pipes gurgled into life. Ellie made repeated promises to never listen to people through a glass on the floor again. After assuring each other for the hundredth time it had all been a silly misunderstanding we had both ventured to bed. I slept badly in my big double bed alone, wishing I had someone with their arms around me making me feel that little bit safer.

It had all seemed a little better in the morning. It was a bright, warm day and in the daylight everything seemed a lot less

Kreepy. I decided to stop stressing about weird neighbours and go back to stressing about other things in my life.

I was helped along by Richard, always keen to maximize my stress levels at any opportunity. After delivering another batch of letters to my desk he then informed me that I had to write a 1,000 word article about 'Dealing with Death' for next months issue of the magazine. I wondered how Richard as Head of Features had the authority to demand this of me but my defences were low and I was still scared to do anything else that might put Victoria's nose out of joint.

'Of course Richard I'll just dash something off for you now shall I,' I said sarcastically, pointing at the letters in front of me.

'We're all busy Angel,' he sighed pompously.

'I know,' I gritted my teeth.

'It shouldn't take too long,' he insisted, 'Not for an agony aunt of your calibre,' he smiled, 'And just think you'll have an article in the magazine! Not just some little letters.'

'Just think,' I repeated petulantly.

'I've popped in a few leaflets to help you with your research,' he pointed to the pile.

'Right thank you,' I said giving him a strained smile and hoping he'd leave me alone now.

'Don't make it too disheartening,' he said.

'Fine.'

'And don't make it too dark. Remember the magazine is being read by kids,' he pointed out helpfully.

'It's about death Richard,' I said slightly exasperated.

'Yes but we don't want it to be depressing. It's got to encourage people to deal with death,' he explained with a little smile on his lips.

'You want an upbeat piece on death,' I summed up.

'By next Friday,' he nodded curtly. I watched him walk back to his groupies at Features and mouthed a silent expletive at his back.

I started doing a little research on the article. Reading stories from the internet. Scanning the leaflets for advice on how to deal with people passing on. Suzie came over to talk to Tally about the arrangements for their latest photo shoot. When she looked up at me I had an exasperated look on my face.

'You alright Angel?'

'The lovely Richard has landed me with yet more work,' I moaned, 'He wants me to be upbeat about death,' I wailed.

As Deputy Editor she could do little but nod her head and look sympathetic, 'Has Mary written recently?' Suzie asked to change tack. I begrudgingly let her change topics.

'She did actually. Yesterday. Just a short note.'

'Well how did it turn out with Bernard and the mistress from the Patisserie Section?'

'She reckons it's finished between them because he's been a little bit more attentive this week. She actually sounded infuriatingly optimistic.'

'And you know that he'll just be scheming something else while she thinks everything is going to turn out fine,' sighed Suzie.

'I know, but maybe we're pessimists Suze,' I argued, 'Maybe he will change?' I looked hopeful.

'Men never change,' said Suzie flatly.

'Oh Angel,' called Richard as he passed, 'Deadline's been cut a little shorter. Monday OK for you?'

I scowled at him.

Suzie smiled sympathetically again.

Tally looked up at me,

'If you had to choose would you have long hair all over your body or a life long marriage to Richard?'

I smiled weakly at her, 'Long hair.'

Fortunately all the extra work load put me off worrying about my meeting with Nick later that night. By the time I was home I barely had time to panic. In a massive hurry I flung my clothes off in the corridor and jumped into the shower. Forty minutes later I was dressed and made up and yelling good bye to Ellie. She came to the flat door to wave me off.

'You look gorgeous, it's totally wasted on him,' she sighed.

'Ellie don't...' I said picking up my keys.

'I know, I know you have to talk to him. Fine. Just be careful.'

She sent me off like a concerned parent on her daughters' first day at school. 'So just a drink and don't stay and chat too long. And if he tries to kiss you on the lips tip your head. He must apologise. And promise to treat you better. Oh, and find out if he was sleeping with anyone else behind your back. And good luck.'

Well maybe not exactly like the first day at school.

After a tube journey smoothing my hair and re-applying my lip gloss on I stepped out onto Liverpool Street. Ahead of me was a billboard saying 'More people are coming back to BT than ever before,' an advert for a phone company or a sign from the gods saying 'Reconciliation is on the cards'?

He was already sitting at the bar. His long legs were stretched out in front of him and he was casually flicking through the FT, his blonde hair flopping over his face as he read in earnest. My heart flipped over and I was suddenly a million times more nervous.

'Hey,' I said shyly.

He looked up from his reading to kiss me on both cheeks and then motioned to a chair by the bar. I didn't really know what to do next. So I sat there while he ordered me a Vodka and Diet Coke trying to repeat Ellie's earlier advice in my head. But it was already swimming around in a jumble. Make sure he tries to kiss you on the lips and stay long and treat him better. No, no that wasn't it. Stay long but make him tip his head. I took a mental deep breath to steady the nerves... Calm blue ocean, calm blue ocean.

I started running through a nice opening question. Something safe about his job, his current work. Nick sat back down and looked at me. I sipped my drink. Then without so much as a 'Would You Like A Pack of Peanuts,' which on closer reflection I realised was probably a dud offer as this was the kind of place that sneered at the common or garden peanut, he looked right at me and said, 'I'm sorry it didn't work out Angel.'

He then shrugged and knocked back his beer. There goes asking about his day...

'Oh.' I took a sip at my drink.

'I'm too young to be tied down I guess. It was time to move on.'

'Right... time to move on?' I repeated, looking genuinely confused. Wasn't this the part where he was meant to look at me in my new Karen Miller top, note my perfectly applied make up, gasp, tell me I look amazing, that he was gutted we'd been apart so long, that he'd been a fool to have left someone so gorgeous so suddenly, and that we simply must, must get back together this instant? Or at least try to kiss me. Or pretend we'd never broken up at all and it was some horrible misunderstanding? He certainly wasn't meant to be launching into the reasons why he didn't want to be with me. That was not part of the script at all.

'This... this got too much,' he gestured between us.

I looked at him.

'It just moved too fast Angel.'

'Too fast. But...'

'I don't think I was ready,' he nodded solemnly.

'But...,' I gesticulated a little in the air, 'I gave you your space didn't I? And we had a good time didn't we? You didn't complain before. I thought it was going well.'

'It was, it was great Angel.' My heart lifted, it was Hope raising its head again. Maybe this was the moment where he would reconsider and take it all back. I looked expectant as he went on. 'But I missed my freedom and I'm too young to be tied down babe.'

Tied down, there it was again. I slumped on my stool, anyone would think I was some frantic nagging fishwife, 'home by six so baby can have a bath and be settled, you can bring home them work things n all.' But I wasn't, we'd had fun, he'd just confirmed that, so it wasn't some bizarre illusion I was under. But I could almost hear how un fun I was being now. The whine was slowly creeping into my words.

'Could we just try again maybe?'

Oh Angela where is the request for an apology? Where is your cool? Where is your self respect? I couldn't help myself. Maybe I have an illness? But I had to say it didn't I? I had to keep going. I'd sunk low enough now. I had to finish with a bit of unrestrained begging for good measure.

'...I promise I'll give you lots of space and won't tie you down.' I petered off into another silence and Nick finally had the decency to shift uncomfortably in his chair.

'No I'm sorry, look maybe its best we don't keep doing this,' he said gesturing between us again as if I was constantly meeting up with him to beg and plead. I had only done it the once for gods sake.

'Do what?' I said trying to make light of the fact that my stomach had felt like someone had punched me in it.

'This Angel.' The gesturing was repeated just to bang the point home. 'Maybe its best to not see each other for a while.'

'Oh yes. Right. That's fine. I would have said the same thing,' I said putting on a brave face about three weeks too late and trying to gloss over the previous comments about wanting to be with him again forever amen. 'Best thing.' I muttered as he drained his beer and stood up.

'Well I think that needed to be said. Sorry babes. I'll see you round.'

'Oh yes OK. Yeah.'

He kissed me on both cheeks and I watched him move easily through the crowd and out of the doors.

See you round.

That hadn't gone exactly as I'd hoped. I got up to go.

'You going to pay for that drink or what,' the bar man asked.

'I'm sorry' I said looking up.

'That, Vodka and diet coke wasn't it. Four pound forty.'

'Oh, of course, I'd thought he'd... doesn't matter.' I paid him and left the bar in a daze, drifting to the tube station and trying not to cry.

The next couple of days were miserable. I felt even worse which was an impressive feat when I thought I'd felt pretty crappy before. At least then I'd had lovely denial, reliable solid denial always there to give me a bit of hope and let me carry on with my day. Now I just felt so rejected. He didn't want me, I'd tied him down. I hadn't meant to but I'd made him feel cornered. When did it start to go wrong? Why did I have to do that? When did I do that? How did I do that? When had I become so over-bearing, such a drag, such a stone weighing him down. I missed denial. All I had now was misery. Misery, misery, miserable misery.

Dear Angel,

I think my boyfriend might be cheating on me as he won't let me ever read his messages on his phone. I've been snogging his best mate from football practise though and he hasn't been told yet so I reckon we should break up, but he says he loves me a lot so I don't know. And the football practise guy has snogged my other mate in the shopping centre so I don't know whether he's right for me. Should I stay with my boyfriend then?

Cerys, Swansea

As if I am meant to know the answer when you don't. I've never even met him, or you. You all sound horrendous, you deserve each other.

* * *

Everyone was doing their best to rally round me and make me forget to mope. Rick, now convinced that he was in the early stages of psoriasis because of a slight rash on his elbow, had only emerged from his fervent study of the condition to join the trend to cheer me up. We decided to go to the cinema, bonding without the need for too much talk and dark enough to hide Rick's dissolving elbows.

I'd let Rick choose the movie which was a re-run of the film 'Hero,' which I hadn't seen the first time round. It was chosen by Rick 'in an effort to expand our minds.' And to impress his new Pilates instructor who told him about it. It's a martial arts film. Not usually my cup of tea but I go along with it... crouching tigers hidden dragons, I know my martial arts jargon. Hi ya.

Keen to ensure we had adequate time to buy popcorn, soft drinks, pic 'n' mix and ice cream we had arrived suitably early. They weren't letting anyone in for a few minutes so we sat on a nearby bench waiting eagerly for the doors to open.

'How's the situation with Nick?' asked Rick, never one to skirt round an issue. 'Have you heard from him?'

'Well I was talking to Suzie who suggested that we should attempt to pursue a platonic friendship for the time being,' I quoted.

'Meaning?'

'You know, maybe I was the cause of all the antagonism in our relationship and I was unable to recognize that we were drifting apart so now it's probably best to...'

During my spiel I noticed Rick looking at me in bewilderment. I brought it down to his level, 'OK you know that film where Julia Roberts plays that horse lady.'

'Is that the one with Richard Gere?'

'Er no, that's Pretty Woman.'

'Right... Is it the one where she keeps getting married?'

'Runaway Bride.'

'Yes that's it, with Richard Gere,' he said triumphantly.

'No, not that one. And Richard Gere isn't in it.'

'Pretty Woman's the one about the hooker.'

'I know but... Well anyway Rick it's not either of those films. It's the one where she plays this horse lady.'

'Right.'

'Do you know which film I mean Rick?'

'Yes.'

'Who's in it?'

'OK, No.'

'OK well it doesn't matter anyway – she is married and her husband cheats on her and then she goes to vet school.'

'Oh I know this one,' interjected Rick with a burst.

'Good, well...'

'Bit of an obscure one...'

'I know but well... you know the bit where she invites him round for dinner and...'

'Are you meant to be Julia or the sister?' Rick mused.

'It doesn't matter...'

'Oh right, because I don't think the sister's anything like you.'

'That's not the point. Listen. It's at the dinner that she realises she pushed him away long before he cheated on her. Do you see?'

'How do you mean she's a horse lady.'

'She looks after horses,' I said exasperatedly, 'But that's not the point.'

'Right.'

'Do you see?'

'Yes. Absolutely.' He said solemnly. 'Oooh I think they're letting us in now,' he said jumping up.

I traipsed behind him to settle in front of a screen for a couple of hours.

The film seems to be essentially about an assassin who goes to assassinate the emperor and then doesn't. He then gets killed by about 100,000 arrows. As deaths go it is fairly conclusive. There are characters called Moon and Snow and Broken Sword. There are lots of characters who seem able to swoop through the air at any given moment. Gravity apparently being an unheard of concept in martial arts films. There was a lot of wailing, clashing of swords, swirling and flying. Moon does a lot of poofy crying for a man who knows how to kill in three movements, and there's a passionate double suicide on a mountain in the desert. We both leave determined to take up Tae Kwon Do and hungry for a Chinese takeaway.

'So what do you think will happen with you and Nick?'
'Well Ellie says he wasn't the right guy for me.'
'How do you mean,' he said slurping the last of his drink.
'You know the film 'My Best Friends Wedding'?'
'Oh god, why are you always comparing yourself with Julia Roberts?'
'I'm not.'
'Sure. You're not.'
'So in the film…'
'Is Richard Gere in that one?'
'No.' I said quickly; keen to not start that up again.
'Who is then.'
'The guy who was in 'Friends' for a bit. But it's not relevant, so anyway in the film she thinks she's right for him but she's not. He knows that and ends up shagging Cameron Diaz and she dances with Rupert Everett, who's like you.'
'Why because he's gay? He's nothing like me Angel.'
'Fine, he's nothing like you.' I said rolling my eyes to move on to my reasoning.
'Do you fancy Julia Roberts Angela? Because you talk about her a lot.'
I ignore him.
'…and the bloke and her they stay friends,' I said with emphasis, 'So maybe Nick will stay friends with me.'
'Angela you don't want to be friends with Nick, you want to have sex with Nick.'
'So.' I said petulantly.
'So Angela, friends aren't meant to walk around secretly lusting after each other.'
'Why not,' I said, knowing that I sounded pouty.
'Because well, what would you advise your readers to do?' He asked, unfairly handing me the baton back.
'I would… I'd… Oh… They're just kids, that isn't the same.' I whined. There's a bit of a silence after this.
'Rupert Everett and I couldn't be more different. He is a totally different kind of gay man. I represent the group of gay

men who...'

I make a mental note never to talk about Julia Roberts again.

* * *

I managed to get through the next few days. I had been trying particularly hard not to become too bitter in my letters. I wrote the article 'Dealing with Death.' Richard had only made me rewrite it twice. I made a voodoo of him out of photocopying paper. I had been visiting the gym; I was a regular at Body Combat classes (I had a lot of aggression to vent). I had even half dialled the phone number of BOS Productions about seeing them for an audition. Soon a couple of weeks had passed. I had survived.

Everyone was trying to keep me busy. Suzie and I had been out for a huge number of 'working lunches' and Ellie kept making me come with her to her yoga classes. Mel had been feverishly discussing wedding food and bridesmaids outfits with me and I had now agreed to accompany her to Zac's end of term parents meeting as Peter was working. It seemed my friends believed involving me in any activity was an improvement on leaving me alone with my thoughts.

Zac attended a day school in South London. As we drove through the gates of the school I was suddenly transported to another world. Everywhere I looked coiffured mothers stood about pulling their jackets about them, chattering to their other mummy friends and simultaneously wiping chocolate off the face of their little darling. They looked years older than Mel who in her suede A-line skirt and heels looked like a fresh faced teacher and not a mother of one. I suddenly realised her desperation in wanting me there.

Various signs herded us towards a large hall. We were bustled in with the other parents and stood looking around as to where to start. Around the walls were signs announcing, 'Biology,' 'Religious Studies,' 'Physical Education' and beneath them sat a little row of staff behind tables talking sincerely about their pupils. Queues had already formed leading away from these tables. At the back stood huddles of mothers and fathers talking animatedly about what they'd just heard and what they were about to hear. I noticed a little corner with a few desolate looking tables and a counter with two large urns being manned by two large women.

'I'll get us some tea,' I said delaying the crush for a queue. I approached the nearest tea lady who looked suspiciously like she might be a witch. She had managed to pile her almost jet black hair into a bun on top of her head. Her large arms were encased in a black top and she had the compulsory mole on her face. I quickly checked for six fingers. They were hidden by the urn. Well of course they were. I wouldn't go about broadcasting my supernatural qualities.

'Two teas please,' I asked the witch. She popped two tea bags in the cups and started filling them up from the urn. Her hands moved too quickly for me to count the digits.

'Milk?'

'Sorry, oh... Yes please.'

'Sugar?'

'Um... one with, one without please.'

I was handed two cups on saucers, the tea in one already slightly swilling over the side.

'How much is that?' I asked witch woman.

'We're raising money for orphans in Africa,' she said rattling a tin at me. 'Give what you feel appropriate,' she said glaring at me. I quickly put the two teas down on the table in front of me.

'Oh right, I see, I'll just find my purse,' I said, slightly flustered. Was she asking me what was appropriate for a cup of tea, or appropriate as an offering to help the plight of a nation of starving children? My panic was rising, made worse by the continued rattle of her tin as she stood waiting for me to hand over any life savings I'd just happened to stash in my bag. Was 50p going to make me look like a tight-fisted cow? I started fumbling for change. Moments passed as I sorted past a mobile phone, two boiled sweets, about eight pens...

'Difficulties?' came a voice from behind me.

'Something like that,' I replied triumphantly locating my purse amongst the various paraphernalia in my bag. The witch was still staring at me, no doubt placing some ancient curse on my well-heeled head. I scolded myself for looking so middle class and well orf.

The voice behind me piped up again, 'Parents meetings always throw me into a spin.'

'Hmm,' I replied distractedly, 'Absolutely...' I finished, at last pulling out a shiny sovereign for the witch's rattling can. I popped it in quickly before she could finish her spell and turned with the teas to acknowledge the voice in my ear.

I found myself looking up at a tall man with scruffy dark brown hair. He was dressed in a suit and tie and was looking at me with piercingly blue eyes.

'So which one's yours,' the lone father enquired.

'I'm sorry,' I stammered, thrown by the eyes.

'Which one's yours,' he repeated.

'Oh er... Er... that one,' I said without thinking, pointing to a group of boys near the end of the hall. The man peered over, looking confused for a brief moment.

'Who? James?' he asked.

'Er... yes. Sure. Why not.' I picked up the two teas again trying not to catch his eye.

'I know him,' the man nodded. Damn.

I tried to steer the subject away quickly. 'Oh yes, parents meetings, so hectic,' I tutted, rolling my eyes in what I hoped looked like a knowing motherly way.

'Yes the kids don't like them.'

'Oh I know,' I said over-enthusiastically (it was the eyes again. They had some kind of magical effect.) 'Little Jimmy always gets very nervous.' Well done girl that is just the way to gloss over the lie.

I thought I saw a glint of amusement in the eye of the attractive man, 'Little Jimmy, eh.'

'Yes... well er, that's just a pet name I like to use for James, he's such a sweet boy.' I said doing a good job of looking dreamy about little Jimmy as if he were Tiny Tim and it was Christmas time. I had absolutely no idea what I was doing talking lovingly about an imaginary child to a ridiculously attractive man but the actress in me was prompting all my lines.

'I think these meetings really do little to improve his performance in class... they just make me nervous...' I said laughing in a light tinkly way as I thought any mother would.

'Absolutely, well I best get on, it was nice to have met you Mrs er...' he held out his hand to me, which left me helplessly gesturing with the two cups of tea.

'Oh er...' I started, 'It's Miss actually.' The attractive man raised one eyebrow at me as I rushed on as if I were on the stage of Trisha and about to tell all.

'Jimmy's er... father and me never er... married,' I finished. What was I doing? Why? Why was I still talking?

'Oh how sad,' he gave me a warm smile, 'Right well Miss... Miss, I must get back.'

'Right of course,' I said quick to realise that he was obviously used to listening to strange single mothers and their broken homes at every parents meeting, and all he was really here to know is if his little nipper is going to get on to the cricket team that year. As he walked away I realised I'd forgotten to ask about his children. Lucky things to have a daddy like that. Kodak cameras could hire him for their adverts. Man running along beach with child on back. Man gazing lovingly at wife in sand dunes etc. I'd love a daddy like that, all gooey eyes and gorgeous smiles. Although Freud might have a thing to say about it all. Suddenly realised in my warped daddy musings that the two teas I was clutching were getting cold. I craned my neck to search for Mel and spotted her hemmed in by a woman wearing a sour expression and a nasty tangerine neck scarf. She caught my eye in what was clearly a call of distress. I rushed over.

'Mel, your tea,' I interrupted.

'Oh thank you,' Mel said overly politely and clearly relieved at the intrusion.

The woman began wrapping up, 'Well I'm glad I got a chance to talk to you Melanie. I hope this puts an end to it,' she said and then with a flick of her tangerine scarf she was gone.

'Who was that?' I asked, handing the teacup to Mel.

'Mrs Coles. Her son's in Zac's class. She says Zac keeps calling him a 'Donkey Head' and it's upsetting him,' she sighed.

I stifled a laugh.

'Surely there are worse things than a Donkey Head. Donkey Bum would have been much more rude.'

'Apparently her son's got paranoia about his front teeth poking out or something.'

'What so he actually looks like a Donkey?' I asked.

'Slightly I suppose.'

'Sounds like Zac was just being honest,' I said with a grin.

'Right well why don't we start. You do English, Science and

P.E, because that's what he's best at, and I'll take Maths, History and Geography. I'll meet you back here at 12.'

'OK then.'

I looked around the walls for the sign for 'English' and then made my way through the clusters of parents. I stood sipping idly at my tea in the queue looking around the hall. I heard proud fathers booming glowing reports at their meek wives. Confident mothers were smoothing their skirts down preparing themselves for the proud news that yes, one day, Suzanna could study law at Cambridge and Richard could definitely stand for Parliament. Then there were one or two more hopeless cases. One woman in the Maths queue was gripping her hands together in silent prayer. These poor children. Such expectations. At 5-11 could they really tell? I neared the front of the queue beginning to get a little nervous that Zac wouldn't be quite up to scratch.

Glancing at the teacher under the sign announcing 'English' I started. I looked again. Oh god. Mr Kodak Camera was a teacher. I froze for a second and then when I'd just made my mind up that I would turn and run in the other direction it was my turn. The woman in front got up positively glowing from the chair at his desk and Miss Miss was being beckoned forward. It took me a few seconds to recognise this was my cue. I sat on the chair and gave him a weak smile.

'Hello again,' he said in a friendly voice.

'Yes,' I said vaguely in reply. We sat there a little longer; he was looking at me expectantly.

'Right well you'll want to know Little Jimmy's progress in my class?' he prompted.

'Well... I.'

'I'm afraid I don't have the pleasure of teaching him.' He spoke with a twinkle in his eye. I shook myself.

'Er... no. I know you don't, but I would like to talk to you about Zachary Beecham.'

'Oh dear. Is there some kind of a problem with Zachary and Little Jimmy?'

'Er... no, not exactly. Well I'm friends with Zachary's mother and she's asked me to see if he's doing well in....'

'Miss Miss.' I stopped mid-flutter and looked at him; fortunately he was giving me a repeat look of that melting, warm smile. 'Zac's doing very well in my class.'

'Really,' I said trying to sound business-like whilst shifting uncomfortably in my chair.

'Yes he's a good kid and a pleasure to teach.'

'Oh well. That's great. Super,' I muttered.

'He's got a good grasp of grammar and spelling and a very creative imagination.'

'Yes I can imagine,' I said, thinking back to the Donkey Head comment.

'Is there anything else you'd like to know?' he asked.

'No, no, that's all... well... best get on,' I said in a terrible gun ho style voice only just stopping short of slapping my thigh enthusiastically. I raced out of the seat and looked back in time to see a shapely blonde, complete with set curls plant her rear into the chair after me. I started for P.E. miserably. I was such a Donkey Head.

There were four P.E teachers sitting at the table waiting to talk to the queue of parents. Most were fathers wanting to talk sport or ogle the tennis instructor, or both. They bunched up towards her end so the queue moved surprisingly quickly. I listened as a butch looking woman in a tracksuit, tried to sign up someone's daughter to the Under 8's England netball team. The mother in question was beaming with pride. Another, slightly balding, coach next door was saying that Kirsty was a lovely little footballer with (from what I could pick up) excellent ball skills. Lucky Kirsty. Wish I had them. I was left to talk to the mousey looking woman who ran the Trampoline. She said Zac was very good on it and we left it at that.

I finished up with a visit to Science where I was told that Zac might possibly be the most talented biologist the school had ever known. No one, he insisted, took up with more enthusiasm, the offer to dissect a frog. No one was so fascinated by the internal organs of a woodlice. No one wanted to experiment so much with the effects of acid on cloth/metal/wood/skin. He was gushing and I let him carry on feeling a glow of pride for the child that wasn't mine. As he rattled off more and more facts I noticed Mel nearby looking for me. I shook the man's hand happily and went to meet her. By the time I had pushed through the milling throngs of eager parents I found her wearily slumped shoulders.

'How did it go?' I asked in a voice still buoyant over the last report.

'Oh, you know the usual; sits at the back, says little, doesn't appear to be interested etc, etc.' As she went on it was like listening to the report of an entirely different person. This wasn't Zac the Scientist, Zac the trampolinist. It sounded like Zac the Nightmare.

'But how about you?' she asked. I soon cheered her with tales of English success, trampoline triumph and biology glory. She started to look a little happier. I decided now was not the time to mention that her son sounded like he had some kind of split personality. I'd have to save that for another day and a better mood.

'Right well shall we go,' she said looking around for Zac.

'Absolutely.'

We both headed towards the exit and freedom. There was a scuffle behind me and I saw Mr Kodak heading in my direction. I looked away hurriedly only to hear, 'Um excuse me, Miss Miss.' I turned towards him. Mel, noticed and stopped in her tracks. The English teacher stopped in front of us and looked at me.

'Excuse me I was just wondering if I could possibly take your telephone number. I just want to keep you posted about little Jimmy's progress in his classes.' Mel was gaping as he spoke.

'Oh that's very kind. Of course,' I said solemnly, scribbling my number on a bit of paper and handing it to him.

'Excellent,' he said, 'Well it was very nice to meet you Miss Miss. You too,' he nodded at Mel. 'See you soon perhaps.' He said pocketing my phone number and giving me one last melting smile for the journey home. I watched him as he was swallowed up by the huddles of parents.

'Mummy,' said Zac rushing up to Mel.

'Hello darling, time to go,' she said taking his hand. 'Is that OK by you Angel,' she said with a little smirk.

'Fine,' I said flushing, turning back around, 'Absolutely.'

We headed out of the hall in silence. When we reached the outside and the fresh air hit us she started giggling.

'So who was he?' she asked.

'English teacher,' I said suddenly a little embarrassed. I didn't divulge any other details and I could feel Mel looking at me enquiringly.

'That's Mr Stamford,' said Zac in a moment of attention. I tried not to seem too interested. Mr. Stamford...

'He teaches you then does he Zac,' Mel asked.

'Yes, he likes me because I can do the snakes voice in 'The Jungle Book'?'

'Does he now,' she said smiling, 'He sounds nice.'

I got into the car without another word and we drove off. Mel kept sneaking amused glances at me in the passenger seat. I tried not to notice.

'Don't look at me like that Melanie,' I said slumping stubbornly in the car seat.

'I'm not looking at you Angel, I'm looking in my mirror. Anyway,' she added with a smirk, 'Why would I want to look at you.'

'No reason,' I mumbled sinking lower into my seat and letting my thoughts drift back to nice man at weird meeting.

'MUMMMMMEEEEE,' came the screech from the back seat.

'MUMMMMMEEEEE,' it repeated just in case Mummmmmeeee had a major hearing impediment. Mummmmeeee didn't.

'What darling?' Mel asked of the voice. Such a reasonable tone for such an unreasonable greeting. Children could get away with everything. If I yelled MEEELLLLLAAAANNIIEE she'd hit me.

'Sweetie Stop, Sweetie Stop.' Mel rummaged around in her bag for a spare mint to feed the infantile beast. Her search was hopeless. I had wolfed the last one. We were now moving at a snail's pace down the Fulham Road.

'I haven't got any darling,' said Melanie.

'Hold on. I can jump out and grab you some if you like,' I said, pleased at the change of topic.

'Alright,' she said when we reached another red light.

I opened the car door and hopped out trying to avoid the London traffic inching past me. Apart from a rogue cyclist doing more than 15 mph I was in no imminent danger. I turned back to the door.

'So what do you want? Fruit pastilles? Mints? Chocolates?' As I waited for Zac to make up his mind my eyes scanned the street for the nearest sweetie vendor. On the other side of the road I saw an elegant blonde girl laughing up in the face of an equally elegant blonde man. I paused to smile at the scene. They looked really happy. Then I realised with a slow horror that I knew the elegant blonde girl. It was Georgia of Members-Only-Club fame. Slowly the blonde man turned and all my fears were confirmed. Nick. Looking happy and elegant and beautiful. Without me. I felt around for the car seat and slumped back in next to Mel, the colour draining slowly from my face. Zac was still mulling over his sweet choice but Mel had noticed something had gone wrong.

She looked over to where I'd been staring, 'Oh shit,' she said and put her hazard lights on. 'Are you alright,' she asked turning round at me from the driving seat.

I nodded distractedly.

A few beeping horns revived me enough to close the door so she could start the car again.

'Mummmmmmeeeee what about my sweeties?' came a wail.

'Not now sweetheart. We'll get some when we get home,' she promised. We drove off.

I sat in a bit of a daze replaying their smiles and happy glances. They had obviously been having a whale of a time. There could be no other explanation. Nick had clearly moved on, which was simply not on. In my opinion once you have broken up with someone they should be permanently evicted to an island of eternal celibacy, to be with your other exes. There they are allowed to meet freely with each other to discuss the delights of being with you, share the pain of losing you, concoct plans to win you back, and then top themselves. I was certainly not a fan of the plan to merge them right back into society with no kind of qualms that they have experienced any form of emotional meltdown. This was pure absurdity.

Although he might have just been cheering himself up with Georgia I thought hopefully. They might have just been having a lunch so that Nick could talk through our relationship with a woman's point of view. It might have just been a friendly get-together. I mean I had been laughing and teasing with Mr. Stamford five minutes before hadn't I? If Nick had seen that he would have thought the worst wouldn't he? It could just be an innocent, platonic lunch. Nothing more.

It was ridiculous to be upset anyway. Even if he was out with Georgia I wasn't with him anymore. We'd broken up and I had no claim on him at all. He was a free agent. He could do what he liked, which was clearly what he was doing. Or rather who he was doing more to the point.

Mel dropped me at home and I waved a miserable good bye. If I hadn't been so distracted I might have noticed the police car parked in the street across from our house.

* * *

I walked into our living room to see two uniformed police officers standing looking solemn. Policemen make me nervous. I always feel irrationally guilty, as if they are suddenly going to produce a list of crimes from inside their jacket. What had I done? What could they take me down town for? I had read somewhere that a police man couldn't arrest you if he wasn't wearing his hat, so I tried to motion to Ellie to move them away from their grasp. Ellie however was sitting on the sofa sipping tea as if she were on the set of Police Academy and they were not doing some kind of a drugs bust in our flat.

I suddenly realised they might not be here for me. I was surprised. Ellie had never seemed like the criminal type. Always friendly and chirpy, she didn't seem like your average offender. But thinking about it, she used to speak of an Italian Great Aunt, mafia link perhaps? I should have paid closer attention.

'What's going on?' I asked a little nervously.

The two policemen looked around. One was tall and lean and good looking. If he hadn't been trying to finger us for a crime I might have asked him for his number.

'Hello Miss Lawson is it?' asked the shorter, fatter one, holding out his hand to shake. Was gripped with a sudden panic that he might try and handcuff me. My hand wavered in front of me before I made the decision to give it up.

'That's me,' I said, afraid to add anything extra for fear of incrimination. I shook his hand quickly and then joined Ellie on the sofa.

'Can we help?' I asked laughing nervously for no reason at all. Well done Angela, now they definitely think you did it.

'We were wondering if either of you might be able to help us with our enquiries,' said lean good looking one.

'As we were telling your house mate here we are currently investigating an event that occurred two miles from here, in parkland on the night of the 4th. Of this month.'

'Where were you on the night of the 4th?' asked the shorter, fatter one.

'Um...' I tried to rack my brains.

'It was a Monday night if that helps at all,' added the lean good looking one.

I smiled graciously at him, best to try and get on their right side, and continued to look thoughtful. Guessing that most weekdays were not spent living it up out on the tiles I plumped for Option a) At home in the flat.

'I think I was here then,' I said.

The lean, good looking one made a note of this.

'At 10.48pm a woman was attacked in parkland not far from this house, did you hear or see anything unusual on that night around that time,' asked his partner.

'No, I'm afraid not,' I said.

'No,' said Ellie miserably, 'How awful.'

'We are currently looking for Mr. Helm to help us with our enquiries,' claimed the shorter, fatter one.

I looked at Ellie shocked. Kevin, they were looking for Kevin. Kevin Helm. It suddenly didn't seem like such a surprise. Oh God.

'When was the last time you saw Mr. Helm,' asked the lean, good looking one looking at me.

I mentioned that I'd seen him a couple of weeks ago before I went jogging. He had been returning to the house at around eight in the morning.

'I haven't seen him since then,' I said.

Then Ellie piped up, 'We haven't seen him but we...' she looked at me, embarrassed to admit we'd been behaving like two nosey curtain twitchers, 'we heard him a about a week ago shouting at someone in his flat.'

'Well they were both shouting,' I corrected, 'They were having a row.'

'What about?' asked the shorter fatter one. There was a pause, we blushed.

'Don't know.'

'Couldn't hear,' we both mumbled simultaneously.

'About a week ago could have been the night in question. Did you hear him shouting on the Monday night?' pointed out the shorter, fatter one.

'Oh yes it would have been that night,' Ellie nodded working it out.

'At what time did you hear them shouting,' asked the lean, good looking one.

'Um... it would have been around seven,' said Ellie.

'Yes I'd just got back from work,' I said backing Ellie up.

'Do either of you know who he was shouting at?' The lean one asked pencil hovering over his pad.

'Well it was definitely a woman,' claimed Ellie.

'There is sometimes a blonde woman who visits the property. I've never seen him have any other visitors in fact,' I said, already beginning to talk like a policeman.

'So you think it might have been this person?' said the shorter, fatter one.

'I'd assume so, yes,' I confirmed, 'But I wouldn't be 100% sure.'

'We haven't been able to find Mr. Helm at this address so please if you do see or hear from him give us a call at the station. Don't approach him, just give us a call. We need to speak to him.'

'Is... is there a problem?' Ellie piped up.

'We would just like to eliminate him from our enquiries,' said the lean good looking one.

I laughed nervously again, this time with good reason.

'Well I think that's it for now,' concluded the shorter, fatter one closing his pad, 'Thank you ladies, and if you think of anything else please do give us a call,' he said handing us a card with their phone numbers on it.

'We will,' I muttered, the situation beginning to sink in.

'We will,' Ellie nodded looking worried.

'We'll see ourselves out.'

As they left I realised we had hardly asked them a thing. It had all seemed so bewildering. Ellie and I looked at each other in shock. It was surreal. What had Kevin done? We managed to work ourselves up into a frenzy of panic fairly quickly.

'He'd said he'd killed someone,' I admitted the moment I heard the front door slam shut.

'But that wasn't late at night and they want him for something that happened late at night,' Ellie said, aware that we hadn't offered this information up to the police.

'How do you know?' I asked.

'Because they said didn't they?'

'No they didn't say when, they just said she was attacked in parkland.'

'No they said at night.'

'He was yelling at her before the night,' I said.

Ellie looked afraid, 'Maybe he followed her out and... followed her there... to the park?'

We fell into silence

'But then who did he kill, if he did say he killed someone? It couldn't have been her because he told her,' I said, confused now.

'And the police would have said if the girl from the park had been killed wouldn't they?' said Ellie looking for reassurance.

'They wouldn't leave us alone in this flat if he was a threat would they?' I said shocked.

We couldn't agree on much. The argument that night had become a blur and neither of us were sure what had happened to the girl in parkland. The only thing we could agree on was that Kreepy Kevin was undeniably Kreepy and had always had a dangerous air about him. I repeated my story about seeing him in the corridor the other day leaning threateningly against his door and leering at the blonde girl. If I recollected correctly I had sensed at the time a tension between them, a possible explosion to come. Ellie nodded sincerely at me, telling me in turn about the time he had passed her in the downstairs corridor looking bloodshot and scowling. She told me it might have been the breeze but she thought she had heard him whisper threats at her under his breath. I nodded animatedly at the tale. And we were living above this time bomb.

In all the confusion I had completely forgotten to tell Ellie about seeing Nick and Georgia. And about meeting Mr. Stamford. I went to bed that night wishing I was lying next to someone who might make the bed seem much less empty, and the flat seem much less eerie. Mr. Stamford's face swam before my eyes and I smiled. Then sleep overtook me and he transformed into a laughing, carefree Nick. Throwing his head back in the wind I shivered as his face turned back towards me. It was Kevin, clutching dead plants in his hands, and staring at me with a twisted smile on his haggard face.

* * *

I was still thinking about Kevin in the office the next morning, as I waited for the kettle to boil. What did he do late at night? He often went out, we often heard the door closing, and I'd seen him with my own eyes returning early the next morning. Who was that girl I'd seen? What had he done to her? What had he done to other girls before her...

'Aaaaaaggghhhhh,' I spun round, grasping the kettle in my hand to fend off an attacker.

A guy was standing in the doorway of the kitchen, a look of shock on his face and his hands held up in mini surrender.

'What?' he gabbled eyeing the kettle in my hands.

I lowered it immediately.

'I'm sorry, you scared me' I said panting.

He stayed frozen in the doorway.

'I'm sorry,' I said putting the kettle back on the counter and blushing as I realized how mad I'd seemed.

'Are you alright?' the man asked side stepping into the kitchen as if at any moment I might spring another attack on him. I started laughing with the sheer stupidity. He looked at me as if I'd really lost it.

'God I'm being stupid, sorry, I was thinking about something else. You just surprised me.'

'Right,' he said popping a tea bag into a mug, 'Anything serious?'

'Not really,' I said and then before I knew it I'd told him the whole story.

He looked at me shocked, 'What and they're just letting him roam around?' he said.

I nodded, 'Hence the jumpiness. Not that he'd be here,' I went on, 'I was just distracted. Sorry I don't know your name,' I blurted out.

'I'm Alex,' he said reaching out and offering me a hand to shake.

'I took it, 'Angel.'

'Oh you're the agony aunt I've heard so much about,' he grinned.

I looked at him confusedly.

'I've just started working on Features,' he said as a way of explanation, 'Richard's mentioned you.'

I looked at him and grinned, 'You must have heard only positive and glowing things then. Richard is my number one fan.'

Alex smiled, 'Something like that.'

'Well I best get on,' I said indicating my tea. 'Sorry about before. Nice to meet you.'

'See you round Angel,' he said, 'You take care.'

For much of the day I regaled people with stories about my police visit from the night before. Tally stared at me wide eyed as I described Kevin's ghoulish appearance. A man with the hair of a beast, arms as wide as tree trunks, a threatening swagger and a look of death in his eye. It made me feel better to exaggerate, as if the reality of the fact that he was wanted by the police would stop scaring me.

We should have realised a long time ago that he was a threat. He had always looked so out of it, so distracted. All the late night walks and strange noises. The snake. I suddenly felt guilty that we might have been able to stop him if we'd reported him earlier. Would the girl in the park ever been attacked if we had voiced our suspicions? Then I shook myself. We couldn't just go around accusing people of crimes because they looked a bit Kreepy. How could we have known he was dangerous? He had never actually tried to harm us.

'Have you seen the new guy in the office,' interrupted Claudia propping herself up on the edge of my desk to exchange gossip. It was the second time she had been over to my desk in the two years I had been at the magazine. The first was four months ago to inform me that John (Sub Editor) was sleeping with Crystal (Health) and he had a wife and two kids.

Her lips were pursed together, 'He's quite attractive I think,' she summed up.

I looked over at Alex critically. He looked like a stockier version of a young Robert Redford. Blonde hair, quite a good body, a little short for my usual tastes...

'He cycles,' said Claudia leaning in confidentially.

'Really.'

Tally raised an eyebrow at me from across the desk.

'Debbie says he was working at The Independent. Very intelligent,' she claimed knowledgably.

'Hmm...'

'And under thirty,' she continued in a stage whisper.

'Gosh.'

'I like the way he seems to have just fitted in with the rest. The Features team just love him,' she confided to me.

'Good.'

'He was talking to Richard earlier about some girl called Hannah. Girlfriend I wonder,' she reflected, puffing up her hair with her hand.

'Hmm... maybe,' I muttered.

Tally looked over at me and gave me a friendly grimace as Claudia went on.

'It's so lovely to get some new blood in the office,' she said as if he were a fresh piece of meat.

'Isn't it,' I agreed.

'So what do you think?' She asked me, bored of listing his glorious attributes.

'Yeah he seemed nice, I met him briefly earlier.'

Claudia was instantly all ears.

'And what's he like?' she asked, licking her scarlet lips.

'Well I didn't really talk to him that long,' I said thinking back to my near attack on him with a kettle.

'But what was your impression of him Angela.'

'Yeah nice,' I repeated, realising this would not be adequate for Claudia.

She looked at me disdainfully and then raised herself up, 'Right well, I really must get on. I have so much work to do.' And with a look that suggested I was to blame for her leaving her desk and keeping her from it, she went back to hers.

I rolled my eyes at Tally and carried on writing.

Not long after I was interrupted by the shrill ring of my phone. I paused in my reply and scooped up the receiver.

'Angela, it's your mother.'

'I'm at work Mum so I really can't talk for long,' I explained immediately concerned I might be embroiled in a long and ramblingly pointless discussion.

My mother was fairly to the point however, 'Don't worry Angela I'm only ringing to see if you can make it home this weekend.'

'Possibly, I'm not sure yet,' I said doodling on a nearby piece of paper.

'Other plans?' said my mother instantly curious.
'Not especially Mum I just...'
'Doing something with Nick?' she asked.
'No.'
'How is Nick?' she asked.
'I think he's fine,' I sighed.

My mother, not getting the past-tense hint and the heavy sigh continued to badger me, 'Your father and I want to meet him you know' she chastised, 'We didn't meet your last boyfriend,' she pointed out.

'What boyfriend?' I asked confused.
'Jim, or John or Jack something,' came the reply.
'You mean Pete,' I added.
'Yes that's it. We never met him either,' she went on.
'Mum I went out with him for about 3 weeks.'

Tally looked up and gave me a little smile. I grimaced.
'Well we want to meet this Nick character...'
'Hello Angel,' said my dad picking up the other line in a timely way. Good, I wouldn't have to go into the whole humiliation of informing my mother I had been dumped quite yet.

'I was asking Angel to bring home that Nick,' piped up my mother. Damn. 'We'd like to meet him wouldn't we Michael?'
'Of course,' said my Dad, 'would be good to meet him.'
'Will you please invite him to Sunday lunch,' my mother said. There was no avoiding it. She'd asked a direct question.
'We've broken up actually Mum.'

I heard her intake of breath.

I noticed Richard straining his ears close by, desperate for any piece of information that might be used to attack me. I scowled at him and went back to concentrating on my mother.

'You broke up, oh dear,' she sighed, 'And we never met him.'

'Wouldn't want to. Fellow must be mad,' my Dad scoffed instantly.

I felt a surge of love for him.

'Why did you break up?' asked my mother

I started to explain, 'Well we were...'

I considered opting for something a little cooler. We wanted different things, I wasn't ready to settle down, it was going too fast, I felt that we were pulling in different directions, the cosmos was against us, I wanted to focus on my career, I didn't want to be tied to one person, I'm young, I need to get out there and see what's on offer...

I plumped for the lame 'we just both got really busy' and then petered off into silence.

'Well that's a shame,' said my mother, 'and I never met...'

'DON'T, DON'T,' came a sudden shout down the phone. I jumped. The DON'T's were followed by a banging noise. What was going on?

'Mum? Dad?'

'MICHAEL,' came my mother's shrill voice, 'DON'T YELL AT IT.'

'NO GET LOST,' shouted my father and the banging noise was repeated.

'Hold on Angel,' said my mother into the receiver, 'Have you quite finished?' She asked at her end.

'It's gone.'

'Of course it's gone, you've scared it half to death,' she said exasperated.

'That damn cat on the lawn again,' my dad explained breathing heavily down the receiver from all the shouting excitement.

'Poor thing's frightened,' said my mother.

'It's not frightened, it's evil,' he ranted.

'Will you stop with this obsession Michael, Angel doesn't want to hear it.'

For once she was right.

'It needs teaching a lesson,' he went on, not to be thwarted easily.

'Don't start her on it Michael.'

'I just think she should know,' he insisted.

'I'm sorry about Nick darling,' said my mother bringing the conversation back.

'Thanks Mum.'

'And if you want to come home anyway for Sunday lunch you're very welcome.'

'Thanks, well I better get back to work,' I said motioning at the letters pointlessly.

'Yes you do that. We'll speak soon,' said my mother, layering on her sympathetic voice now she had realised I had been let down in the love department.

'Chin up Angel,' said my Dad realising the same thing.

'Thanks,' I said to both of them, feeling like a loser.

'Bye.'

'Bye.'

'Bye.'

I put down the phone and momentarily sat gazing into space. I thought briefly of Nick and the happy little smiles he'd swapped with Georgia. All the police chaos had dulled the usual ache every time I thought back to Nick. It was almost a relief to have something else to think about. Even if the subject was the gruesome antics of my weirdo neighbour. Suzie however had spotted my distant expression on her walk to the kitchen. She came over and propped herself up on my desk.

'What is it?' she asked instantly.

I was woken from the reverie.

'Nothing Suzie, I was in a world of my own,' I said scrambling for a letter to prove it.

'Nick?' she plumped for, ignoring the scrambling.

'Hmmm... sort of,' I nodded, not really keen to talk about it all.

'He's a pratt.'

'I know,' I sighed, having heard it all before. A hundred times. From everyone I knew. 'I just feel a bit depressed sometimes,' I explained.

'Look Angel maybe it's not just Nick you're down about,' she said seeing my continued gloomy expression.

'How do you mean?' I said looking at her.

'Well it's everything isn't it... it's your life.'

'My life?' I queried, not sure whether this was going to help make me feel better. The start hadn't been promising.

'Well you haven't done any acting for months and you stopped trying to get work when you started seeing him. You were never like this over men at university, because you had things to do, but now you are in a rut. You need something to focus on, to look forward to. You've got to send out some CV's, get yourself a bit of work. You'll love it,' she went on looking at me encouragingly.

I momentarily felt a surge of happiness. That was the answer, she was right. I should send out some CV's. I should get back into it all. I missed it and it wouldn't take too much time to look for some theatre work. But then I was awash with a sad bout of reality,

'It's never going to happen, my agent is useless. The other week he called me Angelica Dawson,' I wailed.

'Well you need a new one,' she said laughing at my despair.

'I know,' I agreed glumly.

'Angel when you asked me for a job you said it was a temporary stop. You are a great actress.'

I looked at her seriously. Suzie didn't usually shell out compliments so I was grateful for this one. I found myself telling her about BOS Productions' phone call.

'They wanted to see you for an audition,' she repeated, 'Why didn't you say you'd go?' she asked, frowning in confusion.

'I don't know. I just think what's the point? I've lost all confidence.'

'Rubbish,' she scoffed, 'You just got distracted. Give them a ring.'

'Maybe,' I smiled at her feebly.

'Do. And no more moping about men. Nick was...'

'... an idiot,' I concluded for her, 'I know Suzie; I'm getting a grip I promise.'

'Well just don't go back there. Move on.'

'I will.'

'You can do a lot better,' she said confidently.

'I know,' I answered automatically, 'And I really think it's made me a much better judge of character,' I assured her.

'Let's hope so,' she said getting up to go.

'What do you think of the new guy?' I asked thoughtfully, catching a glimpse of Alex at his desk. He looked very like Nick from the back. All blonde hair and butch shoulders. Suzie looked at me in horror.

'I think he'd be bad for your acting career too,' she said heading back to the kitchen.

Cross with myself for not following up the audition, cross that I couldn't get my mind back off Nick I started scribbling a passionate reply. This Kate, 15, from Suffolk was concerned about leaving her house, she obviously had the onset of agoraphobia, but I assured her the world was a cruel, dark place and she was probably better off inside. Verity,16, Lincoln was worried that she had an STD, and I agreed with her valid point that nothing good comes out of dealings with the opposite sex. Today you're heartbroken, tomorrow you've got herpes. There was a lesson in there for us all.

Tally had been quietly attaching sequins to a top all morning. It was to be the centrepiece of next months fashion page for teens. A sort of Do-It-Yourself accessorize article. 'How to make your clothes more individual.' I hadn't registered her get up for a break. She was now idly sitting at my desk sipping a coffee and playing solitaire on the computer. I didn't notice her pick up one of the replies I'd finished that morning.

She almost spat out her coffee, 'Angel, you can't send this,' she said looking at me wide-eyed.

'Which one?' I asked looking up from another reply.

'What do you mean which one?' she asked aghast, 'Yvonne from Nottingham,' she held up the letter trying to nudge my memory.

'Yvonne,' I repeated thoughtfully, 'Oh yeah. Why not?' I said looking back down at my work.

'Angel she has written to you saying she is confused about her sexuality. Isn't the usual reply, 'all teenagers go through this, its perfectly natural to be curious, it might just be a phase, talk to your teacher ya dee ya da'.'

'Yes,' I admitted.

'But you have written, I quote, 'Dear Yvonne. I myself have been mulling over the benefits of lesbianism. The problem us women have is clear. Men are quite frankly lazy good for nothings who don't know how to cook, don't take care of us, act selfishly, put us last and eventually cheat on us.'

'Hmmm... accurate isn't it?' I said, pleased with my day's work. Tally went on flabbergasted.

'You go on to advise her to stick to the course of lesbianism 'it will reap far more satisfying rewards.' Angel you can't send this,' she said half laughing, half serious.

'Why not? It's the truth.'

'That's not the point. And no it's not.'

'I'm sure it is,' I said waving her concerns away.

'She'll get even more confused,' she went on.

'She'll be fine.'

'Angel you can't tell her to become a lesbian,' Tally stressed horrified.

'I'm not; I just think she should be encouraged. Can you imagine how easy life would be if we were lesbians,' I said confidently.

Tally looked at me stunned.

'What? It would be brilliant. No more men,' I sighed looking back down at my letter.

'I am a lesbian,' she said shrugging her shoulders, 'And life doesn't seem any easier.'

My head snapped back up to focus on her.

'You're a lesbian,' I repeated, amazed.

'Yup.'

'I didn't know,' I said truly dumb-founded at this information.

'You never asked,' she said grinning at me.

'But you're so... so...'

'What Angel?' She said loving every minute of my discomfort.

'You're so cool,' I said quietly, realising how ridiculous I sounded.

'Thanks. Some lesbians are you know,' she said looking at me solemnly.

'Yes I know,' I flustered, feeling put on the spot.

She held the letter out to me, 'Anyway that's not the point. You have to give this girl sensible advice. She's really confused.'

'But if she can be given a little push in the right direction...' I persuaded.

'You can't send it,' she said more firmly.

'Fine I'll re write it,' I said snatching it back off her,

'Mad woman,' she said shaking her head and returning to her desk.

'Lesbian.'

It was nearing the end of the day and I'd done some re writes and kept Tally happy. Yvonne from Nottingham had been assured that her confusion over her sexuality was a common occurrence among teens, that she had nothing to worry about and should not feel ashamed by her feelings. The rest of the afternoon had been spent in a constant series of questions for Tally including the 'Do you have a girlfriend?' (No), 'Have you always been gay?' (Yes), to the inevitable, 'Do you fancy me?' (No).

When she'd answered 'no' to the latter I was hurt.

'Why not?'

'I see you as just a friend,' she said looking at me critically.

'Oh.'

'Would you fancy me if I were blonde?' I asked sulkily.

'Nope.'

'How about if I wore my hair... up,' I asked piling it on top of my head and looking at her as seductively as I could.

'You're just not my type,' she laughed, seeing Alex striding up behind me.

'Even when I do this,' I said pouting at her a little more.

'Maybe,' she said laughing and going back to her sequins.

I jumped to see Alex swooping down on me.

'Oh Hi,' I stuttered letting go of my hair.

'Just thought I'd check up on you,' he smiled, 'Just as jumpy now I see.'

'Hmmm,' I muttered. Tally was bending right over her work trying not to laugh.

Alex perched himself on my desk. I was aware that Claudia had clocked him approaching. She was staring open-mouthed as Alex leaned over me, 'What are you working on?' he asked, curious to read some of the letters.

'Just writing some home replies to the letters this month,' I said indicating the stack in front of me.

He picked up one in two fingers, 'This is genius' he said starting to read, 'Listen to this,' he said laughing and looking at me, 'This girl is 14 but wants a baby,' he started mimicking a girl's voice, 'My friends all muck around in clubs but all I really want is a man who will take care of me and have a family with. Am I the only teenager like this?'

I smiled weakly at him when he finished.

'Is this what you do all day?' he asked laughing at the letter. 'It's like a soap opera on every page,' he said scooping up the next one. I reached out and put my hand on the top of the pile. Alex's hand rested on mine. I looked at him, suddenly embarrassed.

'They're confidential,' I explained, trying to sound light-hearted.

He left his hand a second longer on mine before smirking and removing it slowly.

'Alright,' he said laughing at me again.

I noticed Tally rolling a sympathetic eye at me.

'Alex have you met Tally, Tally this is Alex,' I said indicating between them to get rid of any awkwardness. 'He's just started working on Features,' I smiled as she arranged her expression into something suitably welcoming.

'Oh right Hi,' she said raising a hand to him.

'Hi,' Alex said looking at her.

'It's your first day isn't it,' Tally said with a slightly pointed look.

'That's right,' Alex confirmed.

'And what do you think?' she asked looking at him.

Alex turned to look at me, 'I think I like it,' he decided.

At that moment Victoria had walked up behind us and made me jump again, 'Everything alright here?' she asked looking quizzically at us all.

'Fine,' I said flustered to have been caught looking so lazy, 'We just met Alex,' I said pointing at him like he was a new stationery item or printer.

'Who's just getting back to work,' he said flashing Victoria a smile.

'Good to see people are making you feel welcome Alex,' she smirked, looking at me, 'See you later.'

'Righto,' he said confidently.

Alex watched her go. 'I suppose I better get back to my desk,' he sighed getting up and stretching languidly.

'Yup, you don't want people talking,' I joked, glad that I could get back to work in peace.

'Haven't they been already?' he said looking playfully at me.

'I have fielded a couple of questions about you, the glamorous new boy,' I admitted, thinking of Claudia's wide eyes, even wider now.

He didn't laugh but held my gaze, 'As long as you like me Angel.'

I blushed and looked down at my desk, pushing a pencil around, 'You're very direct,' I laughed, slightly nervously.

'Not at all,' he said holding his hands up.

'Well I better get back to work too,' I muttered, motioning to the letters.

'I'll only leave on one condition,' he said looking down at me confidently.

'What's that?' I asked, aware of him standing over me.

'That you promise I can take you out sometime,' he asked.

'Maybe,' I smiled up at him. He met my gaze. I was the first to drop my eyes.

'Maybe,' he pouted.

'Yes. Now run along,' I said jokingly, a little nervous again.

'Alright. See you later Angel, nice to meet you Tally,' he said heading back to the Features desk. We both watched him go.

'He seems.... nice,' I concluded.

Tally looked at me and rolled her eyes again.

A few seconds later Claudia scuttled up, 'Soooo... what did he want?' she asked me.

I looked at her, bored of the questions, 'Dinner and a blow job,' I said scooping up my bag and leaving her mouthing like a gold fish.

That time Tally did spit out her coffee.

* * *

Our flat phone was ringing as I got in. I snatched up the receiver before they disappeared off the line.

'Angel thank god,' my mother said the moment I answered the phone.

'Mum what's up, are you alright?' I asked, panicked by the urgency.

'Yes, no, it's nothing. Well it's not nothing, it's your father' she exhaled dramatically.

'What's wrong with Dad?' I asked suddenly scared.

'Oh nothing serious don't worry, he's just. Well I'm a bit worried about him.'

'Worried why?' I thought of my dad. If I had to be worried about either of my parents I wouldn't have plumped for my dad. He was calm, he was steady, he was reliable. He propped my mother up at her most frantic, he calmed her down, he made tea and told her it was fine. 'What's the matter with him?' I gulped, waiting to hear why my mild mannered father was causing my mother so much concern. Was he ill? Was it serious?

She paused and I waited impatiently.

'I won't sugar coat it for you darling,' she warned.

Oh god this was serious.

'OK. Go on,' I urged, What's happened?'

'Your father has gone mad darling. I don't know how else to put it,' she went on in a high pitched voice.

'Mad. What do you mean mad?' I asked surprised at her answer.

'He's done something terrible,' she said getting uncharacteristically quiet.

'Did he hit you?' I asked shocked that my dad had gone loopy so out of the blue. Domestic abuse, I'd read about it in my letters. I would never have thought my dad would be a wife beater though, but it's often the quiet ones.

'No darling of course not,' my mother insisted, 'No nothing like that. He hasn't become violent.'

'So what has happened?' I asked confused.

'He's kidnapped next door's cat. Stolen it.'

'What?!'

'He's holed it up in the garage and he's refusing to let it out. I can't persuade him. He's gone quite mad. Refusing to listen to reason. I've given up,' she said, frantic again.

'Kidnapped their cat,' I repeated, at a total loss, 'But why?'

'Says it's got it in for him,' she said sounding increasingly high pitched.

'Got it in for him?' I said, realising I was no help if I continued to just repeat everything she said, 'The cat?'

'Says that it knows where he goes and deliberately relieves himself there,' she went on, her voice a little choked now.

'But that's crazy,' I scoffed.

'I told you darling. It's serious. He's lost his marbles. I don't know what to do. He just won't be persuaded he's not thinking sensibly.'

'So what's he done with it?' I asked, curious now. What was Dad up to?

'It's in our garage and he is guarding it,' she whispered, obviously afraid the neighbours might hear.

'Right. So is he planning on giving it back?' I asked trying to keep up.

'He hasn't told me that yet and what am I meant to say if I see Mrs. Phillips, it's her cat you know and I... hold on Angela, he's coming in from the garage. I've got to go. I need to talk to him a bit more. Honestly I've got to try and make him see sense.'

And she was gone and I was left looking blankly at the receiver wondering what had just happened to my parents. I knew my Dad didn't like the cat but this aggressive manoeuvre was definitely a first for him. It couldn't be as bad as all that, I'd call back later and talk to him.

At that moment Ellie returned from a day in a new temporary administration job. She was filing for a large company in the city to make ends meet and still talking to the various agencies about her ideal career path. From the loud bang of the door slamming I assumed that filing for a large company in the city was not it.

'Honestly Angel I don't know how long I'm going to last in this one,' she warned, appearing in the doorway with hair askew and a crumpled shirt.

'What now?' I asked sympathetically.

'Everyone keeps insisting on calling me Eloise,' she announced, 'Which isn't even my name. My name is short for Eleanor. They don't care. It's horrendous,' she moaned stomping through to her room.

'Oh, don't fuss Eloise at least you haven't just received a phone call from your mother to inform you that your father is due to be popped into a mental home unless he stops stealing other people's domestic pets.'

This reply stopped her short.

'What?' She asked peering around her door instantly bemused.

I explained the whole Dad turned cat napper story and by the end Eloise had completely forgotten why she had been in such a bad mood.

'That is...' she gaped at me.

'Crazy?' I added.

She nodded at me.

'Do you think your mum's exaggerating?' she asked flinging off her pinstripe trousers and popping on her tracksuit bottoms.

'Probably,' I said going into the kitchen. 'Do you want some spaghetti?' I hollered.

'Yes please.'

We sat and ate and watched soaps and forgot about faceless corporations and mad parents.

'Any news on Kevin?' she asked through a mouthful of spaghetti and sauce.

'Not that I know of,' I said leaning back in my chair.

I hadn't heard or seen him round the flat for days now. Was he even in London? Was he on the run? I was beginning to take it for granted that we were living above a fugitive. We couldn't go around being permanently terrified. We had to hope the police were on to things. I changed the channel to distract us both from fretting anymore about him.

In the midst of a seriously dull drama my mobile started ringing. It was an unknown number and I hoped it wasn't Dad calling from a local B and B/ mental hospital with a bag under one arm and a cat under another.

'Hi is that Miss Miss?' A voice asked as I answered my phone.

It wasn't my Dad in a B and B or a mental hospital. It was Mr Kodak Camera. Much better.

I smiled, 'This is she,' I answered, 'And is that Mr. Stamford of English?' I asked in return.

'It is definitely not,' he laughed, 'It is Charlie, and you are?'

'Angela, Angel whatever you feel,' I said getting up and moving into the kitchen so I wouldn't disturb Ellie too much.

'Anything will be better than Miss Miss,' he said laughing.

'I didn't think I'd catch you at home,' he said.

'Why not?' I asked confused but flattered he reckoned I was such a party animal.

'I assumed you might be taking Little Jimmy out somewhere nice, first day of the holidays and all that.'

Oh god I suppose I better confess...

'Oh um... little Jimmy, well about that...'

Charlie cut me off, 'He doesn't exist does he Angel?'

'No,' I admitted, 'He doesn't.'

Charlie was laughing.

'You knew already didn't you,' I said sensing I was being teased.

'Well seeing as James is a strapping 11 year old it would have made you quite a child-bride,' he chuckled.

'Ah.'

'I felt sorry for you. A single mother of an energetic teenager. It must be a lot of hard work. And how old are you?

At least twenty three and Little Jimmy is eleven. That makes you young enough to be used as an example in our sex-ed class. What not to do as a twelve year old.'

'Look I wasn't paying attention, the tea witch was panicking me and you kept asking me questions.'

'That explains it then,' he said deadpan.

'I bet you've made up stuff in the past,' I said hoping to divert the attention away from me and my mad lie.

'Well my mother still thinks I don't smoke. Does that count?'

'It'll have to.'

There was a bit of a pause,

'So are you planning on calling one of your children Little Jimmy by any chance, because that is a great name.'

'Have you just called to tease me,' I said laughing, 'Or are you going to threaten me with social services?'

'Certainly not. I was just hoping, if you don't have a child to baby sit, I might be able to take you out somewhere this week.'

'That would be lovely,' I said taken aback. Mr. Kodak camera was asking me out. Little me.

'Well how about Friday night? I'll give you a call some time tomorrow and we'll make a plan.'

'OK. Well I'll talk to you then.'

I put down the phone feeling a little skip. It was nice to be asked out I thought as I dreamily thought back to his smile at that meeting. I walked back to the living room with a vacant look on my face. The dreary drama was still playing in the background. Ellie gave up on it.

'Who was that?' she asked looking curious.

'No one,' I started, slightly embarrassed.

'It wasn't Nick was it?' she said, her expression instantly hardening.

'No, don't worry,' I assured her.

'Angel,' she said suddenly sounding like my mother.

'I promise,' I said seeing her continue to look wary. I hadn't heard from Nick since I'd seen him cosying up to Georgia on the road side looking so damn happy together. Then I shook myself. Happier thoughts.

'No, it was Charlie,' I said as if she would know who Charlie was.

'Who's Charlie?' she asked.

'A teacher I met at Zac's school,' I explained.

'Right. Nice?' she asked.

'Lovely,' I sighed, thinking back to his Kodak camera good looks. Blue eyes, dark hair...

'And he's asked you out,' she concluded.

'Yes,' I said not wanting to divulge too much yet.

'Good,' she said struggling to be laid back. Ever since Nick she had been careful not to encourage any more men, until she'd vetted them first.

My phone rang interrupting her questions anyway. It was Suzie.

'Tally told me,' she began.

'Told you what?' I asked caught off guard.

'About Alex,' she said smugly.

'Alex,' I said trying to sound innocent of where the conversation was headed.

'Yes, he asked you out,' she said.

'Asked me out?' I repeated, hoping to put her off lecturing me by repeating everything she said until she got bored.

'Tally told me Angel,' she said, not letting me squirm out of it.

'Well she's a lesbian,' I said defensively.

'I know.'

'Oh.'

'She's not a liar though.'

'No.'

'So?'

'Well he did ask me out but I said maybe and we left it there. I hardly know him,' I protested.

Ellie was following the conversation back and forward like a tennis match.

'Well as long as you are not going to go all gooey over another man quite so soon. Remember what I said earlier.'

'Yes ma'am.'

'So did you call them about the audition?' She asked.

'Sort of.'

'You didn't.'

'No... But I will tomorrow,' I assured her.

'Good. Alright. See you tomorrow. Love to Ellie.'

'Night.'
I put the phone down. Ellie looked up at me.
'Who's Alex?' she asked, her eyes wide now.
'A new guy at work,' I told her.
'Right. Nice?'
'OK,' I shrugged.
'And he asked you out?' she asked.
'Yes.'
'Right,' she paused, 'And who is the lesbian?'
'Tally,' I said.
'Right. Nice?'
'Lovely,' I confirmed.
'And did she ask you out?'
'No,' I started laughing, 'No she didn't.'

I got ready for bed with a little spring in my step. I'd been asked out twice in one day. That was good going. Maybe being single wasn't so bad.

* * *

A couple of hours later, alone in my bed, I woke with a start. Nothing. A cars headlights swept past the darkened curtain and I jumped a little. Nothing. I went to lie back down. Maybe at moments like these being single wasn't so great. I held my breath and listened. I still felt irked that there was something out there. I struggled up to my elbows and strained to hear in the dark. All had gone quiet again and my heart was beating a little faster. I shook myself. It was just the dark. I was getting jumpy. I peered round my room. Normal everyday items had taken on ghostly shapes. My dressing gown was now a threatening dark clump hanging ominously close to me, my hairdryer on the floor could be a foot edging closer to me. I tried to rationalize. There was no armed intruder. The noises could have been anything. It might have been a cat; it might have been some late night revellers. I strained to hear. Something was growing in volume. Something seemed to be making noises, it almost sounded like muffled crying. Then a few louder moans tore through me making the skin stand up on my arms and my body freeze. Suddenly a wailing cry ripped through me. It was horrendous. I screamed as someone appeared in the doorway.

'Get away, what get off' I gabbled as a silhouette neared me from the doorway.

'Angel, Angel it's me,' said Ellie holding her tennis racket aloft and looking petrified, 'Did you hear that?'

'Yes.'

'What was it?'

'I don't know. Sssh... has it gone.'

'Do you think we should go down there?'

'Are you kidding?'

'Do you think we should call the police?'

I gulped, 'I don't know.'

We both sat in the dark in silence. After a while I could hear Ellie's breathing becoming steadier and I whispered to her, 'It's quiet again now. Maybe it was a cat outside,' I said hopefully.

Ellie looked at me doubtfully, 'Do you think it was him?' she asked.

'I don't know. Was it coming from outside or in?'

'I don't know. Angel shouldn't we call the police?'

'And tell them what? We heard someone crying. In the dead of night. They'd think we were just being over sensitive women.'

We waited a little longer listening out for any noise that might be a roving murderer. After a couple more minutes Ellie whispered, 'Angel.'

'What?'

'Can I sleep in here tonight?'

* * *

After my interrupted late night I woke up with a leaden head. I knew instinctively today was not going to be a good day. Waking up centimetres from your flat mate's face is not the most refreshing start. Still, even after this, I hadn't known instinctively immediately. In fact once I had got out of bed the day had started out ok. My instincts weren't yet ready to inform me of any imminent doom. I had got up, dragged myself to the shower, breakfasted and left the house. Unharmed, both mentally and physically. It hadn't been anything to write home about. Which is lucky as if it were, my parents are keeping a fair stack of letters from me after every morning I successfully manage to wake up. No, I only realized instinctively that today was not going to be a good day when today turned into a bad day. It was only that shift that prompted my instincts to kick in and send me negative vibes.

I got into the office to see Victoria standing ominously close to my desk, holding a pile of what might be letters and wearing a stern glare and quite an attractive cashmere jumper. My instincts nudge each other a bit, as if lining up in some kind of formation ready for the first signal. It comes fairly quickly.

'Angela I want to see you in my office. Now.'

The general in charge of my instincts is now waving his boys forward, 'Ominous signal lads pip pip ho ho, tell the lady there might be danger ahead.' I'm too worried to pause and wonder why my instincts sound like squaddies on some kind of gutsy British mission. I follow her into her office. Claudia walks past and raises an eyebrow. Richard is openly gaping. Alex winks at me but I am too nervous to respond.

'Sit down Angel,' she said pointing to the chair at her desk.

I sit down feeling very, very nervous. She looked cross.

'I've spoken to you about your page before and quite frankly I can't believe I am speaking to you again.'

I gulped. I had no idea what I'd done. I could definitely guess, recently my work had been slap dash to say the least, but I couldn't pin point anything specific. Had she found the original Yvonne from Nottingham reply?

'I received a complaint from one of the mothers of our readers and she enclosed the following.' She flung a letter down in front of me. In reply to the girls' concerns about her fear of enclosed spaces I had told her that she should get out more. I looked slightly guiltily at the page hoping Victoria might produce the rest of the letter that was sympathetic, helpful and informative. She didn't.

'I was frankly shocked by the kind of advice you are sending out on behalf of this magazine. I'm afraid unless something changes I'm going to have to reconsider your contract.'

I inhaled sharply. I couldn't bring myself to say anything. I really had no defence.

'Suzie has informed me you've been going through a bit of a difficult patch at home so I thought it would be best to give you the rest of the week off to sort out your priorities.'

Thank you Suzie.

'You must think about what this job means to you. Your readers rely on you for sensible advice and I don't think you're taking your responsibility seriously enough...'

I couldn't look up at her now as she went on.

'...And, though I'm sympathetic about any personal problems, if I don't feel you are doing your job properly I will have to let you go Angela.'

'I'm so sorry,' I said genuinely ashamed. How could I have been so selfish? I hadn't cared what had been written in some of the letters I'd sent out. I had just assumed that they wouldn't make a difference. But what if I had really upset some of the readers? What if I had made them more confused and upset? Tally had warned me yesterday and I hadn't really paid much attention.

'Thank you for, for, well, being so nice about it.'

'Well I will see you back here on Monday and in the meantime I want you to write to this woman and her daughter to apologise.'

'Yes of course I will,' I said reaching out for the letter.

'See you on Monday.'

I scuttled out of the office with the letter in my hand and my tail between my legs.

I started packing things away on my desk in a daze.

'Alright Angel,' said Alex coming up behind me and putting a hand on my shoulder.

'Yeah,' I said weakly, not able or wanting, to prolong the conversation further.

'Are you in trouble?' he said laughing at me.

'Don't Alex,' I said squirming away from his hand.

'Hey. What happened in there?'

'I'll talk to you about it some other time OK? I've got to go,' I said looking around for Suzie.

I wanted to tell her I was sorry that I had messed up. She had got me the job and all I could do was screw it up and then rely on her to get me out of being fired. God knows what she had told Victoria but I didn't think the Kevin worry and my love life amounted to huge personal problems. I owed her.

'Angel don't be boring. Tell me the gossip. I'm the new boy, I need to be filled in,' said Alex leaning on my desk.

'There's no gossip Alex,' I said, aware that Victoria was

watching me from her office.

'Fine,' he said, obviously a little offended I didn't want to talk to him about it.

He walked off in a bit of a sulk but I didn't care.

Tally came over the picture of concern, 'Angel what's happened?' she asked seeing me slinging my bag over my shoulder, 'Where are you going?'

'Home,' I said dully.

'Oh god have you been fired?' said Tally looking shocked.

This managed to raise a smile, 'Not yet, but thank you for the vote of confidence.'

Tally blushed.

'I'm back on Monday. I'm being sent away to think about my priorities,' I said lowering my voice.

'Wish Victoria would give me a week off to think of my priorities,' sighed Tally wistfully.

It was funny I hadn't seen my exit in that light. It would be a week off. I suddenly felt desperate for the time away. Maybe my head wouldn't be in such a muddle at the end of it.

From the corner of my eye I saw Alex bending down to say something to Richard and then, with a gleam in his eye, I could make out Richard snaking his way over to my desk.

'Bye Tally, have a good week.'

I raced out before he could reach me.

In five minutes I was pacing towards the tube station trying to forget Victoria's remarks as quickly as possible. I had been an idiot and felt so humiliated. Arriving at Oxford Circus tube I realized I wasn't sure where I should be headed. I headed towards the ticket barriers and then stood cluelessly by them as various people shunted past me with bits of luggage and scowls. It felt strange feeling so directionless. I stared at the various maps of tube lines and arrows pointing Northbound and Southbound for ages before finally deciding to go home and change before planning my next move. I reckoned Ellie would be in and I felt the need to talk things through with someone.

I was waiting for the Victoria train in another stupor when I managed to get in the way of a babbling mad woman, in a multicoloured sunhat, who was wandering aimlessly around the platform. I snapped out of my thoughts and looked at her in a fond sort of way. She was gazing around the platform probably remembering the days she used to camp here down during the raids in the Battle of Britain, supping tea from a flask and singing 'White Cliffs of Dover.' She had a lost look, possibly the mad thing, but suddenly realised she might actually be lost and all these heartless people where just letting her wander around before her ultimate demise as she wanders onto the tracks. I hadn't achieved my Girl Guide's Badge for Community Service for nothing.

'Excuse me are you alright?' I said gently placing a hand on her shoulder. Her wandering eyes fixed on me briefly. I continued in a slow voice, 'Do you know which platform you want?'

'Fuck off,' she snapped.

I reeled backwards. She was obviously, definitely mad. Fortunately at that moment a tube arrived and I scuttled on to it before she could abuse me further.

Ten minutes later I'm sitting in the silent carriage carefully avoiding eye contact and ignoring the fact that some guy's ipod is playing New Metal, loud. We can all hear it. It's like bad tapped music in restaurants. We can all hear it but as the Tube Etiquette book goes we all pretend we can't hear it. It's only the mad woman in the sunhat opposite that appears to be breaking the code by tapping her head to the beats.

I let the tube carry me off and stared idly around for a couple more stops. 2 suits, 4 books, 3 newspapers, a girl in orange, one German novel, 2 rucksacks, 1 poncho, 5 shirts, 2 ties. At Pimlico a busker springs on. Not that I see him actually springing but I imagine from the jaunty tune he's now strumming, loudly, that that is just what he did. Instantly everyone stares off awkwardly, hoping to ignore the time when he'll be by their side with a little cup for change. Finally I arrive at Brixton and, giving the mad woman one last look, I leave to head home.

As I exit the station my mobile starts beeping and I pick up my messages. It's Suzie calling to check I'm OK and immediately the guilt kicks in again. I dial her number and when I get her answer phone I leave a gushing message about how sorry I am and how terrible I feel about it. I promise to turn over a new leaf to become a much better agony aunt and when I put the phone down I do feel a little better. I do mean it as well. I will become a lot better. Fast.

'Ellie,' I called as I slammed the flat door. No reply.

Kicking off my shoes I dumped my bag on the sofa and went into the kitchen to put the kettle on. Waiting for the kettle to boil I picked up my mobile to call Rick. Even if he could only offer me predictions of his ultimate demise it would still cheer me up to hear his voice. Before I could dial however my phone was ringing. It was Charlie. I hesitated as I looked at his name and then, reckoning I had just enough energy, I answered the call.

'Angel it's Charlie. I was ringing about Friday.'

Of course, we had agreed to go out for a drink. The idea suddenly exhausted me. I couldn't cope with a date with a good looking man. That would require effort and brain power. I would have to make an excuse.

'What time are you free?' He asked cheerily.

I really didn't feel like lying to him.

'Um... well I'm free from today on,' I said gloomily.

'Today?'

'I've just got home.'

'That's early.'

'I got sent home,' I said staring listlessly at my reflection in the mirror.

'Sounds bad,' said Charlie immediately concerned.

'And you're a teacher and you'll think I should be in detention,' I wailed.

Charlie laughed at me, 'Why? What did you do?'

'I've been an idiot,' I sighed, twirling a piece of hair in my fingers.

'Well you can tell me about it in person. I'll take you out for lunch.'

I paused, noticing my sad little state in the mirror. I had bloodshot eyes from my lack of sleep and my hair was tied back in a pony tail to disguise the fact that it hadn't been washed in a couple of days.

'Come on Angel, it'll cheer you up. You'll make my day. No one our age is ever on summer holiday.'

'Give me an hour' I said feeling cheerful for the first time that day.

I quickly washed my hair and got changed into a skirt and pair of flip flops. Popping on a tiny bit of lipstick and sticking a pair of sunglasses over my red rimmed eyes I set off. A little bit of me realised it was wrong to be organizing a lunch date only two hours after being sent home to consider my life's priorities. But a girl has to eat and maybe this was the best way to find the answers to life's bigger questions. I would only know if I tried.

Charlie greeted me easily. As if we were always used to meeting up for mid week lunches when I'd been sent home from a job he didn't know I did, from a place he didn't know I went. Talking on the phone only an hour before and telling him I was an idiot had definitely made everything much less awkward. Charlie was so laid back anyway, instantly steering me into a lovely little restaurant, I don't think I could have felt nervous if I tried.

'So what do you actually do...?' he asked after we'd poured ourselves large glasses of wine.

'I work as an agony aunt on a magazine.'

'Right. That sounds like an interesting job,' he said looking at me.

'I suppose it is when my heart's in it,' I said sipping at my Rosé.

'So it's not something you've always wanted to do?' he asked.

'No not exactly. I read Psychology so apparently I'm qualified. My friend Suzie got me the job. I was trying to be an actress before but it didn't work out.'

'How come?'

'I couldn't act,' I said looking at him and smiling wryly.

Charlie, noticing the edge to my voice, sensibly didn't probe any further.

'So, out with it, why were you sent home?'

I told him about Victoria's telling off and described a few of my replies. Charlie nodded at me to go on.

'I just feel so awful. I was so obsessed with myself I didn't think it would matter what I wrote in the letters. I feel like an idiot,' I said miserably, realising how many letters I'd written just to vent some personal anger, or particular feeling at the time. I had been so unprofessional. I deserved to be sent home, I deserved to be fired. Charlie didn't patronize me, he just sat and listened and ordered more wine. It was a relief to talk to someone about it and I found myself spilling out all sorts of horrible little facts. I was relieved he started laughing when I described some of the replies to Richard's letters.

'He sounds horrendous,' Charlie exclaimed.

I allowed myself a brief smile and a nod of agreement. After I'd exhausted the topic and finished my bowl of mussels we sat back, soaked up the sun and talked about nothing. I felt a lot better and Charlie didn't appear too shocked. In fact I hadn't noticed a flicker of judgment when I'd been talking to him, and there was a lot he could have been judgmental about.

I realised I hadn't asked him many questions at all, so busy unburdening myself under his scrutiny. His Mr.Kodak look had enjoyed a few days off and he looked even sexier now that he seemed less fresh faced. He had dark stubble emerging on his jaw line and his eyes seemed bluer. I made an effort to learn a little more about him.

'Why did you go into teaching?' I asked curious. He seemed so glamorous for an English teacher of 5-11 year olds.

'Well I didn't really know what I wanted to do, and it was anything to avoid going into the city and signing up for an eighty hour week. But I actually love it most of the time,' he said popping a chip into his mouth.

'I know I couldn't do it. I can barely keep my parents in line, let alone a classroom of eight year olds.'

'It's not as hard as all that, you just need to treat them like adults.'

'You make it sound easy,' I sighed, thinking I needed to do just that with the readers' letters.

'There is one brilliant thing about being a teacher,' he said looking at me seriously.

'What's that?' I asked, 'The kids?'

'No. Very long school holidays.'

I looked at the table scattered with napkins, spilt wine and glasses and sighed contentedly. I stretched out my legs in the sun and wiggled my toes. Charlie was going to the park and I started to think I better get home.

'Where do you have to be this afternoon?' he asked.

'No where.'

'Well then.'

He got up to pay the bill. He really did look gorgeous with his brown hair and the start of a tan. All those days off. I smiled after him lazily. I noticed a waitress washing glasses was eyeing him surreptitiously as he chatted to the girl who had brought out our food, and I felt suddenly proud that he was with me. Just for the afternoon, I thought hastily.

We wandered aimlessly for a while window shopping and then discovered a dusty looking bookshop. I had always loved books and happily perused the shelves for an interesting read. Charlie, being an English teacher, was quickly ensconced in the classics section and I dragged him back out into the sunshine before he sunk into one of their leather chairs, never to emerge again. With books under our arms we made our way to the park where we found a good spot away from any boisterous groups playing frisbee/football/rounders/other. I finally relaxed into the novelty of having a weekday off. The area we'd stopped in was practically empty and I lay happily reading and every now again making half hearted conversation with Charlie. He'd seen me in such a state now it really didn't seem to matter that I wasn't making a massive effort to impress. It was lovely just to sit back and do nothing. I inched my straps down a little and closed my eyes with the sun on my face.

I was lying in a poppy field with Charlie. We were right next door to a fairground. Rick was already seated on a blue horse on the carousel and I waved at him as he went round. Suzie was eating mussels at a table nearby and kept telling me not to worry about Victoria. And then a monkey in a hot air balloon came down to try and sell me cheese crackers.

I yawned and stretched, opening a sleepy eye to Charlie. Then I sat up quickly, trying to gloss over the fact that I had been snoozing. Charlie was sketching something on to a left over napkin, the ghost of a smile on his lips.

'What are you drawing?' I asked, embarrassed that I had fallen asleep. My mouth had probably been hanging open, I had probably begun snoring and dribbling and he was too polite to say. Oh god.

He laughed at me, 'Nothing sinister Angel,' he said noting my worried expression.

'Can I see?' I asked curious now.

He looked a little uncertain and then shrugged and handed it over. It was a sketch of me. I felt myself instantly going red.

'It's brilliant' I muttered, unable to make a joke. It was. I hurriedly handed it back to him. I suddenly felt awkward.

He lived near Waterloo so we started walking back along the river trying to avoid any rogue cyclists and enthusiastic skateboarders.

My mobile interrupted the peace and without thinking I answered the call. A familiar squawk from the line made me instantly regret this decision.

'Hi Mum,' I said giving Charlie an apologetic grimace. 'How are you?'

'Why aren't you at work darling, are you alright?'

'How do you know I'm not at work?' I asked confused to know how she had heard so soon.

'Well for one I can hear cars in the background. But I called your office didn't I and I spoke to that nice Tilly girl. She told me you were having the week off.'

'Tally,' I corrected automatically.

'Tilly, Tally it's all the same.'

'Not to her,' I pointed out.

'It doesn't matter. Anyway I'm just ringing to check you are OK and you haven't had some kind of mental break down. I'm convinced they run in the family. On your father's side need I point out.'

'I'm fine and no I am not having a mental breakdown,' I reassured her.

Charlie smiled.

'So why are you not at work?'

'I've just taken the week off to figure out what I'm going to do next.' I explained, keen to not mention I'd been sent home.

'Next in what?' asked Mum.

'Next in my life. I don't know. I just needed to think about what I'm doing with my life,' I said realizing how dramatic it all sounded.

'Well let me know when you've decided dear,' she sounded a little frosty.

'Mum are you OK?'

'Yes I am fine. Always fine.'

'Is it Dad again?' Knowing instinctively mother wouldn't be ringing me just to check on my mental state.

'Your father,' she scoffed, 'Well you'll be pleased to hear your father is still mad as a March hare.'

'Er... right. Oh dear,' I sympathized.

'He refuses to listen to reason. He's still got that cat you know, and do you know what he is doing right now?' she asked breathlessly.

'No, what?' I asked knowing it wasn't going to be good.
'He's writing a ransom letter. A ransom letter for the cat.'
'What?' I yelped.
Charlie looked up at me startled.
'So when I call you from the police station asking for bail don't be surprised. Honestly I don't know what he thinks he's up to.'
'What are his demands?' I asked, amazed at my father's actions.
'He wants it to be forced to go in its litter tray. He says all other cats seem to manage,' she sniffed.
'And then he'll give it back?' I checked.
'Yes, unless it persists in pooing elsewhere.'
'I'll call and talk to him later if you like Mum' I offered, having heard enough.
That seemed to placate her a little. 'Well I hope that might help, the man is beyond reasoning with,' she grunted.
'Right Mum well I'll do that. Don't worry and thanks for checking on me. I better go now.'
'OK,' she said sighing with the world on her shoulders.
'You take care Mum,' I said and put down the phone.
Charlie needless to say was trying hard not to seem too curious. I instantly explained the Dad turns cat napper story to him and the latest ransom twist. Charlie was lost for words. By the time I had finished the story we were walking down my road. I had just about convinced him that these type of events weren't usual occurrences in my life by the time I was walking through our front door. That was just before when we noticed a woman sitting on the bottom of our stairs crying loudly. Charlie looked at me in disbelief. As if this was somehow highly typical.

The woman had her head rested in her arms and I noticed she had blonde hair. I recognized her, but it couldn't be. The girl in the grey jacket... The girl who'd been arguing with Kevin... The girl who was attacked?

I rushed over to her without thinking, 'Are you OK? Are you hurt? I said instantly looking her up and down for any obvious bruises or cuts, she seemed OK.

She looked up, slightly startled at my concern.

She stammered as she got up, 'I'm fine, sorry I...' she wiped her eyes with the back of her hand.

'Can I help at all?' I asked, 'Can I get you anything? What are you doing here? I thought he... well... I thought Kevin... I...'

The girl had stopped sobbing now and looked at me with a horrified expression, 'You thought he what?' she asked.

'Nothing...' I said noticing her expression, 'Sorry would you like to come up for a cup of tea or something,' I said weakly indicating our flat up the stairs. The girl nodded.

'Do you want me to bring this,' asked Charlie indicating the fish tank on the floor. It was full of leaves and... oh god.

'Yes please,' the girl nodded.

I gave Charlie a weak smile as he manoeuvred his way up the stairs with a python in his arms and a slightly confused expression on his face.

Ellie was in the flat and bemused to see me arriving home in the middle of the day with a crying blonde girl and a gorgeous dark haired man carrying a snake in a tank. The girl had stopped crying quite so hard and I tried not to stare at her too much. I was still very confused as to who she was and why she had returned to the home of her attacker. Who was still missing. She sat nursing a cup of tea looking slightly dazed. Charlie had put the tank down quietly in the corner and was now scanning the paper, trying to be as discreet as he could, as Ellie and I sat watching her.

'So you weren't badly hurt then?' asked Ellie sipping her tea politely.

The girl looked at her, a baffled expression on her face.

'We thought you might be in hospital,' said Ellie kindly.

The girl looked confused.

'Hospital. Why?'

'Because of the attack,' said Ellie looking up at Charlie and I in worry. She clearly thought the girl might be suffering from amnesia or burying the attack in her sub conscious.

'What attack?' sniffed the girl, 'What are you talking about?'

'Well the police came round here after they'd found a girl in the park. And it was the night you were shouting at him so we thought...'

'You thought it was me,' she concluded softly.

'Yes,' muttered Ellie.

'It wasn't.' A tear ran down her cheek. I watched its progress, not sure what to do next but listen.

'And he didn't do it.'

I looked at Ellie.

'The attack,' she went on, 'It wasn't him. But the police are looking for him and I don't know where he's gone,' she burst into fresh sobs. Ellie went to make more tea and I sat there frozen.

'So he didn't attack you,' I confirmed.

'He didn't attack anyone,' she said looking up at me angrily. I didn't dare ask her how she knew this for certain.

'I'd know. I'm his sister,' she announced.

I heard Ellie suddenly clatter in the kitchen.

'His sister,' I repeated. She seemed well dressed and pretty, and normal. How could she possibly be his sister?

'Kevin's had a few problems in the last few months but he, he would never do that,' she whispered. She started crying again, 'I've got to find him,' she said and got up determinedly.

I was at a loss for words again. Why had he disappeared if he wasn't guilty? Who had he attacked? Why had they been shouting? It was all still so confusing. Neither Ellie or I dared to tell her we had heard him confessing to a murder.

'Thank you for the tea. I have to go,' she said shaking on her coat.

Ellie put down the mugs she was holding.

'Is there anything we can do?' she asked concerned.

'No honestly I'm fine... but...' she looked at the tank and stopped, 'Well actually,' the girl shifted a little, looking slightly embarrassed, 'if you're sure, there is a small favour you could do.'

'Oh anything,' said Ellie deeply touched by the real life soap opera unfolding in front of her.

'Well I was going to take the snake,' she said pointing at the tank Charlie had carried up the stairs, 'because I didn't know when he'd be back. But it's so heavy. If I could leave it here would it be possible for you to feed him until... until he comes back...'

My mouth dropped open and I noticed Ellie had got quieter.

'... I'm sure you won't even have to, he'll probably be back soon so it's not a problem if you haven't got time or...' she looked close to tears again.

Ellie gulped. 'Um no, no, of course we can. Of course,' she

repeated with slightly more confidence than I know she felt. I was still looking totally horrified.

'Won't we Angel,' said Ellie looking at me.

I didn't trust myself to do more than nod.

'I know it will seem weird but it's pretty simple. He keeps the frozen rabbits in the freezer, I've popped some in this bag,' she said grabbing the carrier bag I had innocently brought up for her, I flinched. '...And he needs to be fed once a week.'

'Right. Frozen rabbit from the freezer. And we just pop that in the tank do we?' asked Ellie trying to sound perfectly laid back.

'Yes, he'll eat it if you leave it in there.'

'Right,' she nodded.

Frozen baby bunnies. In the freezer. To be fed to the snake. I caught Charlie looking at me and suddenly felt a mad urge to start giggling.

'Charlie could you help me put it by the window,' I said smiling sweetly at him, 'Ellie why don't you put the bunnies in the freezer,' I said turning to her.

We manoeuvred the tank under the window. As I lifted it I tried to crane my neck as far away as possible so I wouldn't eyeball the reptile.

'Thank you,' the girl muttered as she left, 'I'm sure he'll be back very soon. You're very kind.'

And with that she left us, the proud owners of a domestic python.

An hour later, after dissecting the whole day with Ellie, Charlie and I had settled down in front of the tank. I had unearthed some more wine, which we'd all needed after the girl had gone. We now sat cross-legged, in silence, staring at the snake. It was lying perfectly still, but you could tell that at any minute it could raise its head, swivel its snake body and attack. Charlie, being a boy, was fascinated.

'It's huge,' he exclaimed amazed.

'I know,' I whispered, careful not to disturb it, 'I've never seen one that big.'

Charlie nodded and continued to stare. 'I didn't even know you could get them that big.'

'Are you sure it's tamed?' I asked worriedly.

'I think so.'

As if on cue the snake slithered forward an inch or so, its whole body curving as it moved.

'WOW,' we both breathed out.

'How can it all fit in there?' I said looking at the tank.

'I know,' Charlie agreed, 'They don't get bigger than that.'

Suddenly a noise interrupted us. A snort of laughter. We both peered round to see Ellie, hand over mouth, shaking in the doorway. 'Sorry you two didn't mean to interrupt such an intimate conversation.'

My brow furrowed and then I realised what she meant.

I looked at her haughtily. 'We were talking about the snake,' I said.

'I heard,' she chuckled.

I blushed, fortunately Charlie was laughing with her.

'Well I don't want to interrupt your snake watch,' she said smirking and picking up her keys, 'I'm going out. Nice to meet you Charlie and thanks for your help earlier. See you tomorrow Angel.'

'Have a good one,' I called after her.

We went back to sipping at our wine and staring at the tank.

After a bit more silence Charlie stirred, 'Well I suppose it is getting late,' he said looking at his watch.

'I know I feel so lazy. I can't believe it's a weekday and I am just lounging about,' I said stretching out my legs.

'You know Angel, you are very strange,' Charlie said laughing and shaking his head. 'Snakes, dangerous neighbours, jobs you escape from... is this just a usual day for you?'

'Not at all. I promise I am perfectly normal,' I said laughing and giving him Scouts Honour.

Suddenly the intercom buzzed through the flat. Ellie must have forgotten her keys. I went to buzz her in.

'Angel we love you,' chorused two voices over the intercom.

It wasn't Ellie. Charlie looked quizzical. I knew instantly who was there.

'Let us in. We know you're there,' chimed the two voices.

'Come up,' I said pressing the intercom.

I heard two people pounding up the stairs and left the door on the latch.

'Charlie my friends Suzie and Rick are about to arrive and...'

I was interrupted by their arrival.

'Angel we bring you gifts to cheer you up,' said Rick bustling in with wine and sweets.

'We have cards, and food, and wine and... it's nice to meet you,' said Suzie drawing up in the doorway when she sees Charlie.

'Hi I'm Charlie,' he said getting up smiling at her.

'Suzie.'

'We're going to play poker,' squealed Rick excitedly bouncing into the room after her, then he saw Charlie, 'Maybe strip poker. I'm Rick,' he said offering his hand.

I looked at him suspiciously, 'Strip poker?' I repeated slowly.

'Yes let's,' said Rick looking at Charlie expectantly.

'No stripping,' said Suzie laughing.

'I agree,' I chipped in.

'Me too,' said Charlie.

'Damn,' said Rick flinging down his carrier bags.

'So poker it is,' announced Suzie clearing the table of strewn magazines.

'I don't know how to play,' I said.

'We'll teach you,' said Suzie.

'We bought some nachos and wine,' said Rick popping everything on the table. 'And Maltesers and the little pink and yellow marshmallow twists.'

'OK I'll get glasses and things,' I said moving through to the kitchen. 'Charlie will you stay?' I asked calling from the kitchen.

He was already shuffling the cards and fielding Suzie's questions about his life.

When I'd settled again Suzie looked at me with concern, 'So Angel have you had an OK day.'

The last thing she'd known I'd been sent home with a slap on the wrists and a guilty conscience. I'd had a whole day however to get used to the idea, plus a large amount of wine. Not to mention the hours of distraction with snakes, neighbours and crying women. This morning seemed like forever ago.

'I've been fine,' I assured her, 'Victoria was really nice and I'm glad I've got this week off to think about things.'

'To think about things,' she repeated, smiling wickedly at me as Charlie looked away. I poked my tongue out at her and poured out some more wine for everyone.

'So you're free this week.' Rick concluded excitedly.

I turned to him pleased for the change of subject.

'Yes.'

'You can hang out with me then,' he announced looking pleased. 'I think I'm definitely on the mend from the psoriasis. My mate Zoe reckons it could have been brought on by all the exam stress,' he explained carefully.

'And what else did she say Rick?' piped up Suzie.

I looked at Rick.

'That it might have been a little eczema,' Rick muttered quietly.

'Well I'm glad you're better,' I said smiling generously at him.

'So you've really been OK Angel,' Suzie said double-checking.

'Fine,' I laughed, 'Really...Well aside from adopting a large python.'

'What?' said Rick eyes snapping up in fear.

I pointed to the tank now installed under our window sill.

With an 'Ooh' Rick got up to investigate while I told them the shortened version of the snake story. Kevin's sister, who we thought was dead, turns up upset and asks us to take care of a domestic python until her brother, our murdering neighbour, returns from his latest killing spree. It all seemed so unreal put like that, which made me feel a lot better. Although his sister was convinced of his innocence I wasn't so sure. But tonight was not the night to worry anymore about Kevin. I did feel relieved that there were so many people in the flat. Safety in numbers. It had been eerie with just Ellie and I in at night.

'So... poker,' I said clapping my hands together, 'Explain.'

'OK,' started Suzie, 'there is a dealer, we all get dealt two cards and then we place our first bet on them...'

'Hang on,' I said pausing Suzie's instructions and running through to my room to rummage through my bedside drawer. 'OK coming.'

I returned carrying a lighter and an ancient packet of cigarettes.

'I didn't know you smoked,' said Suzie

'I don't,' I shrugged.

I started lighting a cigarette a little inexpertly.

'So what are you doing,' Suzie asked as I flicked the lighter on for the third time.

'It seems like we should smoke. Poker's that kind of game,' I said knowledgably, returning my focus to the fuel.

'Absolutely,' agreed Charlie proffering a lighter, 'need some help Angel.'

I scowled at him, 'I'm fine thank you.' It lit and I looked at him triumphantly. He grinned at me.

'Right...' said Suzie expertly shuffling the cards like a croupier in a casino and explaining the gist of the game. '... So a pair is obviously a pair of the same number, as is two pairs, three of a kind etc, then a straight is a run of numbers in a row and a straight flush is a run of numbers all of the same suit.'

'Don't forget the Full House,' piped up Rick.

'A Full House is three of a kind and a pair,' explained Suzie.

And a Royal Flush,' added Charlie, 'is the highest straight run around the table.'

I was looking at them all with boggled eyes.

'I'll just write them down for you to look at...' said Suzie scribbling on a piece of paper.

Charlie leaned forward to chip in with further instructions, 'So you say 'Twist' when you want another card, then we reveal our cards when the betting is finished.'

'Right, I said nodding solemnly at him.

While I was blowing out smoke rings and Suzie was dealing cards Rick, always excited to be introduced to a new audience, immediately settled down to tell Charlie all about his latest run of diseases. I was too busy trying to remember the rules of the game to pay close attention.

'You see I'm worried I'm developing a case of gastroenteritis. Recently I've noticed I've got a little blood in my stools and my friend Gary, who does medicine with me, says it might be that, or kidney failure perhaps.'

Charlie looked a little pale.

'But I haven't been vomiting and I've had no diarrhoea so I'm not sure he's right or what it is...'

'OK we're ready,' announced Suzie cutting Rick off before he got any more graphic. Charlie looked at her in relief. I sneaked a look at him and smiled.

I picked up my cards. Hooray they looked good. They were all red. That had to be a positive.

'Good cards Angel?' asked Charlie innocently.

'Yes... no... maybe.... Why?' I said flustered.

'You just have a bit of a grin on your face,' he chuckled.

'Well I am just pleased we are all here having a lovely night together,' I said huffily turning back to moving my cards around.

'Betting.'

'Twist.'

'Twist.'

'Twist.'

'Fold,' moaned Rick throwing his cards down.

'Twist.'

A few goes passed.

'So hypothetically if I had three numbers the same and two others the same would that be good?' I asked looking at the cards and trying to sound light hearted.

'Yes,' said Charlie, 'that would be good Angel.'

'Angel you are not meant to do that,' said Suzie looking up.

'Do what?' I asked, excitedly punching the air.

'Tell us what cards you have.'

'I didn't,' I protested. 'I said hypothetically. I don't actually have them that would be ridiculous. I was just checking in case I do get them soon.'

Charlie smiled and looked down at his cards in concentration.

In a plume of smoke we played on. I got the hang of it more and more. Rick was terrible. He kept squeaking every time he got a good card. Then when we pointed this out, he insisted he might be double bluffing. He never was. Suzie took it very seriously and I was sure Charlie was sending me up. Every now and again I caught his eye across the table. Today had been a strange day; I felt I knew him so well...

'Angel it's your go,' nudged Rick, 'Ooh I'll swap you a five of spades for that Queen,' he said looking over my shoulder.

'RICK,' screeched Suzie.

It had got dark outside and I had stubbed out one last cigarette, realising that they had done little but give me a nasty ash like aftertaste. We'd been playing for a good two hours now and we had to produce our cards again. Charlie had a pair, Rick had nothing, Suzie had a straight.

'Oh,' I said looking disappointed, 'I just have lots of diamonds,' I said.

'How many?' asked Charlie.

'Five,' I counted, 'Oh I think that's a Flush,' I realised.

Suzie sighed as I asked, 'Does a Flush beat a Straight?'

'Yes Angel it does,' she said gritting her teeth.

'Right... oh I think I have that then' I said fanning out my cards.

'What a surprise' muttered Suzie.

'Does that mean I've won again?' I asked wrinkling my forehead and holding out my cards to her.

She looked at me. 'Angel I am never going to play poker with you again.'

Charlie and Rick were in hysterics.

I couldn't believe that only this morning I had been sent packing from work with my tail between my legs. Charlie and I had spent so much time together today that as he got up to leave I thought I might miss him when he was gone. I walked him to the flat door.

'Thank you for cheering me up today,' I said, handing him his coat.

I suddenly realised we could be in for an awkward good bye kiss.

'Night Charlie,' chorused Suzie and Rick from the living room.

I grinned at him.

'Night,' he yelled back and then looked at me, 'I hope you're OK Angel,' he said. He leaned in and kissed me on the cheek, 'I'll speak to you soon.'

I nodded.

'Night,' I said closing the door.

I leant back against it for a couple if seconds. Then hearing Suzie and Rick bickering next door I went to join them.

* * *

I spent the next couple of days quietly at home with Ellie, talking things through and updating my acting CV. I repeated Suzie's compliment to myself. She'd thought I was a 'great actress.' I thought back to past plays and reviews and felt a glow as I remembered performances I'd been proud of and roles that I had loved playing. I'd been to evening workshops, theatre groups all through school; I'd been on summer courses with the National Youth Theatre and had always wanted to work hard to become an actress. The idea of trying again suddenly gave me a buzz of nervous excitement.

On my high I called my agent to attempt to arrange a meeting with him. His response was depressingly pathetic and my spirits were dulled temporarily. He claimed he was too busy his end to see me, and I wondered exactly what was making him so busy. It certainly didn't appear to be finding me any work. Although I knew I had a full time job at the magazine I felt better for realising I needed to start acting again, even if it was with an amateur group of an evening. I scanned some acting websites and looked up various theatre companies in London to see what they were planning to put on in the near future. On numerous occasions I had thought of Sam at BOS Productions who had called to ask me to audition for them. Now was the moment to take him up on it. I dialled the number with a new optimism.

'Good afternoon BOS Productions, can I help you?'

'Hi,' I started, nervously clearing my throat, 'My name's Angela Lawson, you called me a couple of weeks ago now wondering if I was available to come in and audition for you.'

'Who did you speak to?' came a brusque reply on the end of the line.

'Oh um... Sam.'

'Hold the line.'

I held the phone to my chest. Why had I rung? Of course they wouldn't remember me; they must be ringing hundreds of girls. I considered hanging up. But then I wanted to audition for them. I had to start somewhere and they had wanted to see me.

'I'll just put you through,' said the voice while I was fretting. Then there was silence.

'Hello, Sam speaking.'

I took a breath and repeated my learnt spiel, 'Hi Sam, my name's Angela Lawson, you called me a few weeks ago now wondering if I was available to come in and audition for you.'

'Angela, oh yes, Angel of course' said Sam confidently, 'So are you available to audition for us at all?'

'Well, yes,' I said surprised that he was still interested.

'Excellent,' he said enthusiastically.

I smiled, feeling a little less nervous suddenly.

'We're doing one last casting session for the season later this month. Could you come in on the 27th, that's Wednesday, week after next?'

'Wednesday the 27th. Yes that should be fine,' I agreed, tentatively picturing Victoria's face.

'Would any particular time suit you?' he asked.

'Afternoon I suppose.' That gave me the morning to figure out an excuse for missing yet more work.

'OK, Wednesday 27th, 3.45pm. Is that alright?'

'Yes.... That's brilliant.'

'OK, well it shouldn't be too strenuous. If you prepare a speech for us, no more than two minutes, and then we'll give you some pieces to perform cold. OK?'

'Right. That's fine. Well thank you and thank you for seeing me at such late notice,' I stuttered.

'Not at all, looking forward to meeting you in person Angel.'

'You too,' I said gratefully.

I put the phone down and relief flooded through me. Hooray. One small step...

My mind was already running through the possibilities. Should I do something comic for them, something tragic to make them all start sobbing? Should I fling in a bit of Shakespeare to make them feel I am comfortable with all styles? I was grinning as I got more and more excited about the prospect of planning and rehearsing for the audition. I realised a weight had been lifted. All the months at the magazine, all the times I had been bored hanging around at Nick's flat doing nothing, I had missed having something to focus on. Going out with Nick, worrying about him, had been a good way to ignore the hole in my life, and now, it seemed, I was filling it!

With that behind me, and something to aim for, I felt a lot happier. I sat down to plough through the last few weeks replies I had written. I needed to rewrite around half of them where I had strayed into fantasy/warped musings/selfish observations/madness. I dutifully picked up a pen and worked my way through the stack, pausing to think of similar cases I'd read about and advice that would prove helpful. I wanted to prove to Victoria that I had changed; that I do take the problems, and my advisory role, seriously. I thought of what Charlie had said, about treating kids like adults, and I realised that my approach on the magazine had often been patronizing, belittling the problems because they were just teenagers who didn't know better. After fretting over my life I realised we always have problems we need to sort through, no matter if we're eighteen or thirty-eight.

Still on a roll from sorting out my life (audition planned, letters re written, head feeling clearer) I decided to move on to other peoples. My first port of call had to be Dad. Even I could not ignore the fact that my mother, frantic at the best of times, was clearly going up the wall over his cat napping schemes. I dialled home in the hope of restoring a little sanity to the household, confident that if I could fix my life, I could do anything. Just when I thought I would put the phone down and assume no one was in Dad answered the line. It appeared fate was on my side today. I felt the positive energy was flowing and it gave me a confidence to tackle the problem head on.

'Dad I'm glad it's you, it's Angel.'

'Hello love,' he answered letting out a sigh, 'Glad it's you too.'

I instantly felt guilty that I was about to launch into a mother-inspired lecture.

'Dad I got a call from Mum yesterday,' I said beginning tentatively by immediately shifting blame. My dad let out a slightly louder sigh.

'Go on,' he said preparing himself for what was coming next.

'Well she's a bit worried.'

'Yes I know she is.'

'So...' I urged, hoping he would make this easier.

'I'm not giving it back to them Angel,' he said stubbornly.

'Don't you think maybe you're taking this whole thing... well... a bit far?' I asked.

'Angel you don't understand, that cat makes me mad. It gets everywhere. It leaves muck right in the middle of our lawn. And on the country lane outside, so that my feet stink of it if I happen to walk there.'

'Yes but, well, couldn't you ask your neighbours' nicely to install a litter tray for it?'

'I've spoken to Mrs. Phillips and she says they've got one

but the damn cat just ignores it,' he said exasperated.

'But Dad you can't just take it. I'm sure if you ask them nicely they'll make more of an effort to try and get it to, to... control itself,' I finished.

'I have asked them. No I was forced into the position I'm in and I'm not giving it up,' he said sounding like a general in a war.

'Is it really that bad?' I laughed, trying to lighten his mood a little. To no avail.

'That cat has it in for me Angela,' claimed Dad, mimicking what Mum had told me.

'It knows where I go. It watches me. I'm convinced it's doing it deliberately. It knows. I see it in its eyes. It knows.'

I began to get a little nervous as he went on with his obsession. Mum was right he had lost it. I tried to interrupt him.

'... has it in for me. I'm sure. Well no more. I want it toilet trained. And that is what I have told them. You can have your cat back on the condition that it is toilet trained properly or it will be removed again. Honestly the way your mother goes on about it you'd think I was asking them for money...'

'OK Dad, OK,' I soothed, realising this would be harder than I first thought.

'It's driven me to this Angela,' he pleaded for me to understand.

I was dubious. I really needed to see this cat to get an idea of quite how devious it could be. Dad interrupted my musing.

'Wait Angel, I've got to go, your mother's cars coming up the drive. She'll only lecture me again. I'll speak to you soon love. Take care.'

'Bye Dad... er... you too,' I said hearing the dialling tone.

That hadn't been the huge success I had hoped for. I realised other people's lives could often be a lot more complicated and maybe, for now, it was better to take smaller steps and just fix mine.

There was one small, tiny little glitch on my new horizon. In the midst of all this new found organizing of my life's priorities it had not escaped my notice that Charlie had not been in touch. After spending all day together he had obviously enjoyed his Angel quota for the week and I hadn't heard a pip from him since. I ventured back to the office on Monday and spent the week focusing on other things. Then at the end of the week he texted, apologizing for leaving it so long and asked if I would like to do something the next day. The next day being a Saturday and very soon. A bit of me wanted to play the usual games, leave it a day to reply, not agree to the first time and place, hold out and make him think I was flooded with similar offers but I wasn't busy the next day and I wanted to see him again.

* * *

Over the years I have managed to compile a little list of things to do, and not do, when preparing oneself for exciting date with man/woman/other. Obviously the list has been plucked from my imagination and is in no way based on any past experiences. It is just a list that people should consider before Date Preparation, that is all. Truly. Soooo...

DO ensure you leave ample time to prepare yourself.
DON'T leave all till last minute, decide to put egg on hair in cunning conditioner experiment and then gasp as tall, attractive date arrives ten minutes early.
DO ensure make up beautifully dashed on as if to show date you have just rolled out of bed in an ooh-you've-arrived-I'll-just-get-ready kind of way.
DON'T open door during crazy decision over lime green eye shadow.
DO ensure you smell sweet; of roses or of cute little kittens.
DON'T run out of deodorant so pour Toilet Duck (unscented, and quite painful) over one's body in an attempt to disguise the fact.
DO remember to book yourself into a waxing clinic.
DON'T suddenly wait till moments before, seize a blunt razor, shimmy it up and down your leg, only to see rivulets of blood running down shins.
DON'T greet him warmly after shaving disaster by placing girlish hand on his chest, only to leave bloodied hand marks on his new white Paul Smith T-shirt.
DO make sure any weird freakish looking neighbours with snake/rat/lizard are locked up inside their flat as date arrives.
DON'T be borrowing bottle opener in half-date

preparation from said weirdo neighbour with snake/rat/lizard and seem to emerge from his flat in state of undress to be faced by date.

Today fortunately went off without a glitch. I enjoyed a successful preparation process where I dressed and bathed myself without any physical damage, humiliation or embarrassment. I set off to meet Charlie outside Charing Cross station. He was dressed in a casual shirt and trousers and seemed unaware of the effect that tanned skin meets blue eyes, meets dark hair, had. After kissing me on the cheek he announced it was a beautiful day and suggested we walked to the Tate Modern. I agreed without thinking.

As I made my way over the steel bridge however I became a little nervous. Modern art is not a particular speciality of mine. I do not know my Turner from my Tracy Emin. I hoped I would be able to keep up. I was not comforted by the fact that the first thing we were faced with on arrival was a giant 20ft steel spider with spindly legs clutching what looked like an enormous pouch of eggs. It was quite a welcome. I was thankful I didn't suffer from a bad case of arachnophobia. Charlie had gone off to dump our coats in the cloakroom and I hung around waiting for him to come back, not sure where to begin looking. To the right of the steel spider I noticed everyone peering over the balcony edge. I tentatively went to take a look. A lot of people were milling below and there were some temporary railings up in some kind of mysterious snake like formation. I stared a little longer, unsure whether the railings were some kind of modern piece or whether I was just looking at the visitor's entrance. No one seemed to be nodding animatedly at it so began to feel fairly confident that it was not part of an impressive exhibit. Started to move away but oh, disaster, girl on left started taking photos of it all. I rushed back to the side of the railing and leaned further over the edge still scanning the area. I don't get it. And I don't dare ask.

'There you are,' Charlie said from behind me. 'So are you ready to take a look?' he said indicating the escalator with his hand. He didn't appear to be that interested in the display over the balcony so I turned and smiled, but then realised he might have just seen it before. I turned back, took one last look over the railing, nodded and went 'umm' just to let him know I'd seen and appreciated it. Charlie looked at me a little oddly and I scampered to his side.

On the other side of the balcony I was back on a more confident footing. Rows and rows of busts and various bits on plaques had been set up and I knew bust sculptures = art. The girl with the photo is here too, so I began to perk up a bit. At the bottom of each of the five rows of busts I noticed four televisions playing. I shook my head sadly.

'What is it?'

'Oh nothing,' I sighed.

'What?' he persisted.

I looked at him and then with a little indication of my hand said, 'I just... I find it a sad symptom of this society that even here, in one of the greatest art museums of the world, we still have to have the telly on in the background.'

I gave my head another sad little shake and went to move away. Charlie however stayed stock still.

'What?' I asked as I saw his mouth twitch.

'No nothing...'

I overheard a man talking to his children next door,

'...The screens are part of the exhibition boys. That one is Gilbert and George's piece, 'The Portrait of the Artists as Young Men'.'

Ah.

Charlie smiled, 'Here, put these on,' he held out the headphones.

I put them on, keen to become enlightened. After a few seconds of listening to a fuzzy sound of running water I lifted one up, 'I think it's broken.'

Charlie was listening animatedly. I focused back on the television. I looked at the screen with Gilbert in glasses holding a cigarette and George looking intent. There didn't appear to be any dialogue between them but the running water was still on. They weren't moving. The water ran on. I thought the kids on the headphones next door summed it up fairly neatly. 'They're not doing anything Dad.'

I took them off again and gave Charlie a weak smile.

'So what did you think?' he asked.

'Hmm,' I murmured, hoping that would be ambiguous enough.

'Come on Miss Sceptical?' he said grinning and dragging me off to the first floor.

I liked the picture of the guy with combs in his hair. And the piano hanging from the ceiling. And the sculpture of 'the Kiss' next to the room with the toilet. Not the actual toilet. The fake toilet, the one on show. The yellow one. We walked past a Brillo soap pads box, three basketballs in a fish tank, a car made of what looked like cardboard and a kind of grey ventilator. I had walked past assuming it was a radiator, but Charlie had taken a closer look at it and I'd realised it was a work of art. It was not a radiator, even though it looked just like one. The explanation on the wall claimed it was art because the piece mimicked the appearance of a machine–made unit, but had no utilitarian function. Although, as I pointed out, that's how Mum would describe our washing machine. The trouble came when I noticed the grille on the floor to the right of it which wasn't cordoned off but looked suspiciously like the rest of the stuff. I hesitated by it before I realised it was not part of the display.

'Something interesting Angel?' asked Charlie smirking at me.

I poked my tongue out at him.

After I had seen a cleaners wardrobe, a bookcase of shells, (some not unlike the conch we have on our mantelpiece at home – shall have to tell Dad we are seriously in vogue), a room that changed colour and a few pieces of pop art I reckoned I was ready for a lunch break. I looked across at Charlie to see if he might be persuaded to go. He was squinting at the information below a canvas reading about 'Patrick Caulfield and his oil, 'Interior with a picture.' He looked so solemn mouthing the words on the wall. I felt a new warmth towards him. He seemed so inspired by it all and he was so keen to make sure that I was interested. It was lovely looking at all the things with someone there to tell you little bits about the painters, little facts about the pieces. And he seemed genuinely thrilled whenever I took an interest. He was such a nice guy, and as I continued to stare at him I noticed how good looking he was with his scruffy dark hair and his lazy smile.

In the midst of this musing I was suddenly jolted. What was I doing? Was I already ear-marking Charlie as the next man who would break my heart? Had I learnt nothing from the whole

Nick debacle? Was I not meant to be focusing on other things right now, making sure I wasn't defined by a man, ensuring that I moved forward, progressed... And here I was going gooey over a man I barely knew who, underneath his sexy laid back façade, was probably just waiting to mess me up. I didn't know anything about him. We hadn't spent more than 24 hours together yet. He could be a cheat, an aggressive drunk, a lying scum bag or all three. I really had no idea. And I didn't trust my instincts anymore. Hadn't my instincts been assuring me that Nick was the right guy for me? And look what had happened there...

I had got a little quieter with all the thinking. Charlie, taking it for boredom, had frog marched me straight to the cafeteria. A thoughtful gesture the old me would have thought, but this new me was aware of the dangers of this charm. Twenty minutes and a trip to the gift shop later we were nursing our coffees and looking out over Central London. I realised that this was our second date. Really our third as the last one had been so extended. I would be expected to start sleeping with him soon. He had probably already made plans for our first night together. I panicked. I didn't care how attractive he was anymore I finally felt a lot happier and I couldn't just go back into another relationship with a guy that might seem nice but who would soon let me down one way or another. I had to say something.

My mind was running through a million different openers. Charlie looked so relaxed as he confidently flicked through his Degas postcard book. He was probably planning where we'd stay that night. His place, or mine. He looked up and smiled at me. I knew it. I noticed the picture was of some nude washing her hair. It was just sex, sex, sex on their minds. I sat up straight, remembering to heed my own words of advice. He smiled again. The smile suggested things, 'I like you Angela' it said, 'Isn't this going well,' it said, 'You will be mine soon' said its deeper meaning. I didn't need this. I wouldn't be messed around again. I couldn't do it. The smile had suggested promises of a bright future, but it was masking other things. Bad things. But I was ready for him, I knew his game. Something needed to be done.

'I can't do this,' I announced, putting my coffee cup gingerly on the table.

'I'm sorry,' said a startled Charlie. Playing the innocent no doubt. Wrenched from his masochistic thoughts no doubt.

'I just don't think I can do this,' I said again a little louder.

He managed to put the nude down for a minute.

'Do what... exactly,' he asked.

'This...' I gestured between us, 'This being here with you. I think you know what I mean,' I said giving him a long knowing look. His face didn't register knowing much however so I was forced to stumble on.

'I'm sorry Charlie... I just. I don't know... I really like you but...'

I considered giving him the whole 'It's not you, it's me' speech, 'I just have to really focus on other things right now,' 'You see you are so ying and I'm more yang' but he beat me to it.

'Angela are you alright?' he asked.

'I'm fine. I just don't think I want anything to happen between us. I've just come out of a long term relationship and I'm not sure I...'

'Angela that's OK, you don't have to explain it to me. That's fine, absolutely. I thought you might say this, that's fine.' He assured me. 'So are you alright?' he asked with a look of concern.

Pah! I knew his game. I felt angered. I started to give him the spiel...

'Look it's not you, it's me...'

'Do you want to just be friends?' he said breaking into my speech.

'Well... Yes, you see I'm at that point in my life where I need to focus on my...'

'That's fine Angel, if that's what you want. Let's just be friends. I don't want to just not see again. Nothing has to happen.'

I closed my mouth slowly, 'Oh right,' I picked up my coffee again, 'Good,' I said.

'I know how horrible it is ending a relationship. Let's just hang out as friends,' he smiled at me again and then went back to perusing the nudes and I went back to looking out over the Thames.

Dear Angel,
I was going out with this bloke for a year and then the other

day he said he wanted to be friends. I don't know why. What should I do?

Gemma, 17, Hythe

Dear Gemma,
Don't you think being friends, having friends, is so much more important? There is nothing in life more special than having friends, who look out for you and care. Maybe your bloke was right and this is a positive step forward...

* * *

'You're going to be friends,' Rick repeated when I told him about the conversation in the Tate.
'Yes Rick... friends. You know like Bill and Ben, Burt and Ernie, you and me.'
'So friends. Just friends.' He said
'Yes.'
'Why?'
'I'm sorry?'
'Well why? I don't get it.'
'Well Rick it's fairly simple I like him, he likes me so we thought we'd spend time together as friends.'
'Friends.'
'Yes.' I said beginning to tire of the repetition.
'But what's the point of friends?' he said crinkling his nose up in confusion.
'What do you mean what's the point. What's the point of you and me being friends?'
'That's different,' he said.
'It's not different,' I sighed.
'It is.'
'What's so different about it?'
'Well I don't want to stick little Rick in you anywhere.'
'That is charming Rick.'
'Well it's true.'
'It's not.'
'What Charlie doesn't want to stick...'
'Please don't finish that sentence Rick.'
'So do you fancy him?'

'Well I think he's lovely...' I said as if I were in a Jane Austen novel, 'and he's quite good looking so usually I suppose yes, but that's not the point we're better as friends. Don't you see? It immediately makes everything much less complicated.'

'But...' Rick said still sounding uncertain, 'I thought men and women couldn't be friends.'

'No that's just a myth.'

'What like the bible?'

'Er... Kind of.'

'Well I'm sure I heard somewhere that men and women can't be friends,' Rick insisted.

'Well you heard wrong,' I said irritably. 'It's an excellent idea. It means I can get on and sort out other things in my life without stressing about will he call me won't he call me. Why hasn't he called me, maybe he'll never call me etc etc, etc,' I ranted.

'OK psycho I get the picture,' said Rick raising his hands to me.

'Good,' I said relaxing again.

'It sounds to me like you're keeping him on ice,' Rick shrugged.

I looked at Rick aghast.

'Well it does,' he protested.

'I'm not keeping him on ice. I'm just keeping him as a friend,' I stressed.

'Friends,' Rick muttered as if he'd never heard anything so sacrilegious in his life. Which he probably hadn't. Boy friends did not feature hugely in Rick's vocabulary. He was too busy trying to sleep with them. 'Friends.'

'Finished Rick?' I asked watching him muttering.

'Fine. Friends it is,' he shrugged, still visibly baffled, 'Good luck with that,' he sighed.

'Thank you,' I nodded demurely.

'Do you think he's gay,' Rick asked suddenly.

'No I do not Rick.'

'Well why else would he want to be friends?'

I groaned. 'I want to be friends,' I stressed.

'Well maybe I should have a go,' he chirruped.

'A go?' I said looking at him in disgust.

'What? Someone's got to try and have sex with him,' he wailed.

To Rick's bemusement Charlie and I did become friends. We spent a lot of time lazing around watching videos when it rained and lazing around reading books in the park when it was sunny. Every now and again I would catch sight of Charlie looking particularly bronzed and gorgeous and wonder what I was up to. But then I reminded myself how less complicated it all now was. Work didn't seem such a hardship and I was seeing more of my friends. I had visited the gym; I had re arranged my wardrobe. I felt increasingly peaceful. I hadn't seen Charlie for the last few days, he'd been quite busy recently and quite secretive about it I thought, smiling to myself. He'd tell me what he was up to soon enough. Yes, it all seemed to be going well. Very well I thought as I walked into the office after a particularly good lunch break (sushi).

I'd only just sat down when I noticed someone was standing over my desk. Looking up I was surprised to see the receptionist with the peroxide hair chewing gum and looking down at me in contempt. Normally she didn't feel the need to walk this far to make me feel this small.

'There's someone here for you at reception,' announced her whiny voice.

'Oh right,' I flustered wondering who it might be, 'Er... a man or woman?' I asked, fluffing up my hair a little.

'It's a lady,' she said in her finest flower girl tone.

Curiously I followed the receptionist back to reception where she instantly resumed a conversation on the phone, no doubt cursing me for making her do any work what so ever today. I scanned the reception quickly to see the usual array of cushioned sofas, Ikea prints and glossy magazines all in their usual place. There was only one addition to the room. Standing by the water cooler, looking utterly out of place in such a hip neon coloured environment, was a bland looking mousey haired woman wearing a beige raincoat and carrying a tatty bag. I looked at her enquiringly. Then I looked over at the receptionist. Was this the lady? She didn't look up from her telephonic whining and before I had time to ask the woman in the raincoat had rushed forward.

'Oh I recognise you from your column,' she said gushing instantly.

I looked at her in bafflement. Who was this woman? Was there some mistake? Was I on candid camera?

'I didn't know where to go and you were so nice in your last letter,' she went on.

I looked at her again.

'It's Mary,' she said.

I tried to interrupt her spiel and inform her that I thought she must have the wrong person, 'I'm sorry I...' but then I twigged. Mary, 47, Hull.

'Oh Mary, Right... Hi,' I gabbled ungraciously.

She smiled a little uncertainly, 'I'm really so sorry to just turn up, but, well... I left him,' she announced pointing triumphantly to the tatty handbag and then to the floor behind her where a large tatty suitcase was perched. 'I actually left him.' Then she burst into tears.

At this the receptionist looked up. This in itself was a sign that something fairly dramatic was happening, she'd been known to talk right on through fire drills. I was standing staring at Mary agape.

'Oh I... right. Um...'

I really didn't know what to do. This was definitely a first for me. At that moment Nigel appeared through the office doors. Taking in the image of two women talking, one of whom was bawling her eyes out, he turned to flee.

'Nigel,' I said rooting him to the spot. He looked afraid.

'Could you get her a coffee or something?' I asked glancing up at him.

'Er... of course,' he said looking at us both uncertainly and then scuttling off.

Mary was sniffing into an ancient looking handkerchief. '...So I packed a suitcase and took off in the car. I didn't know where to go and you'd said so many nice things in your last letter I knew you'd understand.'

'Of course,' I said gesturing for her to sit down on a nearby sofa. She didn't seem to take it in.

'I just couldn't face seeing any of my friends. Some of them just don't understand see because they've known Bernard and me for years. And you just seemed to understand what I was feeling and...'

'Don't worry Mary there's really no need to explain. Let's go and have a chat somewhere. I'll just go and have a word with my boss.'

Nigel re-appeared with a tray, 'I didn't know whether you'd want tea or coffee. Or whether you'd want milk, or milk and sugar, so I just made a few so you can choose,' he said placing the tray of drinks down on the table. There must have been about seven or eight mugs to pick from.

Mary's reddened eyes widened with surprise, 'Thank you,' she muttered.

'So Mary just hold tight here, I won't be long.' I started for Victoria's office.

'I'll stay with her,' said Nigel, nervously eyeing her fretting over the mugs.

'Thanks,' I said moving back through to the office.

This was madness. But the poor woman looked so awful and I had heard how much she'd been through. I had to help somehow. She just needed to be assured she'd done the right thing.

Victoria was clicking and typing on her computer when I knocked on her door. She looked up from her work and beckoned me in. I explained things quickly and simply.

'She's what? Turned up here. Why?'

'She's left her husband,' I said.

'Yes but what has that got to do with you?' asked Victoria still at a loss.

'She didn't know where else to go. She's been writing to me for a while and felt that I might be able to help. I think she just wants to talk to someone.'

'Well I suppose so, she's not mad or anything is she Angel? You will be careful,' she said looking a little concerned that I'd signed up for some caffeine therapy with a woman with red eyes and a beige raincoat.

'Oh don't worry she's absolutely harmless,' I said, 'I won't be too long. Thanks Victoria.'

'Fine, well don't be hours,' she said waving me out of the office, 'And let me know how it goes.'

'Oh yes I will,' I said closing her door and scuttling back to reception. Mary was sitting looking pale on the sofa, her hands around one of the dozen mugs. Nigel sat next to her still looking nervously at her as if she were about to start crying again at any moment. He had picked up another of the mugs and they both looked up at me with relief when I returned.

'Right, shall we go,' I said indicating the lift, 'Leave your bags here, we can collect them later. Let's just go and get a real coffee.'

'Thanks Angel and thank you Nigel for the tea,' she said leaving the mug on the table and getting up.

I walked her briskly to Ricardo's and we sat down. I ordered her a double espresso and a freshly squeezed orange juice for myself. It was strange to see this woman, who I'd never met, sitting in front of me repeating the stories I knew so well. The time when Bernard had run off with the newsagent. The time when he had made her cut and dye her hair into a blonde bob because he wanted her to look like Marilyn Monroe. The time he had brought a mistress home while she was ill upstairs in bed...

She had a round friendly face that, when it wasn't blotchy, with crying would actually be quite pretty.

I felt sorry for her. She'd known Bernard for years; he was all she'd ever known really. And he had persistently gone behind her back with other women. He had put her down for years. He had humiliated her. Her neighbours had known about his affairs. Her postman knew. Everyone knew. She'd finally cracked. I couldn't believe she had lasted that long.

What do you do after investing so many years in a marriage? What do you do when all your friends, hobbies, your life style revolves around you and your husband? How much humiliation do you take? When do you give up? To hear her despairing over all that was heart wrenching. She had absolutely no confidence left at all. She was constantly referring to things as if they were her fault. 'He wouldn't have carried on seeing her if I'd lost the weight he'd wanted...'

'I failed him,' she kept repeating.

'No. He failed you,' I insisted.

'I just can't believe I left him,' she said staring at her coffee.

'I can. It sounds like you've done absolutely the right thing,' I assured her. 'He deserves it Mary, you are far too nice to carry on putting up with all that.'

She had tears in her eyes as I finished my encouraging speech. She seemed braver as she said, 'I'm going to stay in London for a while and work out what to do.'

'Have you got any friends in London at all?' I asked

cautiously, picturing Ellie's face when I introduced our new room mate.

'Well I've got a girl friend I used to go to school with. She's recently widowed poor thing and I'm sure she wouldn't mind putting me up for a few days.'

'What about going back to Hull?'

'Oh no, not yet. I need to think things through. It's all going to be so awkward, we've got all these mutual friends and Bernard will have spoken to them all first. Saying I've abandoned him,' she started fretting again.

'Rubbish, they'll know you would have been pushed to it. I'm sure loads of the women will wish they could be as brave,' I assured her.

'Do you think so?'

'Definitely.'

'Oh I hope so. You are kind.'

While she sat dabbing at her eyes I hoped she wouldn't keep worrying about him. He didn't deserve a moment of concern. I thought I had had a run of bad luck but Mary was the proof that things could get so, so much worse.

'Get yourself settled at your friend's and then come and have dinner at ours tomorrow night. My flat mate Ellie and I are becoming professionals at dealing with useless men,' I grinned. 'We'll have a girly night,' I went on, 'And you won't have to keep thinking about it all.'

'Are you still seeing Nick?' she asked trying to change the subject. Uncomfortable with all the attention on her.

'No, we broke up,' I said flatly.

'Oh.'

'Mutual?' she asked

'Sort of,' I said, not willing to admit to Mary, 47, Hull that I had been royally dumped.

'What an idiot,' she sighed sadly.

'Hmm.'

'Any other young man for you?' she asked innocently.

My mind briefly rested on Charlie. I hadn't seen him in a little while...

'Um... No. Not right now. I'm just focusing on other things at the moment.'

'Sensible,' Mary announced, another tear welling in one eye.

I diverted any more mulling by some nonsense chat about the magazine, gossip about who everyone was, a few of the letters I'd been replying to that morning and when she seemed less likely to start sobbing into her espresso gave her directions to our flat for tomorrow night. She was also persuaded that her return to Hull was NOT a top priority, that Bernard was NOT a nice man and that she deserved a time out and a good think about what she wanted to do. She returned to the office a lot calmer and picked up her bag. The receptionist was openly following her around the room, her eyes wide, her mouth chewing on gum. I sent her off in the lift instructing her to get a cab to her friends and to call me later.

'Thank you for everything Angel.'

'See you tomorrow night,' I said giving her a last reassuring smile.

I walked back into the office feeling a little bit prouder of myself. It had been a relief to focus on someone else's worries for a while and she was a lovely woman. She had just been pushed to a new low, and I knew a little of what that felt like.

After my extended sushi lunch and my extended coffee with Mary I had a lot to catch up on. I needed to photocopy pages of leaflets to send out with the letters. Pages on Bullying, Self Harming and Dealing with Drugs were placed on pink, yellow and green paper alternatively. My supply of these had been running low and I always stalled the need to use the massive photocopier. I hated the massive photocopier. However I had another letter about bullying crying out for a pamphlet and could put off the moment no longer. I walked over to the machine, piled high with various coloured paper. Popping open the tray I looked at it in bewilderment for a few minutes and then started cramming the various colours in the different sections. I hadn't been fiddling around for long when Nigel appeared.

'Angel I...'

'Hmm...' I mumbled distractedly. Why don't photocopiers come with better instructions? What did the strange little pictures mean? What language is this? These symbols seem mysterious, lots of diamonds and circles with dashes through them. Do you put the paper in horizontally or vertically or just hope for the best, fingers crossed and see what happens? How did you get it to copy your pages in an order and was it just a myth I heard that it was capable of actually stapling your pages together for you? I looked up to see Nigel still standing there, clutching some sandwiches.

'Oh I'm fine thanks Nigel,' I said indicating the sandwiches and turning back to the blasted photocopier from hell.

'No... I'

I looked up at him. He looked at me, blushed and then looked down at the sandwiches. 'Oh right, no... sandwiches,' he said.

He seemed depressed about it. Maybe I should have bought one out of pity? I never knew he took that part of his job so seriously. But then Nigel was not called Fat Nigel in an ironic way. Maybe my rejecting food depressed him. Maybe I needed to sit down some time with him and talk it through. Did I have a pamphlet on comfort eating in this pile? I was on a roll right now, what with the recent Mary success. I could solve anything. I watched him walk off. Then shrugging I turned back to the printer that was now flashing at me and beeping, and not in a good way.

'Bugger.'

Multi coloured pages were being churned out.

'Sod.'

I went to grab them.

Then the machine stopped as suddenly as it begun and went silent.

'Pissing hell.'

I forgot all about Nigel.

A couple of hours later sitting in an exhausted, yet triumphant, heap of pamphlets, I considered getting up to go home. I was so worn out by my day that when Alex came over and told me some people were going for post work drinks round the corner, I instantly agreed. I could drink myself free of all the pressure. Going home would come after that.

I arrived to see Alex propping up the bar. I gave him a quizzical stare and then walked over to join him.

'Where is everyone?' I asked curiously.

'Well they left, but that's OK. What do you want to drink?' he asked looking at me.

'Oh,' I uttered, taken aback, 'I'll have a Vodka Diet Coke please.'

I went down to the loos to pop a bit more mascara on my eyes and make myself look a little less formal in my work attire. Then gave up. Had other people been here at all? Was this Alex trying to take me out for a drink? I shrugged in to the mirror. I didn't have the energy to care and I didn't have anywhere else I needed to be. I went back to the bar and sat down on a bar stool next to him, accepting my drink gratefully.

'So,' I said looking at him expectantly. I sipped at my vodka.

'I'm glad you came,' Alex said raising his beer.

I kept sipping at my vodka. Soon the squelching sound of air on ice was heard and I looked up at the barman who was absently drying a glass and gazing at a couple of women at the end of the bar.

'Could I have another please – Vodka and Diet coke, Alex?'

'Stella please.'

'Right, and one pint of Stella. So how are you enjoying Sweet SixTeen?' I asked, turning to him.

'Yeah it's good. Easier than my last job on the paper...'

'Hmm I can imagine,' I nodded.

'But it's not exactly working on Nuts,' he grinned at me, 'That would be my ideal job.'

'For some reason that doesn't surprise me,' I said smiling.

'For the literature Angel,' he claimed, trying to look innocent.

'Of course,' I nodded solemnly. 'And the pretty pictures?' I added.

'Perhaps.'

'What's it like working in an office of women?' I asked slyly.

'There are some guys working there,' Alex claimed.

'Certainly not many manly Alpha males though,' I added, thinking of Nigel, Clive with the big hair, Ian of IT...'

'How about Richard?' Alex piped up.

'Puh' was my reply. 'Manly? No, no, no,' I shook my head, simultaneously waving the barman over and indicating another round.

'What has happened between you two?' asked Alex, 'There is a lot of sexual tension.'

The remainder of my drink splattered to the floor.

'Sexual tension,' I laughed out loud, 'Sexual tension – NO, tension yes, sexual tension needyadah, uh uh, nil point, no way, ever, never, yeah he wishes,' I panted.

'I think the lady doth protest too much,' said Alex in a sing song voice.

'I do not. Richard is awful. He goes out of his way to ruin my life... it's totally deliberate,' I explained

'Right,' said Alex nodding at me in an irritatingly disbelieving way.

'Drink up,' I said nodding at his drink to change the subject.

'Shall do,' he winked at me, lightly placing a hand on my knee.

Alex wasn't my type, all blonde and butch, and I worked with him which surely made him Out Of Bounds. But after five vodkas on an empty stomach I could half close my eyes and he looked so like Brad Pitt it was spooky. To be fair if I half closed my eyes after five vodkas Ellie might look so like Brad Pitt it was spooky, but in my state I hadn't made this connection. It is fair to point out that at this point I don't remember every little detail of the night to come. I remember a few things, here and there. But I don't remember every single moment.

Sadly I do remember initiating an ingenious two person drinking game.

'I'm guessing a number between 3 and 300, what is it?'

'49?' (n.b. I don't remember the precise numbers, these are estimates).

'No,' and then pointing at him I added, 'AH HAH – DRINK' (I definitely remember that).

Alex joined in, 'OK I'm guessing a number between 5 and 575, what is it?' he asked.

'Um... hold on,' I said pausing to think.

'Angel what are you doing?'

'I'm guessing,' I said sshing him.

'Right, have you thought of a number yet?' he asked after another few seconds.

'Yes, wait, no, I've changed my mind...'

'Angel,' he warned.

'OK yes, 136?'

'No.'

'Oh.'

'368?' I tried again.

'Angel you only get one guess so DRINK and no it was 8.'

'Bugger I was close,' I muttered.

'Yup really close,' agreed Alex sarcastically, 'OK one last

one Angel, I'm thinking of a number between 2 and, I'll make it easier, 200.'

'Oh that is a lot easier. Thank you,' I grumbled.

'That's OK,' he smiled.

'OK is it...' I paused to look at him, hoping like Derren Brown that I could just pluck the number from his aura. If that is what Derren Brown does. I scanned his face.

'Is it 79?' I said finally.

'Yes.'

'Is it?' I squealed.

'No it's not.'

'You bastard.'

I remember that this game soon got tired (which does seem strange) and I remember then leaving the bar, propped up on Alex. I remember kissing him drunkenly in a taxi, and then I remember kissing him drunkenly outside our flat. I remember stumbling up the stairs, without him? Yes, without him I remember and I definitely remember waking up this morning feeling disgusting.

* * *

I walked in to work concentrating on my feet. I didn't want to look up and catch his eye or I knew I might die of embarrassment. Or throw up on him. Tally, surprisingly cheery for a Tuesday morning had clocked my greyish complexion and immediately piped up, 'If you had to sleep with the world's heaviest man or a man whose face was covered in bees who would you?'

I looked at her scathingly, dumping my bag down, 'Tally I can't: I'm sick.'

'You have to choose,' she reminded me.

'Face... bees,' I whispered, sinking into my seat.

She nodded, 'I think so,' and then she went and made me a coffee.

After a few more minutes of sipping and closing my eyes I felt a little better/able to open my eyes. Tally had unearthed a pack of Nurofen from a drawer and I had downed two gratefully with the coffee. I took a sneaky glance at the pile of letters in front of me. Why had I gone out on a school night? I would just concentrate on one letter at a time. One at a time. Small steps. I picked up the first slowly and focused on the words.

Dear Angel,
Recently I have noticed that there is a reddish brown mark on my pants...

The letter floated to the desk, I reared up and half-hobbled half-sprinted to the toilet. Past Richard, already smirking at me, as I went.

I returned back to my desk clutching my stomach lightly. Tally sensibly didn't say anything. I lowered myself slowly back into my chair and moved the offending letter to one side. I picked up the next and had a quick scan. No bodily functions mentioned, seemed safe to go on. I began to write. Not long after my phone shrilled to life.

'Good morning Angela,' chimed my mother as I reached out to stop the ringing disturbing my calm. Sadly I noted my mother would ensure it was shattered anyway.

'You're calling early,' I commented glancing at the clock that had barely reached nine thirty.

'The early bird catches the worm,' she sang.

'Right.'

'I wanted to call to let you know that Elsie's party has been postponed because she's had to go into hospital. It's her hip.'

'Er... right.' Sounded like something I needed to know.

'But Ed will be home for half term so it shouldn't stop you coming home and spending some time with him? He's still very quiet. We're a little worried about him.'

'Fine, yes Mum of course.'

'Lovely,' said my mother in a sing song voice.

'So is everything back to normal at home I take it?' I asked, noting that she definitely seemed more upbeat.

'The cat has been returned if that's what you mean, yes,' she explained.

'Oh good.'

'And your father seems a little calmer about the whole thing,' she whispered to me, as if speaking at a normal volume might threaten to rouse him into another fury.

'Good.'

'He let it out in their garden, with a letter round its neck about toilet training...'

'Hmm...'

'... So we shouldn't have any problems in the future...'

'Great.'

'... And he can go back to behaving like a sensible human being,' she finished.

'Excellent.'

'Isn't it... and... Angel you seem distracted,' she pointed out; disappointed I wasn't sharing her joy.

'Sorry. Busy with work.'

'Oh, well don't let me keep you,' she said still worryingly happy, 'I just wanted to pass on the good news,' she said as if speaking about the Second Coming. 'I'll speak to you soon darling,' she chirruped. Darling. She must be on a high.

'OK Bye Mum.'

'Bye Angel.'

I put the phone down. The cat had been returned. After all my father's ranting I wasn't so sure the war was over. But my mother had clearly won the battle. I wondered what Dad had up his sleeve next? Or would it really be declared peace time?

It was too early to think about it all and I went back to the letters, keeping the answers short, factual, to the point. I popped in a lot of pamphlets to make up for my thrifty replies and hoped they would understand when they were older.

'You look foul,' Suzie commented cheerfully, perching herself on my desk.

I looked up, 'Thanks Suzie I try my best,' I smiled at her weakly.

'Did you go out last night?'

'Hmm...' I shifted in my seat, aware of the lecture if I admitted who with.

'Morning Angel, Suzie,' called out Alex as he passed, interrupting further questioning. I blushed and muttered a 'morning.'

Suzie had turned to reply and I composed myself. Would she be able to tell? Had she guessed? I tried not to get too panicky.

She was still watching him as he walked into the kitchen. 'Do you know Alex?' she asked turning to me.

'A little,' I shrugged, hoping that my face wasn't turning too deep a shade of red.

'Don't you think his eyes are too close together?' asked Suzie thoughtfully.

'Um I don't know. Maybe. I hadn't really noticed,' I said.

'He is a bit cocky,' she pointed out.

'Confident?' I corrected.

'A bit smooth,' she said wrinkling her nose.

'Quite charming?' I defended.

She raised her eyebrow at me.

'But yeah, quite smooth,' I added hastily, keen to not blow my cover. I couldn't face a Suzie lecture this early in the day.

When she walked off Tally looked over at me. I blushed and looked down to concentrate on the letter in front of me.

'If you had to choose would you have glow sticks as fingers or Pom Poms as hands,' she asked innocently. Then before I could reply she added, 'You pulled him didn't you?' she asked.

I blushed, 'No I, no I... how did...' I petered off.

Tally was giggling, 'I won't tell I promise.'

I smiled at her pathetically.

'Dirty hoe,' she said looking down at her stitching.

'Glow sticks as fingers,' I decided.

'No one ever chooses Pom Poms,' she said not looking up.

On my way out to lunch I walked past Richard, smirking at me again. I could only assume that he had been informed of last night's antics, or that he had yet another plan up his sleeve to wreak havoc in my life. Maybe an article on Dealing with Diddling Your Colleague? I smiled at him sarcastically and pushed open the door. How is it that a man can go around snogging half the office and be labelled a stud, then a woman does the same thing and she is smirked at and presumed, a slut, a slag? I was not a slut, a slag. I was just acting my age. I was taking life as it comes I thought as I descended in the lift. Yeah. I thought as I emerged into the street and the fresh air. Yeah.

After some freshly squeezed orange and an inoffensive chicken sandwich I was feeling a lot better. Almost recovered in fact. I felt happier, more content. I was getting control of my life again. I was worrying about the things I used to worry about (wholemeal bread or white? Custard slice or cream slice...?) I wasn't worrying about my love life. I wasn't worried that Alex and I had kissed last night. I didn't really care. I mean, it would be nice if Richard wasn't grinning at me like he'd just invented the wheel but I wasn't actually, really, genuinely bothered. Lately I was able to focus on me, me, me. I could be totally selfish. I was my own master. I could go out after work, enjoy a night out, have some drinks, have some laughs, partake of some drunken snogging. And who was it hurting? I was playing the field. Acting the singleton. I had nothing to hang my head in shame for; in fact I should be holding my head up and proud. Oh yes.

I pushed my way back into the office with a lot of these positive thoughts whirling around. I couldn't get hurt this way because I would always be in control. I could just drop one man and take up with another. On some nights I could go out with just my girlfriends/Rick and forget about seeing any man. No one would define me. Oh no. No one would make me wait by my phone. No man would make me cry. Oh no. With this new empowering vibe coursing through my veins I confidently started on the next letter. This girl needed my help.

Dear Angel,
I'm fifteen and I'm fairly good-looking. E.g. no spots, medium build, brown hair etc. I have never kissed a boy with tongues. E.g. snogged. I want some tips on: how to kiss a boy. E.g. what to do with my tongue. And how to make him let me kiss him. Thanx,
Lisa, Leeds.

Dear Lisa,
You are a single girl and you shouldn't have any of these cares. You don't need to make a man do anything. The boys will come running; you just sit back and let them. You don't need to worry about the how's and the when's it's the how many's you'll be wondering at. You'll be fighting them off. They should all be grabbing the opportunity to kiss you. You are an attractive brown haired, clear skinned lady and will be in high demand by the men of Leeds town. Be confident. Don't concern yourself with the kissing, it will all come naturally. You just have to make up your mind which guy is the one you want to pucker up with and the rest will be just brilliant.

You go girl. Good Luck.
Angel

After a few more letters, numerous cups of tea and a large slice of chocolate cake – it was Katherine (Features) birthday, it was time to leave. I slung my bag over my shoulder in time to see Claudia giving me a very snooty look. She spun her chair around the other way so as not to have to look at me further. The news of last night had obviously reached her. Suzie looked up from her desk. When she spotted me leaving she made a move to come over, then her phone rang and she was forced back to her desk. By the expression on her face I think the news had reached her too. Did no one in this office have better things to discuss? Had world events not been gripping enough this week? The Deputy Prime Minister had been caught cheating on his wife – was that not enough for them? Did they have to confine their gossip to within these four walls?

I felt relieved as I pushed my way out of the office and into reception to the lift. In less than an hour I could be lounging on our sofa and eating... I heard girlish giggles behind me and looked over in surprise to see the whiny receptionist actually smiling, actually showing teeth. I looked up to see what was bringing on this freakish reaction. Alex was draped over the desk talking to her. During his speech she was following his words with a rapt look on her face. As I pressed the button for the lift Alex looked up. I felt his eyes on me as I waited. I could hear him making his apologies to the receptionist and as I stepped inside I watched him fling himself into the lift as the doors closed. Alex looked at me.

'Hey Angel,' he said smirking.

'Hey,' I said as nonchalantly as I could after a man throws himself into a steel box to greet you the day after you've got drunk and kissed them.

'OK day?' he asked.

'Bit hung over,' I gave him a little smile. This didn't have to be awkward.

'Want to go out again sometime,' he asked. Ah.

'Um... well...' I laughed uncomfortably. Was it hot in this lift or what? Don't they do air conditioning in this building? Alex was waiting for an answer. 'Yeah maybe,' I said smiling at him.

The lift doors opened and a man stepped in. We both turned and nodded to him. Alex moved closer to me. I take it back – this could definitely be awkward.

'Soon I hope,' he said leaning in.

'Hmm...' I muttered watching the lift descend the next two floors. Finally, after a life time we reached the ground.

'Yup sure,' I said, flustered, as I pushed past Third Floor Man, 'Bye Alex,' I waved at him over my shoulder.

'Great,' he called as I scuttled off, 'Bye Angel.'

I turned around and he was gone, back up to the fourth floor to charm the receptionist a little more.

I felt a little calmer as I walked across to the revolving door and freedom. Thank god today was over. I collapsed into a seat on the tube, trying not to catch the eye of the nearby man on crutches who had been lingering by it for quite some time. A quiet night in was on the cards I thought as I exited the tube in Brixton. Mary was coming over tonight and we could have a relaxing time, eating food and cheering her up. It was like doing a charity night for a HelpLine. Then once the counselling was complete I could catch up on my sleep and go into work refreshed and ready for a new day.

It was a quiet night. Mary had come over and been introduced to Ellie, who had made it her personal mission to mummy her as best she could. Never one to like heart break and sad stories she made us pancakes dripping in lemon and sugar, and listened patiently as Mary told her the details of her escape from Hull and Bernard. Mary already seemed far more relaxed. London had really brought on a change, away from Hull and from Bernard's constant criticism she seemed to worry less. After a lot of food and mindless chat she had slept on our sofa, curled up under an old picnic rug of my mothers. The snake sleeping peacefully in its tank, only a couple of feet away.

* * *

Ellie and her arranged to go on a much needed shopping trip the next morning and then join me for an extended working lunch. I persuaded Suzie and Tally to come along and we all headed to Ricardo's for paninis and pointless chatter. Mel who had been selecting china patterns in a nearby John Lewis joined us on a break. She turned up with rings under her eyes deflecting from the engagement ring on her finger. All the organising was obviously proving a strain. I drew up a chair for her and she collapsed gratefully into it, her many carrier bags stored under the table.

We settled ourselves down and ordered a couple of bottles of white wine to begin. We hadn't been long in the restaurant when conversation had crept onto the topic of men, boyfriends, fiancés and husbands. Mary was filling in Tally and Suzie on the latest Bernard phone calls. He'd left a message last night to ask her to come back.

'Only because he's run out of clean socks I'm sure,' she scoffed.

Ellie was telling me about the man from the deli who had smiled at her suggestively that morning when she'd brought some milk.

'I don't think it looked like a 'here's your change and your semi-skimmed' kind of smile Angel.'

Coupled with our conversations snippets of the women on the next door table kept floating across to us,

'I had an Egyptian boyfriend who used to tell me that in Cairo there was a mountain there in the shape of a woman's back and when he looked at it it reminded him of me.'

'Aw.'

'Do you think three dates is too soon to sleep with him?'

'Do you think it's too soon to call Bernard?' asked Mary sipping her cappuccino and looking at Ellie.

Suddenly Mel, who had up till then remained in total silence, stood up abruptly knocking her fork on the floor with a clatter and screamed 'NO!'

Everyone turned blinking at her sudden outburst. She looked us over with a piercing glare. The women on the next door table fell silent. I looked up at her with concern. What was going on? The stress had obviously got to her. She had snapped with wedding stress. She was usually so calm, so sorted, so... She started to speak.

'This is ridiculous. Women fought for years for equality. They wanted the same rights for us in the workplace, the vote, to get us all to stand on our own two feet and how do we repay them?' She looked round furiously at us all, 'We sit around constantly obsessing about men.' She punctuated the last few words so that we squirmed in our seats. She didn't give anyone a moment to react.

'... Do you think they sit around obsessing about us in their lunch hours? Do you think they analyse every phone call, every text message from us? Do you think they lie awake at night wondering what nice thing they could do to surprise us? NO...' she said before any of us could utter a reply. 'They don't. They go to work, they talk about football games, they read the paper, they eye up the receptionist, and they don't sit around showing each other passport size pictures of you from their wallets. They don't tell their friends that you said the sweetest thing last night, and isn't it just lovely having a girlfriend who is that pretty. They don't, they won't. They never have, they never will, so why are we sitting around here constantly obsessing about them when they are sitting around obsessing over a Chelsea transfer, or the price of a brand new MG, or the best way to impress their boss? We're going to talk about something else. We're all busy people with busy lives. Angie.' She rounded on me with a determined glint in her eye. I hadn't been this frightened since Leonara, a ninth grade bully, had run off with my lunch money. Why couldn't she have picked on some one else?

'How is your job going?'

I exhaled slowly, 'Er... great thanks.' There was a pause as I stared at her, brow furrowed. The silence continued.

Tally piped up 'Mary you know I think he...'

'NO,' said Mel turning on her, 'Angie, 'she nodded eagerly, 'Continue...'

Tally had her mouth hanging open and I took my eyes off her, licked my lips and willed myself to continue, 'It's er... just great. I wrote replies to most of Richard's letters today so that didn't take long and I re-arranged the stationery cupboard...'

Mel was smiling encouragingly and I continued, gradually warming to the topic as my confidence grew. '...Well that's a really boring job but it only took me half an hour...'

I heard Suzie's voice questioning me, 'Half an hour?'

'Yeah well it looked fine at the start...' I trailed off as I caught sight of her expression. She looked unimpressed.

'No wonder that place is always such a bloody mess when people clean it so half-heartedly.'

'It's not a bloody mess,' I said defensively.

'It's always fine,' said Tally coming to my aid, 'And it's not the most exciting job in the world.'

'Some bits of my job are a bit dull,' I said conversationally to Tally.

'I got you that job,' said Suzie turning to me.

'Yes I know but it's not exactly what I want to be doing.'

'Oh so you're saying you think my job's dull.'

'What?'

'You're saying you think my job's dull' she spelt out.

'Well not to you,' I said.

'Oh sorry my job is only dull if you are very interesting, so I must be very dull and have a dull job. Thanks Angel thanks a lot.'

'She didn't say that,' said Ellie jumping to my defence.

'What?' Suzie rounded on her.

'She didn't say that she...'

'Don't worry Ellie,' I said.

'No it's fine.'

'Leave it.'

'She did say that Ellie, I knew it would come out soon enough,' hissed Suzie.

'I think she just meant it wasn't what she had dreamed of doing,' insisted Ellie.

'What do you mean 'soon enough,' I've never thought that Suzie,' I said hurt.

'She just doesn't want to be doing it forever,' piped up Ellie again.

'Thanks Ellie but Suzie knows that.'

'Suzie knows what?' screeched Suzie.

'Well you know I...'

'Don't raise your voice at her for god's sake it's only a bloody job...' screeched Ellie.

'You only say that because you're unemployed.'

'Hey that's not fair Suze, Ellie is looking for work.'

'I am looking for work you know.'

'And I know working on a magazine might seem dull Angel but a lot of people want to be doing it.'

'I know,' I insisted.

'She knows,' repeated Ellie.

'Does she? She doesn't take it seriously half the time,' Suzie commented.

'What?' I said quietly

'So does anyone want the cheese omelette?' asked Tally desperately.

Mary looked up at her with hopeful eyes.

'And loads of people want to work on magazines Angel,' went on Suzie.

Mary looked down again. Tally fell silent.

'Oh my god I know, and I like my job Suzie,' I wailed.

'See, she likes her job,' said Ellie backing me up.

'I don't want to argue like this,' I said.

'Neither do I,' said Ellie.

'Well neither do I,' said Suzie defensively.

'Fine.'

'Fine.'

'Fine.'

We all fell into a moody silence. I sipped at my wine. Suzie fiddled with the napkin in front of her. Ellie sat with her arms crossed. Tally was gazing off awkwardly into space. I was about to mutter an apology when Mary piped up, 'So have you done talking about work? Can I talk to you about Bernard now?'

Ellie started giggling first and then I caught Suzie's eye. We gave each other a weak smile and then joined in. Mel smiled a weak smile and sank into her chair.

'Sorry.'

'Sorry.'

'Sorry.'

The women on the next door table resumed their conversation.

'So do you think it is too soon to sleep with him?'

After another couple of bottles of wine and some good food we dragged ourselves back into the office feeling full but far better for the break. I waved good bye to Mary who was going off to shop for a couple more outfits, and look round Harrods (she'd never been). I had hugged Mel good bye and watched as she slumped off to continue her search for affordable, yet classy, table covers. She had seemed particularly wound up. I'd never heard Mel the ardent feminist before. Her outburst had been totally unexpected: I hadn't appreciated how busy she was. I hoped the lunch had cheered her up a little. Suzie had raced off to some afternoon conference but had given me a quick hug before she left. I didn't think the argument was going to cause permanent damage. We had shared a créme brulee for dessert after all. I told Ellie I'd see her for dinner later that evening.

* * *

There had been no news of Kevin now for over two weeks. His sister had not returned. The tank was still in our living room and I hadn't been able to eat anything from the freezer due to the knowledge that the bunny bag was nestled amongst our packets of peas and Fish Fingers. But Kevin hadn't turned up. The initial panic we'd had had subsided. Maybe he would never come back? I thought as I piled yet more mail for Mr. K. Helm onto the ledge in the hall.

I got into the flat to find Ellie staring at the fridge freezer. I looked at her.

'No,' I said dumping my bag down on the table.

'No,' I said as she continued to stare at the machine.

She looked up at me, 'It's Wednesday and you know what that means Angel.'

'No,' I said taking her arm and trying to drag her away.

'Maybe it will die,' she said worriedly.

'And that would be a bad thing because...'

'Do you think good things happen to people who kill off murderer's pets?' she said looking at me.

She had a point.

'But... we can't,' I shivered, thinking of what was in that freezer, what was waiting for us.

'I don't think we can put it off any longer Angel. She said it had to be fed once a...'

My phone started ringing.

'Oh damn,' I laughed picking it up.

'Once a week,' finished Ellie hopelessly, going back to staring at the freezer.

'Hello,' I said.

'Do you know what day it is Angel?' came Charlie's voice.

'Not you too,' I wailed.

'So, have you fed it?' he asked full of boy curiosity.

'No,' I admitted.

'You have to Angel, do you want it to die of neglect.'

I paused.

'Oh.' Then he laughed, 'Angel you have to.'

'Oh I know. It's just, well I haven't done it because...' I looked at Ellie desperately, 'Because... I... I thought you would want to do it,' I finished triumphantly.

There was a pause on the end of the line.

I smiled down the receiver, 'Well...'

'Oh Angel I would if I could but I'm really busy this end and...I've... um...' he started laughing, 'Fine. I'll be over in a bit.'

'It's OK,' I said to Ellie, whose eyes were still on the freezer, 'Charlie's going to do it,' I told her switching off my phone.

She slumped in relief, 'Thank god, I'll make some dinner.'

'I'll go and get changed.'

'Helpful,' she laughed as I left.

Charlie arrived an hour later with a dark blue shirt on and an uneasy smile.

'Charlie,' I smiled at him winningly, 'How nice to see you.'

'OK where are they?' he asked following me through the living room.

I indicated to the freezer. 'Still in there.'

'Well don't they need defrosting?' He asked.

'Probably,' agreed Ellie.

I shrugged noncommittally.

Charlie opened the freezer, 'We could microwave them.'

Ellie looked shocked, 'We can't. I'll never use the microwave again.'

'Well then they'll have to be left out over night,' said Charlie reaching in the bag and pulling out a frozen rabbit. It was like watching a magic show for sickos.

I flinched.

Ellie looked resigned, 'Fine, microwave,' she said reckoning, like me, that anything was better than having a dead bunny thawing on our kitchen table.

'Right,' Charlie said clapping his hands together with false bravado, 'Let's do this.'

We both backed away. Charlie looked at us, 'So I'm doing this.'

Ellie and I grinned and nodded. Then, as we watched him

popping the little animal on a plate and switching the microwave on, the noise of defrosting bunny reached us and our expressions became serious again. A couple of minutes later the inevitable 'ping' came. I could barely look as Charlie bought the plate out of the microwave. I would never eat off that again. I watched in fascination as he took it through to the living room and laid it down on the carpet. He slid the top of the tank open and wavered.

'Do you want to stay for dinner?' asked Ellie popping her head round the doorway but averting her eyes.

'I can't, thanks Ellie,' he replied, concentrating on lowering the bunny into the tank without disturbing the 5ft snake that lay beneath.

I felt a little disappointed. He did look more dressed up than usual actually. The dark blue shirt looked newly ironed. His shoes were smart, he was wearing shiny cufflinks. I wondered what was he was all dressed up for.

'Do you want a drink?' I asked when he'd made the drop and quickly removed his hand and slid the top back across.

'I really can't,' he said checking his watch, 'I've got to be somewhere.'

'Where?' I asked curiously.

'Nowhere important. So have you heard from the police again?' he asked changing the subject.

'Oh... um, no.'

'Well let me know if he turns up,' he said getting up.

'Oh are you off now,' I said taken aback.

'Yup I'm sorry. It's just work you know,' he said shiftily.

'Right.'

'Bye Ellie,' he called.

'Bye,' she yelled over the sound of water boiling.

'I'll call you soon Angel. Have a good night.'

'Yeah, you too,' I said as he walked down the corridor to the door.

I frowned as he left the flat. Work? Marking papers at this late hour? In that shirt? And those cufflinks? What was he up to?

* * *

I was still thinking about it at work the next day as I absently bit into a Jammy Dodger. Some kind person had left a pack of them in the kitchen and Tally and I had ensured that most had disappeared by brunch. As I was mulling Suzie had appeared for a morning caffeine injection.

'I'm glad you're here,' she said flicking the kettle on.

'Hmm...' I said looking up.

'I'm really sorry about yesterday's lunch,' she said linking my arm, 'I really didn't mean what I said. I know you take your job seriously.'

'Oh I know Suzie. It's fine honestly. Totally forgotten,' I assured her.

'And I did know what you meant about not being exactly where you want to be.'

'I do like the magazine Suzie, I really do,' I protested.

'I know but you should be trying to act Angel, you're really good.'

'OK you can stop now Suze,' I said blushing.

'When's the audition?' she asked.

'Next week,' I replied, realising I really needed to work on my speeches and stop day dreaming so much.

'Right,' she said patting me on the hand, back to the old Suzie, 'Ready for it?' she asked.

'Sort of,' I said, 'I've been a bit distracted.'

'What with?'

'Oh not much, just things you know,' I said vaguely.

'Alex?' she asked suspiciously, knowing full well something had happened.

'No,' I replied truthfully.

'Good,' she nodded.

I explained about last night's snake feeding session, the fact that Kevin was still missing and carefully avoided mentioning my thoughts on Charlie.

'Kevin still hasn't turned up?' she asked looking worried.

'No.'

'I wonder what he did,' she mulled.

'I don't want to think about it,' I shivered.

'So Charlie saved the day last night,' she smiled with a glint in her eye, 'how very heroic of him.'

'Hmm...' I said deliberately ignoring her smiles.

'And how is Charlie?' she asked not giving up.

'He's fine,' I bristled sensitively.

'Have you seen more of him then?' she asked stirring sugar into her coffee.

'We've spent a bit of time together. He's been on summer holiday so I've done some stuff with him. Just lazed about, nothing special.' I stopped quickly.

'So what's happening there?'

'Nothing,' I said defensively.

'Oh. He seemed nice.'

'He is, but we're just friends,' I repeated.

'Why?'

'That's what Rick asked,' I said aghast, 'What do you mean why?'

'Well he's gorgeous and you seemed to really like him so why not?'

'Because if you haven't forgotten I broke up with Nick little less than a month ago.'

'So?'

'What do you mean so? So I'm not ready.'

'What to start seeing someone else? Does he have a girlfriend?'

'I... no... well... I don't think so,' I admitted.

'Do you think he's good looking?'

'I suppose,' I shrugged trying to be nonchalant.

'So why are you hanging around?'

'You were the one who told me I needed to think about what I wanted from life.'

'Yes.'

'And I am focusing on my career at the moment.'

'Yes.'

'Well then,' I said as if it should be settled.

'Shouldn't stop you sorting out your love life at the same time. Women are meant to be able to multi task you know,' she smirked.

I ignored the comment.

'Charlie and I are just going to be friends,' I said firmly.

'Angel you're just friends so you don't get hurt, but you will get hurt when you realise you do like him and he's with someone else.'

I bristled with her assumptions.

'Rubbish,' I scoffed.

'It's not rubbish Angel its bloody obvious.'

'It is rubbish. We're just friends. I wouldn't mind if he was seeing someone else.'

'Right,' said Suzie thoughtfully. I felt pleased that I'd settled the argument finally.

'Well can I go out with him then?'

I spluttered, nearly burning my tongue on my coffee, 'No... what... why... of course... fine... sure, why would you do that again?'

'What do you mean why?' She laughed, 'What aside from the fact that he's...' she started ticking off his merits on each finger, 'Good looking, amusing, interesting...'

'Yes I know but...' I didn't know what to say. What was my problem? Of course she can ask Charlie out. But then they'll fall in love and I'll be the number two girl in Charlie's life and it will never be the same again.

'But you two might see each other a bit and then fall out and leave all that tension,' I pointed out.

'Angel I wouldn't, don't worry.'

'But you might. Loads of couples do,' I insisted, 'And it would be so awkward if you stopped speaking to each other and I had to be friends with both of you.'

'No Angel I mean I wouldn't ask him out, never. Really. I was teasing you.'

'Right,' I said carefully. 'But you know you can, if you wanted.'

'Yes sure,' said Suzie, 'Thanks. Well I'm going to get back to work,' she said picking up her mug.

'Hmm...'

'See you later Angel.'

'Hmm...'

I thought about Charlie. Was it just that I liked being a friend of his? Did I want more? Last night when he left I'd been disappointed. And where had he been going? Suzie was right, he was gorgeous, and interesting and nice so... I suddenly felt a little uneasy. Who had he been seeing last night? Then I shook myself. We were just friends. Anyway I'd hardly seen him recently; the way he kept rushing off made me realise he probably never wanted to be anything more than friends anyway. Enough. I shook myself, popped another Jammy Dodger in my mouth and went back to work.

I'd only been at my desk for a few minutes when I looked up to see Fat Nigel standing by my desk looking shifty. I glanced around behind me to spot the person he was obviously waiting to speak to about the wonders of double-sided sellotape or the intricacies of the hole punch and realised there was no one there. Then I realised Fat Nigel was there to speak to me. Grrrreat. I adopted my I'm-always-pleased-to-discuss-the-multi-functions-of-the-paper-clip look and looked at him expectantly as he darted his piggy eyes left and right as if nervously anticipating a sudden attack on his person. He shifted his weight from his left leg to his right leg and did a double-take for those sneaky desk thugs.

'Er...' a cough ensued, 'Er... Angela.' Now it always puts the fear in me when people use my full name. Perhaps prompting early recollections of being told off at school, or by parents or...

Fat Nigel's earnest introduction interrupted this last thought, 'Angela,' he said stamping on the word with all his courage, 'I would like to speak to you.'

I didn't feel this was quite the moment to slowly explain to him that that was precisely what he was doing, albeit badly, so I let him go on. Fat Nigel appeared to have a weight on his mind, if you'll excuse the pun. I regally waved him on as if I was Cherie Blair inviting the Pope to a drink.

'Of course,' I said generously, putting on my most patronizing I'm-talking-to-a-Troubled-Fat-Man voice. He was obviously here for some advice and I waited for the implausible 'Well you see my "friend" has this problem' opening remark.

'Well you see lately I have been feeling a little bit,' another attempt to clear that throat of his, 'a little bit lonely and I was wondering, not that I don't have any lady friends, whether...'

Oh my god he's asking me about his love life. What a joke, I would be about as helpful as Britney Spears at giving advice about the secret to holding down a successful long-term relationship. I wasn't exactly doing brilliantly myself at the moment, but Nigel's dilemma was probably fairly easy to fix.

'...you might be able to take my number and...'

But what if he's not here for some advice, oh no. 'You might be able to take my number.' Is that what he had just said? Oh wow, oh it's obvious. He is not hear wanting words of wisdom, oh no. The thought suddenly hit me straight between the eyes.

He was blatantly here under some veiled attempt to seek advice, when someone has clearly told him I'm now single and he's trying to crack on to me. I felt dirty. Fat Nigel wants to sleep with me. It sent a shiver down my spine. Fat Nigel wants to ask me out. Fat Nigel wants to be with me. He would never have had the nerve to ask me if I'd been gorgeous, but I wasn't and he thought he had a chance. Things had really sunk to a new low now. I needed to get back to the gym, buy some edgier work clothes and...

'...You see I noticed your friend, Mary, was it. I thought she looked lovely and I was just wondering if she was single, or whether she...' Mary. Mary. He wanted to ask Mary out. That was why he was here. He'd seen Mary with me and wanted to know if she was free. Mary, not me. Fat Nigel didn't want to sleep with me. A feeling rose up within me, disappointment? Nigel hadn't even, hadn't even tried to pull me. He wanted Mary. He wanted Mary over me. I digested this information a little. What did Mary have that I didn't? I pondered this thought. She was certainly homely looking, but her tea cosy hats and baffling choice of coloured tights surely did not stand up against my suede skirts and knee boots? And yet she had won. Beaten me to Nigel. I mean not that I wanted Nigel, of course, that was absurd. But why I repeated petulantly did he not want me? I don't want him I concluded firmly, but a little voice was nagging, 'It would have been nice of him to at least ask.'

'So then my wife died a couple of years ago and ever since I've.... Angela, Angela.' Nigel's beseeching voice infiltrated my brooding over the last rejection and on hearing my name I burst out of my bubble and looked at his expectant face.

'That's fantastic, 'I gushed, 'Super in fact, absolutely marvellous.' Nigel looked at me more than a little baffled and I felt a little guilty about being quite so horrible to him. It wasn't exactly his fault that he didn't fancy me. I was obviously more hideous than I initially imagined. No wonder Charlie hadn't tried anything. I was grotesque.

Why was I telling Mary to behave more like me and my friends? Perhaps I needed to become a little more like Mary. If that was the case I could start eating a lot more I decided. What was the point of all this life improving stuff when I should be sitting at home piling on the pounds and darning my own tights?

Don't people tell you to 'be comfortable in your own skin,' and Mary was, I needed to let go. Let it all hang out. But then maybe I would go too far. Lose all self respect. Grow to a size 28 and shop for clothes solely in Oxfam. Just give up, let nature take Her course and let it all hang out. I could imagine it now, a life of crisps and Pepsi's and sweets. I'll end up sitting in my flat in a big fat chocolate heap. Actually will not be able to live in the flat as there are too many stairs so will have to move out, leave Ellie and rent a bungalow. I will forever be forced to live inside my one level home, shopping on the internet and not mixing in public places. Children will come to stare through the window at me. They will point and they will snigger and they will say... 'Look at the big fat chocolate monster. Look at her.' and then I will turn my chocolate smeared mud mouth to them and yell, 'Oi you kids ge' away from my 'ouse' (as my concern for good grammar will have gone, along with my lithe and little figure). Oh god. I can see it all now. It was heart breaking. I am destined to become a disgusting 300lb whale of a woman. Those who worked with me will tut their heads and say, 'Just think she used to call Nigel fat.'

'Angela are you OK, is this a bad time?' My hands were gripped to the side of my desk. My face was obviously telling the world about my future misery.

'No, I'm sorry,' I said snapping back to the problem in hand.

'Don't worry about telling me straight,' said Nigel earnestly.

I focused on him. 'Right. Mary. Um... Yes, she's sort of free. She's just left her husband though so it's a bit of a sensitive time.'

'Oh yes I know, she told me a little about it, well if you could pass on this note I'd be most grateful,' he said holding a bit of paper out towards me.

'Right... of course,' I said glumly taking it from him.

So Nigel loved Mary. And no one loved me. I felt awash with self pity. What will become of me?

I looked down at the next letter in a daze and instantly started to scribble.

Dear Angela,
My boyfriend says that he'll dump me if I don't sleep with him. Although I really like him I don't know whether I'm ready.

We are both 16 but I haven't slept with anyone before. I don't know what to do please help.
Louisa, Kent.

Just stay with him. Do whatever he wants. Read the karma sutra, learn to cook, surprise him with gifts and don't let him go. Ever.

I was too drained to do anything but pack up for the day. Nigel's rejection and Suzie's comments had got to me a little. What was I doing pretending to be friends with Charlie? What if Suzie was seeing him? Not that she would. What if a Suzie, another girl, wanted to see him? Would I care? I shifted uncomfortably. I had got very used to Charlie being around. Recently I had seen less of him and I... I had missed him. Just a little I convinced myself. Not a huge amount. Nothing to really report, but well I suppose I had wanted to tell him a few little things about my day and wanted to ask him advice about my audition and wanted to plan something to do later this week and...

Maybe I needed to get a little distance from him; I wouldn't worry about him so much if I was spending less time with him. Did I like him? I think maybe I did a little. Then I thought of his face and I gulped. Maybe a bit more than a little. So when he called later that day I looked at my phone, finger hovering over the reply and then... didn't pick up. In fact it wasn't until I'd calmed down a few days later that I decided I was fine, I had just got a little worked up, and was now able to accept his call.

'Charlie,' I said in an airy way.

'Angel. I've been calling you for the last five days,' he said sounding confused.

'Oh I've been soooo busy,' I said rolling my eyes in a way that exuded power and control. Not that he could tell, but it gave me some extra confidence.

'Oh right. Well I was just wondering if you wanted to go to the cinema?'

'Well,' I faltered. This was all very direct, shouldn't he skirt around the issue a little bit? Send a few cryptic messages? Blow hot and cold? Why damn it he just asked a straight forward question. That wasn't in the rule book... hmphh. Dirty play. 'Well I?'

'Do you not want to?'

'No it wasn't that, I was just keeping some distance, you know.'

'Some distance?'

'Yes.'

'Why um... distance?' he asked.

'Oh,' I said realising I couldn't go into the whole I wanted to ignore you because I fear I might like you and I don't want to like you because then I'll worry and fret about you, but I also don't want anyone else to like you, so essentially we are all in for a very long term of celibacy and... 'Oh I just wanted to um... focus on me right now,' I said well aware that I sounded very American and very pretentious.

'Right so you do want to go out, you were just keeping a bit of distance... to focus,' Charlie summed up a little baffled.

'Er yes.'

'Right. Well in that case,' he said seemingly cheerily. 'Do you want to go to the cinema tonight? Unless you are focusing on you right now,' he said with a hint of a smile in his voice.

'Yes please' I said quietly.

So a couple of hours later I was getting ready to go to the cinema. I was excited. What should I wear? Not that it mattered, I hastily corrected myself, because we were just good friends. And that's why I was fine with whatever. I held up one of my favourite black tops and looked at myself in the mirror. What was I doing? Why was I going to the cinema with Charlie? I had other friends I could go to the cinema with. Was I going to the cinema with him, to get close to him? Was I beginning to like Charlie? Pah. Beginning. What a lie. I knew I liked Charlie. I didn't want to get hurt, that's why I shouldn't go to the cinema. And Charlie had been acting very strangely. Could he be trusted really? Did I need all this? And in a couple of days I had my audition. Did I want to get messed up before that? Did I want a re run of Nick? No. I got worked up again. I called and cancelled the cinema.

'To focus on you,' Charlie sighed.

'Er... yes.'

* * *

I hadn't been thinking about Charlie that morning. I had put the last night's cinema saga to the back of my mind and focused on my work instead. I was fine. And then like a well written soap scenario it all unravelled. It had all begun after Suzie had returned from a trip to Spar. She had been laden down with biscuits, coffee and chocolate for the kitchen and had come via my desk to offer me a snack. I had selected something to keep me going until lunch. An innocent tube of Smarties. These Smarties however had sent me over the edge. I hadn't been thinking about Charlie all morning. Not a jot. Then I opened the tube and what did I see as I removed the lid.

A large 'C.' And what does a large C stand for?

'What's the problem,' said Tally noticing my aghast expression.

I asked her, 'What does a large C stand for.'

Tally, not knowing it was a rhetorical question, came up with: chlorine, crabs, carbon monoxide and cystitis.

'No,' I muttered, cross (which begins with a C too she pointed out).

'It is the first letter of the name Charlie,' I pointed out.

'I know,' said Tally, confident in her alphabet, 'Your point is?'

'I have no point,' I grumbled, not wishing to discuss anything any further, but now cranky (see above) that I was thinking about him. It had all been fine before I had wanted to gorge myself on chocolate. Nothing good ever comes of it. I went back to the letters trying to block out all thoughts of Charlie's with C's. I had an audition to do and I had done the right thing. We were just friends.

Hi Angel,
I want to kiss me boy friend but he often ignores me. I'm so depressed that yesterday I tried to hurt myself by scratching my arm with a compass. Help.
Fiona, 15, Glasgow

This poor girl I thought rattling the tube of Smarties into my mouth and writing her an emotional reply. Us girls had to stick together. Self harming with stationery items was not the answer. I wrote a heartfelt reply, bucking her up, letting her see this boyfriend of hers might not be the one for her. I thought of

Charlie again. Why was I thinking about him? I had only broken up with Nick a month ago. Although I had to grudgingly admit that I hadn't thought of Nick in the same way. I didn't miss going out, being seen in the coolest bars with him. I hadn't liked his friends, hadn't been that interested in his job and hadn't ever truly felt that we were compatible. I'd fancied him. A lot. But now that I hadn't seen him in a while I realised I didn't miss spending time with him. I didn't want to tell him about my day, knew that he wouldn't be interested particularly if I did... Whereas with Charlie...

I went back to the letter. Poor girl, poor girl, I repeated. Then I moved sharply on to the next one, not thinking anymore about him. Tomorrow was my audition. I spent the rest of the afternoon surreptitiously learning lines for it, and successfully managed to get home without worrying about men anymore.

I pushed open the flat door and threw my keys down with a sigh. They landed amongst a pile of debris. Various key chains with no keys, left-hand gloves with no right-handed friends, chocolate wrappers with no chocolate, all lay on the table graveyard and every morning was like a mini adventure to fish out the correct item. After the usual nightmare of tackling the rush hour on the tube it was good to be home away from the hecticness. I leaned against the door and a small sense of satisfaction flooded through me. I had achieved something today. I had got up, got to work, actually undertaken a little work and got home relatively unscathed, both mentally and psychically. Yes I felt a small glow of achievement.

I looked down at where we kept the post and noticed someone had dropped off a package for me by hand. I picked it up curiously and ripped it open. There was a little note saying 'Read this and I'll see you soon, Charlie,' I frowned and turned over a book he had wrapped. A self help book entitled, 'Focusing on You Right Now.' I snorted with laughter and reread the note. That had been kind of him. I should get a grip and ring him and...

My train of thought however was suddenly halted by the sound of muffled sobbing. I stood confusedly for a few seconds and then sprung into action. Ellie. I rushed down the corridor listening to further snivelling. It must be Ellie, the only other possibility being some traumatized burglar who'd had an overwhelming feeling of guilt and broken down in tears in our living room. But I doubted it. I ran into the sitting room to see Ellie in a ball on the sofa, legs tucked up under her chin, her face hidden by the hood of her favourite grey top, sobbing. The television was blaring but she didn't seem to notice. I rushed over the assault course of pizza boxes and half-filled glasses of unidentified liquids and crouched down by her to look at her tear-stained face.

'Ellie – what's happened? What's wrong?'

Tissues littered the sofa around her and I gingerly removed a few as I waited for her to reply.

'Is it Kevin?' I said suddenly scared. Had he come back to claim his snake? Had he threatened her? My grip on her arm grew tighter as she shook her head.

She looked at me through glazed eyes, tried to speak and then let out a wail.

'Oh Ang,' she sniffed.

I stroked her arm trying to coax out the cause of her current state. She started to stutter a reply through intermittent sobs, 'It's.. it's J.. J.. J... Jack,' and then followed in a whisper, 'he's dead.'

I reeled with shock. Dead? I hadn't expected that. I'd have plumped for a bad job interview, Richard and Judy being axed, that kind of thing. Not this. This was serious. My mind was racing trying to work out who exactly Jack was without looking like a really bad friend and having to ask. Was he a friend she'd mentioned? A kindly uncle? A friendly work mate? Jack wasn't ringing too many bells.

'Oh Ellie I'm so sorry,' I soothed. God, how awful. Her face looked grief-stricken.

'It happened today – I just didn't expect it, he'd just got married to Ruth and she's – she's – p, p, pregnant.' A fresh bout of crying ensued. She tried to get more words out, 'He didn't even know about the baby – and now he's d.. d.. dead.' I was totally thrown now, this was awful. More than awful, it was horrendous. Poor Ellie. Poor Ruth. Poor Jack. Poor fatherless baby. This was catastrophic. She looked so helpless curled up in a ball. I waited patiently for her sobs to subside and swallowed the questions I had. Jack? Ruth? She would tell me in her own good time. After a few moments Ellie rubbed her eyes with the balls of her fists and sat with me in silence. I stayed on the sofa, not wanting to leave her.

After a few moments of silence she looked at me through a miserable bloodshot gaze. 'I just can't believe it.'

I rubbed her back assuredly, 'I know, I know.'

'It was so unexpected,' she went on. Her lip wobbled again, 'He was just driving along and the women came out of nowhere. Poor, poor Ruth, pregnant and alone.'

A niggling doubt emerged in my consciousness.

'Er.. Ellie – Jack is... is... who is Jack exactly?'

Ellie looked at me in disbelief, 'Jack is.. was,' she altered dramatically, 'Ruth's husband, he worked in the newsagent. He'd just saved enough money to set up his own business. He was so young.' Realisation dawned in my mind.

'Ellie,' I ventured, 'Is Jack real?'

'Of course he's real,' she snapped, and burst into fresh sobs.

I persisted, 'Ellie is Jack a character in a daytime soap?'

Ellie looked at me through her tears and nodded her head slowly, 'But Angel,' she protested, 'he was real to me.'

'Bloody hell Ellie you had me really worried,' I burst out.

'Sorry,' she sniffed wiping her eyes dry.

'I thought you might have heard from the police again. Or been cornered by Kevin.'

Ellie looked appalled, 'No of course not.'

'Ellie you really need a job.'

'I know,' she said miserably, 'I just don't know what I want to do.'

'Well don't think about it now. Do you want a cup of tea?'

By the time I had returned with the mugs Ellie had managed to dispose of the tissues and pizza boxes.

'Come on you can help me learn my lines,' I said throwing my speeches at her.

We spent a couple of hours on them and lying in bed that night I ran through them obsessively until I fell into a fitful sleep.

* * *

This obsesssion continued all morning at work. Mouthing the words at the photocopier, the computer screen, the telephone, the kettle... If I kept it up much longer people would be dialling the nearest nut house to enquire after free beds. I couldn't put it off any more. Tally gave me an encouraging hug on the way out and Suzie texted me from her conference to wish me luck. It was like psyching up for a first day back at school. I went off gripping my handbag tightly and clutching a photocopy of the pieces I'd chosen to do to study on the tube there.

When I arrived at the correct building, on the correct floor, I emerged to see a girl ticking off names at a table. I approached her apprehensively. This was it. She looked up at me and smiled as I deposited a CV and photo with her. She informed me that she'd let me know when they were ready for me. I felt like telling her I'd inform her when I'm ready to see them.

I frantically ran through the lines one more time in my head, trying to minimize the mouthing as much as possible. What did it matter if it went badly? I was only getting back on my feet. I was only here to see if I could do it. I was only here because they had wanted to see me. I was only here because my parents would be disappointed if I gave up, I'd be disapp...

'Are you ready?' the girl asked giving me another sugary smile. My thoughts screeched to a halt. I nodded at her dumbly, not trusting myself to speak.

The studio was huge. Sunlight streamed in over the floorboards. A camera on a tripod stood at the far end. Next to it a table of three people were staring at me. My feet clip-clopped automatically over the floor to them.

'Could you remove your shoes please,' a man barked looking at my shoes in disgust. 'This is Oak Markant Plank parquet flooring and they will mark it,' he said pointing at my feet.

'Oh sorry, I...'

I hurriedly bent down to remove the offending footwear before I was able to cause thousands of pounds worth of damage. In my haste I hadn't time to notice that one of my socks was pink and the other had Santa on it.

But the man approaching had, 'I'm Sam,' he said offering his hand, 'You must be Angel.'

Before I had time to shake the hand the shoe obsessive had stepped in, 'You can put them over here,' he said pointing at the corner of the room where a row of trainers were lined up. I felt a small piece of relief that everyone else had been similarly chastised. I placed them down carefully and turned back to Sam, hoping that the shoe debacle might have had a line drawn under it. The other man continued to look at me suspiciously, as if at any moment I might whip out a spare pair of high heels and run amok across the varnished surface. Sam indicated to the middle of the room and sat back down at the table which was piled high with various scripts, CV's and photos.

'So what are you going to do for us today?' he asked smiling at me encouragingly.

I felt a swell of confidence. I was off. The next quarter of an hour moved by in a whirl. The camera recorded my every move as I was transported form Angel of the nerves, Angel of the Flustering to Angel the Actress, escaping into someone else's body and mind. I raged, I swore, I cried hot tears of frustration and then I smiled, I chuckled, I skipped across the stage. (In two different scenes I wasn't playing a schizophrenic or nutcase). When I finished I looked up at them sitting in their formidable line at the table and reverted to myself. Nervy little me, slightly breathless, but definitely relieved. I hadn't forgotten it, mumbled it, I hadn't tripped up, fallen down and I didn't think I had scuffed the floor. It hadn't gone badly.

'Excellent...,' announced Sam, which I'm sure he said to everybody, but was still nice to hear. He switched off the camera, 'Well Angel thank you for coming in. You'll be hearing about re calls in the next couple of weeks, if you are successful or not,' he explained. That was it. Over. Done. The dismissal. It was all so sudden.

'Right OK,' I gushed, rushing over to scoop up my bag and coat.

The shoe obsessive rose from his seat and came and stood next to me as I scooped up my heels from the row of footwear.

'It was nice to meet you,' he said looking at my feet. I looked at him worriedly. Was concerned that he was suffering from a bad case of Obsessive Compulsive Disorder. I briefly considered him offering him the number of a helpline he could call but I thought I best leave it. I didn't want to ruin this roll. I nodded at him.

'Well thank you,' I turned back to Sam, 'Have a good day,' I smiled as if auditioning for the part of American Waitress. And I was out of there. Past the women at the table, past another actress and a man talking about pretty ping pong balls (vocal exercises or international table tennis champion?) into the lift and out into the fresh air.

I felt suddenly elated as I left the building, buzzing with adrenalin. I exhaled in relief. That hadn't been so bad. And fine I might not get a recall, even though it went quite well, but I could say that I did my best. I had tried. But surely if I don't get it and it went well that is worse than not getting it when I've done badly. At least I can blame that and just say I'm crap. At least I won't get rejected after doing well. That is surely worse. I started fretting about this fact. If I heard nothing now I would know for sure that I was not good enough. But then maybe it was subjective and Sam and Shoe Man might reject me but others might think I'm the next Julia Roberts. At this thought I smiled. Rick would despair of me. What was my obsession with her? Maybe I had a crush on her? I did love her in Pretty Woman. Was I fretting about Julia Roberts now? Or my audition? My heart was still beating and I still felt fairly hyper. I couldn't do anything now, I just had to wait.

I checked my phone. Mel had left me three missed calls. With no plans to return to work when I had escaped so successfully I called Mel to suggest a meet up.

She answered on the second ring.

'Mel you called,' I sang out, realising I was still on post audition high.

'I did. Zac's with his grandparents today and I was wondering if you were free?' she said immediately.

'I was just ringing to see if you were free,' I said happily, 'Shall I come over I'm quite close to your house I could be there in...'

'No,' interjected Mel suddenly.

'Oh.'

'No I'll meet you. Where are you?' she asked.

'Oh I'm by that French creperie place you love, the one by South Ken,' I said taken back by her abrupt efficiency.

'Right I'll see you in there in tcn,' she said and hung up.

I frowned at my phone as I heard her rung off. She seemed unusually tense. Not like Mel at all. But then recently table settings had managed to send her off into an orgy of worry. She was probably fretting over the seating plan for the big day.

She turned up moments later looking fraught with the same shall-we-have-beef-or-lamb worry in the eye. I did not envy anyone planning a wedding. There seemed to be hundreds of little details you never signed up for. I still thought saying 'I do' was the taxing bit. Apparently not. It was in fact similar to taking your Gold Duke of Edinburgh Award. It was like taking up an enormous challenge right at the beginning of your marriage as a test to see if you're going to make it. I reckoned a lot of engaged couples must have broken it off haggling over the issue of cotton or linen napkins for the guests. Whether the service sheet should be in bold or italics... Mel had this kind of nervy look in her gaze. She was in a different place where children wore little culottes and carried rings on pillows.

I steered her into a seat and started telling her about my audition. Anything to postpone the inevitable stress about wedding cake. Should it be fruit cake or Victoria sponge? Should it be three tiers or two? Should she let her mother in law order it? I battled on with my story. She sat nodding at me, a weak smile on her lips. She seemed strangely subdued.

'Mel are you alright?' I asked nudging her, realising she was not remotely with it. She hadn't moved her face in a good thirty seconds.

'Hmm...' she said as if noticing me for the first time.

'Are you OK?' I asked suddenly concerned. I thought back to her outburst in the café a couple of days before. It had been very unlike Mel. She had seemed excessively touchy and aggressive, she was normally so in control.

She turned to me and said flatly, 'I can't do it Angie. This wedding. I can't.' She then burst into tears. I stopped mid-sentence, my mouth gaping open a little as the tears trickled down her cheeks. She sniffed and looked at me but I was still uselessly staring at her, unsure what had just happened. It took only a couple more seconds and I was on auto-pilot.

'What do you mean Mel? Don't be silly. Of course you can do it. You've been so excited about it.'

'That's just it Angel I've been rushing about ordering flowers, sorting out the bridesmaids dresses, telephoning relatives and I haven't stopped for a moment to think. Is this what I really want? Is he the right man for me? It's all too much.

I can't do it.' And the tears were back again. I tried to soothe her, my mind racing for helpful words of wisdom. This was deeper than I had imagined.

'But, but,' I struggled, 'Your wedding should be one of the happiest days of your life.' I trailed off realising how crap I sounded.

Mel sniffed a bit more, 'What's there to be happy about? Any moment now I'm going to be gripped by an uncontrollable urge to pop out five more babies, buy a Labrador and a bloody Land Rover. Angel I'm petrified. We've been good up to now, great in fact. Maybe it will all change with marriage.' She looked at me in panic, 'Maybe he'll run off with his secretary.'

'I didn't know he had one.'

'Well he does,' she said rounding on me, her voice growing increasingly hysterical, 'And she was a beauty in her day.'

'Er Mel... how old is she?' I asked tentatively, careful not to tip her over The Edge.

'What does it matter' she rattled on, 'you are always reading about men chasing the more mature lady,' and then in a slightly quieter voice, 'Sixty-ish.'

I chose to ignore the last bit and ploughed on in true Agony Aunt mode.

'But didn't you want to get married? Haven't you been waiting for him to ask?' I reasoned.

'Yes... but... well... I've changed my mind. Things should just stay as they are,' she said firmly.

'Look Mel maybe you're just getting a bit of cold feet. We see it on television all the time.'

Mel looked aghast, 'And normally they divorce, or they change their mind on the day and don't turn up or cheat on each other with their neighbours.'

I realised comparing her life with TV soaps had not got me to a good place fast so I changed tack.

'Mel you're just winding your self up, Peter and you love each other. You have stayed together for years, even when everyone thought you'd break up. You've raised Zac together. You let him clip his toenails in front of you.' Her sobbing had slowed down to the occasional sniff. 'You should get married; you are perfect for each other. It will be absolutely fine,' I soothed.

'Maybe you're right, maybe it's just the nerves,' she said trying to persuade herself, 'But I don't know. I'm worried that it will change things.'

'It won't Mel. It really won't. Peter is absolutely lovely and you've been great together the last few years. It will be an amazing day. Honestly,' I said earnestly.

She looked at me, willing to believe. I went on.

'Do you remember our dinner party?' I prompted.

'How could I forget?' she gave me a watery smile.

'Well anyway,' I blustered on. 'He was looking at you all night and I remember Suzie turning to me and pointing it out. We both saw how much he loves you.'

'Did he say that?' she asked desperate for the reassurance.

'In everything he does Mel. I promise,' I said expecting the romantic finale music to click in right about now.

She looked at me through her red-eyes and smiled. 'Thanks Angel.'

How cool am I? I thought as I nodded and handed her a serviette tissue to dry her eyes.

'Look why don't you have a day off from all the organising so you and Peter can spend some quality time together.'

'I can't Zac's on school holidays. It's a full time job at the moment,' she sighed.

'I'll look after Zac,' I said, confidently waving my hand at her.

She looked up, 'Really?'

I paused. Ah. How hard could it be?

'Fine yes fine, drop him by whenever and have a lovely day with Peter just relaxing,' I said confidently.

'That would be amazing Angel, thank you,' she said dabbing at her eyes. She looked exhausted but happier.

I felt relieved. Disaster diverted.

'So tell me about this audition,' she said looking almost like the old Mel.

As I walked to the tube I couldn't help feeling a little smug. I was putting out fires all over the place. I felt a little glow of satisfaction that I had helped. Mel had needed a bit of sympathy, a bit of advice. She had needed reassurance and encouragement and I realised how vital it could be. I suddenly really realised how important my job was. The teenagers who wrote in often needed just that. A few words of understanding: a little bit of compassion for whatever problem was occupying their minds. I felt overwhelmingly guilty for the number of times I had belittled or laughed off their concerns. The amount of time I had underestimated the importance of the letters, dismissed the need to show some empathy. I had forgotten what it was like to be confused and needing advice, often with no one to turn to. I often claimed the issues were small problems, they were teenagers, they'd get over it. But they felt lost, in the same way that Mel had sunk into a crisis. No one needed people to buck them up more than me. Wow. I stopped in the street suddenly. I was like Paul on the road to Damascus. It had all become clear. If I kept up these thoughts I was about to become an excellent Agony Aunt. I think I had really started to care.

* * *

I reminded myself of this when Zac was tearing across our living room, roaring his car along the floor whilst Mary was on the end of the phone babbling at me. I cared. I repeated. I cared.

'So Bernard told Sylvia that I'd had a nervous break down and she'd said she wasn't surprised because of all my history of anxiety attacks. Which I don't have so god knows, excuse my language, where she got that from. Then Kathy rings me to tell me that she's seen some fat cow, excuse my language, hanging around outside my house yelling at Bernard through the letter box. And Kathy thinks that that's the woman that her husband Sid saw at the Travel Inn with him in March. So maybe they're having difficulties, not that I care, because quite frankly they deserve each other. So Sylvia, bless her, is going to make sure that everyone knows I haven't had a breakdown but that I've left him because he was sleeping with half the town.'

'Good for you,' I encouraged, moving the phone into the kitchen to carry on whisking the Angel Delight.

'I just can't believe some of things he's saying,' she went on, 'It just makes me realise how stupid I was for staying with him for so long,' she sighed.

'But no one will believe him Mary. Don't worry. They'll know you had just had enough,' I assured her.

'Oh I hope so,' she said sounding a little sad again, 'I never thought I'd leave him you know,' she said in a quiet voice.

'I know' I said stopping the whisking for a minute. There was a pause as I heard her taking a breath.

'At least it is easier being in London and not having to deal with all the gossip,' she said sounding more positive.

'Absolutely,' I agreed.

'And everyone here has been so nice to me,' she went on.

'Good.'

'You know that Nigel from your office has called me a couple of times,' she said sounding a little embarrassed, 'He said he wanted to check I was OK. Isn't that nice of him? she said.

I tried my best not to sound too infantile. No 'wooooh' or suggestive 'Really?' or 'Oh yeah baby.'

'That is nice,' I said surprised, but pleased, that Nigel had been bold enough.

'Do you know what would make me feel better?' Mary asked, 'A bit of an image change. I used to be blonde when I was younger, and I think I want to go back to that.'

'Good idea,' I said catching sight of my hair in the mirror. It had last been cut and styled circa 2002, 'Maybe I'll join you,' I added.

'Oh do Angel,' said Mary getting keener on the idea by the minute.

'OK I can book us an appointment at the hairdresser if you like?'

'I would like,' she said sounding pleased, 'I'm free whenever.'

'How about tomorrow?' I said in a fit of organisation.

'Grand,' she said in a northern tongue.

'OK I'll do it now, and see you then.'

'Excellent thank you Angel. I don't know what I would have done without you, you know.'

'Not at all,' I said quickly, embarrassed by how touched I was.

I put the phone down blushing slightly. Although Mary was ranting and reporting back the gossip from Hull she definitely seemed cheerier and less mousey I thought spooning out the Angel Delight into bowls and popping on the toaster. He really was despicable that Bernard. Thank god she'd escaped. And what was that that she had mentioned about Nigel? He had obviously begun a campaign to woo her. Or maybe that was my corrupted mind. Maybe he just wanted to be a friend. Either way I was pleased. She definitely seemed more confident. Well done Nigel. The doorbell rang in the midst of my musing. I frowned, was Mel early? Very early I thought as I opened the door. Mel wasn't early. It wasn't Mel. It was Charlie.

'Oh,' I exclaimed, taken aback. This was not expected. I was suddenly very conscious that I had one sock on, crazy hair and a pot of marmite in my hand.

'Have I interrupted something Angel?' he asked curiously.

'No I'm just surprised,' I said.

'Mr. Stamford,' came Zac's welcome as he raced into the hallway.

'Zac. Hello,' he said looking at him with surprise, 'Is Angel babysitting you today?'

Zac nodded and roared off again.

I gestured after Zac with the marmite, 'Babysitting,' I repeated pointlessly.

'I can come back if you like?'

I nearly dropped the marmite in all my eagerness to make him feel welcome.

'No, no come in sorry it's fine we were just babysitting. Well I'm babysitting, so do... would you like a cup of tea? Or a bowl of Angel Delight?' I asked racing through to the kitchen to scan my reflection in our kettle. I wiped some stray mascara from under my right eye and pulled fruitlessly at my hair.

'Tea would be fine,' he said manoeuvring his way around the toys already scattered about. Nearby Dolly Mixtures were being crunched into our carpet by a less bothered Zac.

'Is something burning?' he asked sniffing.

'Oh shit,' I said popping the toaster back up just before it could do its worst.

Charlie watched me as I clattered through cupboards and fridges for tea items. Sugar, milk, kettle on, tea bag, or should we have a pot? A pot of tea. Yes. Am I my mother? I thought as I dusted it down from the back of our cupboard. The kettle was boiled and I had put mugs and teaspoons down on the table in front of a bemused Charlie.

'So what did you want?' I asked turning around to pour from the pot and nearly scalding him as some sloshed onto the floor.

'Angel could you stop flapping around you're making me nervous.'

'Sorry,' I breathed unable to explain my sudden jitteriness.

'I did want to talk to you about something though,' he said, noticing the pot of tea with a raised eyebrow. I blushed.

'Oh right what's that?' I asked sitting down opposite him. I couldn't seem to relax.

'Angel,' Zac wailed as he ran in to the kitchen.

'What is it?' I asked relieved with the distraction, I was feeling very self conscious.

'There's something in the tank with the leaves,' he said whispering to me and looking at Charlie over his shoulder. He obviously assumed it was not a manly trait to show fear.

'That's our snake Zac,' I said with a reassuring voice, 'He's very friendly.'

Zac looked at me with wide eyes, mirroring my expression when I'd been introduced to Percy (so named to seem less scary).

'Come on we'll go and take a look at him shall we Zac?' I said taking his hand and leading him grudgingly back through to the living room. Charlie followed.

'He's huge,' expressed Zac.

'Hmm.'

'He's like the snake from the Jungle Book isn't he?' suggested Charlie. Zac, pleased for a chance to show off the voice of his favourite character, began to hiss like mad. Charlie grinned at me over his shoulder.

That danger diverted we all stared into the tank together for a while before Zac decided that Percy wasn't such a threat after all and demanded to play cars again.

For the next half an hour I was very aware of Charlie's presence in the flat. I was playing with Zac in a strangely high-pitched voice a lot of the time. His amused smile followed me as I pushed various cars across the floor. Various conversations were struck up and then abandoned as Zac found ways to infiltrate our boring adult chat. Realising he might not get a moment to talk to me without interruption Charlie got up to go, 'Angel I'll call you later and talk to you then,' he said shrugging on his jacket and making his way to the door, 'Bye Zac' he waved.

I followed him to the door.

'I'll speak to you later then,' I said looking at him, suddenly shy. What had he wanted to tell me? Zac rushed to my side.

'Say good bye to Mr Stamford, Zac,' I said nudging him.

'Good bye Mr Stamford.'

'See you soon Zac,' Charlie turned back to me, 'And I'll call you,' he said leaning in. We kissed. On the lips. Then we froze. Then we looked at each other for a second. I was the first to break the awkwardness, 'Right, yes, I'll speak to you soon.'

'Right,' he muttered straightening up quickly.

'Bye then,' I said almost hitting him as I slammed the door.

'Yeah... bye.'

I stood rooted to the spot for a few seconds. I could hear silence on the other side of the door. Had he gone? Or was he standing there wondering, like me, what just happened? And what did just happen? It had all seemed so normal, so... no that isn't normal. I don't kiss Charlie like that. How did that happen? Did he want it to happen? Did I kiss him? Oh my god maybe he had been leaning in to kiss me on the cheek and I had brazenly gone and... There was a noise on the other side of the door. Someone was walking quickly down the stairs and then the front door slammed.

'Angel can we play with the Lego now?' It wasn't until the sixth repeat of this question and an accompanying tugging on my sleeve that I looked down and noticed Zac was still around to be entertained.

'Is Mr Stamford your friend then?' he asked as I followed Zac back to the living room.

'Um... yes, yes he is sort of,' I said quietly. I idly played with some Lego as I replayed the good bye in my head. It could have just been a mistake; I hadn't willed it to happen. But then why was my stomach feeling jittery every time I thought about it.

'Angel you make the bridge and I'll make the castle,' instructed Zac.

Not long after the kissing confusion Mel came to pick Zac up. I opened the door to see a different looking person. She looked relaxed and rosy cheeked. I, on the other hand, had my hair tied up in a tangled knot, milk spilt down my top and Lego in my shoe.

'Did you have a good day?' I asked.

'Heavenly,' smiled Mel, 'Thank you for looking after Zac. I hope he was OK.'

'What? Hmm, yes he was fine,' I assured her.

'You seem a bit distracted' she said looking at me, 'Tired?'

'Hmm' I muttered, tempted to burst out and tell her what had happened earlier.

Mel however had been bowled over by an enthusiastic Zac.

'Mummeeee.'

'Hello darling,' she hugged him, 'Did you have a good time with Angel?'

'Yes. We played with the cars and the Lego and Angel gave me jelly and Mr Stamford came round too.'

'Did he? How nice,' she said raising an eyebrow and grinning at me.

'Not for very long,' I said blushing.

'Angel kissed him,' Zac said rolling his car up Mel's arm with a roar.

Mel started laughing, 'Oh, did she?' she said looking pointedly at me.

'No she didn't,' I blushed 'It was a kiss good bye that's all.'

'Right. Sure it was,' said Mel moving in to the front room to pack up toys, 'Come on Zac, help Mummy put this stuff away.'

She left with another irritatingly knowing look and a 'Speak to you soon Angel.'

'Bye,' I muttered as I closed the door behind them.

I tried to concentrate on my book as I waited for Ellie to get home but my mind couldn't help wandering over the kiss and back. I began to get quite excited in my musings. What had he wanted to talk to me about? Why couldn't he have talked to me in front of Zac? Had he wanted to tell me he liked me? Had he wanted to ask me out? This idea made me realise I wanted him to ask. I wanted him to tell me he liked me. Then I shook myself. Hadn't I decided to keep Charlie as a friend? He was so lovely and I didn't want him to turn out to be another useless boyfriend, and worse, to then leave my life forever. Then I thought back to the kiss and realised it had felt right. Maybe I should just admit that I like him to him and... oh I don't know. Where's Ellie? I fumed. The clocks hands seemed permanently frozen in their places and I was desperate to talk to her about it all and hear what she thinks. I almost jumped on her when she walked through the door,

'Ellie you'll never believe what's happened?'

'Angel you'll never believe what I just saw.'

We both stopped, looked at each other and laughed.

'You first,' she said flinging her bag down on the table.

'No you first,' I said.

'Well...' Ellie said moving in to the kitchen and flicking on the kettle, 'Guess who I just saw in Tootsies having a very intimate little coffee with a pretty tanned blonde.'

I hazarded a guess, 'Rick,' I said. Maybe he'd finally emerged from his self-imposed isolation. Last week he had been concerned that he was coming down with an infectious glandular disease because one of his lymphoid glands was up.

'Nooo,' Ellie said slowly, enjoying the guessing game.

'Um... Suzie, Mel um... oh... Nick,' I said, suddenly realising I didn't care if it was.

'Nooo... Charlie,' she said.

'Charlie,' I repeated slowly, then my head snapped up, 'Charlie, Charlie,' I said to double-check I understood her.

'How many Charlie's do we know?' she laughed. 'So there he was in Tootsies with this stunning girl, one of those perma-tanned blonde types who ski all year round and sail for the rest of the time.'

'Did you... did you talk to him,' I asked quietly.

'God no, I didn't go over,' she said looking shocked, 'I would have totally cramped his style. Anyway they were very deep into conversation. He looked so happy Angel honestly it was sweet.'

I felt sick. Really. Like someone had just punched me.

'So,' she smiled cupping her tea with both hands, 'What was your news?'

'My... oh, oh that. It's nothing. Nothing at all. The... the gas people came and did a reading.'

'Oh,' said Ellie wrinkling her nose, 'Gripping.'

'Hmm... Well I might go to bed,' I said moving distractedly through to my bedroom.

'Bed? Angel it's 6.30pm.'

'Is it?' I muttered 'Right.'

I was gutted. Who was she? What had I been thinking? Why was I jealous? Why was I moping after Charlie? He was a friend, just a good friend. I didn't have any claim on him: I wanted him to be happy. And earlier had been a mistake, I'd known it at the time. Of course I had. It was just a silly mistake. I had just got a little carried away. I felt miserable. What had he wanted to tell me? Maybe he had come to tell me about her? Oh, I didn't want to know. When he called my mobile later that evening I didn't answer. I didn't want to get hurt all over again. I would stay away for good this time.

* * *

I was still gloomy the next morning when I met Mary for our joint outing to the hairdresser. She, on the other hand, was buoyant. So keen was she for the hairdresser to get her hair just so she had brought along photos of both Camilla Parker Bowles (for the right style) and Gwyneth Paltrow (for the right colour). She didn't notice my miserable expression and I was quick to distract her.

'What did you get up to last night?' I asked.

'Nothing much,' she said suddenly, looking a little coy.

I looked at her confused, 'What?' I asked knowing instinctively something was up.

'Oh it's nothing,' she stuttered trying to sound breezy. She was a terrible actress. 'But well we were going to the cinema and then Nigel called on the way out and we got chatting and... I missed the show,' she giggled.

'Oh really,' I said raising an eyebrow at her.

'He's asked me out one night later this week,' she admitted, breaking into a little smile.

'Dinner?' I asked curious as to what Fat Nigel, no, Nigel had offered.

'Maybe. Or he said he might be able to get tickets for a West End show. He remembered I told him I'd never seen Les Miserables,' she said sounding distinctly happier, 'And he thinks he might be able to get us tickets for that.'

'Good,' I said smiling at her, 'Well your new hair style should blow him away,' I said confidently. She blushed at me.

'I'm sure he's just being friendly,' she said in an echo of what I had thought a couple of weeks before.

I reverted to thinking about Charlie. My smile faded again.

'Come on lets go in,' I said pushing open the door to the salon.

'I want an image change,' announced Mary sitting in the leather chair, 'I want to go blonde. I was blonde when I was younger,' she added.

The hairdresser hummed and aahhed at her as she combed her hair, 'Man trouble?'

It was like being near the Oracle.

Mary laughed at her, 'Spot on.'

We engaged in idle chat with the two hairdressers who in between streaking our hair in dye were bitching about their exes and asking us questions about our love lives. Mary had told them the entire story of her marriage and seemed more able to laugh at it than ever before. She was becoming a different person. When they left us under the dryers I finally told Mary what had been bothering me. I admitted that maybe, just maybe, I was an insy little bit attracted to him, and maybe just maybe should have admitted it to myself. And I obsessed a little more about what he might have wanted to tell me.

'Now it's all too late,' I moaned.

'Oh Angel,' she paused craning her neck a little under her dryer. 'Do you think he likes you?' she asked.

I thought about it, 'I don't know,' I conceded with a sigh, 'I think he did when we first met. But then we became friends and Ellie saw him with that woman looking happy,' I spat indignantly as if it was an absolute sin, which of course it was.

'Maybe he isn't the one for you,' Mary pointed out, 'But you haven't been able to find out so you assume he is,' she said logically.

'Maybe.'

'I mean they often aren't right. Look at Bernard,' she scoffed, 'And Nick,' she exclaimed waving a finger at me, 'He obviously wasn't right for you, and your letters used to be full of praise.'

'Hmm.' I mumbled.

'And then you dumped him.'

I'd forgotten I hadn't reported that story quite so accurately.

'Hmm...'

'He clearly wasn't good enough,' she claimed confidently.

'Well yes but...'

'He sounded very selfish,' she went on, 'And you're a lovely girl. You need to be treated better than that.'

'Yes I know but, well, Nick wasn't like Bernard,' I scoffed, unable to keep it in any longer. Mary craned her foil covered head towards me a little more.

'Do you really think I would have married Bernard if he'd always been like that?' she asked.

I opened my mouth to reply, found I didn't have anything to say, and shut it again.

'We all make mistakes,' she went on, 'When I met Bernard he was lovely, just charming,' she explained seriously, 'But he had bad blood in him,' she went on, 'I used to see little things in him I didn't like. Maybe he wasn't that attentive, maybe he started criticising my life, my choices... My job in Argos for instance. He used to laugh at it.'

I shifted uncomfortably thinking back to Nick's comments about my work. His inattentiveness...

'He sometimes didn't call for days...' she went on. I sighed. Yes. Again.

'... He would go out drinking all night with the men he worked with...'

I couldn't hear anymore.

Fine so Nick hadn't been right. But what about Charlie? Charlie hadn't done any of these things. Charlie had been lovely. And now I'd missed the boat. Not that I necessarily wanted to catch the boat. But I'd never know now if other women were riding on the boat. I wasn't the kind of girl that let two people on the boat at one time so I'd have to wait my turn. He might have warned me that there would be a queue forming. I might have considered things a little quicker. Maybe that was why he had turned up at my house though? To tell me about her? Maybe he wanted to let me know so I wouldn't make a fool of myself? Maybe he had wanted to double check that I still wanted to be 'just friends'? Maybe I am being a twelve year old about all this but grr....

'Oh bloody men,' I fumed out loud.

The hairdresser caught this last exclamation. Leading us over to the sinks she said, 'I've got some great tricks off some friends for when yer fella is up to no good you know.'

'Oh, well I...'

'Go on,' interrupted Mary. I fell silent.

'Well you could try the number game,' she said, 'Or the one where you put his mobile number in the personal ads, sell his car for two hundred quid or something.'

'He doesn't have a car,' said Mary with a hint of regret in her voice.

'Well that doesn't matter does it. They don't know that. His bleeding mobile will be ringing all day with people asking after it and trying to haggle with him.'

'What was the numbers game?' I asked curiously.

'Oh OK. Well let's say you cut a three in his jumper, he knows he has to find a one and a two somewhere.'

We both looked at her blankly as she continued her explanation.

'So you scratch an eight in his car, so he knows he has seven other nasty surprises to find.'

We nodded at her, transfixed by the range of possibilities.

'... Like burn a six into his lawn with weed killer,' she continued, 'Or shave a five into his dog, or post him nine bones in a bag...' She became more and more impassioned as her examples raged on. At the bones in an envelope point I looked at Mary who was sitting with her mouth open like a goldfish. This hairdresser was obviously from the revenge school of psychopaths. We had both gone silent as she finished on, 'Ten dead rats in his bed...'

I suddenly felt a little nervous. What was she going to do to our hair if we fell out with her? I smiled pleasantly. Mary had had the same idea and we speedily tried to change the subject. The weather seemed the best bet.

'Hasn't it been sunny recently,' I piped up. Mary immediately started gushing in agreement.

* * *

It was later that I thought back to the hairdresser's sadistic monologue. She had clearly been screwed over one too many times in the past. Were good men really all that hard to find? Was every man just waiting to mess you about? How did you find the good eggs amongst the rotten apples (and by this I still mean men, I am not hinting at shopping difficulties). Mel had been worried about Peter. The hairdresser had lost it. Nick had cheated on me. Bernard had caused Mary no end of trouble. Was Charlie another in a long line?

I thought he might be the right man for me. But how did I know he was the right man? No one ever knew for sure. I was desperate for a world where all men came with labels. '97% reliable, 3% a total ass, don't mix with alcohol and blondes.' Or be made to wear badges with stars ranging from 0-5. Like the old McDonalds system where you knew never to go for the guy with no stars (suggesting inexperienced) but you also knew never to trust the ones with a full five stars (suggesting an arrogant, done-it-all attitude). No, no, you craved a guy with a couple of stars, like a kindly recommendation from an ex and a nice auntie. Someone who was still keen to improve himself. But surely knowing men they'd forget to wear them/lose them/drop them/eat them, and then where would we be? There was also the possibility that they might refuse to wear them. They had a point; didn't World War II begin with badges?

I started to conjure up a slightly more cunning vetting system, one that we could spring on them totally unawares. I imagined a first date. Him sitting across the table, his face flickering, mesmerised, in the candlelight as I regaled him with another story. Then he takes my hand, leans in, his face moves closer, his eyes shut, his lips pucker.

'Do you have two minutes?' I say. I whip out a typed form and a biro and wave it in his face, 'Just a couple of quick questions. I've not had the best run of luck with men so I've compiled a little questionnaire. Would you mind? OK Question One...'

Or we could just do a random spot test in the street, like those charity-people who harass you in the funny-coloured bibs.

'Good afternoon Sir, I'm just doing a bit of market research, do you have five minutes to fill out one of our forms? Ah you don't, is that because you are a) busy for a meeting at your hugely successful company that is run single-handedly by you and your family members and is all about saving injured bunnies? Or is it b) that you don't have time to talk quickly to a sweet, friendly and attractive girl in the street? Or is it c) simply because you feel you are so important that you can't spare two seconds making someone else's life that little bit happier...'

Questions covered would include:
- Are you:
  a) single
  b) married
  c) a bigamist

- Are you:
  a) 14-18 years old
  b) 18-35 years old
  c) over 55
  (If you answered a) or c) to the above question you are now free to go).

- Is your annual income:
  a) so terrible you can't pay your rent
  b) enough to get away over holiday periods
  c) so incredible you don't know where to stash it all.

- On a first date where would you choose to go:
  a) Burger Van
  b) Posh dinner
  c) Paris

On completion of the forms there would be a follow-up telephone interview for any man scoring over twenty five points on the test and then call-backs for the most successful. Points will be deducted for not filling out the form fully/filling out the form half-heartedly/filling out the form 'with a bad attitude' or filling out the form in blood.

But this approach did seem like a lot of effort and in our buzzing capitalist world, hadn't I learnt it was all about supply and demand? There was clearly a large demand so supply needed to be improved. Surely capitalism has gone so far now that some Western states are advanced enough to create Men Malls, 'For girls on the hop, a handy male-filled shop.' Where there could be an easy in-store magazine to browse through with different sections, 'Business, Bastards, Goth, Prude, S and M, Students, Flings, Foreign...' You could pre-order so you are prepared for what you are getting, 'Business, age 28, annual income: £40,000 height, 6ft 2' eyes: blue, interests: eating out and Elton John. Discount due to unbalanced ex-wife.' You could then send them back if they are faulty, as long as they are unsoiled by you.

Or perhaps the police could be given the power to clear the streets of attractive, straight, single men to be used in a line up in jail? They could arrest them for some petty crime they won't be too bothered about. Then women could just pop into the station and select a number from the group. The positive of that plan is that the women get their date and the men make £12 a day doing it. So everyone's a winner.

This wasn't exactly classy though. For the more sophisticated customer with fatter pockets (due to money bulging out, not weird bits of fat underneath where pockets should be), there would be another alterative. Perhaps the richest girls could get the equivalent of a personal shopper. If Miss-High-Powered-Investment-Banker can't miss crucial time at the office on frivolous dates she could send out her girl to test the goods, so to speak. Her personal man shopper would do all the hard work for her and rate him on return. He would be called back if she had had an enjoyable experience.

I was in an absolute daze as I roved through these various possibilities in my mind. Surely if these systems were in place many of womankind's man problems could be solved. It would be a greater achievement than world peace. Well, perhaps not world peace, but a greater achievement than the Millennium Dome.

But then it struck me that perhaps we could never find the right man, because there was something fundamentally wrong with mankind. And I mean this in the literal sense of MANkind. The problem was that MAN was not normally too KIND. It was an eternal dilemma. It was all in the letters I read. They cheat, they lie, they deceive...

But then I was drawn up short. It wasn't always men. I'd read only this morning that some footballer's wife has been sleeping with another footballer who has a wife. Who isn't her. Women are at it too. Maybe the problem is in our modern day society. My next letter confirmed it...

Dear Angel,
My mum and dad have always argued the whole time. Now

they refuse to speak to each other at all. I didn't like the yelling but this is worse. I think my mum is seeing someone else too but my dad doesn't know. Please help.
Kerry, County Durham

Even my parents weren't happy at the moment. I thought back to my mother's complaints about Dad and the cat. What if this developed into a bigger problem? What if it was already part of it? Was I too stupid to see? I had been hood winked by Nick hadn't I? Did I really think my parents were totally innocent? I re read the letter and then tried to imagine what it would be like if my parents weren't speaking to each other. I realised I had always taken their relationship for granted. I mean my mother and father could pee in the same room so it was surely a given that they would be together forever? (I mean obviously they don't pee in any room together, that would be disgusting. No, no they pee in the bathroom, but the fact that they seem comfortable enough to pee in each other's presence meant something to me. It was my security blanket). With a surge of daughterly love I put the letter and my thoughts to one side and picked up the phone to dial home wanting to hear the familiar squawk of my mother. I was greeted with the engaged tone and placed the receiver back with an affronted jolt. The house phone should never be engaged. It's always so humiliating to be faced with the realisation that your parents have more of a hectic social schedule than you. As my fingers drummed on the receiver I assured myself it was just the gas people or the bridge club discussing some meeting or bill. But then I looked down at the letter in front of me again, I thought about cheating, I thought about the recent cat rows and then I thought... Maybe it was a lover...

So many of the letters from these teens convinced me that quaint domesticity was really hard to achieve, what made me so cock-sure that my parents were living together happily? They did niggle away at each other. And recently it had been positively cold war in the house. I was so naïve. I didn't know what they got up to during the day. Fine, I assumed their separate worlds revolved around bridge (mother) the cat (father) ballroom dancing (father- I know – and we've had words), but I couldn't be certain. I thought about the hours my dad worked. My mum could easily be conducting a daytime affair. Her 'partners' would ring in the day so as not to arouse suspicion (from dropped calls at night) and arrange to meet her at some seedy secret location to do seedy secret things. The idea repulsed me.

I quickly dialled home again willing the panic inside me to be subdued. The engaged tone. I slammed the phone down a second time prompting Tally to look up at the noise. Oh god it was all happening. She was on the phone to her man, her bit-on-the-side, her piece of crumpet. Within a flash I was picturing my miserable future torn between a buoyant mother and a devastated father. I would be forced to ring up Trisha and go live to the nation. 'Daughter in Dodgy Love Triangle Tells All.' My mother would emerge wearing some leopard skin lycra top. She'd waltz in swinging her hips and pouting her lips in the way that she thinks makes her look like Audrey Hepburn. She'd be clinging proudly to the hand of her lover and swearing blindly she's never known love like it. Meanwhile Father would be crying helplessly in the seat beside me. The family would be ruined. No more Sunday lunches. No more Christmas meals. More and more thoughts cascaded through my mind. Would I be forced to take on my mother's role? Support my dad, make meals for my brother and sister and jam for the local fete? Would I have to give up my job, leave my friends in London, move to Guildford and live at home forever?

The injustice of it all angered me. My mother could be so selfish. Doesn't she realise I have a life too, I have dreams and her actions impinge on all of us. And has she forgotten that Dad loves her. Dad will always love her, and I'm sure she could learn to love Dad again. Yes, yes that's it. I would MAKE her love Dad again, I would get them to meet by accident on an anniversary, or a birthday or something, yes on my birthday (I don't know their anniversary) and they would talk. Dad would wear that jumper Mum likes and she would remember. She would remember how much they had in common; gardening, Countdown er... and then she would move back in. It would be hard at first, but she would build up Dad's trust again and soon they'd be peeing in the same room once more. It was going to be OK. It was going to be OK. Steadying my nerves with this thought I dialled the number once more, vowing to not act suspicious if she answered.

'Yello?' A male voice grunted. Oh god. It was Friday morning, Dad was at work. What other explanation was there? He was there, he was in the house. Grubby whore.

'Yello,' the voice repeated.

Then with a swell of relief I remembered my brother, his new manly voice, and the fact that he must be on half term by now.

'Oh hey, it's Angela... Ed?' I said uncertainly.

'Hey' he grunted again. The overly enthusiastic greeting wasn't particularly unusual; he'd never been one of life's great talkers. Perhaps having two older sisters had scared him into silence. We'd spent most of our childhood carting him round the garden in a pram with his hair done in pigtails. My father was still worried to this day as to whether that experience had affected his sexuality. So I did the sisterly thing and checked for any early signs.

'Girlfriend at the moment?' I queried casually.

'No' he grunted.

'Anyone you like?'

'No... all girls are stupid.'

Riggggghhhhht, he was definitely still in his I-hate-girls-stage. Best not tell Dad.

'Mum in?'

'No.'

'Dad?'

'No.'

'Well where are they?' I questioned, pushing an image of my mother leisurely draping herself over a four poster bed at the local Holiday Inn with Clive the builder, to the back of my mind.

'Mum's out shopping and Dad's waiting in the garden with a gun.'

'What? Waiting, why?'

'Dunno.'

'With a gun?'

'Yeah.'

'Why?'

'Dunno.'

Exasperated I realised I could still be having this conversation in twenty years time. 'Well could you tell them that I calle...'

He'd already gone.

All thoughts of lovers and cheats flew out of the window. What was Dad doing with a gun? I'd ring Mum on the mobile. It was an emergency after all.

Phones and my family just don't mix. My mother recently tried to embrace mobile phone technology by purchasing the latest Nokia model with the most up-to-date features. Much to the annoyance of my sister whose mobile resembled more of a brick. My mother barely knew how to turn the thing on, let alone how to use photo messaging and all its WAP capabilities. Infuriatingly she had it permanently switched off, 'to save the battery,' making the word 'mobile' one big joke. When pressed to turn it on she had argued that, 'If it was really important people could ring the land line.'

In the unlikely event a) it was switched on and b) that she could actually locate the phone from amongst her handbag of Things That Time Forgot she would fluster about tapping various buttons until I was yelling exasperatedly, 'Yes, Mum, Hello, Put the phone to your ear,' as I heard her confused muttering in the distance. She remained totally oblivious to the fact that her phone was so high tech it could take photos, organise her diary, send emails and solve crime. She just knew it cost her forty quid a month. Money well spent. It probably averaged about ten pounds a phone call. When she eventually got through to me she would screech questions down the phone at five times the appropriate volume, under the impression that at any minute one of us would go through a tunnel and lose all reception. It made calling her mobile a stressful affair and I avoided it as much as possible. But this was important. My father had clearly gone mental and I needed to double check my mother was aware of the fact and was taking appropriate steps to help. Four hours and about thirty missed calls later she answered.

'HELLO... HELLO,' yelled my mother. A rustling then followed.

'Mum, Hi it's Angel,' I said quickly before she hung up on me and I was lost for another four hours.

'ANGELA,' my mother yelled, 'HAS SOMETHING HAPPENED? WHY HAVE YOU CALLED?' she asked, instantly assuming it was a national disaster as why else call The Mobile.

'I can hear you Mum and I'm fine but I want to check on Dad.'

She exhaled loudly her end. I persisted.

'What's Dad doing with a gun?'

'Don't talk to me about that man Angela.'

'What's he doing with a gun?' I repeated, reckoning the gun issue was serious enough not to be ignored.

'He's camping out there for it isn't he.'

'It?' I asked, relieved that he wasn't targeting innocent visitors to the Old Vicarage next door.

Mum ignored my queries and went on, 'Honestly earlier he tried to get me to bring them tea...'

'Them?' I asked.

'Can you hear me Angel. Is it the mobile?' she asked concerned I kept repeating her.

'I can hear you fine Mum, who is them?' I asked.

'Well he's brainwashed Ed into helping hasn't he. Boys will be boys but this is going one step too far. They've been lying on a picnic rug, one of my best I might add, waiting for it to cross our boundary and then bam they're planning to shoot it.'

'Shoot what?' I asked exasperated.

'The cat of course. Angela pay attention.'

Oh.

'Shoot it?' I repeated, shocked, 'They can't do that, they'll be arrested.'

'That's what I said,' said Mum a little calmer now to be talking to someone on the right side of the RSPCA. 'They won't listen though. Like animals they are. Savages. It's like Lord of the Flies round here.'

Oh dear.

'I thought this whole business was finished,' she went on, 'But no, no, no he was just waiting for another chance to...'

'Mum they won't stay out there all night,' I interrupted thinking logically.

'I wouldn't put it past them,' she grumbled.

'Tell them it's steak for dinner, they're bound to come in for that,' I persuaded.

'Me, cook for them?' she scoffed, 'I don't think so.'

This was hopeless.

'Well Mum tell them you'll ring the police or something.'

'The police...' she stopped and thought, 'That could be a good idea Angela, that would sort it.'

'No, no Mum don't actually ring the police, just tell Dad you're going to,' I explained.

'No Angela the police is an excellent idea. They'll put a stop to this,' she said decisively.

Oh god, what had I done? I said a miserable good bye to my mother who was sounding far more purposeful. So now not only might they be heading to the divorce courts, but Dad might be heading down town.

Great.

I put the phone down hoping that somehow things might magically get fixed without the need to raise any bail money. My previous worries about affairs and cheats had died a death, eclipsed by further cat concerns. By the end of the day I was ready to sink onto a sofa and never emerge. I felt absolutely drained after my day of fretting. Which had of course been all my fault. If I had just behaved like a normal human being when I'd first met Charlie maybe it would all have turned out well. I wouldn't ever know. Although I could still tell him. He had come round to see me and I had never let him say what he had to say. Well this time I would say something. With a confident surge of feeling I realised it didn't have to be too late. I didn't really have anything to lose. I had to talk to him before I lost the plot entirely and signed up for an all female commune or evening classes on the politics of the female. I wanted to see him. Friend or not. Blonde woman or not. Missed boat or not. I just missed him.

With a determined air I set off after work, full face of make up for the going-into-battle-look. As I arrived outside his house I saw a pretty blonde woman leaving. She held the door open and I smiled and thanked her, feeling a lurch of nerves when I got inside. Then I froze half way up the stairs. She had looked like a tanned blonde, a thin blonde. The blonde that Ellie had described? My confidence faltered. I forced myself to walk up the stairs to his flat. I rehearsed a relaxed opening line. Then I stopped. This was Charlie for goodness sake, we had fed snakes together, we had hung out together for hours. We had read books, we had laughed about my letters, we had watched movies in the middle of the day together. What was I flapping about? I raised my hand to knock. I paused. But I hadn't seen him for ages and everything had got so awkward and now I was about to confess that maybe I had a crush on him. Oh god. Oh... sod it. I boldly knocked on his door before I could think anymore. Within seconds Charlie had flung open the door with an impatient, 'Yes.'

He was wearing frayed shorts, a shirt buttoned up all wrong and his cheek was smudged with a black streak. He looked absolutely gorgeous and my voice just didn't connect. Seeing it was me he looked startled.

'Angel,' he said hurriedly, 'Hi, Angel,' he repeated clearly baffled by my sudden appearance.

I immediately felt embarrassed. Why had I turned up on his doorstep unannounced? No one did that anymore. That was what American people did to welcome their neighbours with brownies, before they had their mobile numbers to text them first. And I had just popped in, presuming it would all just be a really nice surprise. As I was thinking all this Charlie had come out into the corridor, quickly drawing the door toward him.

'Angel, um... what are you doing here?'

I felt ridiculously awkward.

'Oh nothing really, I missed you, I mean I missed seeing you and thought I'd pop by and see how you are... but it doesn't matter. You look busy and I've got lots to get on with...' I said turning away quickly.

'No wait, look, give me two minutes and I'll meet you outside.' He said looking back into his flat nervously.

'Er... ok,' I said not daring to suggest the polite thing might be to invite me in. What was going on?

'Right... why don't you go to that little coffee shop over the road?'

'Sure ok... see you in five then.'

He scuttled back behind the door and I was rooted to the spot until I shook myself and went back down the stairs.

I crossed the road in a daze immediately regretting ever coming. I had lots I could have done today. I didn't need to humiliate myself like this. Maybe I should just leave now? He seemed distracted. I didn't know he'd even be in. Maybe he was busy? Maybe he hadn't wanted to see me? He had been acting very strange and jumpy, not like Charlie at all. But I had just turned up on his door like some... Oh my god maybe someone else had been in the flat? Is that why he didn't let me in? Or had the blonde I'd seen on the way in just left? I concentrated on flicking through the pages of an abandoned magazine as I waited. A few minutes later he turned up without the black smudge, the shirt buttoned correctly and a pair of worn in flip flops on his feet. He was instantly apologetic and produced a large latte and a slice of carrot cake to make up for it.

After a few more minutes I was feeling relatively relaxed again. Charlie was making me laugh. That morning he'd received a phone call from some friend of his who had managed to fall asleep on a train to Luton. He was trying to get Charlie to pay for a flight back from Glasgow for him. As he talked I noticed the shadows under his eyes. The usually piercing blue eyes were smaller and slightly bloodshot. He looked tired. Probably all the sex, I found myself instantly thinking. I bristled to think of it. He yawned. I tried to concentrate on what he was saying but I felt my gut twist as I thought of him with someone else. I didn't want to know anymore. I didn't want to hear it. It was so nice to sit and eat cake and listen to him that I couldn't bear to mention why I'd turned up so out of the blue. Maybe it was worth just being friends if we could do this. But then is it wrong that as he's talking and we're sitting here I'm re playing the accidental kiss we shared the other day? Is that a platonic friend thing to do? I didn't think so. But it was so comfortable with him that I didn't want to ruin it. His voice drifted over to me interrupting my thoughts.

'Angel I know I've been distracted recently,' he said.

I thought back to the tense greeting outside his flat. I hadn't expected to be sent to the nearest coffee shop. Why hadn't he asked me in?

'You were a bit strange just now,' I said laughing hollowly.

'Yes about that Angel I'm...'

I put my hand up not wanting to hear about the blonde girl. 'Not at all. Don't worry, please don't explain.' I couldn't face hearing it.

'No I want to. Angel you see I've been...'

'Don't Charlie,' I interrupted him.

'But Angel I've wanted to tell you I'm...'

'Don't Charlie,' I said harshly. He jolted at my abruptness

and tone. 'I don't need to know,' I said a little more quietly.

'Right, fine...' He seemed annoyed.

My mobile suddenly started ringing before I could apologise. Oh, I should have let him explain. I was his friend after all. I would have to hear about it sooner or later. I picked up the phone half heartedly. The voice was frantic on the end of the line. My face drained of colour as it went on.

'Of course. No... Don't go anywhere, I'll come now,' I arranged quickly. I put the phone down, all thoughts focused on one subject.

Charlie was looking at me worriedly, 'Is everything alright? Are you OK?'

'Apparently Kevin has come back. Ellie's called the police,' I said looking at him a little shocked. Then I jumped into action, 'I've got to go home' I said picking up my bag.

'Yeah you better go,' Charlie said a little sadly.

'Charlie,' I reached out for his hand, 'I'm sorry about before I didn't mean to offend you I...'

He shrugged my hand off trying to sound laid back, 'I know Angel don't worry about it.' He smiled slightly. 'Hey, you better see if Ellie is OK.'

'Yes of course,' I said standing up.

'Do you want me to come?' he asked.

'No its fine, I'll go alone.'

I didn't want to see him anymore. I knew I couldn't really be friends with Charlie. It was impossible to think I could. I walked briskly off to the tube not looking back.

* * *

I arrived home in a rush to see Ellie standing in the corridor of our flat talking frantically to someone on her mobile. When I burst in she made her excuses and hung up.

'So,' I panted, 'What's happened, are you OK?' I asked.

'Angel thank god. I'm fine but he's still here,' she said.

'Here?' I looked confused.

'He's still in the house,' she said lowering her voice to a whisper.

'WHAT?!' I yelped, 'I thought the police would have taken him away,' I said feeling the panic rising.

'Well they don't know he's back do they?'

'Why not?' I asked.

'Well unless they've been following him, how would they know?' She pointed out.

'Because you rung them,' I said exasperated, 'Didn't you?'

'Not yet,' said Ellie.

'Why not yet? What are you waiting for, a drum roll, another death?'

'Well I rung you.'

'Well when were you planning on ringing the police, after you'd rung me, your mate Lizzie and your Mum?' I said knowing I sounded like a bitch. But this was no moment to go soft.

'I will now,' she said seeing the look in my eye; she picked up the phonebook lying nearby and started flicking through the pages.

'What are you doing?' I asked.

'Looking for the number to ring.'

'It's 999 Ellie,' I said instantly grabbing at her mobile.

'Shouldn't we ring the local police?' she said dubiously, still flicking to 'P.'

'If you want to be put in a line of people looking for their lost cat, their ten pound note they left in Asda and their passport that got stolen then, yes, continue to look for the local number. 999 should get us fire, ambulance, helicopters etc. Back up, we want back up. I'm not having him prowling this place a minute longer,' I punched in the number.

Five minutes later I hung up disgruntled.

'What did they say?' Asked Ellie concerned.

'They told me to ring the local police.'

Ellie, being not a bitch, went to get the card the policeman had handed us. I went to get a saucepan to stand by the door with (just in case).

We rang, then we waited. Not too long afterwards we heard the downstairs buzzer go and people moving about. Then silence. I ventured cautiously out onto the landing just in time to see Kevin being led out of the front door and into the back of a police car. I breathed with relief.

'He's gone,' I announced, 'They've taken him.'

I was slightly disappointed. It had all seemed surprisingly

tame. I had been expecting machine fire, a few 'Come out with your hands up' on the megaphones, a couple of TV crews and of course a violent struggle where at least one officer was shot in the line of duty. This had all seemed frustratingly English; they'd probably accepted tea, before handcuffing him in silk and leading him politely downstairs to, if he didn't mind terribly, take him to the station for more tea, a couple of biscuits and some questions. Still he was gone, he'd been found and he was with the police. I felt relieved.

The next few days in the flat were relatively quiet. I was out in the evenings a lot. I had dinner with Rick one night who was trying to get me to sign a petition to give to the government. Something about getting them to buy in more vaccines for the approaching hit of Bird Flu.

'Honestly Angel, it's spreading across Asia through poultry, this government are totally unprepared, it could be huge. We must get them to stock up on vaccines, or the cost will be human life...' I'd signed merely so that we could move away from the subject for the evening. Another night was spent with Mel who seemed a lot happier now the wedding was so soon and the organising had been largely done. She was walking down the aisle next Saturday. I couldn't believe it was really happening; I was so excited for her. Then I had been spending time at Suzie's watching videos and eating pizza. I'd hardly seen Ellie in the last few days, getting in after she was in bed, or back from wherever she was. I felt calmer about being in the flat now that I knew Kevin had been with the police. I didn't hear any doors opening and closing late at night, no Kreepy sounds in the early hours. All was relative calm.

The one excitement came at work a few days later, at around midday, from my mobile. It started ringing its little ring and I had picked it up in a nonchalant fashion.

'Hi Angel it's Sam from BOS Productions, have you got a moment to talk?' He asked.

I nearly slammed the phone back in shock. But maybe this was a rejection phone call, it had been a while since the audition, maybe he wanted to give me useful feedback? I gulped. Did I really want to hear this? Sam was still waiting for a reply.

I whispered a tentative 'Hmm Yes,' and waited for the executioners axe to fall.

'Excellent, well we loved the speeches you did...'

But... I predicted.

'and of course I've seen you perform already at the Kings Head so I know you're flexible and can be directed...'

But... I waited.

'And I think you could be really suited for our new season here but...' he said.

BUT I knew it, I bloody knew it. They always build you up so they knock you down. A simple no would have been adequate; a simple 'thank you for coming' would have been polite. A long drawn out, 'you're great but you're just not grrreat,' is what I hate.

'But some of the scripts aren't completely finished. I'd love you to come in and see what you think so far. I know it's last minute. But would next week suit?'

But again. But What? Rewind. Was I listening? All the but's had thrown me off track. I think, I think he was actually saying something positive.

'Sooo,' I drew out, trying to buy me a bit of time.

'So we'd love to see you again if you're keen,' said Sam.

'Again,' I repeated, dumbfounded, 'You'd like to see me.'

'This time obviously you won't need to prepare anything. Just come along and we'll have a go with some of the extracts from the plays we've got coming up. See what you think,' he rattled on.

I don't remember a lot of the rest of the conversation. It was a slightly out of body phone call with me agreeing to everything he said and Sam telling me more and more unbelievable things. Evening rehearsals, a weekly wage, comedy, physical theatre...

I mustn't get my hopes up I repeated to myself firmly. They might be recalling hundreds of girls.

'We saw a lot of girls, and we're only recalling the few we think we want to work with, so if it all goes OK we should have a brilliant cast,' he said.

Still, still I thought trying to calm down, there was still a possibility they might not think it 'goes well.' History hinted that I wasn't the most lucky of beings.

'I'll be in touch with details as to the venue and date but very much looking forward to working with you Angel.'

I was back to whispering again. 'Thank you, brilliant,' I

murmured, waiting for the final crunch, the final no thank you, the final let down. It never came. Sam hung up with the promise that he would be in touch in the next couple of days. I couldn't believe it.

I was still in absolute shock when Tally, who had apparently been talking to me for the last five minutes, finally gave up and threw a doughnut at my head. This did wake me from my reverie.

'What the fu...' I said, my hand dusting off the sugar the doughnut had deposited.

Tally was busy wetting herself and couldn't speak for another few little gasps.

'So what was all that about?' She asked when she'd caught her breath.

I told her. And then when Suzie came over to tell us to stop wasting perfectly edible doughnuts Tally told her. There were hugs and congratulations, and a small bit of me worried maybe they were a little pre-emptive, but a bigger bit of me had started to realise that maybe, just maybe, things were going to happen. I couldn't believe it. They had liked me and now I had the chance to work with them for a season of theatre. I called an early lunch break to distract myself from getting too excited. We spent much of it discussing what I was going to be doing.

When I got home that night there was no Ellie to report to. She was out again. I curled up and watched a video, ate half a tub of dip with cracker bread (I really needed to go shopping) and day dreamed about stages, bright lights and colourful costumes. I fell into a peaceful sleep and was still on a high when I went into the office the next morning.

I'd only been working for a couple of hours however when I noticed Victoria making a bee line for my desk. Instantly I was alert and on edge, all happy, fluffy thoughts about stage make up and playwrights went out of the window. What had I done? I racked my brains. What could she want with me? Lo and behold a few more seconds found her standing over my desk and I rolled the sleeves up on my top to delay the moment I would have to look up and acknowledge her. Sleeves rolled there was nothing left to do. I looked up.

'Angela,' she said, 'Could we talk in my office at a convenient time?'

'Of course,' I said gulping a little.

'When is convenient for you?'

I was tempted to reply Never, but realised I might as well get it over with.

'Now is fine,' I shrugged getting up.

'Right, excellent,' she said turning on her heel so I was following her through the office like a child in the wake of the Pied Piper. Eyes followed me curiously as I walked. We entered her office and she motioned to a chair.

'There are a few things I want to discuss with you Angel.' She sat down and looked at me as I settled myself. I didn't prolong the suspense by replying, she continued, 'Firstly I received a letter from a parent today.' Oh god another complaint. This was it I was fired. In one week I had managed to gain a job and lose a job. It was an impressive feat my life. No one could write it.

'She claimed that the letter you sent to her daughter about her parents' divorce helped the daughter open up to her mother and she wanted to thank you for excellent advice and for seeing them through a crisis. It was a very touching letter and I was very pleased to see you have obviously been giving the letters a lot more thought.'

'I have,' I nodded, remembering the letter and pleased that I had helped her work it out.

'But I am concerned Angel with things as they stand,' she went on seriously.

I looked up at her worriedly. Was this still it, was it over? Just when I had actually become a lot better at it, when I'd actually become satisfied with the job? Was it going to end?

'I was speaking to Suzie earlier who informed me that you might be busy working in the evenings with a production company,' she went on.

I didn't say anything.

'Would you be happy to continue on the magazine if this happened?' She asked.

'Absolutely,' I said nodding earnestly, 'I'm really enjoying my page, and the workload will be fine as a lot of the rehearsals are evenings and weekends.'

'Well I think I have an alternative.'

That was a new way of putting it. 'An alternative.' So she was firing me because BOS wanted to see me again. And what if I didn't get the job with BOS, would I be able to come back and...

'Don't worry Angel it's nothing sinister,' she said seeing the expression on my face.

I composed myself.

'I don't see why you can't go freelance,' she explained, 'Work for the magazine from home so that you can go to your acting things without it clashing with office hours.'

My mouth gaped open. Any minute I was expecting a TV crew to spring out and laugh at me. Was I being framed? But the silence continued and Victoria was definitely looking at me expectantly.

'Are you serious?' I said having to double check.

'Of course,' she said, 'Obviously I will expect you to answer all the months letters as per usual and you can work in the office on your monthly page and any articles we need for two or three days a week. We can be relatively flexible about when your hours are, as long as you put them in. But if it all works out I don't see any problem with it.'

'That would be amazing,' I said staring at her in disbelief.

'It's a trial. Keep me posted as to how you think it's going and obviously I'll see you every week in the office anyway.'

'Thank you,' I spluttered, unable to say much more.

'That's fine. Good luck with it all. We'll make Friday the 16th your last day, pack up what you need and we'll arrange your hours week by week.'

'Right,' I muttered. I remained in my seat.

'That's all,' said Victoria going back to doing whatever it is she does.

I got up and walked out of the office in an absolute daze. Eyes followed me back to my desk. Richard was busy rubbing his hands together in delight. He would miss taunting me, but it was only right, natural selection and all that, the weaker species always died out first. Wouldn't he be depressed when he heard what had really happened in the office. She was offering me freelance work. So I could do the letters, come into the office for a few days and finish the page, and get to do any acting work around it. It was brilliant. This week was surely going to have to be recorded as 'The Best Week of My Life,' in my career calendar. Which I would now have to buy. I was on a roll.

* * *

Life continued on this high, and I was so much happier now I had things to look forward to and focus on. More nights were spent visiting the gym, getting myself into shape for the recall. I had become a semi-professional at Body Combat. Lots of jabs, and kicks and karate inspired movement. The woman with the pot belly had told me she was really impressed by how I'd come on so quickly. It was like being given a gold star. I had ruined a lot of the good work by spending other evenings in the bar near work saying prolonged goodbyes to Tally, Suzie and co over a bottle of wine. Other evenings were spent with Mel, drawing up fancy table settings in pretty fonts on the computer and playing guessing games with the honeymoon destination (Peter was keeping her in the dark).

By day I was sorting things out to take home to work on. I had heard from Sam and booked a time to go in and meet the rest of the company and work on some of the plays they were planning to put on in the next few months. It was amazing and my confidence soon grew as I realised that I had got the work from an audition. They had wanted me. This fact had made me relax, and I knew I could tackle the parts they gave me. I got home exhausted but happy and had time for a bowl of cereal and a hot chocolate before I collapsed into bed. I needed to leave a note out for Ellie about everything; I hadn't spoken to her for nearly two weeks. It was madness. As I drifted into sleep I thought I heard voices in the flat, but I was too tired to take them in. Then it was too late. I was back to dreaming about flowing skirts, elegant speeches and, for some reason, Harry Potter.

The only thing not going my way was, unsurprisingly, my love life. I hadn't heard from Charlie since the day that Kevin had returned and I was glad to be busy, I didn't have time to think about him so much. It was good that everything was going well career wise, I just wished I could tell him about the acting. I knew he'd be pleased for me. But he was with someone else and I had realised I didn't want to be, couldn't be, just a friend. It was ridiculous to think I thought I ever could. I was jolted from these musings by Alex who had sauntered over to my desk to give me a Hob Nob. I accepted politely.

'I'm going to take you out for dinner Miss Lawson,' he said confidently perching himself on my desk and biting into his.

'Oh Alex I don't know I'm really tired,' I said looking up at him apologetically.

'I don't do 'no' Angel,' he said lobbing a piece of paper into the bin.

'But I...'

'I don't do 'but I' either,' he said.

I laughed at him. Where was the harm? It had been ages since I had been out to dinner (n.b. with a man who would pay the bill).

'Fine, OK, that would be lovely,' I said trying to be a little more gracious. It was nice to be asked out to dinner. We'd had a good, if not drunken, night before. Who was I to refuse free food?

'Tonight?' he confirmed, 'Leicester Square at seven?'

'Alright,' I smiled at him, 'Let's do it.'

'Let's,' he said suggestively and strolled back to Features.

I looked over at Tally who was staring at me. She looked hurriedly down at the page in front of her. I went back to my letters.

'Hi Ellie, Bye Ellie,' I said racing in and out of the flat that evening. No reply. I really had to spend some more time at home. Ellie might have grown her hair long, she might have joined a cult, learnt Yiddish, moved out? Little did I know. As of next week I'd be spending a lot more time with her when we'd both be working from home. I could catch up with her then I thought as I rumbled along in the tube. I was only a few minutes late for Alex which was acceptable under the terms 'Fashionably Late.' He was wearing a crisp suit and some fairly strong aftershave that made me sneeze when I greeted him. I was glad I had dressed up slightly. I was wearing a skirt and boots, with a fitted black top and jacket. We looked fairly glamorous strolling into Soho together.

'You look great,' commented Alex as we sat down to eat in a Chinese restaurant he had recommended.

'Thanks,' I smiled. He was waiting for more, 'You too,' I added.

He laughed, 'Thank you, the shirt is from Hawkes and Curtis,' he mentioned as an aside.

I nodded in a 'hmm-good-to-know' kind of way.

We ordered. The dinner was fine. Alex talked a lot about his latest cycling tour of the Lake District and I found myself drinking a lot of the Rosé. As we spoke I realised we didn't have a huge amount in common, but he was making an effort and we could always fall back to talking about work through the trickier silences. Somehow it had seemed a lot easier to get on with him on the night of the Five Double Vodkas but it was still nice to be dressed up and eating Chinese.

Alex paid the bill and we sat sipping at the wine and chatting a little more about people at work. During the midst of a passionate rant about Claudia and her obsessive calorie counting I froze. Emerging from the revolving doors of the restaurant was Charlie, with his hand on the small of a woman's back as they were shown to their table. I watched them crossing the room. He bent to pick up some women's napkin from another table and as he returned it they laughed about something. I felt my stomach twist. He hadn't seen me. Alex had faded into the background. We had to go before he saw me. It was too late. Charlie went to sit down, he locked eyes with me. Then he started. An unreadable expression crossed his face and he sat down, then half stood up, then sat down again.

As Alex started on another story about cycling on the tracks around Lake Windermere I spent the time casually glancing over at Charlie's table to glimpse the action. On a couple of occasions we caught each others eye, but then he would be drawn back into what looked like an animated discussion from the woman at his table. I looked up at Alex gesturing through parts of his story (something about the gears and a steep incline) and felt the urge to flee as fast as possible. I didn't want to keep obsessing about Charlie's dinner partner; he could eat with who he chose. I didn't need to sit like some restaurant voyeur and watch moment by moment. I didn't really want to be here with Alex anymore. I wanted to go home, climb into bed, listen to some music, anything but hang around here transfixed on someone else's meal.

'Can we go now Alex?'

'What right now?'

'If that's OK with you,' I said trying to smile naturally at him.

'Are you trying to seduce me again?' he asked mockingly raising an eyebrow, 'How about a drinking game?' he said thinking back to the last time we'd been out together.

'No,' I blushed, 'I'm just getting a bit restless. We could go on somewhere else,' I suggested.

From the corner of my eye I could see Charlie getting up from his table. Was he coming over? I didn't want to know.

'Come on Alex,' I said grabbing his hand, 'Let's go.'

I dragged him off through the tables to the doors and saw Charlie looking confusedly after me. Then the blonde put her hand over his and he sat back down. I suddenly felt like crying. I wanted to go home and forget about the whole night.

Alex spun me round and kissed me.

'Come on darling lets go back to yours,' he murmured.

Thrown by the suddenness of the kiss, and realising we could still be seen by the restaurateurs, I made a quick excuse.

'Oh I can't. I'm... I'm on my period,' I gabbled, totally out of the blue.

Alex looked suitably disgusted and let go of me.

'I better go home,' I said stepping out to hail a taxi.

Alex caught my hand, 'Angel don't go.'

'Sorry Alex I'm quite tired,' I said feigning a yawn. My eyes darted back to the restaurant but I couldn't catch a glimpse of Charlie.

'Tired? Angel...' he whined pulling me towards him, 'Let's go back to yours,' he murmured.

'It's miles away,' I said not wanting to take him anywhere.

'It's not that far,' he insisted.

'Don't you live by here? I asked suddenly realising we were in Soho and Alex lived in Holborn, a short walk away.

'Sort of, but...'

'So why can't we go back to yours?' I asked suddenly suspicious.

'We can't.'

'Why not?' I persisted struggling out of his clutches.

'No reason,' he said looking shifty.

'Alex,' I repeated, sounding my most intimidating.

'My girlfriends' there,' he admitted.

'I thought you didn't have a girlfriend,' I said quietly.

'Well I don't she's just, well, I've been trying to end it for ages Angel but she just won't go. The flat's half hers after all...'

I'd already started walking off.

'Angel where are you going?' he called out.

'Leave me alone Alex,' I called back.

What was wrong with me? There seemed to be a worryingly recurrent theme going on here I had noticed. Nick, cheating scummer, Alex cheating scummer. Then I find someone absolutely lovely who is attractive and interesting and amusing and I of course tell him I want to be his friend as if we're living in the 19th century and then I kiss another cheating scumbag as if I haven't had enough of kissing the other one. And now Charlie is with someone else and they are both going to be in love and get married and be a beautiful couple laughing and japing and he won't have time for me anymore and...

I didn't want this to happen. But I couldn't do anything about it. It was clearly too late.

'Angel,' Alex whined.

I hailed a taxi. 'Brixton please.'

'Angel,' he repeated.

I slammed the door and sat back in the seat, a couple of tears escaping. It was too late.

* * *

I did not feel like getting up and going into work. I did not. But at least today was a little different, at least I could be too busy to actually deal with anyone else's problems. I was cleaning out my desk and collecting together the things I needed to work from home. I spent much of the morning photocopying and avoiding Richard's incessant smirking. Alex had clearly spun a tale of his own. I really didn't care. I just kept thinking miserably back to Charlie on his date in the restaurant and the black gloom descended. Both Suzie and Tally had tried to buck me out of it. Tally with, 'If you had to choose would you have breath that smelt of fish the whole time or seven fingers?' And Suzie with the offer to take me out for a caffeine pick me up. (Seven fingers by the way).

The café was pretty cramped, but we'd managed to squeeze ourselves into a little corner table, after clambering over numerous prams/plastic spoons/babies. Following hot on our trail, after spotting the opening we'd created, were two guys with gelled hair, tight T-shirts and deep tans. They managed to squeeze themselves around the table next door and I smiled awkwardly at one of them as I dumped my hand bag on his foot.

Too nice to tell me 'I told you so' Suzie listened as I launched into the entire sorry story of the previous night. Suzie had the good grace to not point out that a) she had warned me to stay away from Alex and b) had warned me that this exact scenario would happen with Charlie. She nodded as I explained seeing Charlie with his blonde dinner partner and cocked her head to one side when I told her that I liked him, and had only just realised. She looked at me kindly and sensibly. She didn't mess up by saying anything silly, in fact she didn't say anything full stop. She let me continue.

'He told me he was working really hard at the moment. She didn't look like hard work to me,' I said glumly.

'All men are scum, lying, cheating scum,' she explained matter-of-factly.

'I thought he might be different,' I moped stirring my drink dejectedly.

'So did I,' she said looking at me sympathetically.

'Hard work,' I scoffed.

She nodded in agreement at my indignation.

'Astro physics is hard work. Quantitative Mathematics is difficult. She is not hard work. She looked like easy work. Actually no,' I corrected myself, 'She just looked easy.'

At this one of the guys with the gelled hair and deep tan looked up. Suzie smiled weakly at him as I, unaware, repeated again.

'Hard work. Pah.'

Suzie nodded at me once more.

'I just didn't think he would go for someone like that. She was all girly and blonde with pouffy bouffant hair.'

'Pretty?' asked Suzie.

'If you like obvious blondes,' I scoffed.

'Obvious blondes are the worst,' Suzie nodded.

'Shut up,' I said smiling in spite of myself. 'Yes pretty,' I admitted.

'Oh.'

'One of those girls who puts her hair in rollers overnight,' I muttered.

'So how is the agent search going?' asked Suzie in a valiant attempt to change the subject.

'What a bastard, what an absolute bastard,' I burst out, 'Hard work my arse. And why didn't he just tell me he was seeing someone? Angel I'm seeing someone, Angel I'm seeing a blonde with stupid pert breasts, a lilac jumper and...'

'Poufy bouffant hair,' chipped in Suzie.

'Exactly,' I agreed, glad that she was taking sides.

By now the two gelled hair, deep tans had stopped their own conversation and were following ours back and forth.

'Maybe she was just a friend,' suggested Suzie.

'Well why hasn't he mentioned her before? And why has he said he's working when he's hooking up with blondes the whole time and why...'

I was interrupted by one of the gelled hair, deep tans waving his hand in the air.

'Ladies, ladies,' he piped up.

I stopped abruptly, unsure how to react. Suzie and I looked at him. This was London you didn't just turn around and start talking to perfect strangers. You needed a friend of a friend to introduce you as Paul, who works with Jennie who designed Sue's dress. Or you needed to be pissed. Or requiring urgent medical attention. You didn't just turn around for a chat.

'Ladies, ladies.' They sounded foreign. They looked foreign. They must be foreign. No one had explained our English ways.

'Ladies, we listen to you but we don't like,' piped up the other one. Suzie and I exchanged a glance.

'You think men are bad, in our country we treat you like, how you say, like queen of the palace,' said one.

'You speak that this man was lying you to about this woman...' said the other.

Suzie, too surprised to berate them for such blatant eavesdropping, was sitting listening dumbfounded.

'... Who should do that no, it is not right yes.'

I stared at them as they carried on,

'You tell her this man should speak about this woman and we agree.'

Although I was still in shock that they had gate crashed our coffee I was pleased to receive further support, albeit from two complete strangers. I had soon recounted the entire tedious story of the past couple of months, the break up with Nick, the news that Charlie was now seeing this blonde girl. The Spaniards were deliberating over their verdict of the events.

'Do you have a cartoon in your country. A blue man with a white hat?'

'A smurf?' I said frowning.

The Spaniards started laughing, 'Yes a smurf. This Charlie is a smurf.'

I joined in, 'I suppose.'

'You, you are beautiful girl and this Charlie does not know himself what he is doing.'

I blushed and mumbled a thank you.

'You are both the beautiful ladies and we call you to go out one time,' said the other, glad to see his friends chat was going down so well.

'You come out with us and we go to the dance together yes?' said the other one.

'Oh I...' I looked at Suzie for help.

'We're OK thanks,' said Suzie politely. 'I think we're best staying away from men altogether.'

I nodded in agreement.

'Ah but...' protested one of them.

My phone cut across their efforts to pursue us further. I dived on it in relief leaving Suzie to continue to fend them off. The phone announced it was Rick. I said Hello. He sounded cross.

'Don't move. You little cows. You are having lunch together. Tally just told me. I rang you at work. And you didn't tell me. Wait there I will be five minutes and I am cross.'

'That was Rick. He's cross,' I explained putting the phone down. Suzie had managed to rid us of the deep tan tight T-shirt brigade and now gave me a big smile.

'What a shame I have to go back to work. But you can wait and see him. It is your last day in the office after all.'

'Well not really, I'll be in for three days next week,' I argued.

'Yes but it will be different. Today is the end of an era. You should stay and celebrate that.'

'But you deserve the time off Suzie. Maybe you should wait for him as I have a lot to pack up,' I offered.

'Oh no really. I'll let you stay. I'm Deputy Editor see so I can do that. I have that power,' she said with a wicked smile on her face.

'Thanks Suzie.'

'Not at all,' she said patting my hand.

So I stayed on to wait for Rick. Who was cross, as promised. He arrived cross. Suzie didn't have time to do more than ruffle his hair on her way out, which did little to help his mood. He ranted at her back as she left grinning at him. He then proceeded to try and ignore me during his order, when all I wanted was some Demerara sugar. Flinging himself down and throwing the sugar aggressively towards me he sulked a little longer, then realising he was bored of the silence had piped up, 'And what were you two discussing?' He then couldn't resist adding, 'Behind my back,' to show he was still hurt by our secret lunch meeting.

'It wasn't behind your back and the answer is nothing much. Girl stuff,' I said sprinkling some of the sugar at him.

'Boys,' he guessed rolling his eyes.

'Yes,' I said rolling my eyes back at him because I knew it was actually one of his favourite topics.

'Charlie?' he sighed, clearly believing himself to be some kind of mastermind.

'Perhaps,' I shrugged.

'Is that all you are worrying about?' he sighed patronizingly, 'I think I might have testicular cancer and my two best friends are discussing boys.'

'What?' I looked up.

'Yes. This morning I felt lumps on my testes.'

'It's serious Rick.'

'I know it's serious. The book told me the symptoms can include: lumps, tiredness, and ultimately death,' he finished in a half whisper.

'No not your weird made up illness Rick. Charlie. That's serious. I saw him with some blonde with my own eyes. And I like him,' I moaned.

Rick sighed again.

'I don't know why you're so worried about him. I'm dying, worry about me.'

'You're not dying Rick.'

'I am.' He said obstinately.

'You're not and anyway I'm not worrying about him. I've given up on him,' I announced dramatically.

'No you haven't and yes I am.'

'Rick you're not dying. You're fine. Look at you,' I gestured as he shovelled the rest of his muffin into his mouth.

'Youdonchtnknowwhatisworongwithmethoughdoyou,' he mumbled through crumbs.

'I can't understand you and you seem fine to me.'

He swallowed, 'I'm not fine,' he said dramatically, 'I'm far from fine.'

He then proceeded to outline his plans for after he had 'passed on.' He claimed he had booked a solicitor's appointment to draw up a will 'just in case' and was now enjoying a few more macabre moments fantasizing over which songs he wanted us sobbing to at his funeral (Take that's 'Back for Good' apparently I know). I sat quietly pushing stray bits of sugar into a pattern on the table. Gradually he became bored of mulling over his own demise and steered the conversation back.

'I don't want to talk about me though,' he said, after he just had, for quite a few consecutive minutes without pause for breath, 'I want to get to the bottom of your worries over Charlie,' he said.

'I'm not worried about him,' I repeated.

'So if you're not worrying about him, which you clearly are...'

'Am not,' I squealed.

'So if you're not, why were you discussing him with Suzie?' he asked triumphantly.

'Because she was worried about him,' I said petulantly.

'Sure.'

'I don't like your mood today Rick. You're being very hostile. It doesn't suit you,' I said, sounding very like my mother.

'That's because you have completely bypassed the fact that I might in fact be terminally ill.'

'Rick have you ever heard the story of the boy who cried Wolf?' I asked.

'Ages ago,' he grunted.

'Well I forget the exact details, but I know the boy comes to a sticky end,' I warned.

'That's because he made up a stupid lie, about a wolf getting him, whereas mine is not a lie and based on medical fact,' he finished.

I groaned and went back to pushing sugar. Anything was better than a full scale fight over the presence, or not, of small lumps in his testes.

'And I might come to a sticky end,' he sulked.

'Rick' I whined, 'Don't.'

'Fine. So what's the exact problem with Charlie anyway?' asked Rick not yet bored of the chance to make me squirm.

'I explained the problem Rick; the problem is I keep seeing him around town with this other girl.'

'What once.'

'Well yes, but Ellie saw them too.'

'So.'

'Well he's obviously seeing her.'

'So.'

'What do you mean so?'

'Well I thought you two were going to be 'just good friends',' he said, taking a stab at mimicking my voice for the last bit.

'I don't sound like that,' I pointed out. Rick just rolled his eyes again.

'And we were going to be friends but then something changed,' I went on.

'What?' asked Rick

'Well he became a pratt.'

'So why does it matter if the pratt is seeing someone else a lot?' He asked irritatingly rationally.

'Because he's a pratt, but I like him,' I wailed.

Rick sighed, 'I told you men and women couldn't be friends,' he said looking a little too smug. I glared at him.

'We could have been,' I argued, 'If he hadn't want to sleep with half of London,' I raged.

'What? One blonde woman?'

I grunted, 'Why stop at one?'

'Well my argument precisely but I don't think Charlie thinks the same,' Rick pointed out.

'Don't you?' I said looking up.

'No,' he assured me. I looked at him, slightly comforted. 'He's probably just sleeping with that one,' he said.

I groaned, 'Thanks Rick.'

'What? It's OK because you're not worried about him remember.'

'Yes I know.'

'And he is a pratt,' he repeated.

'Maybe.'

'And you'll move on. You won't be bitter about it.'

'No.' I said glumly.

'And you'll do one of the readings at my funeral.'

'What? No Rick.'

'Why not? I've chosen some beautiful ones. Real tear jerkers.'

I slouched back to the office to pack up the rest of my things and organise files for home, photocopy more leaflets and steal as many office stationery items as I could without being caught. I felt glad to be moving on and making changes I thought as I packed a large hole punch away. It would be exciting to do some different things and I couldn't wait for my recall at BOS Productions.

My mobile rang. It was Mary. I hoped she was OK. I hadn't spoken to her for a few days.

'Hello.'

'Angel,' came Mary's voice.

'Yes.'

'I rang Bernard this morning,' she announced, immediately getting to her point.

'And...' I breathed suddenly nervous. Would she scuttle back to him and revert to mousey Mary? She had seemed so confident since leaving him in Hull.

'I gave him what for,' she said, sounding pleased, 'He really sat up and paid attention. It was brilliant,' she announced, 'He apologised for it all.'

'So... are you going back to him?' I asked, reckoning that he could do more than just apologise to her for everything he'd done. He hadn't even bothered to ring her to tell her he was sorry. She had been forced to call him.

'No. I've asked for a divorce actually,' she said quietly.

'What? Really? And is that what you want?' I asked.

'Yes. Yes it is. He hasn't been good to me for years.'

'Well then that's great,' I said.

'And you'll never guess what...' she giggled like a school girl, 'I'm seeing Nigel,' she announced.

'Nigel,' I repeated.

'Oh he's been absolutely lovely to me Angel. And he's such a nice man. He's been through a lot he has...'

I looked over at Nigel's desk. I couldn't see him. I was really pleased. Mary and Nigel. It was brilliant. They both deserved to be with people who could look after them.

'... and he's booked us in for a spa weekend at one of those fancy country hotels. I can't believe it. Me in one of those fancy hotels. I'll feel like Posh Spice,' Mary went on excitedly.

'That is great,' I said, trying hard to avoid too many images of Nigel in a mud wrap.

'And we'd never have met if it hadn't been for you,' she gushed. She really did seem happier. I was touched.

'Well you keep in touch Mary and good luck with everything,' I said.

'You too Angel. Take care.'

I put the phone down, pleased that Mary seemed so excited. I pictured Bernard sitting miserably in Hull working out which mistress might iron his shirts. So Mary had Nigel and I had my career I thought as I looked at the box of items. I went back to packing, popping in a pack of yellow highlighters. My recall was in less than a week and I was ready for it. The letters had recently become a lot more satisfying. I genuinely felt helpful I thought as I placed a couple of pads of lined paper in. Life was looking sunnier.

Then I turned to look at a load of paper clips and thought about Charlie, not that these two things were in anyway linked. Charlie in no way reminded me of a load of paper clips, or any stationery items come to think of it. Which had to be a positive. But as I looked at the paper clips the feeling of misery and wasted time washed over me and I found myself welling up again. Nigel and Mary. Together. And I had no one. Honestly I would be excellent as a character in a soap. Constantly on the verge of ecstatic joy or excessive sobbing. I shook myself. There were other men, he hadn't been anything special. Then I thought back to our first date. Of his drawing of me. It had just been a little sketch with a biro on a napkin but it had been so accurate. My hair was falling into one eye and an arm was resting under my head. I'd looked peaceful. He'd just listened to me and taken everything in, he'd got on with my friends, he's made me laugh and... fine it doesn't matter. I'd move on.

I picked up the box and moved to the door saying a brief good bye to Tally. It felt odd leaving work so early and I waved meekly at Victoria on my way out. She nodded at me officiously. I nodded curtly back, trying to communicate with her in her world. It was a little like the army I imagined. Without rush hour to tackle my journey was made a little easier, although transporting an entire box of belongings, most of them stolen stationery, was not something I was used to. How did burglars manage it all the time? They must work out. I was lightly perspiring by the time I had reached our house. I was sweating profusely by the time I manoeuvred my way up the stairs stopping every now and again to huff a little. I really did need to get back into the gym, but there wasn't time to worry about it now.

I dumped the box on the floor the moment I could and threw my keys down on the table.

'Hey Angie,' called Ellie from the living room.

Oh good Ellie was at home. I felt relieved to hear her. I hadn't seen or spoken to her in so long. I had always been out and she had spent less time in the flat. Did she finally have a job? I'd have to catch up with her.

'Hey honey I'm home. I went to...' I walked into the living room and drew up short.

Ellie was sitting on the sofa chatting to a tall, good looking guy, light brown hair, nice stubble, long legs.

'Oh hi,' I said, in a voice that suggested I was un-used to seeing attractive men sprawling on our furniture.

The man smiled and nodded at me, Ellie got up.

'Hey I was just going to make tea, Angel do you want some?' she asked moving into the kitchen.

'Oh sure, I'll help you,' I said following her in with another quick sneak at the man on the furniture.

I watched her switch the kettle on and when it was safely bubbling away whispered, 'Well done Ellie, he's lovely.'

'Hmm... she muttered getting three mugs down from the cupboard.

'Where did you pick him up from eh?' I giggled at her. 'You sly thing.'

Ellie looked at me in a confused way, 'It's Kevin Angie.'

'Kevin,' I mused, trying to place when she'd spoken of a Kevin before, 'Is he the guy that used to work with you?'

'No Angie, Kevin, you know...'

'Kevin,' I mulled, 'Oh is he the one you met at New Years?'

'No Angel... K E V I N. Kevin from downstairs.'

'Kevin from down...' slowly the realisation sunk in, 'KEVIN, KEVIN, you mean Kreepy Kevin from down, oh my god, Kevin from downstairs Kevin, as in snake Kevin, murdering weirdo Kevin...' The kettle switched off, 'That Kevin... KEVIN.'

'Can I help at all,' came a polite voice from the living room.

'No, no, not at all,' I bristled in a squeaky voice, Absolutely fine,' I said hysterically, rushing about the kitchen holding a teaspoon and looking for an exit we could clamber out of. I grabbed Ellie and pulled her down so we were crouching next to the washing machine. I started frantically whispering at her. 'How do you know he's not some psycho axe murderer or whatever the police wanted him for. He's a wanted man Ellie. We should be calling them for back up or something, not giving him bloody Earl Grey...'

'He's not a murderer Angie. Don't be ridiculous. He was a witness to a crime. He told me about it, the police just needed to rule him out as a suspect. He was just in the wrong place at the wrong time.'

I snorted.

'It's true,' she whispered urgently.

'Yes but they always say that and then don't you always read stories about people being cleared and they've actually really done it and everyone finds out a year later and its always like 'Girl from Barnsley said if only the police had listened to me'.'

'He didn't do anything.'

'Well of course that's what he'd tell you, he's not going to go around telling people he did it, is he?'

'What?'

'Well a psycho doesn't normally tell his next victim he's a weirdo murderer.'

'Angie he's been around here loads in the last couple of weeks and he's never threatened to take my life.'

'Round here,' I said questioningly, 'Loads,' I repeated.

'Yes, you've been at work and he's been round here. He's had a rough year Angel; he's a nice guy honestly.'

I snorted.

'How are you getting on with the tea?' asked a voice from the doorway. We both jumped and blushed red. The grip on my teaspoon got a little tighter.

'Just fine, fine, fine...' I babbled.

I craned my neck over the serving hatch and sneaked a peak at him on the sofa. A couple of seconds staring at the back of his head was enough. It just wasn't the same person. Where was the Kreepy snake, the massive beard, the bad shirts...? And yet... and yet... this was Kevin. What was Ellie thinking? Had she lost it? Had everyone in my life gone mad? Was there something in the water? There was nothing else to be done. I had to go and drink tea with the murdering weirdo. Maybe this is how he found his next victim? I sat sipping my tea and sneaking him suspicious glances when he turned his head. He didn't appear to be outwardly shouting homicidal maniac, but what was that phrase 'it's always the quiet ones.' Ellie and him seemed to be getting on very well. Ellie was probably brainwashed by him I thought as I looked at her comfortably chatting to him.

We had lapsed into a silence and realising from Ellie's jerk of her head that I was meant to be making polite chit chat, I struck up conversation.

'So um... the snake. How... how is he?' I asked noting that the tank had been removed from our living room. Did this mean the bunnies were out of the freezer because I had been craving potato waffles and ice cream...?

'He's fine, thank you for looking after him,' smiled Kevin. This was not the same person. I couldn't believe it. Was this Kevin's twin brother/better looking cousin? Was this in fact Kevin in another man's skin? Isn't that what that guy had done in 'The Silence of the Lambs.' I shivered as I thought about it. Kevin looked at me enquiringly. Oh god, could he read minds? Was I next?

'So...' I coughed, 'So... how many do you have?' I asked.

'Snakes?' asked Kevin frowning.

'Er yes.'

'Just the one,' he nodded.

'Right.'

There was another silence.

'And is he...' I searched around for another question, 'Is he... nice?' I asked lamely.

'Well I like him,' he answered.

'Right.'

There was a silence.

'Yes of course you do,' I said to fill the gap.

I noticed Ellie smiling into her tea.

After a few more minutes of strained conversation Kevin made his excuses and left. 'I'll give you a call later Ellie. Bye Angel nice to meet you properly,' he smiled at me.

'Yes nice to meet you,' I said raising a hand at him, 'So what is going on?' I asked Ellie the moment I heard he was safely back in his own flat.

'He's nice isn't he?' she urged.

'Well he seems fine for someone who is going to kill us in the next few hours yes.'

'Honestly Angel he's not. You can ring the police and ask. He witnessed the crime, it all got too much and he went to stay with a friend for a few weeks. He told me everything.'

'Honestly.'

'Yes,' she insisted.

'So when did you too become best friends?' I asked, slightly curious now.

'I met him a couple of weeks ago. He was sitting on the stairs looking so lost and I felt sorry for him. Then he started telling me a little bit about himself. Angel his Mum died six months ago and he blames himself. She was in a hospice and was miserable. He took her back to their family home and she died there two days later.'

'I killed her,' I muttered.

'What?' said Ellie.

'That's what he said wasn't it, I killed her, he meant his Mum,' I looked at her.

Ellie nodded.

'And the attack in the park just brought it all back, he said he felt helpless, although he managed to scare off the attacker,' she said with a hint of pride.

'So all those months he locked himself away was over his Mum,' I said slowly, beginning to understand.

Ellie nodded again, 'It really shook him up. He told me they were really close. His Dad had walked out on them when he was younger and his Mum was all he had. Honestly Angel it sounded like he was on the verge of a bit of a break down.'

'No wonder he always looked such a mess,' I admitted begrudgingly.

I was still suspicious, 'What about all the weird late night outings?' I pointed out, still keen to expose Kevin the Kriminal.

'He had insomnia after his Mum died,' she said, 'He used to go walking around London at night. He told me he sometimes took flowers for her.'

I thought back to my morning jog. I'd seen him clutching some dead plants. It hadn't made sense then. I suppose it added up...

'Is he OK now?' I asked suspiciously, still refusing to totally trust her.

'He's been prescribed some sleeping pills,' she said.

So that was why I hadn't heard him leaving and returning in the small hours recently.

'And he shaved his beard off a few days ago and he just looks better... happier,' she said.

There was no denying this fact. The Kevin I just met looked like a perfectly normal, walking, talking member of the human race. The Kevin of Christmas Past looked like a drug addict in a mac. But no, no, this couldn't be right.

'What about the snake thing?' I pointed out, my one suspicion remaining.

'He just likes snakes,' Ellie laughed.

Over the next few days I spent a lot of time with Ellie and Kevin. They were sweet together. She fussed over him and he was a completely different person. No scary bloodshot eyes, overgrown beard, weird hint of madness. Gradually as I got to know him I realised how messed up he'd been. He was constantly referring to his mother, telling us little stories. His sister had been round to the flat, much less hysterical, and seemed so relieved to see him looking well. I had to admit I really liked the man. And I felt safe in his company. He was very thoughtful around Ellie, helping her search for jobs in the day. He freelanced as a reviewer for a music magazine in South Ken, writing music and film reviews for their bi-monthly magazine, so had plenty of time to spend surfing websites for her ideal job. Predictably they started seeing each other, and they were such a lovely couple I felt a little envious that I was alone. They made me ache for Charlie, I missed him. I missed his quiet understanding, the way he knew when to just sit and be with me and the way he made me laugh at myself. I sighed; I would just have to get back out there and meet people, move on and forget him. Tomorrow I would get my first opportunity. It was Mel and Peter's wedding. Didn't people always say everyone meets their future spouse at weddings?

* * *

I woke to a blue sky and birds twittering. Mel would be pleased. It was a day out of one of her catalogues. As I munched quietly on some cereal, keen to not disturb Ellie who had been out last night with Kevin, I planned my outfit. I'd brought a green dress from Zara for it, which looked great with my vague tan and long brown hair. I had my curling tongs already heating up and some subtle summer wedding make up planned.

As I moved back into my room to curl my hair I caught sight of the photo of my parents on my dressing table. I really must ring home and check on everything there. It had all got a little too crazy for me last time, but I had assumed that no news had been good news. Surely my mother would have rung if Dad had been put in prison for crimes against animal welfare? As if she had known my very thoughts my mobile started ringing. The screen announced, 'Home.'

'Mother,' I answered, 'I was just thinking about you.'

'I'm ringing to tell you it's OK Angela.'

'What exactly is OK?' I asked.

'The situation,' she whispered.

'Oh good,' I exhaled, 'Good.' All was back to normal in the Lawson household.

'It's dead,' she went on.

'What?' I yelped confused. 'Who's dead?'

'Not who darling, it, it was an It, we never knew its name.'

'Are we talking about the cat?' I double checked.

'Of course the cat.'

'Dad killed it,' I said genuinely shocked. I did not see my

Dad as the cold blooded killer type, but I had been getting it all very wrong recently. My who's-a-killer radar was way off.

'No the gun only had blanks in it,' she said.

'So he shot it and a blank killed it? Isn't that just as bad?' I asked.

'No he didn't shoot it darling.'

'I didn't shoot it love,' said Dad coming onto the other line.

'Oh hey Dad,' I said slightly nervously; best not to get on the wrong side of him. No idea what he's capable of.

'No it got run over yesterday by Mrs Harrison from down the road,' chipped in Mum back to whispering about it all. I think any talk of death was done in whispers. That and any threatening illnesses/my sister/news of the homosexual vicar who lived two doors down. 'She was horribly upset but I can't say your father was that sympathetic,' she raised her voice slightly to show her displeasure.

'Bloody right. Thing will never be able to crap all over my garden again,' he said cheerfully, 'When are you coming home love. Soon I hope.'

'Soon,' I assured him.

'That would be lovely. Well I'm going to get back, the cricket is on.'

'OK Bye Dad.'

'Bye Angel, hope all is well your end.'

'It is Dad, see you soon.'

I was left to say good bye to my mother.

'So that's all settled then,' I said, relieved my Dad was not home on bail.

'I suppose it is,' said my mother. She sounded a little nervous, 'But Angel I don't dare tell him what they're planning next...' said Mum in a whisper.

'What?' I asked curious as to what could be worse.

'Well I was talking to Mrs. Phillips this morning. You know, next door. She was a bit upset you know. She said they're going to open a cattery in his memory,' she finished.

My mouth fell open. Poor Dad.

'Well anyway,' she said in a louder voice, I think my Dad was still in hearing distance, 'That's great Angel, great.' Then she whispered to me, 'Alright Angel, don't mention anything will you.'

'I won't.'

'Alright then, speak soon, I best get on.'

I put the phone down shaking my head. I picked up my tongs which were now ready for action and rolled my hair up into them. I was glad I wasn't going to be at home when Dad discovered the neighbours' plans. Would they sell up ad move out? Would Dad be pushed over The Edge? I dreaded to think. Light pink blusher was popped on my cheeks, mascara was applied, the dress was on and I was fastening a little butterfly clip into my hair. I had a cream jacket to wear in church and a little clutch bag just big enough to carry lip gloss and half an eyeliner. I looked at myself in the mirror and breathed out slowly. I was nervous for Mel. It was time to go.

I needn't have been. As Mel walked down the aisle I had a lump in my throat. She looked so beautiful and Peter looked so proud waiting for her to arrive next to him. A single tear ran down my cheek as I watched them hold hands and smile at each other. Zac was behaving impeccably as a page boy and joined me in the front pew to watch them exchange vows. As I stood up to say the reading I was aware of all eyes on me and realised how nervous I was. This was an acting part I really cared about, where if I messed up it wouldn't put me out of a job; it would devastate me to think I might have ruined the service. I slowly read the chapter from 'The Prophet' trying not to let another tear escape. It was such an appropriate passage for them, about loving each other but always remaining individuals. They had spent so many years together getting on with their lives, yet always being there for each other. I was convinced it was their secret. I finished and made my way back to the pew. Mel and Peter smiled at me as I passed. By the end there wasn't a dry eye in the place. Those that hadn't cried in the service were caught out by the beautiful rendition of Pachelbel in D that the harpist played on our way out.

I arrived at the reception with a massive smile on my face. Clutching Mel's hand I gave her a big hug. 'You look amazing,' I said.

She had a permanent Cheshire Cat grin on her face, 'Thanks Angel, the reading was beautiful.'

'Absolutely,' chipped in Peter who had turned to kiss me hello, 'Excellent.'

The reception was elegant and moving. The speeches were

peppered with some suitably embarrassing anecdotes, but it was obvious to everyone there that they couldn't be more pleased. Mel's mother was absolutely resplendent in Laura Ashley; she had been waiting for this day for the past seven years.

The dinner was incredible. Fillets of beef and amazing vegetables dripping in butter. I was sitting next to a lovely man who had bonded with me when I'd asked to swap my unwanted potatoes for his unwanted mange tout. He was telling me about his wife and little girl, who wasn't yet old enough to read 'Sweet SixTeen.' I'd told him a little about my job and the fact that I was going to get back into acting.

'I definitely think you should,' the man nodded at me over the pavlova.

'Where were you a year ago?' I laughed, explaining my crisis in confidence to him and my recent decision to have another go.

'Angel we have actually met before,' the man said.

I blushed, how useless was I? 'Where?' I asked apologetically.

'Oh, don't worry, it was for about three seconds, after a show you did at The White Bear.'

'Oh,' I said surprised.

'I thought you were excellent in it.'

I blushed again as he continued.

'I was working for ICM at the time but I've recently set up my own agency,' he explained, 'I actually mentioned to Peter that I was interested in representing you,' he said. I thought back to Peter's comments at my dinner party. He'd mentioned this then and I'd brushed it off.

'I'd be very interested,' I said smiling at him. My agent had barely bothered to email me once in the last year and still thought I was called Angelica. Anything was a step up. At that moment Zac raced past us, 'Angel,' he squealed waving at me, then he was off again.

The man laughed, 'Here's my card, do give me a call next week and we'll talk more then,' he smiled getting up from the table.

'Thank you,' I stuttered, 'Brilliant. I'll call,' I said pocketing the card in my clutch bag. It just about fit.

He blended into the gathering and I was left sitting in disbelief. Maybe things were looking up I thought.

At that moment Mel sidled up behind me with an innocent smile, 'Good seating plan wasn't it,' she said slyly.

'You did that deliberately,' I said hitting her playfully.

'Of course. Sooo,' she said looking expectant and settling down into his empty chair.

'I'm calling him next week for a meeting' I told her.

'Excellent. Oh I have to run; Peter's mother keeps talking to me about her second husband's brand of bug buster. She's heading this way.'

I watched as she rushed off to hide behind Peter.

I hadn't been given fair warning however and was caught. Peter's mother had decided I was just as good a sounding board as her daughter-in-law and begun her spiel. She was now listing the benefits of using insect repellent from a spray can, not a plug in. I tried to keep alert. Suddenly in the midst of it I heard a child shout, 'Mr. Stamford.'

I turned around confused to see Zac rushing to the door. There in the doorway stood Charlie looking around the room. I couldn't believe it. What was he doing here? Suddenly his eyes lighted on me and he started to walk over. Mel's mother in law continued to insist that household pets would not be harmed by it, only the insects, and her voice became a blur as I watched him getting closer.

'So... I said to Neville you should have some at the garden party because of all the wasps...'

'Excuse me,' I muttered barely looking at her. I turned towards Charlie.

The mother in law turned to someone else and began a new spiel, about the terrible asparagus season we've been having. I moved forward.

'What are you doing here?' I asked looking at him dressed in a ruffled shirt, tie askew and hair crumpled.

'I didn't have a morning coat.'

This was not an explanation.

'I called Mel yesterday. She said I was welcome.'

I continued to stare at him.

'You look stunning,' he said taking in my dress and newly cut hair.

I blushed.

'Angel will you come with me?'

'Um... I...' I gestured around the room helplessly. I couldn't think what to say, to do.

'Angel please.'

He was giving me such strange looks I found myself nodding instantly. 'OK.'

I followed him out of the room, past strewn wedding cake and crumpled napkins. What did he want? Why was he here? I suddenly felt awash with misery again. I'd missed him. He led me out onto the street. I looked at him expectantly but he was hailing a cab.

'What,' I said startled, 'Where are you going?'

A cab pulled up and he grabbed my hand, 'Where are we going,' he corrected. Then he opened the door of the taxi.

'But I... I can't just leave her wedding.' I said in a fairly lame voice.

'Please Angel.' He looked at me and I got in.

Charlie leaned forward and directed the cab driver. 'The Buchanan Gallery Please.'

The name rang a bell but I was still staring at him like he was mad. He didn't say a thing but looked straight ahead. What was going on? He shows up, I haven't heard from him in days, I've seen him out with his blonde girlfriend and now he's sitting next to me in a cab and we're not talking. I realise that this is in fact called something, kidnapping, but resist the urge to tell him that. His face looks serious and suddenly I'm totally confused. More confused than ever.

In the midst of my musing the taxi stops and Charlie steps outside, telling the cabbie to keep the change.

'Charlie what's going on?'

He points to the window of a neat terraced house on the corner. In the window is a sign announcing,

'Charlie Stamford's Exhibition 4th September-11th September. Preview 3rd September.'

'I don't understand... that's... you,' I said reading the sign again.

'Yes Angel.'

'Oh my god how amazing,' I said breaking into a smile; all past scenes momentarily forgotten as I read the words. I'm proud of him.

'But when, how did you... I,' I was overcome. Charlie, an artist. It didn't make sense.

He led me inside, 'That isn't what I wanted to show you.'

When I step through the doors I see people milling about inside drinking champagne from flutes, laughing and chatting. Ellie and Kevin are standing chatting to Rick and Suzie and they all grin at me as I arrive. They are standing around a large canvas, a charcoal sketch of a girl. I realise with a gasp that it is an enlarged sketch of me, the picture he scribbled in the park when we first went out.

'I've called it 'Angel',' he said standing close by my side.

I couldn't believe it. It was an incredible picture.

'Angel,' he went on, 'I was trying to tell you about all this before, I wanted to ask if you'd mind me using it, but then you were so strange, and I saw you out with your new boyfriend and...'

'He's not my boyfriend,' I whispered.

'I know Ellie told me,' admitted Charlie.

'Well I saw you with your new girlf...'

I trailed off as I saw the blonde woman I was about to mention walking towards us with her arms out. She was wearing a glitzy black dress, which plunged to her ample cleavage.

'Well done Charlie. It's a success. We've had reviewers from Time Out promising to give you a great write up.'

I stiffened. Here she was, this was the blonde from the restaurant. This was the girl he was seeing. She was so glamorous. A little older than I expected, but very pretty. He had wanted to show me his exhibition. He had wanted to ask my permission to use my picture. He had brought me here and now I was going to have to be polite and say hello to her when all I want to do is run away and...

'Helen meet Angel,' Charlie introduced us. I shook her hand slowly. I knew my face looked miserable. This was hell.

'Hi you must be his muse,' she smiled, 'I'm Helen. I own the gallery.'

I paused. 'His... muse,' I spluttered. '... and this is your gallery?'

'Yes, well mine and Benji's, my husband. Benji darling come and meet Angel,' she beckoned to a nearby man. She was married, and owned the gallery, so he had been working, she wasn't his new...

'She lives with Ellie, we've offered Ellie a job here, she's perfect, fits right in, so welcoming to people...'

I couldn't take anything more in. I shook Benji's hand in a daze and turned to look at Charlie. He was looking at me seriously. Everyone else blended into the background as he took my hand and pulled me away from the noise.

'I'm sorry about everything Angel. I just wanted it to be a surprise and then everything got so strange and I had to work on this. We were really pushed,' he said raking a hand through his hair. 'I...'

'I'm sorry,' I said interrupting him. 'Sorry for being so useless. This is amazing,' I said gesturing around.

He grabbed my hand.

'Angel I know you might not want to go out with a humble English teacher.' I opened my mouth to protest but he went on, 'But how about a struggling artist?'

I looked at him looking at me so solemnly. I felt a rush of happiness.

'Yes please,' I whispered with a watery smile.

And then we kiss, a slow melting gorgeous kiss, and I know I've found Dream Man. He found me.

Dear Angel,
I think I've found my Dream Man, but how can I be absolutely sure?
Anon

Dear Reader,
I think you'll just know.
Love Angel xxx